SINCERELY,
SECRETARY
OF *Doom*

SINCERELY, SECRETARY OF *Doom*

JENNIFER KROPF

SINCERELY, SECRETARY OF DOOM

ISBN Ebook: 978-1-990555-32-9
ISBN Paperback: 978-1-990555-33-6
ISBN Hardcover: 978-1-990555-34-3

DEDICATION

I'd like to dedicate this book to J.M. Barrie and C.S. Lewis for creating the stories that made me believe in magic.

CHAPTER
BEFORE WE BEGIN...

0

Kate Kole and the Day After Book Release Day

(Three months ago)

Candles covered the bistro tables, the café lights were dim, and the fireplace cast a warm glow over the space as the sunset burned against the freshly cleaned windows. Everyone except for Kate and Cress was upstairs being suspiciously quiet. Kate was sure Cress was trying to be romantic, and it would have worked if it wasn't so painfully obvious that he was only doing it to make up for how he'd totally ruined her book release day yesterday by compelling her to shove her face full of cake in front of a room of reporters. Unfortunately for the fae Prince, Kate wasn't ready to forgive him quite yet. Also, it was sort of nice having him try so hard like this. He got frustrated easily when she didn't buy into his over-the-top romantic gestures, and that was probably the best part of it all—

his face muscles tightening, his lips thinning, his smile transforming into a weird, stretched line. Kate caught a glimpse of that face when she didn't accept the bouquet of flowers he'd ripped out of the neighbour's garden after the interview, or the heaping stack of handwritten letters he'd brought her on a literal silver platter two hours later, or the way he'd pushed her aside so he could open the door for her with a dramatic swing, nearly tearing the door off its hinges.

It was glorious.

But tonight, he was smiling, his turquoise eyes aglow. Tonight, he didn't seem to have any doubts that whatever trick he had up his sleeve was going to work to win her back.

"What is it this time, Cress?" Kate asked, folding her arms and waiting for his shenanigans to begin.

Cress yanked her arms free, and he held her hands. He cleared his throat loud enough to echo through the café. Then he dropped to a knee.

Kate sighed. "Unreal," she murmured. "Cress, I hate to break it to you, but in *this* realm, guys do that when they're going to propose. Humans don't grovel at each other's feet to beg for forgiveness." She glanced toward the staircase, hoping none of the others were nearby to witness this nonsense.

Cress cleared his throat, *again*. He squeezed his eyes shut like he was nervous, and Kate drew back in surprise. Cress wasn't one to get nervous. It made him look curiously sincere. "I know I fell fast and hard, and I turned to a complete fool for you, Katherine," he said, and an unexpected patter rose in Kate's chest, "but fairies fall in love fast. It's how we are. And it certainly doesn't mean my feelings for you aren't real. I want you to be mine forever. I want to take care of you for Grandma Lewis—"

"Wait… is this an actual proposal?!" Kate asked.

"—and if you say no, I will hunt you to the ends of the human realm until I change your mind. I will appear in your dreams and nightmares, and I will put an enchantment on every instrument in this entire land so that each song you hear for the rest of your human life will make you think of me." Cress stood and gazed into her eyes. He reached into his pocket and pulled out a wooden ring with tiny branches wrapping a dark blue gemstone. "Marry me, Human. Immediately."

Laughter tumbled from Kate's mouth. She was unsure if it was nerves or amusement. "I don't even know what to say," she admitted through giggles. Marrying Cress had never crossed her mind; mostly because they hadn't been dating for that long, but also because some days she still woke up wondering if it was all a dream that four fae assassins had once shown up to kill her and ended up running her café instead.

"Say yes." There was a poorly concealed demand in his tone. "Say yes, Katherine."

Kate looked him up and down as her chuckles ceased. She'd always imagined that if she got proposed to one day, it would be through a sweet question on a jumbotron at a hockey game while eating nachos, or at least the question would pop at a fancy restaurant. There wasn't even food here. Not a single snack.

Even after all the years that had existed in the universe, men still failed to understand that the way to win a woman's heart was to provide her with endless snacks. A hungry woman was the beginning of all life's problems.

Kate sighed.

"Well, I guess I can't argue with all those threats," she said. She stole one last moment to herself, thinking about having this lethal, turquoise-eyed assassin by her side for the rest of her life.

Could she do better?

Probably.

Did she want to?

A fresh smirk found her face when she realized that no, she would never want someone else. Anyone with eyes could see that Cress was crazy, but he was hers. And the truth was; she was so flattered, she could have cried and kissed him right there.

She lifted Cress's hand to study the ring, and she smiled, but she didn't take it. "I love you, too, Cress. Some days I'm not even sure how it happened. But this totally doesn't excuse what you did at my book release with that red velvet cake."

There it was—Cress's lips thinning ever so slightly, his eyes narrowing and looking like they were going to pop from his head. It was all Kate could have hoped for. "I just asked you to be my betrothed. Say. *Yes.* Katherine," he articulated.

Kate looked off, pretending to think about it. When she brought her attention back, a streak of fear crossed his face.

"Katherine…" Cress was begging now. "I'll never force you to eat cake again," he promised. He took a hold of her cheeks and declared, "I will hunt down your enemies. Any male who hurts you will have his eyes gouged out with a human toothpick—"

Kate felt her smile twist into something horrified as she tried not to imagine that.

"—I shall guard you with the fierceness of a thousand wild forest beasts," he announced. "I shall…"

Kate sighed as he rambled on for another few minutes. Finally, once she deemed he'd suffered enough, she peeled his hands off her face, took the ring, and slid it onto her finger. Sure enough, Cress's undying oaths went quiet. He stared at her hand. At the ring. Up at her face. He could have been enchanted by the way he looked at her in this moment, and Kate's heart did an unexpected flip.

"We," Cress whispered, moving in while staring at her lips, "shall have—" he tilted her chin up so their mouths were almost touching "—seventeen childlings."

Heat filled Kate's stomach, and she tore back. "What?"

"Fine. Sixteen," he said. "But I won't negotiate for less than that. My powerful bloodline must be carried on." He smiled, but not quite in the way that assured her he was joking, more in the way like he was imagining seventeen pointy-eared children running through the café. "And I got you a betrothal present. It sounds like he just arrived," he added.

Kate looked down at her stomach, having a fully awake nightmare.

"Come in!" She was only half conscious of Cress calling to someone.

The bell rattled and Kate tore her gaze away from her *betrothed'* to see Connor wandering in, timid and twisting his police cap in his hands. He stopped before Kate. Then he dropped to his knees at her feet.

"Just so we're clear, *this* is what grovelling looks like," Cress whispered to Kate with a satisfied smile.

"I'm sorry, Kate!" Connor said. He didn't look her in the eyes. "I should have never gone near you. I see that now! I'll never reach or look or..." He paused to think.

"Breathe," Cress reminded him.

"...or *breathe* in your direction again. I've brought shame to the great name of the police department, and I don't deserve to be a cop after how I've behaved! Please forgive me?" Connor pleaded.

Kate turned to Cress. "Seriously? You made him do this?"

Cress's smile turned sheepish. "It was worth a simple and harmless scare tactic, don't you think?"

For a split second, Kate almost laughed. But she bit it back and pulled Connor to his feet instead. She cleared her throat and cast Connor Backs a serious look. She'd been waiting a long time for this moment. Frankly, it wasn't that terrible of an engagement gift. "I forgive you, Connor. Go be a good cop. Your coworkers are the best cops on the planet, and you should be, too," she said.

Connor nodded, *bowed*, and rushed back out of the café as quickly as he'd come in.

"You didn't enslave him or something, did you?" Kate asked. "You promised you were done enslaving people." The temptation to remind Cress once again that he'd made her stuff her face with red velvet cake in front of cameras was nearly impossible to resist, but by the grace of God, she managed.

"Of course not!" Cress waved a hand through the air. "I just told you; it was a simple scare tactic. I merely growled a little. Broke a few non-valuable things. Ripped a cookie from his mangey paws and flung it at the window and all that."

It was a mild comfort, though Kate desperately hoped Cress hadn't caused the scene he'd just described at the police station. She folded her arms. "Well, at least you didn't gouge his eyes out with a human toothpick," she said sarcastically.

Four seconds of comfortable silence went by as they stared out the café windows where Connor had left. Cress wrapped an arm around Kate's shoulders and hugged her to him as they watched the spring breeze dry the streets outside. Then he muttered, "Yet."

There are three things you should never do when chasing a story about an evil, deadly creature of legend.

1)   Don't knock on its front door out of curiosity. (Remember, curiosity kills cats and on some rare and unfortunate occasions, it also kills humans.)

2)   Don't let it talk you into taking a job.

3)   And don't, no matter what, no matter who, when, how, or where, under any circumstances, fall in love with it.

If you fail to succeed at number three especially, you're doomed.

CHAPTER

1

Violet Miller and the Phone Number that Led to Nowhere

In the grand scheme of things, one should always carry at least six pens for emergencies. One to write down a great article idea, a witness quote, or to keep track of the facts. Another as a spare in case the first one runs out of ink. And the third, fourth, fifth, and sixth... Well, these spares can be useful tools for stabbing in self-defence should one find themselves facing certain death.

As the calm spring drifted away and summer crept into the streets of Toronto, a young, aspiring journalist with a chip on her shoulder walked at a brisk speed, stress eating a cinnamon roll. But despite her icing-splattered blouse, her ugly scowl, and her loudly clicking heels, Violet Miller wasn't angry. Moreso, she was desperate. And possibly a little dizzy, though in this instance, her anemia wasn't to blame.

The fragrance of kissing the spring days goodbye and welcoming the sunny heat laced the air as Violet headed up the stairs into the reporters' lounge of The Sprinkled Scoop—the most hipster online news outlet in the city. Only the most elite journalists had blogs on this channel. Only the prettiest and most well-known reporters got to appear on the video stream.

"Have you seen this?" Fil was asking the other interns as Violet came in. He waved a newspaper around. "I haven't seen a real print newspaper in like five years. And who calls their paper *The Fairy Post*?"

"Don't feel threatened by some newbie reporter trying to drag everyone back to the stone age," intern Uriah mumbled as he adjusted the lid of his coffee.

"I think it's cool. I miss real newspapers," Alice piped up.

Violet ignored the insignificant gossip of her fellow interns and marched past, sneaking into the hallway leading to her boss's office. She pushed her way through his half-open door, her pink faux-leather purse slapping against the doorframe and announcing her presence—cinnamon and icing-speckled blouse and all—to her boss sitting in his chair...

And the four other people in the room.

Violet shrank an inch, but she kept her chin up.

"Violet?" Her boss Cedric stood from his chair. "Would you mind explaining this extremely unprofessional interruption?" The way he emphasised the last few words made it clear she was ruining her chances by barging in like this.

Violet cleared her throat.

"Don't cut me," she said, stealing a glance at the clock. She'd made it with less than a minute before The Sprinkled Scoop owners' meeting was supposed to end.

Five sets of uninterested eyes blinked at her. Violet brushed the crumbs from her blouse and stood a little straighter, sure this was the first time any of the owners, or Cedric, had seen her in such a sloppy state. Typically, she was meticulous about her hair and makeup. It was one of the few things people paid attention to her for at The Sprinkled Scoop. "I've submitted all my articles on time since day one," she said to all those in the room. "I've gone to every site in the city related to the *memory-loss case*, and I'm always at work on time. I'm also always the last one to leave. I know my writing style is unique, but—"

"Unique?" Cedric grunted out an almost-laugh. "Your writing style is weird. *Whimsical* at best." He folded his arms and puffed his chest. "We hired you because your life story was interesting, and we thought your presence here would bring in new readers. But this is one of the most sought out news outlets in the city and we have to be picky. People read our articles for the facts, not for the pretty spin we put on things." He chewed on the inside of his cheek for a moment. "We've gotten complaints, Violet. Like, actual *real* complaints!"

Violet rubbed her temple. "I can sharpen up my writing. My expressive descriptions are just a habit. It doesn't mean I'm not a great journalist—"

"You're not a great journalist." Cedric said it flat out.

One of the owners turned his head away, but not before Violet saw his smirk.

"I've trusted you with plenty of stories and they always turn out the same. Your facts are great, but reading your articles is like reading a bad fiction novel. I'm sorry to tell you this, Violet, but you're not going to make the cut. We just finished making our decisions, and we're announcing to the whole office who we're offering full time positions to in a few minutes. You can wait outside with the other interns."

Violet's mouth itched to protest. But…

"You're not a great journalist."

No one had ever said it so bluntly before.

The hallway seemed bland on the walk out. Violet hardly noticed the printed articles in frames along the walls—all showcasing work by other interns. She saw a blurry vision of the dull grey carpet as she made her way back to join her fellow *permanent-position-hopefuls* at a vastly different speed than when she'd come in.

Fil was still going on about The Fairy Post, loudly rejecting the paper's authenticity, announcing to all within earshot that it wasn't reliable news and that most of what was written didn't make any sense.

"You're jealous," Violet said.

When seven heads turned in her direction, she realized she'd said it out loud.

But why should she care? She wasn't going to be working here after today. None of these people had gotten to know her during the year they'd spent together. Most of them only wanted to be her friend because of her fame, and Violet was sure it was because they thought she might bring them a moment in the spotlight. Since day one, Violet had been asked almost a dozen times by her fellow interns if they could interview her for a story of their own. Fil especially; she'd mistakenly thought he was on her side in the beginning until it became evident that the boss didn't like Violet's writing style. Then Fil had avoided her and once even made her feel stupid for trying to sit beside him in the lunchroom.

Violet looked at Fil with new eyes now. No longer would she be subject to his egotism. No longer would he ask her in front of everyone to clean up after him and refill the coffee filters. Fil thought he was a god, but he was just Cedric's nephew and therefore got special "family ally" privileges. He wasn't even good at keeping facts straight.

Violet marched over and grabbed The Fairy Post from the god himself. She scanned the front page where artistic, flowery pictures were nestled into the margins like fairies were peeking out from behind the words. It was weird but also kind of adorable.

"You're jealous, Fil," she said again, lowering the paper and looking directly into his face this time. "This paper has been gathering a big readership in the past few months. Young people like the vintage feel of a real paper in their fingers. And unlike you and your boring unchecked facts, some people like to believe in magic."

Fil's cheeks reddened. "Jealous? Vintage?" He looked off and sniffed, bringing his hands to his hips. "There are still lots of real newspapers in print, Violet, even in Toronto. There's nothing *vintage* about this." He moved to take the paper back, but Violet jerked it away and held it out of his reach. Fil glared. "Of course, someone like *you* would

4

be interested in frilly, unprofessional articles about nonsense. Keep the paper. Maybe it can entertain you on your bus ride home once you're let go from this place."

Violet opened her mouth to object but realized she couldn't. She *was* being let go. Even if the interns didn't know that for sure yet, she did— and apparently, so did Fil.

She swallowed whatever words she might have said, her throat feeling thicker than a second ago.

Violet remembered getting the acceptance letter to The Sprinkled Scoop. She'd cried tears of joy that day, and her Aunt Zorah had baked a gooey cherry pie to celebrate. Being a journalist was all she knew how to do. It was her only dream. Her one goal. There was no other.

It was only a matter of time before everyone heard she'd been kicked out. After she was gone, Cedric and Fil would have a field day harassing the women in the office the same way they'd harassed Violet all year. She stole a sympathetic look at Alice, wondering if the only other female intern would make the cut.

With that in mind, Violet rolled up The Fairy Post and tucked it under her arm. She headed for the door in silence. She didn't make it outside before she heard Alice whisper to the others, "Was that icing on her blouse?"

Violet untangled her hair tie as she walked, freeing her chestnut locks to fall around her shoulders. She whacked the icing bits off her blouse in rigid motions as she headed for the bus stop. "So embarrassing," she muttered to herself. She couldn't remember the last time she'd gone out in public looking this bad. If the owners' meeting hadn't suddenly been moved up, she would have showed up on time, looked a thousand times more presentable, and she would have had a convincing speech prepared.

Shouts of reporters filled the street, and Violet leaned to try and see around the hoard of people extending microphones. Some of them were even wearing jackets with *The Sprinkled Scoop* embroidered on the arm, and for a split second, she imagined herself wearing one of those prestigious jackets. Being one of the lead journalists trusted with the expensive microphones, capturing the story.

She realized they were gathered in front of the mayor's personal, offsite office building when a young girl in a private school uniform stepped backward, hugging an armful of books to herself. The girl's wide eyes darted from one reporter to the next as they inched in, holding their microphones toward her face. The sight turned something in Violet's stomach.

"You're the former mayor's daughter, right? What do you think of your father's behaviour?" one of the reporters asked. Before the question was finished, Violet hurried over the sidewalk to reach them. She cut through the pack and found herself in front of the former mayor's daughter. For a second, Violet wondered why she'd chosen to put herself in this spot. It had been a while since she was on this side of the cameras. She turned to face the reporters.

"She's in elementary school," Violet scolded the pack. "Let her go do her homework."

A few reporters grunted; some rolled their eyes. One or two tried to reach around her with their mics, ignoring her completely. Violet pulled the newspaper from beneath her arm and held it up like she was going to smack the next reporter that didn't back off. The journalist closest raised his hands in apology and finally took a step back.

"Hey, isn't that Violet Miller?"

Violet flinched. Somewhere in her consciousness, she was aware of rainclouds moving overhead. Of darkness crawling over the street and cold drops hitting her cheeks and shoulders. Of reporters pulling out umbrellas to save their cameras.

There was a time Violet would have gladly smiled for the cameras when she was recognized. But not today. Today she'd been let go from her dream job. And before that, she'd stress-eaten a cinnamon roll on the bus ride that had ended up exploding all over her blouse. And now her hair was wild instead of in its original smooth ponytail, and she was being rained upon.

Once, she'd been proud to be the pretty, mysterious girl in the spotlight, but for the first time, she wanted to run.

All it took was one reporter in the group to ask, and suddenly half a dozen microphones were held inches from Violet's mouth. She swallowed, lowering her newspaper weapon and blindly reaching behind her for the former mayor's daughter. She tucked the girl in her shadow as she looked right into the cameras and said, "Yes. I'm Violet Miller. *'The girl in the purple dress.'* If you want an interview, interview me instead. I'll give you a good story."

Ten questions fired in her direction at once. Violet felt the girl slip away behind her. The sound of the mayor's office door slamming shut filled the air a second later. It was a small relief.

"Do you still forget *everything*?" asked the closest reporter, stepping forward and cutting off all the others.

Violet tried smoothing down her dark hair, knowing it was no use trying to look decent right now. She wrung her fingers as she tried to sort through the questions. She'd avoided interviews for the past year while she'd focused on her career. She'd done it believing she could be known for her journalism instead of her peculiar life story. But she could hardly think of answers past the realization that on this side of the camera was where she might be trapped forever.

When she finally reached the bus stop, Violet entered the plexiglass waiting shelter and plunked onto the bench. Rainwater gushed from her skirt and dripped off the ends of her hair. Thankfully no one was around to see her sopping wet, miserable state. She leaned back against the glass wall and closed her eyes, wondering if she might be lucky enough to just evaporate right there.

Paper and ink, blogs and facts, catchy titles, and trending hashtags. Big news and entertaining stories, fact-filled articles—especially about the weird and unexplainable. Those were the things Violet had lived and breathed for a whole year. She'd been following the *memory loss case* for over half of her internship. She wasn't sure she had it in her to let it go. There were still mysteries to be solved. People still needed answers. She still needed answers.

Violet tugged a hand through her unruly hair and sighed. She unrolled the newspaper, glad she'd saved it from Fil's recycling bin. Despite her rotten day, the sketches on the front page of The Fairy Post brought a smile to her mouth. They reminded her of children's doodles; not super detailed, yet charming. As her gaze raked down the page, it snagged on a box of text at the bottom:

JOB POSTING

The writer of The Fairy Post is seeking an individual capable of being a somewhat decent secretary.

That was all it said. Violet turned the paper over. There was no job description, there was no office address or contact name. There was just a phone number in very small text.

"That's it?" she mumbled. She flipped the newspaper open but found only articles with warnings of common fairy tricks, fairy sightings, and an odd crossword puzzle that wasn't built with straight boxes but instead twisted around and connected at unusual points. There wasn't a single word more about the posting, like the person who wrote the paper had gotten distracted and forgot to include it. Maybe Fil was right. The Fairy Post did seem a little unprofessional. Violet released a small laugh. She closed the paper and tucked it back beneath her arm. It didn't matter if there was no job description. She didn't want to be a secretary; she wanted to be a journalist.

Though… she needed to buy groceries this month. And she'd been eyeing a new pair of heels in a storefront window every day on her way to The Sprinkled Scoop.

And how in the world was she going to tell Zorah that she didn't make the cut and was now jobless? Zorah would have a heart attack, then probably drive to her own surgery wing at the hospital and perform emergency surgery on herself. Then she'd come right back and smack Violet over the head for screwing up her life by not doing *whatever it takes* to get the job she wanted.

Violet released a huff and pulled her phone from her purse, dreading the inevitable conversation with her aunt. She opened the newspaper and held it close to her face to see the phone number. It was almost too small to read, but she plugged in the numbers with her polished nails and cleared her throat, pulling the phone to her ear as it rang. And rang. And rang.

There was no voicemail—the line just clicked off. She tapped the corner of her phone, scanning The Fairy Post again. On the back, right at the bottom, the last article ended with:

—and if any faeborn fool has a problem with this, feel free to come meet me at the cathedral on Roll Street, and we will duke it out fairy to fairy.

Violet shook her head with a smirk. The writer of The Fairy Post was odd, but at least he or she had a sense of humour, unlike most of the journalists she'd been working with up until now.

The bus rolled up to the curb and Violet stood, dragging out her bus pass from her pocket. She boarded in silence, was met with an evenly spaced crowd of smelly city people who didn't own cars just like her, and found a seat far at the back. When she was seated, she eyed the phone number on the job posting again. She tried dialling one last time.

It rang once.

Beep.

Heavy breathing came over the line.

Violet sat up straighter. "Hello?" she said when the person on the other end didn't speak first.

A loud smashing sound filled the speaker and Violet nearly sprang out of her seat. Other sounds followed—shattering glass, metal objects clattering to the ground, and other unidentifiable sounds that left Violet guessing. "H... Hello?" she tried again. There was a grunt, then a startling growl-like screech.

Violet pulled the phone away from her ear and looked at the number to check it. She'd dialed the right number for The Fairy Post office. When she put the phone back to her ear, it was silent. She realized whoever had picked up on the other side had hung up. Or maybe their phone had smashed during whatever was happening at the office.

Violet slowly slid her phone into her pocket. She wanted to be a journalist anyway. She was about to put the newspaper in her purse when she spotted that last article again. The one inviting her—or anyone who had problems with The Fairy Post, it seemed—to a certain cathedral on Roll Street.

CHAPTER

2

Mor Trisencor and the Dangers of Flowers

Glass sprayed over Mor. He spun away to shield his eyes, but a shard stabbed into his back, clean and sharp. That's where the irritating wedge of glass stayed as he spun back and slammed his fairsabers against the set of short, black fairy swords that looked identical to his.

The fairy intruder wore a black mask concealing the lower half of his face, but Mor could see the fellow's eyes plainly. A cutting blend of cold, dark browns and sparkling silver, mirroring the flecks embedded in every Shadow Fairy's eyes from the enchanted Silver River where those from the Dark Corner drank.

It was like looking in a mirror. Only this fool's hair was as richly red as the bloodthirsty look in his gaze.

The two fairies fought in the dark cathedral, destroying the fireplace in the living space first. The furniture was next. Then the main level windows and every shelf in storage. Railing spindles, grey brick chunks, and unwashed glass littered the storage room floor all the way to the foyer.

A horrid mess if Mor ever saw one.

The intruder smashed Mor's left fairsaber from his grip. It flew ten feet and pierced the wall so hard it stayed impaled that way. Another thing Mor would have to clean later.

Not that the cathedral's cleanliness mattered in this moment.

Not that anything mattered in this moment apart from dealing a deathblow—or eight. Time was running out, and if Mor wasn't careful—

Mor ducked a sharp swing and plunged his fairsaber toward the intruder's rib, but the Shadow Fairy spun away, doing a full flip in the air and landing with infuriating grace on his light feet.

If only this Shadow Fairy wasn't so faeborn *fast*.

Mor was sure his chest would explode soon. He couldn't keep this pace for much longer, but he couldn't stop, either. His gaze slid to where his phone had landed in a pile of gray rubble.

There was a time when he might have blown a screaming trumpet for help at a moment like this. But no. He could not call for help. It was out of the quest—

A cold, sleek blade entered Mor's side. His fairy blood rushed to the cut, sprinkling out as the intruder tore the saber back. Mor fell to his knees, lightheaded, while a strange, fast heat rushed through his body from where the fairsaber had touched. The room became a fuzzy picture, and he blinked. Worry spread through him; he lifted an arm, pointing his fairsaber at his enemy in warning. He couldn't quite keep his blade from wavering.

The Shadow Fairy approached, his boots echoing over the cold wooden floors. He nudged Mor's fairsaber away, took hold of Mor's left arm, and in one fast jerk, he snapped it. Mor growled as his arm fell limp at his side. He tried to stand, but his legs didn't seem to work. His mouth worked just fine though, so he ran it.

"Numbing flower pollen..." he gritted out. "How brave of you." He glared at the tiny yellow speckles on the intruder's fairsabers that had stolen all function of Mor's cursed limbs. But despite the glower he gave his opponent, Mor's heart tore itself in two, beating and yelling even while he didn't speak.

Though he fought a battle in the dust, Mor Trisencor was at war with himself.

He stole one last look at his phone in the wreckage, swallowing as he considered if he might really die before he caved and called for help. When he brought his attention back to the intruder, he found the Shadow Fairy staring at him from dark, silvery eyes, ever glowing with a power Mor would never possess.

As always, the Shadow Fairy intruder said nothing. He stood over Mor as Mor struggled to keep his faeborn lungs working. As Mor snapped the bone in his arm back into place. He felt himself teeter. Four more seconds, maybe less, until he would be a numb heap on the floor. And then he didn't know what would happen. He expected no mercy from the Shadow Fairy.

Mor imagined Cress's face when he would get the news. The Prince would go wild with rage and reveal himself to every dangerous fairy in the Ever Corners. Then Shayne. Dranian. And the humans. Mor's chest ached at the thought of what his death might do to them.

Perhaps he should have made the faeborn phone call.

His body tumbled onto its side; Mor barely managed to catch himself on his elbow. He dragged his unfocused gaze up to the intruder for one last word.

"I know who you are," he rasped as the numbing pollen took the rest of him, wrapping itself around his veins, muscles, bones, and limbs. He toppled to the floor, lashes fluttering, but he kept his gaze on that Shadow Fairy.

The Shadow had no expression. He didn't blink, or breathe, it seemed. He simply stared.

After several seconds, he stepped over Mor and headed for the nearest broken window. "Then you know what's coming," he said as he climbed onto the sill and hopped through the hole, avoiding the jagged glass teeth. In a wisp of wind, the fairy was gone, leaving only the cool night air slipping in from the window and flooding the cathedral's storage room now painted with wooden splinters and Mor's leaking blood.

Mor breathed a sigh of relief that echoed up into the room's rafters. His faeborn skin prickled. It was the first time the Shadow Fairy had spoken a word since the two of them had begun this war in the human realm darkness two months ago. Mor wasn't sure he could endure it much longer. He wasn't sure how many more fights he'd live through.

And that voice...

He indeed knew it well.

It was a miracle of the sky deities he was still alive.

It took two hours for the numbing pollen to wear off. Mor winced as he curled up to sit from where his body had been frozen on the floor. He traced a hand over the blade wound in his side and then reached back to try and flick out the shard of glass still clinging to his flesh like a pesky leech.

Queensbane. How had it come to this?

He looked toward the window where the Shadow Fairy had disappeared. A storm had come and gone. Mor had watched rainwater sprinkle in through the broken glass and run down the walls. There were puddles in the storage room now.

What a mess.

What a faeborn-cursed mess.

He climbed to his feet and kicked a wood plank across the room. It sailed into the furthest shelf—the only shelf that hadn't fallen—and with a loud, mean creak, the shelf tipped forward. Its contents smashed over the floor, a box of sheet music flinging into the air and sending a choir's-worth of weightless pages fluttering to the ground seconds after everything else.

"Unbelievable," Mor muttered now that everything was, in fact, destroyed.

He shoved his fist against his bleeding side to plug it up, and he strode from the storage room to get his coat. He needed to go find medicine and sink into the sort of scathingly hot bath that would burn away the memories of everything that had just happened in the last three hours.

Exactly eight months ago, Mor and two of his fellow assassins had followed their Prince across the gate into the human realm. Their human target had been harder to kill than expected, and Cress, being the flimsiest of all, had fallen for the human with barely a nudge in her direction. That was the turning point for a lot of things.

Exactly three months ago, Kate Kole had released her first book just in time for spring, titled *High Court of the Coffee Bean* after the new High Court the assassins had decided to form in the human realm. Shayne had quickly called dibs on being High King.

And exactly two and a half months ago, Mor had been delivering coffee and muffins to a business by the harbour when he'd spotted a red-haired fairy standing in a nearby park, cloaked in a black jacket with a hood and a black mask. It was clear when Mor locked eyes with him that the fairy had been watching him rather closely.

When Mor blinked, the fairy was gone. It was like it had been a dream. Like his mind was playing tricks on him, dragging something from his childling years into the present. Punishing him for all the unresolved things he'd left behind with the memories he couldn't forget.

Mor tried to imagine it was just in his head. But he got up in the night and packed his belongings while his brothers slept, just in case.

The next day, when Mor was at the grocery store picking up flour for Cress's new baking show, he spotted the fairy again, lingering by the fruit baskets. The Shadow Fairy lifted a melon and glanced across the chilled area at Mor. It was then Mor knew for sure it was no dream. And that he had a terrible decision to make.

There were a lot of perhaps' after that:

Perhaps Mor should have kept walking on by.

Perhaps Mor should have pretended he never saw.

Perhaps Mor should have gone back to Fae Café that day.

But he didn't. Instead, he'd slipped into the air and mapped every street, searching for abandoned buildings in the city. And when he found one, he closed himself inside, and he never went back.

CHAPTER

3

Violet Miller and the Creepies

The article in The Fairy Post hadn't been joking when it mentioned a *cathedral*.

From where she stood, Violet stared up at the spokes and the bell tower spearing the clouds. The morning was darker than most mornings, overlayed with grey haze and filled with thin, whistling wind, making the cathedral look even more terrifying. Clearly this building was abandoned; there wasn't a single light on inside, and some of the windows were broken. Bits of glass littered the lawn out front. It reminded her of a haunted house in a movie, the exact sort of place every horror flick lover would know to avoid.

The great wooden doors were sealed shut. An elegant inscription was written across the door in what looked like fresh ink: TRESPASSERS BEWARE. MONSTERS LAY WITHIN. Violet chuckled as she stepped up the stairs and knocked a few times where the wood varnish was peeling off. If she got the job, at least her boss would have a sense of humour at the office. Though... this looked nothing like an office.

Perhaps The Fairy Post owner just happened to own this building. Maybe the main office was somewhere else. Violet leaned back a little and looked both ways down the street as the thought crossed her mind. There weren't any other buildings close by. Most of the block was taken up by the cathedral yard and a small graveyard a stone's throw away.

"Super creepy," Violet mumbled to herself as she knocked again. She was an expert on creepy things, having gone to plenty of crime scenes for her articles. But this place was a whole different level of weird.

It seemed no one was home. That or she wasn't knocking loud enough.

Rain began speckling Violet's shoulders, and she threw her hands over her head to guard her hair. Once she had finally dried out after the last rainstorm, she'd spent over an hour at home curling it into waves before she came. Her makeup had almost taken that long too after she'd redone it from the catastrophic mess it had been this morning. She came to the cathedral ready for an interview on the spot, and she wouldn't take no for an answer.

Well, unless the rain completely destroyed her look first.

She tried the doors. They were locked.

Violet winced up at the sky where not an ounce of blue light could be seen, and a small moan escaped her. She looked back the way she'd come, thinking of racing for the bus stop in her overpriced stilettos. But...

She'd be eating nothing but instant rice and ramen all month if she couldn't land a job. Zorah would fill the fridge with groceries and tell Violet to enjoy them, but Violet would feel too guilty to eat anything if she wasn't contributing to the bills. And since it was just the two of them living together, Violet hated relying on her aunt for everything when she was a grown, capable, legal adult who could work.

The Fairy Post claimed *this* was where the owner would be—right here in this old building. It didn't seem probable that anyone was inside, or that this was really an office, but Violet knew she'd never stop regretting it if she didn't at least peek inside.

The grass was already sparkling wet, but Violet hopped off the stairs, mumbling an apology to her non-waterproof shoes. Her heels stuck into the ground as she wobble-hopped around the base of the building, crunching over hidden stones and glass. She came to a blown-out window, and she leaned forward to peer inside.

It was too dark to see. The rain picked up as she sighed, trying to imagine why this building was in such rough shape. It didn't seem safe to try to get inside if locals were going around bashing in its windows.

"Forget it," she mumbled. "This place looks like a death trap." No job was worth this kind of risk.

She almost tripped when she turned to leave, and she looked down to find her stiletto heel stuck deep into the earth. With a huff, she dropped her purse onto the grass and tried to yank her shoe free with the hook of her toes. The only thing that could make this day worse would be if she had to step on wet grass in her nylons. She tugged again, hopping back with the other foot to balance, causing her heel to hit the windowsill. There was no stopping herself from tipping backward after that and rolling right through the window.

Her shriek was loud enough to shake the city as she fell. For a split second, she forgot how to breathe.

Her elbows hit the floor first, then the rest of her body unfurled like a thrown blanket. She laid there, blinking up at a dark room, hardly believing what had just happened.

Violet sat up and looked herself over, checking her elbows for scrapes, her knees, her rear. She released a high, sharp sound when she noticed the dust covering her best interview skirt. Then she sneezed. It echoed, and it occurred to her how huge the room was. It was also… completely destroyed.

She jumped to her feet and gaped at the broken furniture in the corners, chunks of drywall and stone, and the shredded wallpaper coating every surface. This did *not* look like an office.

She was in a deep basement, and the window was too high to climb back out.

Violet strode out of the ravaged space and up a trio of stairs, praying it was just a fluke, but the lobby was covered in broken glass, too. She nearly tripped over it trying to reach the large entry doors, but when she made it, she grabbed a cold handle and tugged. The doors squeaked a little, but they didn't budge. There were no locks on the inside, and she hadn't seen any on the outside, but somehow it was locked both ways. All the broken windows she could have reached had tightly fastened boards over them, drilled into place.

"Oh my gosh..." she breathed as she turned to take in the huge, unlit, creaking cathedral. "I'm totally trapped!" And like a genius, she'd left her phone outside in her purse.

Glass crunched beneath her heels. She nearly rolled an ankle with every other step as she rushed from room to room, looking for a way out. Every area appeared closed off to the outside world, and like it hadn't been touched in ages. A thousand half-melted candles covered tall shelves, and old books with aged ivory paper were piled in mountains on tables like she'd found herself in some mad potion-mixing wizard's hideout.

She entered a vast room that took up most of the first level of the building; a sanctuary. She wasn't sure how she knew what it was. She didn't remember being in a cathedral before, but that little voice inside her—the one that only came out when she was experiencing déjà vu from a life she didn't remember—told her she'd been in a church, with a sanctuary like this one, at least once in her life.

Violet rubbed her temples. "This is the worst day, ever," she decided. Her hair was wet again, she was sure her makeup was smeared, and now she was covered in dust and stuck inside a building she stupidly mistook for a newspaper publisher's office.

"Idiooooot." She dragged the word out, letting it sink in to punish herself.

"Hello?" she finally tried. Her voice carried up through the heights of the sanctuary and into the balcony above that wrapped the large room. Dozens of wooden pews had been pushed to the sides, making the space open and lonely without furniture. A dais filled the front, covered with more dusty candlesticks. It might have been a pretty place once—she imagined the lights on, the pews set out, warmth in the air, and a congregation of people singing hymns. But now...

It looked like a vampire's lair.

She sighed and turned back the way she'd come, returning to the lobby and going for a large set of stairs covered by an aged emerald carpet. "Hello?" she called toward the upstairs rooms. She headed down the first hall, peeking into doors that were open. "Hello...?"

A lamp was on.

Violet stopped outside the door. A wooden desk inside was stacked high with newspapers. The cozy room looked completely out of place in the gloomy cathedral. Cut out articles were pinned to a wall, and a ceiling-height chalkboard filled the other side with notes: headlines, dates, names. She took two steps in, spotting a familiar article flapping in a stormy breeze creeping in from the open window. It was pegged to the wall just like all the others, but... She knew that headline.

Violet had written that article.

"This has to be a joke," Violet breathed. Her heart began to thud, her heels sliding back toward the door as she took in the other columns, realizing there wasn't just one article of hers, there were *dozens*. Articles she'd written while working at The Sprinkled Scoop. They were tucked in around other columns penned by various journalists who'd only dabbled in the story Violet had spent so much time obsessing over. Articles about the strange occurrences of young women waking up in various places around the city over the last six months and being unable to remember how they got there, their pockets sometimes full of small rocks. Some were half starved to death like they'd slept for days without waking up to eat. And in two cases... In two of the twenty-seven cases, the women were found dead. Killed of starvation while comatose, turning the memory-thief case into a possible murder case. People were saying the streets were haunted.

Violet lifted a slow hand to her mouth as it dawned on her: Whoever owned this office had to be *him*; the criminal she'd been writing about. The one creeping from shadow to shadow, snatching young women and erasing their memories with some form of scientifically advanced drug—or some unexplainable, mythical trick from the ancient times. She hadn't ruled out either possibility in her research.

She released a breath and backed out of the room. Suddenly the broken furniture downstairs didn't look like an accident. In fact, everything in the cathedral looked like there'd been a struggle.

All the faces of the young women she'd seen left sleeping in the woods, in the park, on a random streetside bench, began flashing through her mind. Over six month's worth of victims. But not her; she wouldn't be next. Because Violet wouldn't still be here when the killer returned.

She grabbed the sharpest looking pen from a tray on the desk and clutched it, pointy side out, inhaling and exhaling as she charged herself up to stab a cold vampire heart, just in case. She abandoned her heels in the hall and fled on bare feet, scurrying deeper into the cathedral to look for a back door.

The hallways on the second level were darker. Violet murmured prayers, pleading that she wouldn't be tossed into an unmarked grave out back where Zorah would never find her. But she grabbed the wall for support when a burst of dizziness filled her brain. Her hand drifted to her temple.

"No…" She shook her head. "Not right now! Don't do this *now!*" she told her horridly iron-obsessed body. She slid along the wall toward an open door where a sliver of light showed a rickety spiral staircase. She shook the anemic clouds from her mind and raced up the stairs, shoving open a trap door at the top.

Cool wind met her hot cheeks, snapping her out of her dizzy spell. When she looked up, she gawked at an enormous bell hanging above.

She climbed onto the bell tower balcony, open on all four sides except for the decrepit spindles and railing, and white beams precariously holding up a small roof. She could see half the city from this vantage point; rectangular buildings drenched in rain and mist. She could see the bus stop two blocks away. If only she could fly.

There was no way out from up here. Violet spun back toward the stairs—too fast—and tripped over a hanging rope, pulling it down with her. She hit the ground, and the whole bell tower swayed as an ear-piercing musical note erupted over the city. Violet shrieked and slammed her hands over her ears, stuck in the fetal position beneath the ringing bell. She knew she'd go deaf if she stayed here. She inhaled, leapt to her feet, and ran straight into a broad chest.

The bell drowned out all other noise as her eyes lifted.

A black hood shadowed the guy's features. From within, bright silvery eyes looked out at her. The hem of his dark, rain-speckled vampire coat fluttered in the wind.

Violet screamed.

She flinched as his hand flashed out, her eyes squeezing shut.

The noise stopped.

Violet unpeeled her eyelids and dragged her gaze over to find him holding tight to the bell. A flit of worry warmed her stomach as she considered the weight of that bell and how easily he'd been able to stop it. His arm hovered just over her shoulder. She didn't dare move, afraid she's brush against him.

He said something to her—it might have been a question, but she could hear nothing in her ruined ears. It was like being under water; even the wind and rain were faint and muted.

"P… please don't hurt me." Her own voice was distant.

But *he* must have heard. He stared at her for several seconds. It seemed this guy didn't need to blink or even take a breath.

"Are you a vampire?" She meant to ask herself quietly, but she didn't know how loud she was talking anymore. She poked a finger into her ear to try and unplug it, but it didn't help. She stole a look at the trap door, but when she brought her gaze back, she was sure he could read her thoughts about wanting to lunge for the exit.

His gaze grew penetrating, and Violet took a small step back, certain she was being sized up like a meal for breakfast. She swallowed as she searched for a way off the tower balcony, but there was only a small drop to a very steep roof in every direction.

He stepped toward her and lifted his free hand.

Violet froze, fear sinking through her as he reached toward her temples. Suddenly she remembered something from the life she'd lost all memory of. She remembered a faceless person reaching for her temples just like this. Her very first—and only—memory of her past, slamming into her after all this time. And all she knew was that she could *not* let him touch her.

So, Violet chose the crazy option. She jumped.

She toppled over the balcony rail and slammed into the roof, clawing at it with her polished nails to try and stop her fall, sure she could catch herself before she reached the edge. She asked herself what she was doing as she slid further and further down the slope.

Unfortunately, Violet realized too late that she had severely miscalculated.

She fell over the side and dropped off the roof of the cathedral.

CHAPTER

4

Cressica Alabastian and What Happened
Two Faeborn Months Ago

Cress stopped talking when Dranian rolled his eyes. The fae Prince tightened his grip on the rolling pin, quite certain it had transformed into a weapon in his hand in the last seconds. After a brief debate in his royal faeborn mind, Cress dropped the rolling pin onto the table where a scatter of flour, charmed almonds, and other baking supplies rested in view of the camera in Dranian's strong assassin fingers. The pin released a loud clatter through the café and shook the presentation table.

"What?" Cress demanded. "Do you wish to lose your eyes? I know my cooking show isn't boring. My ten thousand internet subjects—"

"You mean your subscribers?" Dranian mumbled.

"—are all the evidence I need. Humans *like* watching a deadly assassin bake things. So, if I catch you rolling your eyes again, Dranian Evelry, you'll be the next thing I use the eggbeater on."

A low growl lifted from Dranian's throat, but the fairy assassin reluctantly went back to his filming, keeping his eyes steady.

Cress cleared his throat to begin his show again. "Now, as I was saying, roll out the fat dough clump—"

"Why must I be the one to do this?" Dranian's monotone voice interrupted again. "You should get Shayne to film your cooking show for the humans."

"Shayne said he was busy, Mor still hasn't returned from the secret mission he refuses to tell us about, our human females are away on Kate's book tour, and Kate's-brother-Greyson is with Shayne in whatever unbeknownst corner of the human world he's run off to. I had no other option for an assistant but the faeborn fool before me who can't keep his eyes from rolling back into his head. Now help me finish *Cookery with A Fae Prince* so we can both be on our way. That's a command."

"By fairy law, you can't command me anymore, Your Highness." Dranian was growling again. "Shayne is the King of our new High Court. Didn't you see his announcement?" the fairy asked as he jabbed his thumb into the camera's button.

It was Cress who rolled his eyes this time. As he did, his gaze settled on the window, through which humans milled back and forth, some stopping at the breakfast tavern across the road in small herds. "That is preposterous. I wonder what our alleged *High King* is doing right now anyway that was so important he needed to steal Kate's-brother-Greyson and leave me with the grumpiest fairy in all of existence?" the Prince asked.

"We could go spy on him," Dranian suggested with a shrug.

Cress's mouth twisted to the side as he thought about that. "You're chatty today," he commented, dragging his gaze back inside. He debated. Then he said, "And that's an excellent idea. I think I like it when you're chatty."

A newspaper was left on one of the bistro tables by the window, sticking out from beneath one of Kate's novels. Cress sauntered over to it, eyeing the paper's title. It was Mor's latest scroll of articles. Even though Mor had been scribing *The Fairy Post* for months now, Cress hadn't bothered to read any of them. Mor's writing was horrendous. It was an outrageous expectation for a gifted poet-prince to be forced to read measly information articles. But his curiosity got the better of him when he spied a black and white painting on the newspaper's cover with the title: 'WARNING TO HUMANS AND FAIRIES ALIKE' below it. He nudged the book out of the way to see the picture in full, and what he saw made him draw back a step.

A painting of a fairy filled the front of The Fairy Post, though the bottom half of his face was covered with a black mask. The creature's eyes were shadowed with a certain violent hunger that dug old memories out from the places Cress had buried them deep within his faeborn soul. The fairy's ears were strikingly pointed. And if he had to guess, Cress imagined the creature's eyes were brown and laced with a ribbon of silver, though the black and white picture could promise no such thing for certain.

"Queensbane," Cress muttered. "What exactly was Mor working on when he left us two weeks ago?" He turned to face Dranian still by the camera with a new worry in his fairy bones.

Dranian's face didn't change much—not even curiosity could move the fairy's ever-scowl—but he walked to where Cress was and glanced at the newspaper. Cress heard the change in Dranian's tone when he mumbled, "Who in the name of the sky deities is that?"

"Perhaps we should go find our High King," Cress said, tucking The Fairy Post under his arm. The Prince looked up at the street again with fresh eyes. "I'm curious if he's gotten through to Mor."

Cress gaped up at the large sign hanging before the congregation of humans that read: HOTDOG EATING CONTEST.

"This is *not* more important than my cooking show!" Cress growled. "Where is our *High King*? He's due for a royal beating!" As he said it,

Cress spotted Shayne marching onto the dais with a wide grin where eight thrones were evenly spaced apart before a long feasting table. Seven large, jiggly humans walked up alongside him, and Cress bristled at the sight of his white-haired assassin parading among them.

Humans began to laugh.

"Get off the stage, muscles!" an audience member shouted, and Cress eyed the man in the blue hat. It seemed the human's jest had been directed toward Shayne. Cress glanced back to the stage to find Shayne taking a seat on one of the thrones. "Can you believe that guy? What is he, a CrossFit champion? He's not even going to finish his first hotdog. What an idiot," the human in the hat added.

Cress's cold, turquoise gaze narrowed on the human.

"Should I go stop Shayne before he embarrasses—"

"Let's sit," Cress interrupted Dranian. He kept his eyes pinned to the back of the human's blue hat as he weaved through the chairs and took the seat directly behind. That hat was where Cress's lethal gaze stayed as platters of hotdogs were carried out and laid before each human—and Shayne—at the feasting table.

"You guys came! Cool." Kate's-brother-Greyson appeared and scooted into the seat beside Cress. "I was going to do this," he explained, "but Shayne wanted to compete so badly that I let him have my spot." The human grinned. "I had to beg the people running the contest to get gluten free buns for Shayne though. They weren't happy about it. And Shayne still complained that the bread would kill him, but I convinced him he wouldn't have an allergic reaction to—"

Dranian stood up so fast, his chair toppled over behind him and into the humans in the next row. "Your Majesty!" he shouted over the group in a panicked tone. "Don't eat the bread!"

Shayne waved when he spotted Dranian. But what he didn't do was keep himself from stuffing his face with bread-coated-meat-tubes the moment a whistle was blown.

Cress and Dranian watched in horror as Shayne slid not one, not two, not three, but *twelve* hotdogs down his faeborn throat in a matter of minutes, leaving the rest of the humans in the contest behind. "How repulsive," Cress said. "This competition is utterly horrifying."

"Yeah." Kate's-brother-Greyson grinned and leaned back in his chair with folded arms.

"Wow," was all the human in the blue hat in front of them had to say about Shayne's performance.

Cress released a gloating grunt. "He's my friend," he loudly announced. "Well, actually, he's my subject. Some would think it's the other way around—" he cut a glance at Dranian "—but—"

"Shhh!" Kate's-brother-Greyson smacked Cress's knee and leaned forward with a wild expression as the contest came to its conclusion. When a bell rang and those on the stage stopped eating, Kate's-brother-Greyson jumped to his feet, thrust his fists into the air, and released a magnificent battle cry over the throng.

A human judge climbed the dais stairs at the front as the crowd clapped and cheered. Cress sighed and joined in, slapping his hands together in the odd human fashion. When the judge announced Shayne as the winner and brought Shayne to stand before the audience, Cress cheered a little. He kept his satisfied smile on, casting subtle glares at the blue-hat-human in the row ahead, until Shayne leaned forward an inch with a pale face and a strange look.

The fairy loudly barfed.

Humans in the front row screamed and wrestled out of their chairs to run as the incident turned projectile.

Kate's-brother-Greyson turned white.

Cress laughed.

Somewhere in the crowd, a vomit-soaked female was shouting threats at Shayne. A contest banner was ripped down as panicked humans tried to run in too many directions.

Dranian was plugging his nose when Cress looked in the rearview mirror. Cress felt an ounce of sympathy for the fool, knowing that of all his assassins, Dranian had the most acute sense of smell.

The Prince drove Shayne's chariot on wheels back toward the café, holding his breath while Shayne moaned and dozed off in the back seat. Finally, Cress couldn't take it anymore.

"That is a *ghastly* smell, Shayne!" he roared. He was sure he needed to roll down the window and spew at the next car passing by himself. "Can you not... hold it in?"

"Hold it in? What in the name of the sky deities are you talking about? You want me to hold in my smell?" Shayne asked.

Kate's-brother-Greyson released a snort-laugh. He was the lucky one who got to sit up front with Cress. Dranian was trapped in the back with the hotdog monster.

The rearview mirror filled with flashes of red and blue, and Cress eyed it suspiciously for a while until Kate's-brother-Greyson seemed to notice them.

"Woah! You need to pull over, Cress," the human said.

"Pull what over?"

"The car! You're getting pulled over!" Kate's-brother-Greyson pointed toward the side of the road, so Cress inched the car that way and crawled it to a stop. "Put your window down," the human added when Cress sat there and did nothing.

Cress sighed, thinking only of a hot shower that might rid him of Shayne's horrid smell. He hit the button and the window lowered. A human police officer was already standing on the other side, waiting.

"Do you know how fast you were going, sir?" the officer asked.

Cress raised a brow. "Precisely as fast as I wanted to. Why?"

"Were you speeding, Cress? You're not supposed to go fast. It's against the law here," Shayne mumbled from the back seat.

The officer leaned to look in the window. The fairy assassins lounged around, waiting for this encounter to be over. Dranian was still plugging his nose, and Shayne was covered in faeborn-cursed vomit. Kate's-brother-Greyson, though, looked frozen and panicked beneath the officer's stare.

"You weren't speeding," the officer told Cress. "You were holding up traffic."

"Holding up..." Cress blinked. "Are you trying to tell me I was going too slow?!"

"Yes. Way too slow. This is a busy city, and you're going to cause an accident if you drive like that. Can I have your license and registration, please?" The officer eyed the fairies in the back seat.

"I don't have any of that nonsense. It's for humans," Cress announced. Kate's-brother-Greyson slapped a hand over his eyes and pursed his lips.

Finally, Shayne leaned forward to help. He nodded toward Cress. "Don't worry about him, Officer Alwing. He's got several raging human mental illnesses."

The officer raised a brow in concern. "Does he?"

"Just let Officer Lily Baker deal with this. She knows all about his... *condition,*" Shayne added, and Cress turned around to glare into the back seat.

"You know Officer Baker?" the police officer said.

"She's my girlfriend," Shayne lied, flashing his lovely fairy smile.

The officer blinked at Shayne for a moment, and his own aged face broke into a smile. "Shayne!" he said. "I didn't recognize you back there. The last time I saw you, you were all dressed up and... wearing shoes."

"Lovely to see you again, officer." Shayne slumped back in the seat and forced another smile onto his exhausted, sick face.

"Are you coming to our department hockey game this summer? I'm sure we could use you on the team—"

"If you don't *mind,* we'll be leaving now. I have a bath to take," Cress stated.

"I'll be there, Officer Alwing. Tell Lily I say hi when you see her!" Shayne called as Cress slid the window back up. Cress pulled the chariot back onto the road, leaving the dumbstruck officer behind.

"Queensbane," Dranian muttered to Shayne. "She's going to kill you."

Shayne nodded. "Yes, she will try. I suppose I better not fall asleep tonight, lest she poison the coffee before we all drink it in the morning."

Kate's-brother-Greyson stared ahead with wide eyes, not moving a muscle. "Yeah," was all he managed to squeak out after a few minutes. "Lily's going to kill you for sure."

Cress debated about waiting until Kate's-brother-Greyson was gone before he got down to fairy business, but the rolled-up Fairy Post beside his seat must have been enchanted to make him obsess over it at all moments.

"Take a look at this," he said, abandoning his worry about the human and tossing the newspaper back to his brothers in the rear seat. Shuffling and sounds of paper-wrinkling followed.

"I'm making a decree," Cress stated when he imagined Shayne had seen the depiction of the Shadow Fairy. "I know full well Mor told us to stay away in his last message. I thought he needed a break from work, but this is something else entirely. This is something my royal gut is telling me will get him killed. The three of us…" He glanced over at Kate's-brother-Greyson who listened with a quizzical brow. "…the *four* of us, I suppose," he corrected, "are now entering into a fairy match. We need to convince Mor to return at all costs. Whichever one of us manages to get him back before it's too late will earn a great reward. But I know Mor. He's sensitive about Shadow Fairies," he added. "If he realizes we're going after him, he'll grow afraid we'll get involved, and he'll disappear. So, I beg you; be discreet."

Kate's-brother-Greyson raised his hand and left it in the air. It seemed as though he had questions of his own to ask, but Cress wasn't really sure if that's what the gesture meant.

"Why would Mor try to handle this himself?" Shayne asked first from the back seat. "Does he think just because he's a Shadow he needs to go head-to-head with this fellow?"

"What reward?" Dranian mumbled too quietly for anyone to really hear.

"He can only have one reason to go it alone," Cress answered Shayne. His grip tightened on the steering wheel until his knuckles turned white. "He must know who this Shadow is."

CHAPTER

5

Mor Trisencor and the TV that Told Secrets

Mor hadn't bothered to take off his hooded jacket, even though it was rain-speckled. The cathedral was empty and cold, and all the candles remained unlit. Rather than warm up the space with light and a log-popping fire, draw a cozy blanket, pick up a book, and wedge his feet into his too-tight slippers, he'd gone to the old "TV" in the basement that the human internet had told him how to get working.

A piping hot tea was nestled into his fingers. He didn't care for tea, but he knew if he drank coffee this late at night, he'd be up pacing and cleaning for hours instead of sleeping. And he might—he *might*—become weary and reckless enough to make a phone call. And that couldn't happen.

So, tea it was. The herbal remedy was the only thing keeping him warm as he watched the pictures on the TV screen flicker. The TV reminded him of Cress. The fae Prince had always hogged the remote for the TV in the café, and then he'd gone as far as to hide it somewhere so no one else could take it. Truly, Mor had found it pleasant to have the TV all to himself these last months. Even if the cathedral did feel a little empty in the evenings.

Mor watched the humans babble their news for half an hour. There was no mention of the tormentor in the shadows haunting the city streets. For a single night, it seemed the human journalists had forgotten that a deadly beast was on the loose, regardless of how Mor had tried to warn them.

Mor sipped his tea and winced. Simply put: tea tasted like dirt. There was no sweetness in it whatsoever.

He set his mug on a low table and lifted the remote, his thumb on the "off" button. But he hesitated when a new face filled the screen.

A young human woman stood there with painted lips, deep coloured hair, soft green eyes, and a modest scatter of freckles mostly covered by thickly smeared cream paint.

"Isn't that Violet Miller?" the on-screen reporters asked amongst themselves, and Mor's pointed ears tilted toward the TV. He crept closer to the screen, eyeing the face he'd just looked into only hours ago in his bell tower.

Violet Miller. He wondered if that was her real name or just the pen name she used to write her articles. He'd never seen her face before to match with her name. His rival in journalism, yet... also his informant, even if she didn't know it. Among a few others.

"Queensbane," he cursed as he realized. If only she'd told him her name in the bell tower. He could have laughed if he wasn't so curious about why she had come to his cathedral in the first place. When he'd first read her articles on The Sprinkled Scoop's human internet pages, he'd imagined her to be old and wrinkled like a mature human who'd been writing for a long time. Not young. Not...

Pretty.

Mor nearly turned off the TV again as Violet Miller started addressing the reporters. Her eyelash paints ran down her cheeks as the rain soaked her face, her hair, her clothes. The journalists all brought out umbrellas to protect their cameras, but not a single one offered an umbrella to the shivering, sopping wet female before them.

Regardless, Violet Miller spoke with clear words, holding a confidence entirely the opposite of how she'd been in the bell tower when she crossed Mor. "Yes," Violet Miller said in response to the chatter, looking right at the screen now. Seeming to look right at Mor. "I am the girl in the purple dress who woke up with no memories. I've also spent the last year of my life working at The Sprinkled Scoop as a journalist, reporting on whatever creep has been taking victims and haunting the streets of our city. Though I'm no longer with The Sprinkled Scoop, I plan to find the memory thief. I'm still going to stop him, and I'm still going to write about him from whichever news base I end up at."

Ah. So that was why Violet Miller had come to his cathedral.

Mor found himself smiling. He tossed the remote back onto the table and folded his arms. He watched the human say several other things aimed at warding the reporters off. After a moment, she excused herself, but not before one last riveting statement:

"To the women-murdering predator of Toronto, I'll say this: I'm coming for you." The reporters went wild, snapping photos and asking new questions, but Violet Miller nodded her farewell and left. The news switched to a different story.

Mor tapped a finger against his chin. What a surprise.

Violet Miller wanted to *find* the monster of the city, while all the other humans seemed intent on avoiding him—the ruby-haired gumiho. The Shadow Fairy. The fox. The memory-stealing monster.

The one fairy in all of existence Mor had wanted to hide from for the rest of his faeborn life.

Fourteen years prior, the Shadow Army had come to the coastal village of Pane in the Dark Corner of Ever in search of childling recruits. Mor had been the only one from his village who'd volunteered to join. It wasn't because he wanted to; it was because he knew a faeborn male or female from Pane would be required to enlist before the army would leave and move on to the next fairy village. While in Pane, the Shadow Army leaders had demanded the locals bring them fresh meat, sweet blossoms, baskets of vegetables, and everything else the folk of Pane had worked so hard to store all year.

Mor was the strongest childling fae in his town at eleven years of age. And though he was the most loved by the village fairy folk—those who worked alongside him gathering shellfish on the seashores especially—he was the only one without family. His aunt and uncle who raised him had passed on when the sniffle spell had rushed across the coast.

So, it was only natural for him to rescue the rest of the Pane childlings from such a fate and offer himself when there was a chance he would survive because of his strength. Most of the other young males or females from Pane either would have frozen to death in the mountains or would have been snapped in half in training.

The Shadow Army was not half as bad as the rumours had claimed. Training was hard in the days that followed Mor's recruitment, but food was never scarce. With ripe white grapes and hogbeast meat to feed on, Mor grew stronger as he grew in years. And even though whispers moved through the Shadow Army that they were planning a war against the North Corner, Mor kept to himself and believed the army could not be so faeborn foolish as to actually go through with it and kill thousands of Northern fairies without just cause.

But as time went on, and he beheld the vicious nature of the Shadows, his belief began to wither away. Eventually, he feared a great deal that the Shadow Army would, in fact, attack the North Corner of Ever and slaughter thousands. All for the sake of a greed that Mor didn't share.

Five faeborn years after the date of his recruitment, he was invited to dine among the army elites where there was feasting, shouting, cheering, and marvels each night.

Mor went, but he never ate their feast food.

He never shouted their praises.

He never cheered alongside the other army elites.

He did not watch the marvels.

He waited.

And when the time was right, he destroyed them all.

6

Violet Miller and the Whack-Job Police Officer

Crumbs of a dream lingered in Violet's mind when she awoke. Her lashes fluttered in the late afternoon sun filtering through the slats in her window blinds. Her hand drifted slowly to her thudding forehead, and she made an anguished sound, dreaming of a tall glass of cold water and an aspirin. A ringing sound echoed through her ears.

She sat up in bed, dropped her hand to her lap, and glanced at her mirror across the room. She screamed.

Zorah burst through her bedroom door with oven mitts on. "What? What? *What?*" she asked. "What happened?" The pretty surgeon in her early thirties looked like she was ready to use her oven mitts as boxing gloves. Her glasses were halfway down her nose and her hair was falling out of its bun, but her eyes were big and alert.

Violet lifted a torn flap of her most expensive blouse. "What happened to my awesome clothes?!" she screeched. She twisted so she could see her back in the mirror. An even bigger dirt stain ran down her spine.

Zorah slapped an oven-mitted hand over her chest. "Gah, *seriously*, Violet! I thought someone came in here and attacked you! Why'd you scream so loud over a measly blouse?" But as her eyes took in Violet's state, her brows came together. "What were you doing last night?" she asked.

"I have no idea!" Violet said, rushing to her mirror to see better. "And where are my heels?!"

"Vi, are you really concerned about your shoes right now?" Zorah slid off an oven mitt and came over, lifting a piece of Violet's shredded sleeve.

"I spent every penny I had on those shoes! I don't have money to buy another pair." Violet dropped to the floor to look beneath her bed. Once on her knees, she spotted a long run down her nylons, and she moaned. "These were brand new nylons, too."

"You look like you played mud football." Zorah tugged her oven mitt back on and headed for the door. "And since you're not hurt, I'm going back to my pie!" Zorah trudged into the hall and trotted down the stairs to the kitchen. "Come try it!" she shouted back up. "The berries came straight from our garden!"

Violet barely heard her. She climbed to her feet and grimaced toward her mirror at the sight of her hair a tangled mess, her lipstick smeared over her chin, and her mascara a river of black down both cheeks. "Is this a joke?!" she shouted at Zorah, or the wall, or the neighbours through the window, or whoever. "Did someone pull me out of a swamp this morning?" She headed into the hall.

In the kitchen, Zorah was dragging a steaming pie from the oven. She grinned and placed it on the hot pads. "Yum!"

"Zorah!" Violet shouted as she came down. She slowed when she looked at the clock in the kitchen. It was the middle of the day.

Zorah turned with her oven mitts in the air. "Huh?"

"What happened to me?" Violet asked in exasperation.

Zorah paused and pushed her glasses up higher on her nose. She looked Violet over. "You got in a fight?" she guessed.

Violet threw her hands up. "You're not at all worried that I look like this?" she demanded, and Zorah shrugged.

"I mean, I *was*, but then you started going off about your heels, so I figured you were fine—"

"You're not wondering or concerned about what might have happened to me for my blouse to look this way?" Violet went on. "I don't even remember going to bed or…"

A large, ear-piercing bell.

A long, black, rain-covered coat with a hood.

Striking multicoloured eyes.

A steep cathedral roof.

Falling…

Violet gasped as bits and pieces of a chopped-up memory came back to her. Parts of it were missing—like a story with gaps. She couldn't remember why she was on a roof or how she got there. But Violet remembered falling. She remembered her throat being too thick to scream. She remembered…

Two strong arms catching her in midair. The smell of flowers and an earthy, tea-like aroma hitting her senses as he hugged her close and broke her fall.

Violet slapped a hand over her mouth. Old fears she'd stuffed away rushed upward alongside the vomit that threatened the back of her throat.

"What?" Zorah raised a brow. When Violet didn't answer right away, Zorah abandoned her to go smell the raspberry pie, but she cast a worried look back toward Violet.

"Zorah, I think it happened again." Violet sank into the closest chair at the table. She could hardly believe her own words. She couldn't trust she'd really just said them out loud.

"You think *what* happened?" Zorah blew lightly on the pie and pulled a lifter from the drawer.

"I think… someone erased my memories."

The pie lifter clattered to the floor. Zorah's glasses fell off, too. She turned to face Violet again without stooping to pick them up. "Are you messing with me right now?" Her words were sharp and to the point like she wouldn't appreciate it if this was a joke. "What do you mean, *someone* erased your memories? You mean you've got amnesia again?"

"No, I think *someone* is to blame," Violet said. "Like what happened with all those other women…" She slowly lifted a hand to her chest, feeling her deep, living heartbeat as she thought of the ones who starved to death while they were sleeping.

"Then how do you remember *me*?" Zorah asked, ripping off the oven mitts and scooting into the chair across from Violet. Her large, unmaintained brows were scrunched together.

"Not all my memories were erased like last time, just…" Violet glanced at Zorah's phone to check the date. A whole day had passed since she was let go from The Sprinkled Scoop. "…just part of yesterday, I think. I remember pieces of what happened, but something is definitely missing." Violet rubbed her forehead, reminded of aspirin and trying not to panic as the familiar feeling of helplessness overtook her senses. It didn't feel real—that she was waking up again, missing part of herself.

Zorah's shoulders relaxed and her eyes softened. "Oh." She almost laughed.

Violet dropped her hand to the table. "It's not funny."

"Oh, I know. I'm just relieved. I thought it was like, you know, a *real* memory wipe or something. Like before." Her aunt waved a hand around, completely dismissing the urgency of what Violet was saying. She even went back to her pie and poked it.

"I'm being serious," Violet said.

Zorah nodded. "All right."

"Zorah!" Violet stood again, and Zorah sighed.

"Yes, I know you are. You look ridiculous and you don't remember what happened. Let me guess, you were out late last night? Did you enjoy some celebratory festivities with your coworkers at The Scoop for getting hired permanently?" Zorah folded her arms.

"No! I didn't go anywhere last night! I remember going somewhere yesterday morning though." Violet glanced off. She'd gone to a cathedral yesterday. She'd gotten the address from a niche newspaper, and she was going to try and get a job interview. But what in the world had happened after that?

She looked down at her outfit again.

"I think I need to go to the police," she said.

"I think you need to sleep it off," Zorah said back. "But if you're worried, stop at the station on your way into work. I'm guessing you're planning to head to The Scoop with a *very* well-rehearsed excuse as to why you missed a whole morning. I'm surprised they didn't even try calling while you were sleeping." She took a long knife from the drawer and carefully began cutting the pie into slices. "Also, can you grab my glasses?" She pointed to them with her toe.

Violet huffed and grabbed the glasses off the floor. She set them on the counter and headed back up to her room to change.

Something had happened. She felt in her bones; the familiar loss of a thing she couldn't put her finger on, the unexplainable feeling of having misplaced something important. She could have walked back downstairs and forced her aunt to believe her, especially because if she didn't have Zorah's concern, she had no one's. But Violet wasn't sure she wanted to force Zorah into this without finding out what had really happened first.

The last time Violet had woken up with amnesia, Zorah had sacrificed everything for her. And while Zorah was a positive person by nature, she'd been a young, struggling student at the time. Even though her aunt had never complained about it, Violet knew it had been hard on Zorah back then to take care of a young girl while carrying the weight of classes and finances on her shoulders.

Violet checked herself over quickly as she pulled off her clothes— arms, legs, fingers, toes—for bruises or cuts. There was nothing apart from a few scrapes on her elbows. She didn't feel like she'd been assaulted or hurt, but if she *had* been attacked and had put up a fight, she'd likely have the attacker's DNA beneath her fingernails. She lifted her hands.

Her dusty-rose nail polish was chipped on the ends and her nails were jagged, like she'd savagely filed them down. It was so bizarre she couldn't stop staring at them.

Maybe after she went to the police station, she could spend the afternoon getting a manicure so Zorah would think she was working. A grunt-moan escaped her as she thought about having to tell Zorah the truth about The Sprinkled Scoop job. It was a true saving grace that Zorah didn't watch the news, or she would have already figured out that Violet had been let go based on that horrid interview Violet had done in the rain yesterday—Why had she done that?

She flopped back onto her bed.

A wave of light-headedness made the room spin, and she wondered if she'd missed taking her iron pills last night. For a split second, she considered maybe her iron deficiency was to blame for her patches of memory loss. But it was too weird. She'd never had trouble remembering quite like this, even during her worst days of dizzy spells.

Her hand came up slowly to her temple as she got up, squirmed out of her clothes, and pulled on a comfortable pink summer dress. Once she smoothed down her hair, washed her face, and redid her makeup, she looked at her reflection in the mirror, reliving her worst day all over again. She had to admit—this felt a little like that day. Lost. Filled with questions. No one waiting at her bedside to tell her what had happened. Her skin pebbled, and she hugged her arms to herself, shivering and shaking the thought away.

The police station was loud and busy. Violet almost turned around and changed her mind, positive she was inconveniencing the Toronto police officers who seemed to have too much on their plates already. She could hardly hear the officer calling her over when it was her turn to approach the desk for crime reporting.

She brushed a hand down her hair to position it back in place, and she ventured over, pushing past a few people to reach her spot. She shifted her purse to her lap as she sat down in the open chair which looked anything but sanitary.

"What brings you here this afternoon, Miss?" the officer across the desk asked as he punched some buttons on his keyboard.

"Um. I'm not really sure. There's a chance I was attacked," Violet said as quietly as she could. She didn't want the whole station to know.

"There's *a chance* you were?" The officer looked up from his computer. It was remarkable he could hear her over the noise.

"I mean, I don't remember. I think my memories were erased. Listen, I'm a journalist, and I've been following some pretty weird, unexplainable stories. Like potentially magic, folktale type stuff." She held up her hand to stop the officer when his face changed. "Don't assume I'm eccentric just yet. I have evidence and all the facts point to something going on in this city that doesn't always seem human in nature. I'm sure you know about the memory loss case—"

"Hey, Baker!" the officer suddenly shouted toward a far desk in the corner, making Violet jump. A young, blonde officer looked up from the desk. She had her sleeves rolled up, revealing two armfuls of tattoos. "This one's for you!" The guy nodded toward Violet as he yelled, and Violet blushed as his volume turned heads. The officer glanced back at Violet. "Go see Officer Baker. She'll listen to your story."

"B... but..." Violet raised a finger to protest, but the officer pointed back toward the corner desk again.

"We have an officer who specializes in... well, you know—weird, supernatural, mythological... anything unexplainable, basically. You're best off telling your story to her," he said.

Violet's jaw tightened a little. She was used to people not believing in the stories and articles she wrote with her opinions on the odd happenings in Toronto. But half of her facts she'd gotten from the police themselves. This officer was clearly uninformed about that. She bit at her lip in frustration as she picked up her purse and weaved through the crowded station toward the waiting blonde officer.

Books as thick as the Bible were piled on her desk. Violet stole a look at the title of the one on top: MODERN FOLKTALES. Another was splayed open with a loose paper tucked in like a bookmark. Notes were written on it in messy cursive. Violet reached over and carefully lifted the cover to see the title: CANADIAN ODDITIES AND OTHER MYTHS OF THE NORTH.

It seemed this Officer Baker person was the right cop for Violet after all.

"Can I grab your name, friend?" Officer Baker said through a wad of gum. She tugged the book away, making the cover slip from Violet's fingers. The officer slapped the book shut and added it to her stack of colourful tomes.

Violet worked her jaw, wondering what this officer was trying to hide from a mere curious journalist. "We're not friends," Violet pointed out. "I don't know you, and you don't know me."

Officer Baker nodded and pursed her lips. "My bad, citizen."

"Citizen?" Violet huffed a skeptical laugh.

Officer Baker settled her gaze on Violet across the desk. She slowly blew a large bubble with her gum, and Violet watched it grow and grow. When it popped, Baker clawed it all back into her mouth with her teeth. She didn't break eye contact once, and for the first time, Violet shifted uncomfortably in her seat.

"You haven't given me your name yet and you complained when I called you *friend*. So, *citizen* it is," the officer finally said.

This time, Violet nodded and sat up a little straighter. She cleared her throat. "My name is Violet Miller."

For a police officer, Baker looked young. Young and pretty. And beautifully tattooed. That felt like a triple threat.

"Violet... Miller..." Officer Baker poked the name into the keys of her laptop, but she paused before she finished. She turned in her seat to face Violet. "The girl who can't remember anything? The one from the TV shows?" she asked, lifting her artful arms to her desk and folding her

46

hands.

"Yeah… That one." Violet glanced off. For the last ten years, her childhood fame had gotten her far in her high school relationships, with the fresh-out-of-high-school internship, and with her online socials. But after being dumped in the street by The Sprinkled Scoop, Violet wasn't sure people would still admire her for being 'the mysterious girl in the purple dress.' Also, she was terrible at social media, so she'd never really kept up with it.

Officer Baker looked Violet up and down. "I wasn't sure about you when you first sat down here, to be honest. But I've always wondered about your history. Maybe we have a few things in common."

"My history isn't why I came in today," Violet said. "I came in because I went somewhere yesterday afternoon—to a cathedral on…" She rubbed her temples as her choppy memories flickered. Officer Baker gave her a moment to think and turned back to her computer to take notes. "Roll Street," Violet remembered. "A cathedral on Roll Street."

Officer Baker's fingers stilled, hovering just above the keys of her laptop. Her gaze appeared glued to her hands.

"What?" Violet asked. "You stopped typing, and you haven't even heard what happened to me yet."

Officer Baker's gaze fired up in surprise like she forgot Violet was there. "Hmm? Sorry… Go ahead."

Violet cleared her throat and tried to piece everything together as best she could. "A crime might have happened. And if so, some of my memories may have been erased to hide it. But not all my memories are gone—it's like only bits and pieces are missing."

The officer reached slowly for her phone resting on her desk. She pecked at a few buttons as she listened to Violet speak, nodding all the while like she was listening.

"All right. And you're sure it was the cathedral on *Roll* Street, right? Why do you think your memories were erased? Did you wake up somewhere with no recollection of how you got there? Sort of like someone was trying to cover their tracks and took only enough of your memory to protect themselves?" she asked, and Violet blinked in surprise.

"Yes!"

"You know what?" Officer Baker looked around the station. "The noise in here is unreal. Do you want to talk outside?"

Violet nodded and stood, relieved since she could hardly hear herself think. She slid out of the chair and squeezed through the officers and complaining juveniles alike to get to the door. When she reached it, she pushed it open and stepped out into the warm summer air, turning to hold the door for Officer Baker.

Officer Baker wasn't behind her.

Violet leaned to peer back inside, but the officer wasn't at her desk, either. In fact, Violet couldn't see her anywhere in the station. She turned back toward the sidewalk and started at the sight of someone there.

A guy stood in a black vampire coat with his hood up, peering at her with silvery brown eyes that glowed in the late afternoon sun.

"Nice to see you awake." His voice was deep and crisp.

Violet looked both ways, wondering who this weirdo was. "Are you talking to me?" she asked.

He marched across the sidewalk and grabbed her hand. Violet's grip slipped off the police station door, and in the blink of an eye, the world around her vanished.

7

Violet Miller and the Teleporting Vampire Lord

The sunlight disappeared, the wind ceased to blow, and everything smelled of dust and damp wood in an instant. Violet blinked to adjust her eyes. Her hands were flat on a hardwood floor—she was on her knees... *somewhere else.* She'd just been at the police station... She'd just been grabbed and taken and...

When she looked up, she saw a wall filled with newspaper clippings and familiar blog articles; articles, she realized, *she* wrote. She quickly looked around and took inventory of a wooden desk, stacks of newspapers, and a chalk board to her right. A whole network of notes covered the chalkboard; details, dates, names...

Her own news stories came to mind in waves. It seemed like she was in an office of some sort—an office of someone who was as obsessed with the monster roaming the city streets as she was. Unless...

It all pieced together, memories of the day before that she thought she'd lost rushing back and slamming into place. This office. These articles. This cathedral... Violet gasped as she realized she'd come to this conclusion before, and she suddenly knew that all the memories she'd lost from the day prior were somehow *back*.

She scrambled to her feet and reeled backward—right into someone who nudged her away again. She spun with her fists raised.

A guy.

The guy.

The one from the bell tower. He must have owned this office. He must have been following along on what the news was saying about his kidnapping, memory-stealing ways.

His hood was still up, shadowing his diabolical face, but the office window brought in enough light that Violet could see his features this time; his smooth, tanned skin. His wild, treacherously beautiful eyes. The shallow curve of his lips that he kept calmly together instead of gaping at her like she was at him.

Violet slid back and bumped into a desk. Her hand flew to it to keep balance, and she padded her fingers over everything in reach. But she didn't take her eyes off the guy. He didn't take his eyes off her, either. He just watched as her fingers wrapped around a cup of pens, and he raised an eyebrow as if asking what she planned to do with them.

They became ammo. She hurled them at him, three pens at a time.

"You psycho!" she shouted.

One pen bounced off his shoulder. Another off his stomach. One even pelted his face.

He looked annoyed, but he didn't retaliate.

When that didn't work, Violet spun for the desk and grabbed a jar of ink. She turned back and raised it above her head, threatening to throw it.

This time, his hands came up like a shield, and he tried to stop her. "Miss Miller—"

She splattered the ink at him—hitting the side of his face and his collar.

He dropped his hands and rose to his full height, eyes narrowing, mouth thinning. But he still didn't try to grab her or shove her or eat her for a snack.

"Murderous, hostage-taking psycho!" she said anyway.

Violet spun for the desk and picked up a thick book to throw at him, but dizziness rushed in, and her limbs grew weak. The book dropped back onto the desk, and she grabbed her head as her thoughts teetered. Tingling sensations washed up her legs and she knew they might give out.

"My iron pills…" she murmured to herself, or whoever. She whirled back toward him, but the spinning only made it worse. Violet tipped forward, grabbing a handful of his vampire coat on the way down. He didn't reach to catch her like a gentleman. He didn't touch her at all as she passed out.

Music was playing somewhere, softly brushed violin strings and a deep cello. Violet opened her eyes.

A canopy of sheer curtains hung between thick, black, gothic-like spokes that held the bed together. It wasn't a room she recognized, and she had to think for a moment before she recalled where she was.

She sprang up, gripping the white bedsheets with all her might when it hit her. Her mouth went dry, and her wide eyes darted around to take in her surroundings. The windows were covered by bloodred curtains, and the furniture around the room was all dark wood and surprisingly clean, yet inexplicably sharp looking.

Classical music, a gothic bed, drawn curtains…

"He is *totally* a vampire!" Violet whispered.

"Not at all."

Violet almost sprang from the bed before spotting the silvery-eyed guy at her bedside. Her mind soared with the thought to fight her way out, but her body wouldn't move. She sat there, pinned beneath his attention, realizing that exiting the bed would only make it easy for him to grab her.

Her eyes dropped to his casual white shirt and gym pants. His creepy coat was gone, allowing Violet to see several tattoos wrapping his neck. His curly hair was pulled back into a bun too, as though he was heading out for a jog like any normal person who got up early to exercise. He looked vastly different than he had in the bell tower and outside the police station. In fact, he was a bit handsome, in a terrifying way. She cleared her throat and scolded herself for having such a thought about a dangerous, possibly supernatural kidnapper.

"Are you the..." What were you supposed to call someone who looked and acted like a vampire? "...*master* of this house?" She said it with an uneasy note—it wasn't really a house. More like a haunted mansion.

"Yes." The guy's deep voice was calm. Deceptively soothing.

Violet glanced at his arms where reddish marks covered his wrists and palms. It was like he'd stuck his hands into an oven and pulled out a hot pan without oven mitts.

"What are you, then? Some sort of dark housemaster of doom?" She scooched backward an inch on the bed, wondering if she could jump off the other side and plunge through the window. She'd have to break the glass with her body, but so be it. It would probably only be a two-story fall.

She swallowed at the thought, rubbed her temples, and cursed her brain fog. She needed her iron supplements before her irrational thinking got her killed.

Her attention fired back up to the Master of Doom. He was folding his large arms, hiding away the burn marks on his tanned skin.

"I'll admit, I didn't plan to ever see you again after you recklessly flung yourself off my roof like a fool," he said. Violet's fingers worked through the knots she'd made in the bedsheets. He spoke with a bit of an accent. "And I would have taken you home after you fainted in my faeborn-cursed office but…" He unfolded his arms and leaned forward, coming over her and bracing his fists against the bed. Violet's insides tumbled into acrobatic leaps she didn't realize her organs knew how to do. His face was less than three inches away, and he studied her curiously—right in the eyes. Exactly what a murderous psycho would do.

Violet's breathing turned shallow when he inched even closer. She imagined him trying to kiss her or some other horrifying atrocity. But his cheek moved past hers and he paused there. He sniffed.

Violet's jaw dropped. He was some kind of pervert.

She slapped a hand over her racing heart.

"You have a scent from exactly a decade ago that shouldn't be on you," the guy said matter-of-factly by her ear, and Violet's wild heart seemed to stop.

She might have been dead on the spot for how still she was. How every muscle inside of her had tightened in an instant. *A decade ago.*

"What did you just say?"

The guy pulled away, stood, and refolded his arms. The room felt colder all of a sudden. He looked at Violet strangely. "Who are you?" he asked. "Why do you smell like that? You absolutely reek of something."

Violet's palms were sweaty, but her bewilderment at his rudeness was what stole her ability to respond. She couldn't have told him if she wanted to—and she most certainly did not want to. She needed to run before he did something. Before he asked more invasive questions. She tossed the sheets aside and climbed from the bed to leave, hoping with every ounce of her being that he'd miraculously let her walk out without seizing her. She was unsure if she was more perturbed about his brief mention of her past, that he thought she stunk, or at how he'd looked at her like he wanted to take a large bite out of her neck with gross, elongated teeth he was probably hiding past his shapely lips.

But as soon as she stood, dizziness pooled at the sides of her brain and she put her arms out to catch her balance. After staring longingly at the door for a second, she sank back down to sit on the bed again.

The vampire lord didn't move. He just watched. He also didn't try to help her sit when she was clearly struggling—not that she wanted him anywhere near her. As her eyes went in and out of focus, Violet took another look at the red marks on his hands, trying to sort out what his problem was and why he was such an arse on wheels.

"What happened to your hands?" she asked, imagining him murdering people in his creepy cathedral basement and getting irritated skin from all the grabbing and holding and destroying.

The guy took a deep breath and huffed it out. "Sometimes it hurts to touch you," he said.

Violet glanced up at his face. He didn't seem like he was the joking sort. Creepy and deadly, maybe, but definitely not the jokester she thought he was when she'd read the inscription on the wooden doors out front warning trespassers that there were monsters in this building.

"This has to be a joke." She rubbed her forehead viciously. The front doors had basically told her to stay out for her own good and she'd still waltzed up to the windows to snoop like a fresh platter of easy-to-murder young woman.

"Why would touching me hurt you?" she asked. "And who gave you permission to touch me in the first place?"

"It hurt the first time we met on the roof. But it doesn't hurt today," he informed her like this conversation was totally normal. "Why is that?"

"I don't know! Don't you think after all your evil deeds this might be some kind of deserved punishment?" she snapped.

"All of my evil..." He blinked. "Queensbane, what sort of faeborn evil mischief do you think I did?" he asked, and Violet released a grunt from the back of her throat.

"Are you joking? How many women are you going to kill before you stop terrorizing the streets?! In case you haven't heard, I'm not afraid of you!" She pointed at him when she said it. Though, she was totally lying. Most of her was afraid, just a small, teensy tiny part of her wasn't. The idiot part of her that was going to get her killed today.

The guy stared, his mouth gaping for several seconds. He released a huff-laugh of disbelief and put his hands on his hips as he seemed to let that sink in. Seemed to realize that she'd figured him out like the brilliant reporter she was. Then he laughed, more to himself. "Queensbane," he murmured again as he rubbed his temple.

"How many?" Violet asked again. "How many more of us must suffer—"

"I'll ask the questions, Human," he cut her off, and Violet felt the blood drain from her face at the word.

"Human?" Every cuss word she knew went off in her mind like a potty-mouth grenade. "Oh my gosh, you *are* a vampire!" She scooted back on the bed and grabbed the sheets, pulling them high up to her neck.

The guy almost rolled his eyes. "Vampires don't exist. Be realistic."

Violet pointed at him. "You have to let me leave your creepy dungeon. Holding me here is a *crime.*"

"I haven't tried to stop you from leaving. And you seem to be under the impression that I want you to stay, which I don't. But I doubt you're able to leave on your own two weak, wobbly human feet in your condition," he said. "You need my help."

"I'm going to have you arrested," Violet promised. "You're crazy, and I'll make sure the whole world knows it."

He stifled an eye roll. "If you're finished with your outrageous threats, I'll ask my questions now. Who. *Are.* You?" he tried again. "Explain why you're painted with such a dreadful scent from—" He thought for a moment. He sniffed. "—at least ten faeborn years ago?"

Violet's mouth hung open in disbelief. Not only was this guy a woman-snatcher, he was also totally bat-spit crazy.

When she didn't answer, he said, "Fine. Play stupid. But at least tell me why you broke in here yestermorning."

Her day yesterday returned in flashes. She had no idea how or why her memories had suddenly come back. But she remembered every detail; her atrocious exit from The Sprinkled Scoop, the bus ride phone call, getting ready for an interview for The Fairy Post, coming to the cathedral... "The job posting," she realized, then grunted.

The guy raised a brow. "The job is yours."

Violet blinked up at him. "I don't want it."

"Too bad." He eyed her and unfolded his arms. "You are my ideal help, Violet Miller. Your writing, your fact checking, your belief in magic, your choice of stories for articles. And from what I hear, you need me now that The Sprinkled Scoop has dropped you like a charmed hot coal. Rest up today, and we'll start tomorrow. Permitting you pass the interview in the morning, of course." He turned and headed for the door.

Violet's lips parted in disbelief. "Why did you make a job posting in the first place? Were you trying to lure in another innocent victim?" she challenged, scaring herself a little. "Am I going to be the next person you leave in a heap with no memories and rocks in my pockets?!"

The guy stopped. He turned, his eyes slightly wider even though the rest of him seemed as uninterested as before. "I posted a job, Human, because I've become busy with other things."

Violet released a revulsed huff. *Other* things. "I can only imagine," she said.

He seemed to think better of leaving. The guy turned and drew back into the room. The corner of his mouth tugged up into a poorly suppressed smirk. He approached until he stood right before Violet, a daunting statue of muscle strength, tattoos, and the devil's eyes. "Worse things than you can possibly imagine," he assured.

Violet swallowed. When he made eye contact like that, the colours of his irises were utterly consuming—like a drug or restraint that pinned her in place and made her believe she couldn't move.

Her stomach interrupted with a growl. She slapped a hand over her abdomen, but he was already glancing at her loud, obnoxious stomach with something of its own to say.

"I haven't eaten anything since yesterday," Violet felt the need to explain for some unbeknownst reason, though she shouldn't have cared what he thought. Her cheeks felt warm.

He sighed. "What would you like for breakfast? I have everything," he said without addressing her stomach music.

Violet glanced back at the window she'd thought to leap through. There was no way she could eat here—with him.

"Toast? With jam?" she suggested.

His face twisted into a scowl. "No bread. How about cooked bird eggs, hog meat, and warm beast milk? And coffee?"

A scoffing laugh bubbled in Violet's throat, but she sealed it in when she realized he wasn't joking. "Sure," was all she said, smile dropping.

He finally turned to leave. Violet stayed still until his footsteps disappeared down the hall. As soon as he was lost to his hunt for *cooked bird eggs* and *hog meat*, she lifted from the bed and used the wall to keep herself balanced while she planned her escape through her brain fog.

CHAPTER

8

Mor Trisencor and the Human on Quick Feet

It took everything inside of Mor to stay leaning back, relaxed against the kitchen counter as he listened to the human struggle. He didn't care to try and help her—the lightly stinging flesh on his fingers and wrists was enough of a reminder that he should never touch her again. But she was astoundingly clumsy. He sipped his coffee as the sounds of her pushing a table across the storage room downstairs flitted through the cathedral and into his lovely, pointed fairy ears, along with a ridiculous amount of female grunting, and a messy climb out the window.

He smirked when it seemed she'd fallen onto the grass outside—with a shriek loud enough to wake the sky deities. At least she'd managed to make it out in one piece. Mor sighed and guzzled the rest of his coffee, sprinkled with the light tastes of hazelnut and cream. He turned and set his empty mug on the counter, then leaned his hands flat against the smooth surface, letting the cool marble ease the hurting flesh on his palms. His skin was nearly healed of her. What a relief it had been when he'd grabbed Violet Miller outside of Lily's workplace yesterday and hadn't been scorched a second time. The pain had been startling when Mor had first caught the human—when she was falling from his roof toward her death. It was like touching cold iron with one's bare flesh, and the irate, prickly aching even two full days later was astoundingly annoying.

His phone beeped. Mor crossed the kitchen and flicked it on to see he had a new speaking message from Shayne. He thought to snap his human phone in half to be rid of the faeborn fool who kept leaving him messages every few days. Shayne didn't seem to understand that when a fairy ignored him, it meant he didn't want to talk.

"Sky deities," Mor cursed, caving and poking the buttons until Shayne's speaking message performed its duty. The white-haired fairy's unmistakable, chipper voice filled Mor's kitchen.

"Good morning, Mor. Today's message is a simple death threat, unfortunately. If you don't come back here, I'll kill you. Simple as that! See you soon, then."

Mor rolled his eyes and silenced his phone. Shayne's first few messages had been sweet and inviting in the beginning, stuffed with luring things meant to make Mor miss home based on how much he was loved and missed and a bunch of other faeborn nonsense. Shayne's next few messages had been tricks. "Cress is bleeding out!" and, "Queensbane, Mor! We need you! Kate was hit by a speeding vessel on wheels and her arms ripped off!" and Mor's favourite, "A flood has rolled in, and the café is under water! Everyone is drowning inside but me! Hurry, Mor!"

Since then, most of Shayne's messages had turned violent. In the last one, he'd laid out the exact fairy gutting Mor was in for if he did not return. It had only been two months since Mor had left the café to face his own beasts, and in that time, he was sure he'd heard Shayne's voice more than anyone who was still trapped in the café with the white-haired assassin.

Mor tossed his phone back on the counter and headed out of the kitchen, through the hall, and down the faded emerald carpet on the stairs. He lifted his coat from the hanger and sniffed it to make sure it still smelled of the crushed dandelions he'd rubbed into the fabric, and not his catastrophic blend of Dark Corner and North Corner fairy scents. He slid the coat on and stepped into an airslip.

The cathedral vanished, and the city appeared around him. He walked casually, at least thirty steps behind the human. Violet Miller boarded a large human vessel on wheels—a bus, as Kate and Lily called it. Mor could never bring himself to ride one, stuffed between all those nose-picking, unbathed humans staring at their phones and completely inconsiderate of those around them.

The air carried a soft blend of fragrances, and Mor sighed, following the most familiar one. The one that a dangerous monster was very likely also following from the shadows. After a nice, brisk morning stroll, Mor left the walking to the humans and slipped back into the air. In a moment's rush, he appeared across the street from Violet Miller's humble garden-fenced home. Colourful flowers blossomed in the vines covering the fence, and baby vegetables sprouted from the greens. For a split second, Violet Miller's yard reminded Mor of the North Corner of Ever with its lush garden villages and the magic air that fed the buds.

He tore his gaze away and glanced down at his feet just as the city bus rolled to a stop down the road. Violet Miller half-tumbled out the vessel gates and put on a horrendous show of trying to walk normally as she made her way to her house. She opened the front door and walked right in, announcing to Mor and possibly all the creatures watching that she kept her home unlocked, even when she wasn't there.

A large living space window permitted Mor to see the human rush to the kitchen cupboard and drag out a bottle with shaking hands once she was inside. He folded his arms as he watched. Violet Miller twisted the lid, dumped a pill or two into her palm and tossed them into the back of her throat. She guzzled a cup of water resting on the counter seemingly without questioning how long it had been sitting there.

The human escape artist dropped into a chair like a rock and leaned forward on her kitchen's feasting table. Mor chewed on the inside of his cheek. Truly, she appeared dead. She was just slightly too far away for him to hear her rhythms, but the twitch of her pinky finger told him she hadn't yet died. Not that he would have rushed in to save her anyway, rude as she was with her name calling, trespassing, and tossing pens and ink at his face.

The air grew a pinch chillier. The human hot season seemed to forget its job for a moment as a dark presence breathed past Mor. Mor kept to his side of the street, his chest tightening as a hint of that deadly, alluring, dangerous scent from his past crawled over him.

"There you are," Mor whispered to himself.

A second later, a fairy folk in a scent-cloaking coat similar to Mor's appeared at the side window of Violet Miller's house. Though the fairy's hood was up, his rich, ruby-red hair peeked out ever so slightly. He peered into the house, watching the human falling asleep on the table.

Mor tapped his chin. "That was far too easy," he muttered. "Fool."

With that, Mor turned and continued his stroll, back the way he had come. The only disappointment he felt was that he would not be there to witness what would happen to the ruby-haired fairy when he tried to touch Violet Miller.

As he left to watch from a distance, Mor prayed to the sky deities the human would resurrect her power to repel fairy flesh in time, lest she become the next victim of the nine tailed fox.

CHAPTER

9

Violet Miller and the Most Epic Blog that Might Ever Exist, Maybe

The world was spinning. Violet waited for what felt like hours before she could move. And even when the iron supplements slowed her mind to a normal speed, she still felt groggy and weak.

She stood to get another glass of water. And some toast. And jam. And three cookies. And a handful of almonds. Everything she could get her hands on, really. The tip of her nose felt numb and prickly. She flicked it, trying to get the feeling back as she scarfed back more food than her body would have been able to handle at a normal snack time.

As she lazily spread jam over her second piece of toast, she grumbled about her blood sugar problems, her iron deficiency problems, her hand-some-vampire-aka-Master-of-Doom problems.

When she lifted her eyes, she startled at the sight of someone looking into the house through the garden window. The butterknife slipped from her fingers and clattered over the floor as she tried to decide if she was dizzy and delusional or if there was actually a peeping Tom on her property. But she blinked, and the figure was gone.

Still, she stared at the window, not really seeing the flower-covered fence outside, or the lengthy crack in the glass, or anything. She was sure she'd spotted glittering, metallic-red hair and a set of eyes that looked like... *his*. The Master of Doom's.

Violet swallowed and glanced at her toast.

She hadn't imagined it. Just like she hadn't imagined anything at the cathedral.

Someone out there had tried to wipe away her memories. Again.

Violet shoved the plate of toast away and headed for the front door. She dragged an old pair of heels out of the closet and threw on a business jacket over her wrinkled, grass-stained, two-days-worn summer dress to try and look somewhat decent. She couldn't remember the last time she'd looked this messy so many days in a row.

She wouldn't go to the police. She couldn't show her shameful face to any reporters either after what she'd said when she was let go from The Sprinkled Scoop. She could never go back to the cathedral again— she wouldn't even if someone paid her to. But she couldn't stay home, either. What if the Master of Doom had the means to track down where she lived? She paused at the front door and glanced back at the kitchen window. Then she turned and jogged back through the house, up the stairs and into her room. She grabbed her laptop. A moment later she pushed out of the house and headed back to the bus stop.

Zorah's gasp filled the entire hospital waiting room. "Did you bring me a bubble tea?" Her 'excited voice' was so loud, Violet cringed. The waiting room was packed today; a mother with a sleeping baby shot a look at Zorah's back.

"Aren't I the best niece ever?" Violet held a cool drink toward Zorah, but she had to wait like that as Zorah quickly dragged her contact lenses off her eyeballs in front of the whole room, stuck them in a case, and pulled out her nerdy glasses. She slid the glasses on as she took the bubble tea.

"You know, that might really gross some people out," Violet said, casting a repulsed look at the contacts' case.

Zorah waved a hand through the air. "I need to wear contacts when I perform surgeries. And who would be grossed out by contact lenses?"

Violet could think of at least one person.

"Have you eaten lunch?" Zorah asked. "I'm starving." She took a loud slurp of her bubble tea.

"I was going to go hide out in a café and write an article. We can go together?" Violet looked warily out the hospital windows before they exited. The parking lot was busy. She scanned the nearby faces for anything out of the ordinary. She had, after all, fled a complete hostage situation. Or was it a hostage situation? She'd been grabbed outside the police station, but technically the guy had offered her a job.

Regardless, it was taking every ounce of her self-control not to freak out about it and start yelling the whole story to Zorah. She would wait until Zorah was sitting down before she told her of the horrors.

"Let's go to the one with the salad bar. I feel like salad and donuts." Zorah veered onto the sidewalk, chugging her tea until the cup was empty and only the tapioca pearls were left in the bottom. She twisted off the lid and tipped the cup back, clawing the gummies into her mouth with her lips like a horse.

"It's a miracle people believe you're thirty-five," Violet said as she tried not to watch the spectacle. "We should start telling people I'm your aunt instead."

"Sure." Zorah tossed the empty cup in a garbage bin outside the café as they reached the entrance. "But no one would believe you're older than me."

"I wouldn't be so sure." Violet tugged the door open, and an air-conditioned gust swept over them from inside.

They found a table and Zorah tossed her purse onto the seat. "I'm going to order. What do you want?" she asked.

"I'm good." Violet didn't mention that she'd eaten her way through half the food in their kitchen at home. She set her laptop on the table and filled the screen with a fresh document. She began typing immediately.

Zorah stood there and watched her for a moment. "What are you working on? An article about bad mealtime etiquette when you're with a friend?"

"I told you I came here to work," Violet said. "And it's an article exposing a real-life villain. I'll let you read it once I'm done." She shifted in her chair, knowing every word could give Zorah a heart attack. Maybe Violet would wait until Zorah had a full stomach before she told her about the whole hostage thing.

Zorah sighed as she left for the front counter, and Violet took the opportunity to come up with a title for her article.

"The Master of Doom's Haunted Mansion?" she mumbled to herself. "Creepy Cathedral Office of Death? Vampire Lair of a Thousand Wax Candles?" Nothing felt quite right, but *Master of Doom* did have a nice ring to it.

Zorah came back a few minutes later with a massive platter of salad and two donuts. She passed a chocolate donut to Violet, then started licking the icing off the top of hers.

"Is this article for The Scoop?" Zorah asked through icing-coated teeth as she sat down. She grabbed a loose lettuce leaf and stuffed it into her mouth.

"Your facts are great, but reading your articles is like reading a bad fiction novel. I'm sorry to tell you this, Violet, but you're not going to make the cut." Violet swallowed. Cedric's opinion would haunt her until the day she died. She wasn't sure she had the heart to tell Zorah what he'd said word for word.

"No. I'm going to start a blog. I'm going to track down real villains and expose them. I have a gut feeling it's going to take off and be really popular in this city," Violet said. She stole a look at Zorah's salad.

Probably around fifteen more mouthfuls to go. Then she would tell Zorah.

"Do you think there's any money in that?" Zorah asked, shovelling in another bite.

Fourteen more mouthfuls.

"It doesn't matter. People need to know the truth, and I'm the only one who will tell it," she said, thinking of Cedric's hatred of her story-telling, and the blonde police officer's betrayal.

Zorah stopped eating for a moment to stare.

Violet looked up from her computer screen at her aunt, then at the salad. At her aunt again. "Keep eating," she invited. When Zorah didn't immediately take another bite, Violet nudged the salad a little closer toward her. "Mmm. Looks yummy."

Zorah dropped her fork to the table and folded her hands. "Something has gotten into you. Out with it. Tell me."

Violet chewed on her lip. "I thought you were hungry."

"I'm suddenly feeling very full."

Everything Violet had been planning to say roared up into her throat and found purchase on the tip of her tongue. But she bit her mouth shut, unable to spit it out now that it was time. She pictured a scenario of Zorah losing her mind in public and talking too loud and everyone turning in their seats and looking at the already humiliated failed journalist a little too hard.

"I'll tell you when we get home," Violet decided, ready to kick herself for chickening out a third time. She focused back on her article. She had yet to pick a title, and not a single word had been written of the actual story yet.

Zorah did that thing where she half eye-rolled, half fluttered her lashes. She reluctantly went back to mercilessly inhaling her salad. The thirty-five-year-old woman was too focused on picking out the croutons to notice when Violet looked back up and studied her.

Zorah. The woman who had saved her life.

A full month was how long Violet had stayed in the *care* of the most prestigious reporters in Toronto. She'd only been thirteen years old. At least, the doctors who appeared alongside her on the talk shows guessed she was probably around that age. Her purple chiffon dress had been washed by the production team, and she'd been told to wear it for all her TV interviews. *The Girl in the Purple Dress* had been a hot topic for every news station. The nameless anomaly who woke up in a forest with no memories. The girl whose DNA had never promised she belonged to anyone on record.

One month. Violet had been ushered around by the city's curiosity, taking interviews by both police and reporters and making waves in people's hearts as Ontarians tried to piece together the history of the mysterious girl, at the protest of child services. That was how long it had taken for someone to show up and claim Violet as their own.

"Her name is Violet Miller, and I'm her aunt. I've been looking everywhere for her! Turn off your cameras before I sue you all!" Zorah's voice had been so authoritative when she'd walked into the interview that day—interrupting it halfway through filming. At the time, Zorah had only been twenty-five. She'd been a thriving medical student who'd seen Violet on TV and had been outraged that a young girl was being put in the spotlight without any concern for her health.

Violet hadn't been outraged by it though. She'd found a strange home in the news stations, had found a bit of magic in the storytelling of the reporters, and for a while, she'd enjoyed the interviews. People gave her their full attention. She got dolled up to be on camera. Those things had made her feel important. They'd taken away some of the sting when day after day went by, and no one showed up to claim Violet.

That day though, Zorah had pulled Violet out of the spotlight, and had brought her home to her one-bedroom student apartment. It was a different sort of home than the news stations had been. It brought different kinds of comforts. For the first time since Violet had woken up in the forest, she felt like she could breathe.

Zorah had taken Violet to a trusted doctor who ran more tests—in addition to the ones the doctors on TV had already run—and had gotten her iron supplements prescribed for anemia, Dr. Wendal was peculiar, but he claimed there was nothing physically wrong with Violet, though some evidence could have disappeared after a month.

"These iron pills are different than regular iron supplements, Violet Miller." Dr. Wendal had said her full name when he handed Violet the first bottle. *"Don't ever trade these out for regular supplements. Only take the ones I give you."*

Violet. Because Violet had been wearing a *violet* dress at the time when Zorah showed up.

Miller. Because that was Zorah's last name.

In a heartbeat, the girl without a name had become Violet Miller, the niece of a brilliant student who'd lost her sister several years ago and had still earned herself a scholarship for medical school during the heartbreak. Zorah took the spotlight only long enough to explain that Violet was the daughter of that beloved sister, and to threaten the reporters not to come after Violet again. The story had fizzled out after that. There was nothing exciting about Violet anymore after all the questions were answered.

Zorah had admitted to Violet the next day that she wasn't really her aunt. That she'd never known Violet before she saw her on TV. But she knew what it was like to feel lost and to have to make a way through the world on her own. As an orphan who was raised by her older sister, Zorah had always had to fight for her success a little harder than everybody else. She expected it would be the same for Violet, but Violet's childhood fame had the opposite effect. When Violet enrolled in high school, everyone wanted to eat lunch with her, give her things, and get her autograph. It seemed her lost memories had given her a life.

At least, it had until the boss at The Sprinkled Scoop decided she wasn't worth his time. It was the first true, real rejection Violet had felt in the parts of her life she could remember. And it shouldn't have hurt so much, but it dragged her back to that month when she was a lost, confused girl waiting for someone who loved her to appear and claim her.

Even in the years with Zorah that followed, no one ever came for Violet.

That simple fact was how Violet realized how unloved she must have been, for not a single person to show up and claim her.

It was the driving force behind why she wanted to be the one to make up the stories, to decide the narrative, to figure out who people really were. It was the reason Violet had chased the memory-thief so hard when the first police report had arrived at The Sprinkled Scoop six months ago, claiming someone had woken up in the park with no memories of the day before, yet their brain showed no signs of physical trauma or anything else that would lead the doctors to believe it was really a case of amnesia.

Violet followed Zorah off the bus. They got off a stop early because Zorah said she needed to run into the convenience store for makeup. Violet waited outside the storefront, tapping a finger against her laptop as people passed by. After a minute, Zorah stumbled back out with four full bags hanging off her arms.

Violet raised a brow. "What in the world did you buy? Christmas presents for the whole world?" Violet reached to take half the bags, but she stopped when she saw a shadow move behind the bus shelter across the road. It was bright daylight, and *hot*, but a person was there wearing a long black coat with a hood up. He leaned back against the poster-covered shelter wall, eating an ice cream cone in the shadow of his hood. His posture seemed way too comfortable after he'd kidnapped Violet at the police station the way he had. Even after all that, here he was, harassing her again.

Violet set her jaw.

She shoved the bags—and her laptop—toward Zorah. "I'll meet you at home, Zor. I have something to deal with."

Zorah said something in objection that Violet ignored. Violet took a quick look both ways before crossing the street, thinking only of informing the no-good vampire that she was going to expose him to the whole world by the end of the day if he didn't leave her alone. But when she set her glare back on the bus shelter, the guy in the coat was gone. She slowed her steps as she came around to the back, eyeing the posters he'd been leaning on. There were a few scattered pedestrians down the sidewalk, and some dark storefronts with rental signs in the windows. She tried to peer into the darkness past the store windows, her nerves getting the best of her. She wondered if she shouldn't have marched over here.

She turned around and jumped, slapping a hand over her chest in surprise to find him there. She opened her mouth to speak, but he grabbed her shoulder and shoved her backward into the shelter wall—the air escaping her lungs. She pulled at his cold sleeve, her other hand diving into the pocket of her business jacket and clawing for her pen. She tore it out and shoved the pointed end against his pale throat. She almost shouted at him, but she stared at that throat instead.

Pale skin. No tattoos.

Her gaze dragged up to a face that wasn't the Master of Doom's.

Lush, metallic-red hair filled his hood, and deep brown eyes with sparkling patches of silver took her in, in a way that made her feel small and very breakable. Her blood heated in her veins. A gold chain necklace fell from the collar of his coat with a bunch of tiny white and red feather-like charms.

He smiled; a slow curve of his lips that was alarmingly beautiful and a little too broad. "Oh dear," he whispered, his voice fluttering over Violet like a song. "You seem to be all alone."

Violet felt like she was being pulled toward him by a magnetic force she could only resist by digging her heels into the ground. When she looked into his eyes, a silent voice seemed to call her forward, fluttering her hair with a cool breeze and tickling the insides of her ears. She shook the feeling away.

"W…" She swallowed so she could speak from her dry throat. "Who are you?"

He leaned his tall frame forward to look her right in the eyes like a grownup addressing a child. "His scent is all over you. Either he did that on purpose so I'd come, or you're an accident waiting to be snatched up. Either way, it's tantalizing," he said, ignoring her question.

Violet felt her grip on the pen waver at his throat as he pushed himself closer, unbothered by the stabbing sensation, seeming to invite it. The pen's tip dug in so hard, Violet panicked and released her hold. The pen tumbled to the ground, bouncing off her high heel and rolling over the asphalt. She looked around to yell for help, but their side of the street had become empty.

The redhead pulled a deep red gem from his pocket and rolled it over his fingers. "Let's have a little chat," he invited.

The sky shifted from bright to dim, and Violet found herself in a sudden shadow. She blinked, more startled by the sudden appearance of clouds overhead than the guy speaking to her. The air felt like it had changed in a split second, too—it had been rushing a moment ago, and now it wasn't.

Violet's stare fell back to him as she realized he must have asked her a question. But she couldn't remember him speaking. "I'm going to call the police," she threatened.

The guy's smile broadened. He glanced down at her mouth, and Violet shivered, but she went on anyway.

"You're going to be arrested—"

Before she could stop him, the guy's lips came against hers, sparking a wild thrashing in her chest. Violet released a muffled sound, but his sound was louder. The guy's strained, guttural grunt filled the alley as he ripped himself back. His fingers flashed to his lips, his silvery eyes wild. A fresh-looking pink burn mark covered his mouth, and he glared at her. Violet felt a ripple in the air; a strange, cold breeze that fluttered her hair again and stroked her skin like a limb tracing her throat, ready to cut her open with a long, pointed nail. It wasn't something a human could do, and her heart faltered.

How many of these inhuman beings existed?

Her mind was as dizzy as before, only this time with terror.

The guy dropped his fingers from his swelling lips. "Clever," he growled in a low voice. Without explaining, he grabbed Violet by her jacket sleeve and threw her down the sidewalk into a passing couple.

"Next time," he promised as Violet slammed into a middle-aged man.

Violet stuttered through an apology and whirled back toward the bus shelter. The couple asked her if she was okay. She didn't answer. She just stared at the empty sidewalk, her chest tight, hands shaking.

"Did you see a guy there just now?" Violet asked the concerned pair as she pointed toward the bus shelter.

The couple eyed the shelter. "I didn't see anyone," the man said. The woman was already shaking her head.

Violet swallowed and hugged her arms to herself as she turned and speedwalked down the sidewalk, looking over her shoulder every few seconds until she cleared the block. She didn't know what to think anymore. A week ago, she wasn't even sure that the memory-loss victims had been affected by ancient folklore magic. And a day ago, she'd stood across from another one of these beings who'd been frightening in his own way, but he had at least let her sleep after she'd fainted, and had planned to make her breakfast, and had offered her a job. Though the two beings looked similar, they felt vastly different.

"Either he did that on purpose so I'd come, or you're an accident waiting to be snatched up."

Violet was sure one of those two guys was the villain stalking the streets and doing terrible things in the city. She'd accused the Master of Doom without hesitation. But her instincts were telling her she might have just looked straight into the eyes of the real monster.

10

Violet Miller and a Gift of Surprise Pebbles

The house was in organized shambles. Violet's mouth parted as she came in the front door. Zorah was standing perfectly still in the kitchen, but she turned and cast Violet a horrified, *what-in-the-world-happened-here?* kind of look.

Violet had noticed the gardens outside first. All the rosebush stems were tied into tiny little knots. The petals had been plucked off every flower and neatly organized over the lawn in ten-inch intervals.

It was the same inside. The kitchen table was upside down in exactly the same place it had always been, with its legs sticking up. All the teacups were upside down on the counter, their matching saucers balanced carefully on top. The paintings and pictures on the walls were all turned backwards. But the worst was the pebbles...

Tiny pebbles were everywhere; covering the floor, across the counters, up the stairs… All evenly spaced apart like the flower petals outside. Violet didn't think she could take a step off the welcome mat without kicking them.

"He's messing with me," Violet realized. The pictures. The teacups. The garden…

This was all a joke to the Master of Doom. Some twisted revenge for how easily she'd escaped his clutches. How she'd denied his job offer.

"Who is?" Zorah finally spoke. But she wasn't looking at Violet; Zorah's gaze followed the pebbles leading up the stairs.

Violet wondered if there were rocks left in their beds, and her skin heated. She yanked off her jacket and threw it into the closet without hanging it up. "I'll be back." She left before Zorah could ask any more questions. She clicked down the street on her heels, ready to bash in the door—and possibly the handsome face—of this Master of Doom jerk.

It took her an infuriating three minutes longer than it should have by bus to reach the cathedral. Violet marched her way up to the doors and knocked as loud as her knuckles would allow. She knocked again when no one answered, even bashing the door once with her foot. "Hello?!" she shouted. "Hell—"

A body appeared beside her, and she stifled a scream.

She whirled on him with her finger up to scold him, but he grabbed her arms before she could speak and the world turned to liquid around her.

The guy dropped her so fast, she tumbled to the floor like her legs were missing. He released a strained grunt. Dust was beneath Violet's fingers, and her surroundings were dim. She was back inside the cathedral. When she rolled onto her butt to glare up at the Master of Doom, he was rubbing his hands and wrists where fresh pink marks were beginning to form.

He was the one already glaring. "What did you do between yesterday and today that made it painful to touch you again?" he bit out.

She stared at him as it sank in once and for all that he had teleported.

It wasn't the first time he'd done it, but it was the first time Violet was sure it was real and not a delusion of her dizzied state. He'd moved at a speed unheard of. She'd always believed in the weird and unusual, the things others would claim were conspiracy or fiction. She'd just never met one of *them* in person until this week. And now there were two.

"Why did you destroy my house?!" she shouted at him. "I'm going to have you arrested for breaking and entering! I'll go to a cop you're not secretly aligned with like that bubble-gum-chewing, law-breaking, heartless, *Officer Baker—*"

"Watch it." His words were filled with warning.

Violet's mouth twisted to the side at his defensive tone.

So, insulting the pretty cop girl was off limits, then.

"Fix my house," Violet said without yelling this time. "Fix it now, before my aunt has a heart attack."

Doom exhaled, and his shoulders relaxed. "That wasn't me, Human."

"As if," Violet said doubtfully as she climbed to her feet. "Who was it then? A sneaky leprechaun?"

He actually *rolled his eyes*. Like *she* was the one being ridiculous.

Violet swallowed when she thought of the redhead guy at the bus shelter. That eerie image of how he'd studied her, the feeling of his coldness, the terrifying smile. She didn't want to admit to herself it could have been him who'd been in her house.

Like he could read her mind, the Master of Doom marched over and pulled Violet to him by the skirt of her dress, keeping his hands far away from her skin. He leaned in and inhaled by her neck. Something flipped in her abdomen when he tilted his face toward her jaw.

His grunt sounded more like a growl as he drew back. "He's found you then. Excellent."

Violet couldn't tell if it was sarcasm. The Master of Doom's voice was always so even. He looked her over and went dead still when he glanced at her mouth. The intensity of his lingering stare sent a new wave of flutters through her chest. He seemed like he wanted to ask her a question.

Violet raised her fingers to her lips, afraid she had food on her face. Without thinking, she nudged him back a little at his covered chest. He dropped his fistful of her skirt, questions unasked.

"I think it's clear we both know who messed with my house then," she said. "Who is that redheaded weirdo, and why did he come after me?" Her cheeks felt warm, but she didn't dare reach up to cool them with the backs of her hands. "You're obviously the only one who can give me answers." It wasn't like she had any other reason to come back here.

"He and I have a history," was all Doom said.

Violet shook her head. "Okay, well good for you. But why did he come after *me*?"

"He smelled me on you. You slept in my bed, Human." He said it like *smelling people on other people* was the most normal thing in the world. "My faeborn scent will take at least a month to wear off, and even then, it may never wear off completely. That fool has mistaken you for my lover because of it."

Violet blinked. "You seem pretty relaxed about that, considering this is all clearly your fault. What am I supposed to do if that creep comes back? He tried to kiss me—Actually, he *did* kiss me. It was the worst."

The guy stole a quick glance at her lips again and Violet got the feeling he'd already figured that out. "Did it burn him?" he asked like he couldn't stop himself.

"Yeah."

It was the first time Violet saw the Master of Doom try to suppress a smile.

She looked down at her hands for a second, considering that she'd somehow managed to harm both Doom and the redhead guy with a simple touch. Scientifically, it made no sense. But maybe she was done trying to understand things with science.

"You never answered my question." She dropped her hands to her sides. "Who is he? *What* is he? And while I'm at it, what are you?" Violet didn't mean to take a step back when she asked the last one, but for a moment she'd forgotten he'd teleported. She scanned him up and down.

"*He* is called many things, but mainly, he's a deadly creature with nine lives. And I've been hunting him. He's a master of hiding because the shadows are his, and he lives in the air, slipping from place to place on the breath of the wind," he said.

"That's poetic," Violet mumbled.

"And he knows my weaknesses, which is why he's been beating me thus far. Unfortunately, he has no weaknesses to speak of. Only a wildly powerful advantage." Doom folded his arms and glanced toward the big wooden cathedral doors that didn't look nearly strong enough to stop a mythical creature like the redhead she'd met. "Which is why I had to get creative," he added.

Violet's brows came together as a thought leaked in. Her scowl returned. "Wait—did you use me as bait?"

The guy lifted his shoulder into a shrug. "A little. Not on purpose. At least, not on purpose at first." He didn't look surprised. Or sorry.

Violet's jaw dropped. "You *wanted* me to escape from here?"

"No, you performed that circus act all on your own, Human. I just decided not to bring you back because I knew you were wearing my scent. Therefore, I knew he would follow you. It's an easy trick I wagered would give me an advantage, and so far, it's working."

Violet wanted to smack him. No, she wanted to grab his bare arm and burn him all over his pretty tattoos. She was a dangling worm waiting to be swallowed by a red-haired fish, and this Master of Doom was going to bait the hook himself.

The nerve.

What exactly would happen to her if the redhead came back to finish the job? He'd been to her house. He'd knotted her garden and spread pebbles all over her…

Pebbles.

"Wait." Violet shook her head, a thought piecing together, slamming into place. "It *is* him," she realized. "He's the real serial-attacker I've been writing articles about." She said it through a dry voice.

Several of the women with missing memories of the previous day had woken up with their coat pockets full of pebbles. Violet lifted a hand to cover her mouth as it dawned on her like a mallet plunging through her brain. She'd found him—the *real* culprit. He'd been in her house; the serial attacker she'd been obsessing over for half a year. "Oh my gosh," she rasped. "He knows what I look like! I've written terrible things about him... I challenged him to come find me on the news!" she shouted. "He's going to kill me!"

Doom tilted his head back and forth like he was weighing that. "Probably not."

"Didn't you see what he did to the other victims? You were following that story, too! I saw your article in the last Fairy Post. You know how he left the people he attacked!" Violet's voice had grown uncharacteristically high.

"Yes. And *most* of them he left alive," Doom said.

Violet's jaw dropped. "*Most* of them?!" She slapped a hand to her forehead, feeling a sudden lack of necessary iron supplements. Her knees were weak.

He shrugged. "I mean, the odds are in your favour, if you want to be picky about it."

"Picky? You're talking about my life!" Violet snapped. Then she whispered, "What have you gotten me into?"

The Master of Doom uncrossed his arms and sauntered over. "I got you into nothing, Human. You came here all on your own and broke into my house and rang my bell."

"Is that *all* that happened?" Her glower fired up to him. "Because for a while I was missing part of the memory of when we first met."

His jaw slid to the side. "Fine. Yes, I tried to steal your memory of coming here on that first day." Violet slid away from him, nearly stumbling over a broken chair. Her eyes were wide, she was sure she'd heard wrong. "But your faeborn-cursed flesh burned my fingers and I only got fragments," he added. "And besides, I gave the memories back to you once I thought better of it. You should have realized by now they've returned."

Violet wasn't breathing anymore. If she was, she didn't feel it.

It should have been obvious the moment he'd teleported her in here that he was magical enough to do other things too, like wipe memories. But she hadn't known the cold, definite truth until this moment. Even if the serial-attacker and Doom were two different beings, they both stole memories from people. She thought of the crushing pain she would go through again if she lost her precious memories with Zorah, and everything else she'd experienced the last ten years. The only memories she had left. She shook her head in denial. She didn't want to lose a single one of them ever again. Not even a minute.

"Who are you?" she asked for the hundredth time, only this time, it came out cracked, and worn, and a necessary amount of afraid.

He seemed to notice. Seemed to consider the waver in her words. "My unhidden name is Mor," he finally said.

Mor.

Just, Mor.

She wouldn't call him that. That was a clean name meant for someone harmless and normal. He was not normal. He was an animal. A bringer of destruction; a stealer of life. He was…

He was Doom.

Doom right before her eyes.

CHAPTER

11

Mor Trisencor and How it All Began in the Shadows, Part 1

Mor was no longer a childling when the Shadow Army reached Windswiple, the northernmost fairy city on the cusp of the Dark Corner, where sunlight filtered in and chased the ever-clouds away. The army always washed in like a black flood, taking over homes for beds when they grew tired, robbing the villagers of their milk beasts when they were thirsty, and at times, stealing the villagers' hard-earned coin.

No one seemed to wonder what it was, exactly, that the Shadow Army was protecting. It certainly wasn't the citizen fairies of the Dark Corner.

But Mor never asked questions. He never said much of anything, to his army comrades' discontent. When he turned thirteen years of age, he stayed silent for over a full faeborn year. At first, his fellow Shadow Fairies tried to get him to speak by means of prodding, poking, and trickery. But they grew silent when Mor volunteered for combat training that year and brutally and violently defeated them in the training rings. No one seemed bothered by Mor's silence after that.

The day he broke his silence was the same day the Shadow Army entered Windswiple. Mor was exactly fourteen and twenty-three days old.

The trees were different in Windswiple. They were greener, livelier, lush. They bore giant fruits unheard of in the rest of the Dark Corner due to the great toiling cloud—a cloud the Queene of North Corner had cursed to remain over the land of the Shadow Fairies for their insubordination. Harvests were difficult in the shadows. But the toiling cloud didn't reach the vibrant city of Windswiple on the outskirts of the Corner.

The Shadow Army came for supplies in waves. Mor's division came in the second wave, so the humble city streets should have been mostly empty. But when Mor entered on the back of a crossbeast that morning, followed by the army folk his own commander had entrusted him with, he saw a fairy childling squirming in the tight grip of a ruby-haired war fae. It wasn't the first time Mor had witnessed such scenes. He often looked away, swallowed his words, and let the memory slip from his mind into another place afterward.

But perhaps… perhaps that day, while seeing the sunlight for the first time in several years, Mor felt he'd had enough.

Mor slowed his crossbeast to a stop, bringing the lesser fairies under his command to a halt. His glistening, iridescent, black pearl armour clapped together at his shoulders as he slid off his beast. Truly, Mor never even knew there were rainbows in his armour until he saw it in the light for the first time that day.

"State your real name, Fairy. So that I might return to you the torment you've given this childling. Unless you're a faeborn coward."

His first words. In over a year.

Mor did not look back at his lesser fairies even though he heard one or two of them gasp.

The ruby-haired war fae in the street slowed his wrangling. He didn't remove his pale-skinned grip from the childling boy's arm, however. Rather, he turned to face Mor, and Mor gazed upon a folk who was just as tall as him, and possibly even more shapely in his muscled frame. The fairy's sharp, pointed ears twitched as though he wondered if he'd heard Mor correctly. And when he smiled...

Queensbane, when he smiled.

The darkness of midnight and a glisten of the moon were in that evil smile.

Mor felt a ripple of fear move through the lesser fairies at his back. Even the crossbeasts groaned and shuffled as the wind picked up and the air turned cold. The childling boy stifled a wail and dropped a handful of ripe sugar blossom seeds to the dusty path where the mud instantly swallowed them. Pink sugar buds sprouted at the childling's feet. He stared down at the fresh flowers in dismay.

The ruby-haired fairy seemed uninterested in the sugar blossoms now.

"Don't you know who I am, fool?" he asked Mor. The tone of the fairy's voice told Mor he had missed something important. It was a tone that weaved a tale of a certain authority Mor had not picked up on during his approach. A master, maybe? A High Lord? No, the fairy wore the same black pearl armour as he. A golden necklace rested at his throat with exactly nine scarlet, feather-like tails with pure white tips. As Mor studied the clues, the fairy released his grip on the childling. The boy raced off on his tiny faeborn feet, dropping his spare sugar blossom seeds the whole way.

It was only then that Mor spotted the twisted threads around the Shadow Fairy's wrist—crimson in colour and woven into a four-strand braid. Heaviness sank through Mor's stomach. Yet, when he lifted his gaze to the fairy and saw not even a speck of remorse, his jaw hardened.

"I don't care who you are. I'm detaining you in accordance with the Shadow Army's fairy law." Mor's hand was around the fairy's wrist in a heartbeat. He yanked an enchanted vine from his pocket and slapped it on—first on the ruby-haired fairy's wrist, and then on his own, tethering them by flesh, blood, and body, until whenever he might decide to break the vine by his own teeth.

The Shadow Fairy's wicked smile melted. "You're doomed, you fool."

"And you're going to face the wrath of the commanders for harming a childling," Mor promised.

"If you look at that childling—" the Shadow Fairy pointed in the direction the boy had run with his seeds "—you will see he is unmarked, apart from a few scrapes he gave himself while fighting me. I simply wanted his sugar seeds to present as a gift to my father." He angled his head like a crossbeast. "I suppose you don't know who my father is?"

"I imagine he's one of the faeborn army commanders based on your wristlet. Let's go."

Mor tugged the fairy who followed without objection.

They rode through the city on Mor's crossbeast, wrists bound together. The Shadow Fairy made no comments on the trek to the temporary Shadow Army base in the woods, though, even his silence told a story. Howlings chirped at the group of fae as they rode beneath the black branches and pushed through silver shrubs. Even the lesser fairies who followed at Mor's back were silent—likely afraid for their faeborn lives simply because they'd been in Mor's company when he'd arrested a commander's son.

The scent of crisping hog meat wafted through the trees as they reached the tall cooking fires. Mor slid off his beast and the ruby-haired fairy followed in what seemed like mock respect. "You'll die today," the fairy said as they rounded the path and approached the circle of stick thrones erected for the high leaders of the Shadow Army. Mor had never entered their circle before. He'd never had a reason to.

The leaders—commanders and strategists and even a low prince of the Dark Corner—were still filing into their seats for the evening meeting when Mor entered the circle, without permission and without being announced. If the most powerful of the Shadow Army didn't know Mor's face up until this day, they would know it now.

"I beg an audience," Mor stated simply, drawing the brown and silver eyes of his own commander up in surprise. His commander had never heard Mor's voice. He had disregarded Mor as a mute fool after several months of unanswered questions.

"What in the name of the sky deities are you—"

"The High Prince has arrived," a fairy announced, making the commanders close their mouths.

When High Prince Reval entered the circle by a graceful sweep of his white and red robes, his aged gaze settled on Mor first. Then on the Shadow Fairy at Mor's side. He glided to his seat, his long crimson hair brushing over his shoulders in a chilly wind. And Mor's eyes slid closed in disbelief as he realized exactly who this was, and who the fairy beside him must have been.

"What brings you before the inner circle, Son? Did you manage to capture a childling with sugar blossom seeds for me like I asked?" The High Prince lowered onto his twig throne, and the enchanted vine wrapping Mor's wrist grew hot.

The Shadow Fairy at Mor's side stepped forward and performed a shallow bow toward the High Prince. "Nearly, Father. But this fairy stopped me." He nodded toward Mor, and the stare of every eye around the circle warmed Mor's skin as much as the vine.

Mor took in the High Prince, heir to the throne of the Dark Corner of Ever. The most powerful and rumoured to be the most wicked of souls. The one who owned the Shadow Army, who held them in their place under his royal thumb.

Mor saw the choices before him and for a moment, he considered releasing the Shadow Fairy and begging for mercy. But the eyes of the High Prince were just as darkly unapologetic as his son's, and for that, Mor found he could not let it go.

"I detained him for harassing a childling in the open street." Though Mor's voice was naturally softer and quieter than most, he stated it clean and clear. "It's a crime to harm a childling, regardless of where the order came from." His tongue felt heavy. He knew he might lose it soon. "I was ashamed travelling the streets today beneath the eyes of the sky deities. Ashamed to wear the same colour of armour as this fairy." He jabbed his thumb toward the Shadow Fairy. "Ashamed to be riding among the cruel hearts of this army. I cannot lie about that."

There were no gasps. The commanders knew better. But there were glares. Fingers tightened on twig armrests, and Mor's own commander leaned forward with a promise of forthcoming torture in his eyes.

High Prince Reval rose from his twig throne. He drifted over the grass that shivered in his wake. When he reached Mor, he looked down upon him intently. "Those feelings you have," he said, "they will bring pain and death to your door if you cannot get them under control."

"Kill him, Father," the Shadow Fairy said. "Do it terribly."

When the High Prince's aged face warped into a smile, it was just as beautifully alluring and dangerously broad as his son's. "What faeborn justice that would be," he said in a dark, musical voice.

His hand lashed out and grabbed for a fairy throat—but it was not Mor's. Mor nearly jumped as the High Prince dug his black nails into his son's neck. Cold power and strength made the air shudder as he lifted the ruby-haired Shadow Fairy off his feet, tugging the vine at Mor's wrist.

"I was very specific when I told you to snatch a childling in *secret*," the High Prince said. "Do you want the Dark Queene to find out I'm gathering forbidden sugar blossom seeds?"

High Prince Reval hurled his son into the grass, and Mor was torn back with him. Mor caught himself on his knee, but the ruby-haired Shadow Fairy broke a bone in his arm as he struck the dirt. The fairy growled, clawing at the grass as he climbed back to his feet. His sparkling, metallic hair was dishevelled. He kept his mouth shut as he stared at his father and snapped his arm back into place.

"Go fetch me a childling with pockets full of sugar blossom seeds and do it the way I asked." The High Prince's cold voice drifted across the circle as he made his way back to his twig throne.

"I shall complete my task as you wish," the ruby-haired fairy promised. But his glower dragged over to Mor. "But what will you do about him?" he asked his father.

The High Prince sat and tapped his armrest. "Who is this fool's commander?" he asked the circle.

Mor's commander scrambled to stand. He bowed before the Prince. "I will punish him severely, Your Highness. I will take away his food for three days."

"Nonsense, don't drain him of his strength. He has *feelings*. We must stomp those out of him," High Prince Reval said. He eyed the vine around Mor's wrist, and another beautiful, wicked smile crossed his face as his gaze followed the tether to his son's wrist. "Is he a decent fighter?" he asked the commander.

"Yes. He is one of my best," the commander said. "But up until today, he has not spoken a word in front of me. I thought he was mute until just now. I've been calling him *fool* because I did not know his name."

The High Prince nodded. "And what is your name, young fairy?"

Mor felt the implication. He knew how easy it would be for this High Prince to ask for his real name and force him to do unspeakable things.

"Mor," he answered, because the High Prince had not been specific in his question.

"Do you know how powerful my son is, Mor?" the Prince asked.

Mor did not answer, so the Prince told him. "My son is a nine tailed fox, like me. And you must know that I'm the most powerful of all the fairies in the Dark Corner apart from the Dark Queene herself. Have you heard of foxes before?"

Mor swallowed, and this time, he nodded. "Only in childling books."

Books that had told ancient stories of unstoppable power. Rare creatures with nine lives, the ability to steal secrets, and a special intuition that made them nearly invincible. If the Shadow Fairy beside him was what this Prince claimed, Mor wondered why this young fox had allowed Mor to take him in the first place back at the streetside. He turned and took his first real look at the ruby-haired fairy.

The ruby-haired fairy looked back at him. He flashed a lovely, crooked smile.

"You will become part of my division, Mor," High Prince Reval announced. "I will not make it easy for you. I will ensure that every one of your *feelings* is squeezed out until you are nothing more than a fae folk shell for me to use in battle. You were clever enough to carry an enchanted vine in your pocket that ensnared a powerful fox, so you are worth more to me alive than dead. You start as one of *my* war fairies tomorrow."

It felt as though Mor's blood was draining out right there in the grass. He had spent years staying undetected and quiet. He had been so very careful not to stir the cauldrons or shake the pepper since the day he volunteered to join the Shadow Army. He'd stayed quiet to avoid this exact sort of thing.

"And Son, I've changed my mind. Forget the faeborn sugar blossoms. Your new mission is to turn this Shadow into a true war fairy." Prince Reval's voice was cold and sweet, and it prickled over Mor's skin. "Even if you have to rip out his heart to do it."

A flutter of chilling silence roared over the circle as every commander's gaze settled on Mor.

Mor would never be able to go anywhere unnoticed again.

"And I shall be clear about this," Prince Reval added, looking directly into Mor's eyes. "In this army, feelings don't belong. Once you are a Shadow Warrior, there is no love. There is no care. There is no hope of finding a mate, ever. You will be marked to be eternally alone, but we will all be alone in war together."

Mor was deathly silent for several heartbeats. Then, he lifted his arm and bit the vine with his teeth. It snapped and the plant disintegrated to ash that fluttered away in the cold breeze. As soon as the ruby-haired fairy's wrist was free, he walked around to stand face-to-face with Mor, silvery eyes promising that he was going to enjoy destroying him.

CHAPTER

12

Mor Trisencor and the Present

"I hate you."

It was an unexpected confession from the other side of the room. Mor heard it well enough from where he hauled the bucket of cleaning supplies from the closet in the cathedral's living space.

The human hadn't moved from the same spot on the floor where she'd been standing, staring at him in an entirely different way after he admitted he'd tried to take her memories the other day. Her tone told him she wasn't making a jest; that deep down, a fiery part of her truly did hate him for some preposterous reason that likely had nothing to do with him.

Mor set the bucket down and turned to face Violet Miller, writer of all things dark and mysterious and noteworthy.

"Truthfully, Human, I don't particularly like you either," he admitted. He didn't have to remind her how she'd snuck into his home, called him names, thrown pens at him, and after all that, she'd just arrived at his front door, pounding her fists against it like a childling. "You are the absolute worst," he added.

She released a disgruntled sound and folded her arms. She hugged them to herself tightly as she worked her jaw, looking him up and down with a mix of expressions. She appeared to be calculating.

"But you need me," she said with a note of challenge in her voice.

Mor grunted. Though, he did need her. Desperately.

"You need me, too," he said. "I gather, by your first venture into my abode, that you're in need of employment. I gather you need coin to eat, as well as lodging."

The revulsion that filled her human face was nearly offensive.

"I would never *lodge* here in this hut of darkness and despair," Violet promised.

Mor bit back his retort and smiled through thin lips. "Perfect. It's settled then. You come here to work and keep The Fairy Post alive, and I'll pay you whatever you like to do it. Then you can leave in the evenings."

"Perfect," she mimicked, and Mor noticed her rose-coloured nails dig a little deeper into her flesh. "I can't *wait* to get started." Her sarcasm was ripe, and Mor hissed a laugh.

"Don't get too excited. Just because we need each other doesn't mean I have to make things comfortable for you here. I imagine you'll see all sorts of atrocities from now on that will turn your insides," he said.

"Is that a threat?" the human asked as Mor picked up the cleaning bucket again.

"*If* and *when* I threaten you, Violet Miller, you will know without having to ask," he promised, turning away to carry it to the coffee table.

She still didn't move from her favourite spot, as though her heels were glued to the floor.

A pair of fluffy slippers with kitten beast ears rested on a stool by the broken fireplace. They were one of the things Mor had stolen on his way out of the café, back when the morning air was still chilly, turning the wood floors cold. If Kate had noticed her slippers were missing from her apartment, she hadn't bothered to call him and complain about it. Maybe she hadn't yet realized.

Violet finally moved. She inched toward the stool and lifted one of the slippers, casting Mor a judgemental look. It was very female-y. In fact, most of her looks were rather feminine in nature. It wasn't that Kate and Lily *weren't* feminine, but Mor hadn't caught those two wearing dresses often like the one Violet Miller fashioned now. This human was a different sort of female—dark polished lashes, golden earrings, coloured nails. Plum-red lips. Pretty in a strange, colourful way.

Her personality was garbage though.

And worst of all, she wore masks; one of over-the-top boldness to hide her fears, and another mask of colour to hide her real face. For a moment, Mor wanted desperately to see what she looked like without face paint. He wondered how different she might appear if she let her hair be its natural way without forcing its shape. He imagined she might be a different sort of pretty.

"Did you steal these from a *girl?*" Violet asked in a tone that told him she was trying desperately to be mean, likely the result of the energy and fear channelling through her veins. The rhythm in her chest was loud and wild even though she seemed to be pinching her face to keep it composed.

Yes, she was a few seconds away from a full-fledged human meltdown. And trying very hard to make Mor feel foolish for owning slippers that resembled something a female might wear.

The joke was on her though. "Yes. I stole them from a girl," was all he said.

She didn't seem to know what to say about that as he began tidying up around the fireplace, kicking aside brick chunks and wiping the stone crumbs from his fireside chair. His catastrophic fight with the *intruder* several days ago had destroyed nearly the whole main level and basement of the cathedral. What a faeborn disaster.

An old Fairy Post rested on the end table beside the chair. Mor picked it up and scanned his reports from last month.

"Oh. Well, that's… super weird." Violet tossed the slipper back where it belonged. "What kind of weirdo steals from girls?" Even though she mumbled the last bit, it wasn't all that quiet.

"You're making small talk because you're terrified of me," Mor said, flipping the page of the newspaper. "That's far more weird."

Violet didn't reply for several seconds, so Mor glanced up. Her face said it all. Moments ago, she had been determined to verbally assault him, and now it seemed she'd lost her tongue. All because he admitted to stealing a few patches of a memory. Queensbane, she looked at him like he was a monster.

He closed the paper.

"I searched for you," he said.

She blinked. "What?"

"On the human internet. The web of information. Your name—Violet Miller. I searched for it yesterday with the buttons." He didn't mention that he'd also called Lily and asked her to investigate Violet Miller. Lily claimed there was no information on Violet, and that the whole city had already tried to place her several years ago. But Mor hoped Lily might be compelled to look deeper since he'd asked.

"With the buttons," Violet said quietly to herself, shaking her head. "You talk like you're a hundred years old." She bit her lips after she said it. Swallowed. And then, "Are you?"

"Am I what?" Mor walked past her to fetch the broom and began sweeping up the debris in the living space. It would be nice to be able to inhale without tasting dust again.

"A hundred? Or like... older?"

Mor stopped. He turned back to her. He blinked.

"Two hundred, then?" she tried, wincing a little. Her eyes widened when he didn't answer. "Oh my gosh... Are you *three—*"

"Are you out of your faeborn mind?" Mor growled. "Do I look a hundred years old to you?!"

Violet bit her plum-coloured lips together.

Mor released a snarly huff and began sweeping in rigid strokes. He'd hoped to clean in peace today. It seemed that was a wild dream now. He got only four sweeps in before he spun back on her.

"*Three* hundred?" He glared. "*Three hundred* years old?"

Violet folded her arms. "You're obviously of the legendary, non-human type," she defended. "My instincts were right. Since the beginning my gut has been telling me you're a vampire. You know, with your creepy stringed music and dark cathedral. And frankly, every time you get close to my neck, I think you're going to bite it."

Mor burst out laughing, utterly amused. But he stopped when he noticed Violet eyeing his teeth like she was searching for sharp canines. He shut his mouth, set his jaw, and went back to his sweeping.

"I already told you I'm nothing of the sort. You've been reading too many fictional books written by humans. If you like those sorts of stories, I can recommend a few that'll keep you awake for hours when you want to sleep," he promised.

Violet's arms squeezed across her middle, as though she was questioning whether he meant they were such good stories that she wouldn't be able to put them down, or if they were so terrifying, she'd be too scared to go to sleep afterward. He tried not to snort a laugh at her dilemma.

He heard Violet swallow again. "If you're not a vampire, then what are you? Tell me right now and don't drag it on any longer. I don't have the patience for people who beat around the bush. And I need to decide if I can stomach…" she cleared her throat, "being here."

Mor finished his sweeping and leaned the broom along the fireplace mantle. "Will you write an article on me if I tell you all my secrets?" he challenged.

"Probably," she admitted.

"Why?"

"Because people need to know the truth." She seemed perfectly serious. Mor imagined her trying to expose the fairy assassins living quiet lives in this bustling city. But Kate and Cress had written a book about such things, and still no humans believed it was real. His chances seemed fairly good.

"Very well, Human." Mor marched over to the end table and grabbed The Fairy Post. "You want to know what I am?" He turned the paper to show her. He didn't point anywhere, he just held it up and waited for her to figure it out.

She stared at it. A strange look crossed her face, and she lifted a pretty brow. "A fairy?" She almost laughed. "As in… a cute, little, magic-wand-wielding fairy like in Cinderella?"

Mor's fist tightened around the paper, crumpling the edge. "Cute?" he asked, and Violet's smile faded. He lowered The Fairy Post and stepped toward her, eyes becoming deadly and threatening. He let just a flit of his power ripple off his skin. A strand of her deep brown hair brushed back over her shoulder in a breeze that had no business being inside an enclosed building. "Do I seem *cute* to you?" he asked when she was blanketed in his shadow.

She tried to take a step back. Mor took a step right after her.

"Are you trying to scare me?" she asked from a seemingly dry throat.

"Yes," he said darkly. "Is it working?"

She nodded a little.

"Do you still think fairies are cute then, Human?" he asked. If only she knew half the things he'd done. Half the things he could do still if he wanted.

"I think you're evil," she stated with more gusto than what showed on her face.

Mor nodded, satisfied. "Good." He drew back and grabbed the dust-pan off the chair. He'd just turned to sweep up his dirt pile when she spoke again.

"But even if you're evil, I don't believe it was you who hurt all those young women," she said.

"Also, good." Mor sloshed the dust, dirt, and brick into the dustpan. He carried it down the hall and into the kitchen. The ruckus of her heels trailed after him, though she wasn't stomping anymore.

Mor dumped the debris into the garbage bin and put the broom away. He washed his hands at the sink and dried them on the towel, knowing full well she was watching him. Marvelling, perhaps, that an evil, dangerous fairy also had the skills to tidy up his living space when it was required. He hid a small, gloating smile.

"You are like the fairytale fairies," she said from the kitchen doorway. "I bet you flutter around and cook and clean for princes and princesses." Laughter filled her voice.

Mor slapped the towel down onto the counter and turned to face her. "I don't regret using you as bait," he told her matter-of-factly. "I'd do it again a hundred times over. You are as obnoxious as a moonbug scurrying into a perfectly good spiked citrus and spoiling it."

Violet thought for a moment—not revealing a thing in her expression now. She sauntered in, seeming to decide she was no longer afraid of him even after he'd flexed his power in her pretty little human face. "Do it, then," she said. "Use me as bait."

Mor's gaze sharpened as she came to stand before him. The speed at which her resolve had changed was astounding. He couldn't determine her ploy, or her reasons.

"Use me to catch that devil. And stop him," she articulated through her plum lips. "I might not like you, Master of Doom, but I hate him more. He's the one going after helpless people."

Mor stifled a fairy curse. She wasn't even joking.

The scent of her flourishing home garden wafted over him this close, along with the scent of himself—still too potent. She clearly didn't realize how much trouble she was in. "You would regret it if I did. I already used you once, Human, and now I know I can draw him out with my scent alone. I don't need to put you in harm's way again to trap him." He carefully slid around her so their bare arms wouldn't brush, and he headed out of the kitchen. She followed.

"Wait! Where are you going?" she asked, her heels clicking faster this time. "You can't leave me trapped in this haunted mansion again!"

"I'm going to undo your scent problem," Mor stated, stretching out his hands. Lightly touching the almost-healed burns on his palms.

"I just told you that you could use me. Now you want to erase my

Doom Perfume? Why?"

Mor stopped walking and turned back. He flexed his fingers, thinking of the sting about to come. "Because I lied about your odds, and my tongue is burning from the falsehood. The truth is, you likely won't survive the next twenty-four hours if I don't do something about this."

He grabbed her around the waist and pulled her to him. A burst of flaming heat erupted from everywhere their skin connected as they vanished.

CHAPTER

13

Violet Miller and the Whole Sweater Thing

Violet couldn't get used to the world dissolving around her and sharpening into a different scene. The ground disappeared, and for a split second, it felt like she was falling.

When she was steady enough to not scream, Violet realized she was gripping tight handfuls of Doom's shirt. It was his low, pained grunt that made her drop her grip and step back. Her elbow hit a wall and a ball of yarn tumbled off a shelf beside her.

Mor—he'd claimed his name was—was facing her, standing remarkably still. Violet blinked the rush of teleporting away and shrieked when she realized *why* he wasn't moving a muscle.

A dozen sharp knitting needle points were aimed at the back of his neck. A small crowd of women held them, and for the life of her, Violet couldn't figure out why they all looked ready to stab. Behind them was a wide, storefront-like space covered in pastel-coloured wallpaper and filled with hundreds of baskets of yarn.

"Doom…" Violet rasped and pointed toward the women. "There's a bunch of ladies behind you. I think they want your attention."

"I'm aware," Mor said. And then, "Doom?"

"Master of Doom. That's what I'm going to call you in my article," she said, swallowing. She pointed back to the women with needles. "Now, um… maybe you should—"

Mor turned and the women armed with needles crouched as though taking a defensive stance. Like they thought Mor was going to attack them.

"I'm in need of a sweater," Mor's deep voice declared to the room.

"For you?" one of the women asked in disgust—an older lady with gray hair. The only one who still sat knitting on a couch. "Never," she stated.

"Not for me, you foolish females. For her." Mor nodded back toward Violet.

Some of the women leaned to peek around Mor. They studied Violet standing there, plastered against the wall.

"I already have a fairy goddaughter. I don't need another," the old woman said from the couch as she wound pale blue yarn around a long needle. "Toss him out."

The rest of the women reached for Mor. Mor sighed and shoved their needles away from his neck. "Forget it, then. I'll find one myself." He seemed about to leave but the old woman piped up again.

"If you learned the ways of the yarn, Assassin, you could make your human lover a sweater yourself," she said, and Violet felt a pinch of warmth on her cheeks.

Mor snarled. "She's not my—"

"That's what it smells like from here. She stenches like she's wearing your faeborn clothes—flowers, dirt, Shadow blood, and… dandelions." Her gaze darted up to Mor for a moment at the last one. "Now, don't ever airslip in here again. It's against the rules we made with your brothers." The woman slid her needle out and held up her work—a single thick blue

97

mitten.

Violet watched a muscle feather in Mor's jaw. He seemed to think better about leaving. "If you didn't want us to visit, then why did you move your foul-smelling faeborn store right across the street from our café?" he growled.

A younger woman with a long red braid snorted. "To make sure you stay in line. And especially to make sure you don't blow our cover, you faeborn fool," she said as she twirled her long needle over her fingers.

"And to watch over Kate, of course." The old woman began unwinding a fresh strand of blue yarn. "I don't have an ounce of faith in you male assassins to keep her safe. That Prince of yours is an idiot."

Mor took a threatening step toward the old woman, forcing all the needles to return to his throat. "Watch your tongue—"

"We stayed hidden here for more faeborn years than I care to remember now, and the first chance the North Prince got, he started an online cooking show," the old woman cut him off again and snorted. "Queensbane, if I thought my fairy goddaughter would listen to me, I never would have allowed her to get betrothed to that wicked fairy who killed so many of my sisters as we fled."

Mor released a heavy breath and unclenched his fists. He turned toward Violet and grabbed her by her sleeve-covered shoulder. "I think we've had enough. Forget the faeborn sweater."

He guided Violet to the door, reaching to shove it open in front of her, and he pushed her out into the warm street. Cars puttered by and faint chatter drifted from nearby places. The door slammed shut behind them.

"Where in the world did you just take me?" Violet asked as Mor guided her down the sidewalk.

"A knitting club of pompous, crabby females. That's all you need to know," he grumbled.

Violet looked back toward the store. A pink sign hung out front that said: YARN & STITCH.

"They're giving me an extra-icy shoulder because I hid an enchanted cricket in their store a while back. It chirped for seventeen days without ceasing. It nearly drove them faeborn mad when they couldn't find it." A shadow of a smile crossed his face, seeming to ease his mood.

"I actually can't tell if you're joking," Violet admitted.

"It's not a joke. They moved in across the street, and we didn't like it. And despite our asking politely, they wouldn't move away, so I hid the cricket," was all he said to explain. "And now that you know what I'm capable of, Human, perhaps you should consider showing some respect to your new boss?" He cast her a look with a brow raised.

Violet released a grunt. "Because of a little cricket?"

The Master of Doom's lip curled. "I can do far worse things than hide a cricket, Violet Miller. It's best you know that." He turned his attention ahead as they crossed the street.

Violet glanced back at Mor when he wasn't looking, considering that. She rubbed her temples, feeling like it was all too much to take in at once—the job, the knitting club, literal talk of enchanted crickets. The fact that Mor said she wouldn't survive the next twenty-four hours if she couldn't get rid of his scent. She wanted to go home, drink tea, and take a bath full of fresh rose petals and peppermint leaves so she could think everything through.

Mor stopped before a quaint café with a purple awning. He finally released her shoulder when he opened the door, and a flood of chatter told Violet the café was packed full.

Her gaze fell on a pair of pointed ears inside the café, and Violet stopped walking, causing Mor to bump into her back. He leapt away before their skin could brush.

An athletic-looking guy—the one with the pointed ears along with a styled sweep of pure white hair—turned toward them at the sound of the bell. His face broke into a wide, stunningly attractive smile that made Violet forget where she was.

He was another one of them—this guy with nice hair and a smile for days. He was like Mor.

Mor nudged Violet into the café, and she staggered forward on her heels. She pushed a lock of her hair behind her ear when the white-haired guy came over. A burgundy apron hugged his torso.

"Nice haircut," Mor muttered at him. "Looks like you forgot to leave enough fur to cover your faeborn ears."

"If it isn't our brother who disowned us," the white-haired guy said, beaming. He looked around quickly, then reached for something on a nearby table.

"I'd never be so lucky," Mor returned.

"Who's this?" the white-haired guy asked as he extended a golden-topped butter tart to Violet on a flat hand. "For you, pretty human," he said. Violet fought a strange smile and reached to take it, a *thank you* on the tip of her tongue.

"She's my secretary." Mor smacked the white-haired guy's hand and the tart tumbled to the floor in a tasty looking heap. "And don't you dare feed her the butter tarts, you fool. I'm warning you, Shayne."

Violet's jaw dropped as she stared at the ruined dessert. She turned to scold Mor, but the white-haired guy—Shayne—spoke first.

"I'm just trying to make sure she comes back here." He winked at Violet. "Don't keep her all to yourself, you greedy hogbeast," he said to Mor.

Shouting lifted from the back of the café, and Violet's gaze darted to a tall, turquoise-eyed guy behind the counter. He was going on about a wedding cake, talking over everyone else in the room.

"Don't mind him. He got betrothed a few months ago and he's transformed into an absolute bridezilla," Mor said to Violet as he pushed past her and Shayne.

Violet stayed by the door and watched Mor approach the counter.

As soon as the turquoise-eyed guy saw Mor there, his face went from moderately perturbed to shocked, then to cold, wild, and demanding. Violet thought Mor might get into a fist fight right in the middle of the café after everything else that had already happened in the last hour. A few low words were exchanged, but Violet couldn't hear what they said over the chatter in the café, even when she strained to listen.

The turquoise-eyed guy reached below the counter and drew out a pink sweater. He threw it at Mor. Mor took it without another word and carried it back through the tables, making a few coffee-drinking-girls lift their heads to stare. Violet snorted a laugh. Those girls would probably run away screaming if they knew what Mor was.

Mor stole memories. Mor ruined lives. Mor—

Shayne sauntered into Violet's vision, bringing her attention to his pointed ears. "You're pretty," he stated. A mischievous look entered his blue eyes, and his smiling mouth twisted to the side. "How about a kiss, pretty Human?" he offered, and Violet blinked.

"What?"

Mor was close enough to have heard. Shayne stole a look at him like he was waiting to see his reaction. But Mor appeared unfazed as he reached Violet. The Master of Doom even released a grunt-laugh.

"Please do," he said, and Violet's jaw dropped. "I would love to see how that goes for you," he added.

Shayne studied Mor for a moment, but he didn't try kissing anyone. Another guy emerged from a narrow hall and stood beside Shayne. He had auburn hair, thick arms, and wore oven mitts. He was also scowling and didn't bother to say hi or introduce himself like Shayne had.

Mor handed Violet the pink sweater. "Put this on," he instructed.

"Right now? In this summer heat?" Violet looked at him like he was crazy. "I'll die in that."

"You're far less likely to die *in* this than *out* of it," Mor said back. "It's fairy yarn. Any fairy who comes near you will smell the Sisterhood of Assassins and know to stay away, lest they risk the wrath of the Sisterhood. It's like armour."

Violet took the sweater. The material was extremely soft, the kind you'd want to snuggle up in on a blustery winter day to keep warm. The complete opposite of what anyone would want to wear mid-summer.

Apparently feeling Violet had been thinking too long, Mor stole the auburn-haired guy's oven mitts and put them on. He grabbed the sweater back from Violet and used his lobster-mitt hands to take her arm and wrangle her into it.

"Ow!" Violet complained as he stuffed her hands down the sleeves.

The two guys behind Mor just watched. Shayne winced a little. He leaned over with a cupped hand to whisper to the auburn-haired guy. "He's like an infant trying to rip the legs off an insect," he said way too loudly.

The auburn-haired guy nodded, straight faced.

When Mor's sweater attack was successful and Violet was well snuggled into it, the Master of Doom put his hands on her shoulders. "Shall I take you home with me, rebellious secretary?" he asked. "Or would you like to sleep here for the next day or two until I can solve your scent problem?"

Violet raised an eyebrow. "Are you joking?"

"Not at all," he stated. "You have two options. Make a choice."

Shayne raised a hand behind him. "I vote she stays here. If you let me kiss her, I can even make sure she stays here *forever.*"

"I'll cut out your tongue if you try feeding her anything, Shayne, including your mouth," Mor warned. He looked back at Violet, glancing back and forth between her eyes, waiting for her decision. A decision Violet would never make in a million years when Zorah was still back at the garden house.

A second later, Shayne mumbled, "I can still kiss her without a tongue. Won't be quite as good but—"

"I'm not going to stay in your creepy cathedral," Violet blurted at Mor. "And don't get any ideas about holding me hostage again, you heartless vampire!"

Shayne slapped a hand over his mouth, failing to hide a laugh. The auburn-haired guy's solemn mouth twitched, too.

"Well, you can't go back to your human home now that it's been fairy tricked. Anything you touch will alert the Shadow Fairy that you're there, even nudging a single pebble," Mor said. He released her shoulders and dragged the oven mitts off.

Shayne and the auburn-haired fairy exchanged a look.

"Is this the same Shadow Fairy you refuse to tell us about, Mor?" the auburn-haired guy asked in a deep voice. Shayne smacked the auburn-haired guy in the stomach like he'd given away a secret.

"So much for not letting Mor know that we know about that. No fairy match prize for you," Shayne whispered through his teeth.

Mor's expression fell a little. He didn't reply to the question. Instead, he turned back to Violet, and he waited for her to give him an answer; the brief, sad look in his gaze dissolving in an instant like it had never been there.

Across the café, the turquoise-eyed guy pinned Violet with his stare as he sauntered around the counter and walked toward them. There was a certain coldness to his eyes that made Violet shift her footing when he reached the group. Mor passed him the oven mitts, and the turquoise-eyed guy yanked them to himself like Mor had violated them with his touch.

"I'm not going to hide away in that cathedral," Violet stated, deciding once and for all.

Mor nodded. He walked around her and shoved her toward Shayne—she shrieked, barely catching herself on her heels.

"Keep her, then. For now," Mor said to the other guys.

Violet turned and cast him a disbelieving, accusatory look. "I have a house!" she objected. "And an aunt who's probably worried sick about me!"

Mor seemed doubtful. "That human woman is not your aunt," he stated, and Violet blanched.

"How… How did you know…"

Mor spoke over her to the guys, looking especially at Shayne. "If you want to help me, keep her here even if she protests. Don't let her leave. I'll come back tomorrow to pick her up for work."

"What?! Don't you dare leave me here!" Violet demanded.

Mor slid his phone out of his pocket and tossed it to her. She almost didn't catch it. "Take my calls," he said. He turned and headed for the door, pushing out without another word.

Violet tried to step after him, but the auburn-haired guy's hand flashed out and took her arm, keeping her in place. He instantly tore his fingers back and gawked.

"What is wrong with your skin, Human?! It hurts!" he said through a growl.

"Ah. No wonder Mor wanted to see me kiss her at first. Sneaky fool." Shayne grinned.

Mor glanced back through the windows with a satisfied smile that implied he'd not only heard Shayne's comment *through* the glass, but also assured Shayne that was exactly what he'd hoped for.

Shayne shook his head with a smirk as he went to the café door and turned, folding his arms and leaning back against it, blocking the whole thing with his body. Violet didn't have to be a genius to see she'd never get past him.

As though he could read her thoughts, Shayne winked.

"What about my aunt?" Violet tried, scanning the café for alternate exits.

"Mor didn't tell us to guard her, pretty Human. Just you," Shayne said. "And I've been waiting exactly two faeborn months and eighteen days for Mor to show up here. So, I'm not going to screw this up."

CHAPTER

14

Mor Trisencor and How it All Began in the Shadows, Part 2

His unhidden name was Luc Zelsor. The brutal, ruby-haired fairy not only commanded the respect of the High Prince's division of the Shadow Army, he also tormented them when they didn't do what he wanted. The High Prince's division was tweaked and trained into the most brutal, unforgiving batch of war fairies in the whole Dark Corner. If they disobeyed, their flesh was scorched with cold iron. If they did not kill when instructed, they paid for it with their tongues or fingers. Mor always obeyed without question, as was his duty, but what he did not do was learn to respect Luc Zelsor or High Prince Reval. And even though Mor had come out of his silence, he did not speak unless spoken to. He did not give Luc the satisfaction of punishing him for an errant word spoken.

Instead, Mor left venom petals in the fox's drinking goblet that sent Luc into unpredictable fits of stomach pain and fairy gas for three days. Luc could never prove it was Mor, but he retaliated by placing a handful of freshly birthed starbugs in Mor's bed. Mor awoke the following morning with bright red spots all over his flesh and an itch that lasted for two weeks. That had been the beginning of their fairy games. Every trick got worse and more annoying, until the whole Army unit was whispering about the rivalry between Luc Zelsor—the fox, and Mor Trisencor—the lowly orphan from Pane.

"You two shall be a unit," High Prince Reval said on a dim, cloudy morning in his private hut as he stroked his long, glittering scarlet hair. "I wish to send you across the border as Shadow spies, so you can report back to me what the High Queene of the North is plotting. And if you find a clever way to murder that North Prince while you're there, see it done."

Queene Levress—Queene of all the Corners of Ever but one—the Dark Corner's greatest threat. Rumour claimed Levress had a ward that was tearing through the Shadow Army division the Dark Queene had finally sent to attack the North Corner villages. The Dark Queene wished to claim the golden fields under the sun to fill her own storehouses with gold wheat. Shadows whispered that the ward's name was Cressica Alabastian; a peasant boy turned assassin. The fairy war had only started a single month ago, and already news of this dreadful assassin had reached the Shadow Palace and struck fear and rage into the hearts of the Shadow Army commanders. High Queene Levress did not need to fight herself when she had *him*.

Like every other fairy in the Shadow Army, Mor knew to avoid Alabastian and his brothers in navy and black shells. He would not dare approach the North Prince in his facborn lifetime, lest he be torn apart limb by limb. But Mor had to admit, he was relieved to hear the fairy gossip of the ward's existence. Relieved the North had been able to defend itself against the Shadows.

"A unit?" Luc said in disgust on the day his father stated his decision. "With this mute peasant?" Luc's silvery glare shot to Mor. "What's to stop me from killing him the moment we're out of the Dark Corner and performing this mission on my own, Father?"

High Prince Reval tapped a finger against his folded arms. The canopy of vines around their division's newest cove shuffled outside, and an icy breeze leaked in through the hut's windows and scurried up Mor's spine.

"I am not only sending him for your sake, Luc," Prince Reval stated. "I am also sending him for *his* sake. So, try not to kill him."

Luc did not stop glaring at Mor. Only this morning, Luc had dumped a barrel of seeds into the grass and demanded that Mor pick every single one of them up as punishment for sleeping in. Mor had worked through the whole morning gathering seeds before any got too moist from the dew and began to sprout. So, Mor had placed one in Luc's pitcher of drinking water. He could hardly wait to see the fool drink down the seed, followed by the plant sprouting and growing up Luc's throat and out his mouth.

In fact, Mor was a little worried the blossom might burst out right in front of the High Prince. If he'd known he and Luc would be meeting Prince Reval this hour, he probably wouldn't have pulled the fairy trick. There was no way for Mor to tell if Luc had gotten thirsty and guzzled his water before they came.

"This fool is my greatest enemy here, Father. Haven't you heard the rumours of our rivalry? Don't you feel the ice between us?" Luc gloated. "Hasn't anyone told you of the death threats we generously give each other on our way to our sleeping quarters each night? If you send him with me, I will kill him." Luc stole a quick glance at Mor, like he wanted to see how Mor would react to his claim.

Mor stifled a scoff.

Frost surged over the grass, turning the fairies' toes to ice and making them gasp.

"There are two reasons you must take him." Prince Reval's eyes flared at his son as he stood. "The first reason is for you. The second reason is for him. First, you are loud, Son, and he is quiet. So, between the two of you, if one needs to stand in the shadows to eavesdrop for hours without moving a muscle or peeping a word, it will be him. Second..." The Prince came to stand before Luc. They were nearly the same height, nearly the same build. Both too violent for their own good. "He still feels things."

Mor's skin pulled tight. He refused to speak up for himself or meet the Prince's eyes.

Luc's lip curled into a snarl. "I have ensured that he does not." But the ruby-haired fairy's tone wavered like a bass string being plucked. He didn't dare look at Mor now.

Prince Reval's gaze stayed on his son. "You're wrong. His feelings will poison this army if you can't get him under control. It's why he rarely speaks, you fool—so we can't hear the stories in his tone. He's hiding himself from us," he said. "I want him never to care for another living soul again. I have tasked you with this, and you have failed thus far."

It was at this moment in time that Mor realized the High Prince was taking over Luc's task. Prince Reval would steal Mor's memories and wipe his mind clean. It was a promise the Prince did not need to say aloud.

Once upon some faeborn years ago, Mor had lived on the coast. He'd fed the sea monsters and swam with the blue-scaled water dragons. He'd plucked berries in the fields and had carried baskets of fresh fruit and blossoms to the neighbours. He hadn't a care in the whole faeborn realm. The dragons and the fairies of the coast had become his family after his relatives had passed. They had clothed him in petals and water dragon scales. They had fed him their shellfish and forest beast stew. They were the family he missed, a family that might only remember him in their stories and songs.

But now he was this. Now he was an object that belonged to a vicious fox Prince. And no longer would he be allowed to remember the Jade Ocean or the blue-scaled water dragons. His past would be a blank slate, an uninhibited void for lies the Prince himself would use to bend Mor to his will.

Unless he accompanied Luc to the North Corner and injured the son of the High Prince, buried him in a mud pit he couldn't get out of, and abandoned the Shadow Army forever. Mor held his breath as the thought entered his mind. He heard the shift in his rhythm, and begged the sky deities the High Prince would not pick up on it.

What an absurd, dreadful thought.

It was disgustingly, beautifully perfect.

Mor only half listened to the rest of the conversation between the wicked nobles of the Dark Corner at his side. He had been quiet for a long time. He could remain quiet for a while longer. He would not speak and give away his plans.

During the nights that followed, Mor stared up at the murky skies where not even the stars were permitted to shine. He searched the dark, ever-moving cloud for the moon that rarely showed itself, asking the sky deities how a simple village fairy was to outsmart a nine tailed fox. And he plotted. He plotted treacherously. And he wrote his plot in code on his arms in enchanted, never-vanishing ink so that after his memories were taken away, he would still know what he was meant to do. A code of the coast that he and the water dragons had come up with. A code only he and the dragons knew. If he was lucky, his muscle memory would recall how to read it, even if he could not remember the dragons who had taught it to him.

A week later, Mor stood before the High Prince and awaited the invasion of his mind. The Prince lightly touched Mor's temples and hot power trickled in. All the army commanders were present to bear witness to the trial. But the verdict had already been decided. The High Prince deemed the fairy childling from the coast was no longer permitted to remember his origins. Mor felt the memories slide away, one by one. He said goodbye to his neighbours, to their kindness. He said goodbye to the sea monsters and the water dragons, the quiet forest, the dirt street of his childling village, and even to his aunt who had raised him on honey grape pudding until the day she'd died.

Soon, Mor recalled nothing.

When he opened his eyes, he saw a band of powerful fairies sitting around him on twig thrones. He saw an aged fairy with long scarlet hair wearing a satisfied smile. And behind them, hiding in the bushes, he saw a youthful ruby-haired fairy watching—spying perhaps. The young fairy had an odd look on his face; his brows were drawn; his mouth was tipped down at the corners. He seemed to realize Mor had spotted him. The worried look vanished and the fairy ducked back into the trees.

A date for the mission into the North was set. Mor and Luc were supplied with fresh cold iron fairsabers and pockets full of fairy tricks. They went over the plan thrice in the morning and once before bed each evening, preparing for the day when they would slip across the border and travel the trodden paths into the capital of the North Corner. High Prince Reval seemed quite certain that Luc Zelsor would be safe from Mor. Quite certain that all would go according to plan. And it would go according to a plan—Mor's plan.

Because to Mor's delight, he did remember the code of the dragons. His whole plan hung openly on his arm in tattooed ink, visible for all to see everywhere he went. Yet not a single fairy understood it or beheld the treachery he carried on his flesh. And one morning, as though the water dragons themselves sensed his distress all the way from the sea, Mor caught a flash of a moment when he had been underwater long ago. A memory.

A day later, he recalled another memory. And the day after that, he recalled *every* memory that had been stolen.

It was a miracle beneath the eyes of the sky deities. Perhaps a favour of the water dragons.

Mor smiled to himself for the first time in many years. He kept his plan of treacherous escape to himself, kept his memories concealed, and avoided speaking as he waited and prepared for a mission where he would leave the Dark Corner of Ever, perhaps avenge the fair folk who had been wronged by Luc and the High Prince, and never return.

He watched Luc as he counted down the days. The ruby-haired fairy had gone strangely quiet over the last week. It seemed odd that the fairy had lost his voice when Mor remembered him being shamefully out-spoken before. Luc had stopped his pranks, too. Mor checked his bed every evening, checked his water every morning, and checked his armour every midday before training. There were no bugs, no enchantments, no tricks. Perhaps Luc didn't care to torment Mor anymore now that he believed Mor had lost all his memories.

But everything changed one evening at a fire feast. The Prince's Shadow Army division took over a large cave palace from a noble family. The great cave was notched deep into the mountainside, concealing the noise of the army as they feasted at long tables and entertained themselves with shouts and stringed music.

Mor did not eat the enchanted food. He waited for the evening to pass like all the others, only this time there was a different smell in the air. His left ear twitched as a pair of scout fairies passed by his table. Mor looked up for the first time since entering the cave, and what he saw sent a wave of warmth through his faeborn abdomen, bringing back all the feelings he had so carefully hidden away. Cheers lifted through the cave as the scout fairies tugged a living being to the lit area at the front for all to see. "Look what we snatched up across the gate, Prince!" one of the fairies shouted to High Prince Reval. "Shall we feed her our special sugar blossoms and make her dance for us?"

Mor had never seen a human before, but he had read stories about them and had seen a few black and white paintings in old books depicting their smooth, curved ears. The human girl had a different scent than the fairies. And by the horror of the sky deities, she was frightened. Her rhythms tumbled all over the place, her torchlit human eyes as wide as honey grapes. She could not have been much younger than Mor.

And faeborn plans be scattered to the starless sky, Mor decided he could take it no longer.

CHAPTER

15

Mor Trisencor and the Present

Mor stared at his bedsheets. He sighed, then suppressed a shallow grunt as he realized all he could smell now was the human's overpowering perfume. The entire cathedral was ruined by it. There wasn't a room Mor could go in to get away from the potent vanilla smell. But it wasn't just the artificial scent of her that had attacked his walls and his pillows and his sanity, it was the real ones too, painting the air in shallow, fragrant waves of flowers. Many flowers. All kinds, as though Violet Miller had rolled around in a fresh garden in bloom.

It was obnoxious to have it seem like she was standing around every corner when she wasn't.

Freida's words played through his mind as he turned and left his bedroom: *"She stenches like she's wearing your faeborn clothes—flowers, dirt, Shadow blood, and... dandelions."* Mor huffed. So, she smelled like *him* then, and his whole house smelled of *her*. He ought to scrub every surface and linen with enchanted soap. Though, it would just be a waste of soap. Not even fairy magic could fix this problem.

It wasn't that he didn't like Violet Miller. It was just that he didn't like others thinking he cared for his secretary that way. Their relationship was purely professional—fairy and human, Fairy Post supervisor and secretary.

Gifted secretary. Who could write her way into the hearts of the sky deities if she wanted. Who could probably write her way into other places as well.

Mor headed down the stairs, glancing at his dandelion-smeared coat as he passed it and feeling the hot season heat rushing in from the wide-open cathedral doors, unlocked for the first time. He headed for the kitchen to make coffee, and as it brewed, he prepared the beverage fixings. He was sure his invitation wouldn't go unnoticed.

When the coffee was made and hot, Mor pulled two mugs from the cupboard and poured them full. He added lots of sugar and a dollop of beast milk, and he carried them out to the table he'd set just inside the cathedral entrance. He placed a coffee on either side and sat in one of the chairs. A moment later, the warm air began to shiver, and the wind streaked with colour. A soft patter sounded on the front step outside.

Mor sipped his coffee.

The presence outdoors hesitated, likely studying the open entrance. The table. Mor.

"Your drink is getting cold," Mor said. He shoved a coaster across the table. "Make sure you don't spill on my carpet," he added. "It's vintage."

The fairy appeared across from him, his black coat shuffling in the wind. After a few cold seconds, he slowly sank into the open chair, and only then did Mor lift his gaze. Two sets of brown and silver eyes met.

It was impossible to see if the fairy was smiling or frowning with the mask covering the lower half of his face.

"Take that off, Luc," Mor demanded. "It's useless. Unless you have the human sniffles and don't wish to get me sick."

The Shadow Fairy stared. He took his time raising a gloved hand to pull down his mask.

He was frowning.

Mor fought to keep his faeborn heart steady as he looked at a face he had not seen in full for a long time. Since the day Mor had burned bridges and destroyed many sacred fairy things. Since the day Mor had been decreed a traitor to the Shadow Army for all of eternity.

"You're black-marked, Trisencor," Luc said.

Mor felt as though he was back in a time he wished to forget. He'd once tried to steal his own memories of the time and dispose of them, but it had only led to the years becoming a misty recollection of life events that always rushed back. It was his blessing and his curse—that his memories could not be erased.

"You're marked as well," Mor said, and Luc raised a brow. "By me. I will kill you. Long before you can destroy me."

"I won't aim my arrows at *you*, Trisencor." Luc leaned forward a little. "You know how I operate. Everything you care about with those feelings of yours is going to scream and beg for mercy when I'm through. Starting with the pretty human and ending with the gruesome deaths of your new High Court when I find them."

"And here I was hoping for a nice afternoon of sharing civil fairy gossip over coffee." Mor nodded to Luc's mug. "Drink," he invited.

Luc held Mor's gaze for a few moments longer. Then he lifted the coffee and took a sip. He made a strange face. "It's bitter," he mumbled and set it back down.

"It's loaded with sugar," Mor stated evenly.

"I expected it to be loaded with poison." Luc's silvery gaze flashed up again.

"I will strike you down fairly while looking right into your eyes," Mor promised. "Not to worry." He took a long drink of his own coffee, keeping his level stare on Luc. His tongue grew warm.

Luc leaned back in his chair and draped an arm over the backrest. "All right, let's gossip then. Gossip claims you're part of a High Court here. But you seem very alone in this establishment," the ruby-haired fairy mused as he twirled a finger toward the echoey cathedral. "Have they abandoned you? Perhaps they discovered you're a traitor? Or that

SINCERELY, SECRETARY OF DOOM

you're terrible at picking seeds out of the grass at your master's feet? Or perhaps they simply can't stand leeches."

Mor cast him a fake smile. "They like me too much, actually. Also, I hope you enjoyed your coffee." He stood, dragging his empty mug up with him. "It *was* poisoned."

Luc's face fell. Mor swung the coffee mug at him like a rock. The ruby-haired fairy spun off his chair, barely missing the punch, but it was clear his limbs were sluggish. Mor marched after him, drawing the handle of his fairsaber from his pocket. The blade was out in a flash beneath the afternoon sun, and he struck.

Metal hit metal. Luc's blade was sharper, and as he pressed, a dent melted into Mor's weapon. Mor slid the blade away and threw the mug. To his delight, it smacked Luc in the face and sent the fairy teetering out the front cathedral doors.

"Now we'll make a bargain," Mor stated as he followed the fairy and stood over him on the stairs. "I know you rarely make bargains, Luc. But I watched you ruin a few fairies' faeborn lives with them, so I know you'll do it if pressed. And don't try to airslip, you're far too weak."

But Luc rolled onto his side. "You fool. You should have made the beverage sweeter so I would have drunk it all," he said.

Mor flinched as the fox heaved and spat up the contents of his stomach down Mor's front stairs. In the same instant, Luc vanished, always one step ahead. Mor released an ancient curse and charged into the wind after him.

CHAPTER

16

Violet Miller and the Great Fairy Debate

Apparently, the names of the Fae Café owners were *Kate* and *Lily*. The *Lily* one was nowhere in sight, but Violet watched Kate from across the café, studying the girl's nonchalance about the memory-thieving brutes travelling around her, pouring coffee and coming out of the kitchen with steaming trays of baked goods that made the place smell amazing. Violet's stomach growled.

The late afternoon sun melted over the tables, bleaching them gold after the most bizarre three days of Violet's life. Every so often, Violet glanced at the door and considered making a run for it. But the white-haired whack-a-mole fairy popped up at random intervals throughout the hours like he was waiting for her to try. Like he *wanted* her to try.

She'd considered more than once that if her touch really burned them, she could probably get past him. She just wasn't sure if she was in the business of hurting someone without a really good reason.

Though… seeing if Zorah was okay in that pebble-covered house felt like a pretty good reason.

The most annoying part of Violet being trapped here was that the person Mor was worried about Violet crossing was the very person she'd been studying for half a year. She probably knew more about the redhead guy than anyone—apart from Mor. It was the reason she agreed to take the secretary job. Because as strange as everything was, she wanted to catch the serial-attacker more than anything.

Violet startled when Mor's phone rang in front of her, vibrating against the table. She looked around, wondering if one of the Master of Doom's *friends* should answer it—in case it was official fairy/Doom business or whatever. But everyone was busy serving coffee, washing counters, and taking orders.

Violet grabbed the phone on the last ring and answered. "Hello?"

"Good evening. I'm Fil Selemini calling on behalf of The Sprinkled Scoop. I'm wondering if I can speak to whoever is in charge of The Fairy Post about coming to our station for an interview?"

Violet stood, her chair scooting out behind her. A few choice words punched against the inside of her sealed mouth. Shayne glanced over snoopily from where he hovered by the café door.

"Hello?" Fil said again in his thick, nasally voice that sounded con-descending even over a phone. "I'm just calling as a courtesy—" Violet rolled her eyes, "—because getting an interview with us would be big exposure for you—"

Violet hung up the phone. She tossed it back onto the table and folded her arms. She would die before she let Mor's considerably better and *far* more entertaining Fairy Post be heckled by The Sprinkled Scoop—which was definitely what Fil Selemini intended to do. Her finger tapped on her bicep as she began to pace.

A second later, she grabbed the phone again and punched in the number she knew by heart.

It rang a few times before one of the interns picked up. "The Sprinkled Scoop, how can I help you?"

It seemed they'd put Alice on the phones again, instead of giving her real journalist work.

"I'm calling from The Fairy Post to speak with Fil Selemini," Violet said in a cool, even voice she hoped wasn't recognizable.

"Of course. I'll see if he's available."

In other words, *"I'll go see if he even wants to talk to you, and if not, I'll come up with an excuse about how busy he is."*

Violet paced as she waited, her heels tapping over the floor. She almost walked right into Shayne's chest when he appeared in front of her. His arms were folded. "I'm needed until tomorrow morning on a quick errand, Human," he said. "I expect you to stay put. Dranian will be watching you closely."

"Shh." Violet put a finger to her lips. "I'm on a call."

Shayne raised a brow. "For what?"

"For The Fairy Post." She cast him a look that said, *"What else would it be for?"*

"Huh." Shayne looked amused. "So, you really are his secretary. Queensbane, I thought he made that bit up." He grinned.

"Hello, Fil Selemini here."

Violet turned away from the fairy and focused all her attention on her journalist nemesis. "Hi, I'm returning your call on behalf of The Fairy Post. I apologize for the last call, but we've been experiencing some technical difficulties due to the volume of phone calls and emails we've been getting from our fans. I hear you're interested in an interview?"

"Yes!" Fil sounded maliciously excited. "Who am I speaking to?"

Violet's words caught in her throat. "The Secretary of Doom," she decided. "I'm a little offended you didn't do your research on our staff before calling us," she added on the end.

There was a notable shuffle on the other end as Fil fumbled through an apology, and Violet smiled.

"That's... quite the interesting job title," Fil said, even though it was obvious that *interesting* was the last thing he felt it was. Just like any dull doorknob journalist with no imagination. "My boss and I are very curious about the writer of your paper. From what I can tell, there's only one—"

"There are two now," Violet stated. It was maybe a bit presumptuous to assume Mor would let her write articles for The Fairy Post, but he had said he wanted her to keep it alive. She hoped that meant she'd get to write.

"Ah. Two, then. Well, we'd love to interview them both. Is there a time that might work for The Fairy Post journalists to come to our station and do an interview for our online video channel? We'll also have it featured on our blogs." What he didn't add aloud was, *"And we'll make sure we twist your words and write nasty things about you so no one wants to read your paper anymore."*

"Unfortunately, we only work with print," Violet said.

"Wait… Seriously?" Fil wasn't even hiding his annoyance now.

"But my boss is telling me to formally invite *you* to be interviewed by *us*," she added.

There was a pause. "Well, we don't normally get interviewed… Is there any chance I can speak to your boss directly?" Fil had the nerve to ask.

Violet took a deep breath and tried to let it out without blowing into the phone. "I assure you; this is what he wants—"

A hand came around her and lifted the phone from her fingers. Violet turned and shrank beneath the pair of cold, turquoise eyes glowering down at her. The guy put the phone against his pointed ear. "This is Mor, owner of The Fairy Post, mediocre writer, and terrible friend. How may I help you?" His voice was intimidating and authoritative, like he could convince the masses and become the city mayor overnight if he wanted. Or like he was the real boss around here, not the *Kate* and *Lily* people.

Violet's mouth parted. She didn't know if Mor would want her to snatch his phone back or if she should just let this happen. It wasn't like she could take on this tall, muscular, turquoise-eyed fairy by herself. Her eye caught on his small metal name tag that said: CRESS.

Cress grunted into the phone in response to something. "Don't be preposterous, you fool. Only the truly gifted can handle being on a human internet show. I would know," he stated, and then, "*We* will interview *you*, or there will be no interview at all. You decide." Cress handed the phone back to Violet.

Violet blinked as she slowly returned the phone to her ear. She cleared her throat before she spoke again. "If you'd like to come to our office, we'd be happy to feature The Sprinkled Scoop in our newspaper. With our own narrative, of course. The way you're written into our articles solely depends on whether or not we like you," she said. Her mouth found its smile again.

Justice.

Fil didn't say anything for several seconds. "Uh… I'll have to talk to my boss," he finally spat out when he found his senses.

"Please do. I'll be awaiting your call, Mr. Selemini." Violet hung up. She inhaled and let the breath out slowly.

She was going to need a new dress and some awesome heels. If she was going to face her journalist nemesis *and* her former boss, she had to look like she was killing it in life.

"You're welcome." Cress turned and went back into the kitchen, flicking sugar off his sleeves.

Shayne untied his apron and hung it up in a narrow hallway by the door. "Farewell, pretty human. Don't think that just because I'm not here, I won't know if you step outside. Dranian will call me," he warned. He cast a look toward the back of the café where the auburn-haired fairy came out of the stairwell. He returned a small nod like he was reporting for duty, and with that, Shayne left.

The moment the white-haired fairy disappeared down the street, Violet set her sights on Dranian. From the start, he'd been the quietest. The crankiest too, it seemed. Yes, he must have been the weakest link.

Violet approached him and grabbed her forehead. "I'm not feeling good," she admitted. "I think I need my medicine."

Dranian looked her up and down. "You need nothing, Human. Your rhythms are fine, and you're lying off your human tongue."

Violet braked her damsel in distress act. She dropped her hand from her forehead. "Okay, but seriously, I do have a condition that I need supplements for. I may be fine now, but in the morning, I'm going to get really desperate. Can't you just take me to my house for *one* minute?"

The fairy only growled in answer.

Violet didn't think she'd be able to sleep in one of the chairs by the fireplace, but she was miraculously out like a light the moment she flopped down into it. Whether it had been the day that had pumped her with adrenaline only to crash later, or the plushness of the chair, or the warmth of the fire on her toes, she'd gotten the best sleep of her life.

She woke up from a wild fairytale dream about a handsome mythological journalist that turned out to not be a dream at all.

"You've got to be joking," she muttered to no one in particular as vertigo rushed in. She slapped a hand to her forehead and leaned forward on the chair. Haze clouded her thoughts, and her stomach squeezed, pain leaking through it and burning her insides. "I'm such an idiot."

She'd had two options yesterday—stay with these weirdo fairies or run for the door.

She should have run for the door. Nothing was worth feeling dizzy and sick like this in the morning. She turned to shout at whoever was around. "Hey!" she called. "I need my supplements! It's an emergenc—"

"If you want to wake the neighbourhood for no reason, keep shouting," someone muttered.

Dranian sat on the opposite plush chair, reading a book.

"I'm not messing around this time. I actually really need to go home," Violet tried.

Dranian shut the book, annoyance flickering across his dull expression. "I've realized. Something in your human body changed in the night," he said. He sounded bored.

"I'll die without it," Violet promised. It might have been a bit of a stretch, but feeling like dying was almost the same as really dying. Sort of.

When he didn't respond, Violet tried to stand. She gasped when her knees wobbled, and she teetered to the side. Someone caught her, and Violet's gaze snapped up—her mouth open to warn that her skin would burn them... But it was the café owner, Kate.

"What's wrong with you?" Kate shouted at Dranian. "Why are you being so mean? Just because you're mad at Mor doesn't mean you can let a person faint. Un-*real*!"

Dranian snarled a little. "Maybe if she faints, he'll come back for her," he mumbled, opening his book again. "Then we'll actually get to see him."

"Seriously, Dranian, if Mor finds out you let his secretary get hurt, he'll flip." Kate walked over and yanked the book out of his hand. She slapped it shut and lightly smacked him on the shoulder with it.

Dranian scowled. "You didn't even put in a bookmark, Human! Now you've lost my page!" He yanked the book back. After a moment, his green eyes slid back to Violet. "Tell me where your human medicine is, and I'll fetch it," he stated.

Violet shook her head. "It has to be me. You'll never find it." And she needed to see Zorah.

Dranian huffed and lifted from the chair, cradling his book to his chest. "I wanted to read today," he muttered. "Not accompany Mor's human on a lacklustre stroll." He stomped through the café, tossed his book on a table, and headed outside.

Violet dragged on her heels and headed after him in relief, using the tables for balance as she passed through them. "Thank you!" she called back to Kate.

"No problem. Don't take his mood swings personally—he hasn't had his morning coffee yet. He'll be nicer after he does," Kate said, but then she paused, seeming to think better of the statement. "Actually, he's a bit of a fun-sucker with or without coffee to be honest," she said. "Good luck finding your supplements."

Violet forced a smile as she pushed outside into the warm morning sun. She'd forgotten she was wearing the knit sweater. Thankfully the day wasn't blazing hot yet, but as soon as she could, she'd yank the sweater off. She was dizzy enough without the extra heat, and her skin was already a fairy-repellant machine—she was probably safer armoured in her own bare skin.

Maybe she'd ditch the fairy weirdo, too. Violet had a feeling Dranian would follow her into her house and drag her back to the café after she got her pills. And yes, she needed her supplements so she could think straight again, but mostly, she needed to go to the hospital and make sure Zorah was there for her shift and not passed out in the woods somewhere.

Minutes later, Dranian huffed when she couldn't keep up. "Must I carry you?" The way he asked made it clear he really didn't want to.

"I'm fine," Violet lied. She took in deep breaths. Eventually, she took off her heels and walked shoeless on the Toronto street that was no doubt full of bacteria and contagious diseases.

Ditch the fairy.

Get the supplements.

Go to the hospital and find Zorah.

Violet replayed it in her mind so she wouldn't forget as her brain fog turned into an overcast storm. She winced and rubbed her eyes, teetering a little and grabbing the side of a building as confusion rushed in and everything started spinning. No, she was not okay.

So, when she dragged her eyes up and saw a daunting redhead fairy standing in the middle of the road, she wasn't sure if she was really seeing him or not.

CHAPTER

17

Violet Miller and the Shadows

Violet's sweater was grabbed. Dranian shoved her behind him where she staggered to stay balanced. She dropped one of her heels to the ground, gaping up at his body shielding hers from whoever stood in the road. Then she peeked around, trying to decide if the redhead fairy was really there.

It seemed he was.

"Let him try and take me," Violet scoffed, blinking rapidly. "He'll only get hurt."

Dranian reached back to shove her behind him again. When his fingers accidentally brushed Violet's hand, he stopped. He turned and looked back at her in question, staring at their touching fingers. Violet's mouth parted as she tried to decide if it was real—their hands. Touching. Him not feeling any pain.

"Oh no," she whispered.

Dranian growled and turned back to the redhead. "Great," he muttered.

"Why…" she mumbled manically to herself. "Why now? Why all of a sudden?" She poked the back of Dranian's bare forearm again, but he still didn't react. She poked the other one, and this time, he flicked her hand off seemingly in sheer aggravation.

She felt even more sick than before.

"Oh dear. It seems Trisencor hasn't been abandoned by his rumoured High Court after all. You must be the guard dog he uses when he's desperate." The redhead's cool voice crawled into Violet's ears. She peeked around Dranian again.

There he was. The same lustrous, metallic-red hair, the same silvery eyes, the same strange, dark energy rolling off him. Violet could almost taste it, even this far away.

"Dog?" Dranian's low growl seemed to curse the word.

"Dog. Mongrel. Mutt. Hound. Aren't those what the humans call their pets?" the redhead asked, arching a brow.

"Not really," Violet murmured, and Dranian shoved her behind him again.

"Ah. Violet Miller, we meet once more," the redhead called to her. "Shall we make a bargain, Violet? If you come with me willingly, I won't tear your guard dog to pieces," he promised.

"No, you'll just erase his memory and leave him passed out in the forest somewhere with his pockets full of rocks!" Violet shouted back, and the redhead's face changed. Amusement flickered at the corners of his expression.

"Quiet, Human," Dranian scolded. He spoke to the redhead fairy next. "I wish to challenge you, Shadow Fairy. One fairy duel winner. One dead loser. A simple faeborn fight here in this human street."

Violet gaped. "Wait… what?!" She blinked a hundred times over. "You're not actually going to fight to the death for *me*, right?"

"It seems Mor will only come home once this Shadow filth is dead. So, yes, I will take this opportunity gladly," Dranian stated in a low voice. "Run, Human. You don't want to watch what I'll do to this fool." He pulled out a gold and navy handle from his pocket. Before Violet's eyes, a spear formed, bursting out both ends from the handle, seeming to materialize from nothing. A pulsing, buzzing sound filled the air. Dranian tipped the weapon forward, looking ready to ram the redhead through the heart with it, and Violet reeled back.

"How did you do that...?" She didn't wait for an answer. She dropped her other heel to the street as she raced on wobbly legs toward the nearest alley. She caught the brick wall for support as she looked back, not wanting to watch, yet unable to stop looking.

"Who would win in a fight between you and Mor Trisencor, North Fairy? Have you ever fought him, even in practice?" the redhead asked Dranian, drawing two handles of his own. A pair of black blades formed from them. "Because I have. Many times. And of those fights, do you know how many times I beat him?"

"I assure you, however much you think you hate Mor, I hate you twice as much for hating him in the first place," Dranian stated, refusing the question.

But the redhead answered himself. "Every time," he said. There was a look in his eyes that promised he could kill without compunction, and Violet shuddered, thinking of all the women this guy had lured into the forest.

Violet almost missed it when they charged—the spear and swords shot out in a blur of colour. She scooted another step back, but she marvelled. Dranian was no joke; he deflected and spun like he was a weightless, horrifying creature from a legend. And the redhead...

He was faster. It was almost impossible to tell with their speed as his swords swung with terrifying accuracy. Violet placed a hand on her thudding chest as she watched.

Dranian didn't let him get a hit. He used brute force to shove the swords back, keeping the redhead at a distance with his spear.

A young, screaming couple raced by Violet, snapping her attention to the people escaping in every direction down the street. A few pedestrians pulled out phones to film the scene from their hiding places.

Phone.

Mor.

She had to call Mor.

Violet scrambled through her pockets and pulled out her phone to call him… only it wasn't her phone she had; it was his. She moaned. But when she looked back to the fight, fresh wind swooshed in, and her heart picked up an extra beat.

Mor stood in the street. A glistening sword was in his grip.

Dranian fell back and Mor stepped in like a practiced formation. Violet couldn't believe her eyes as he swung and stabbed forward, body twisting. He landed a punch. She knew he could write, of course. She knew he could manage a newspaper. But never—*never*—did she imagine he could fight like this.

"What am I doing?" she whispered, snapping out of it. Someone was going to die here. If she didn't want it to be her, she needed to leave.

Violet backed down the alley, watching the three fairies the whole way. And she almost screamed when the redhead's blade plunged into Mor's side. Mor ripped himself back, purplish blood speckling the road, and he charged again. Dranian stabbed for the redhead's feet as Mor swung at the guy's head.

Violet turned and ran, hoping she hadn't just made an enormous mistake.

Shadow Fairy. That was what Dranian had called the redhead. Violet had been afraid of him the first time she saw him, sure, but her nerves had subsided when she thought he couldn't touch her. Now it felt like a beast of her childhood nightmares had crawled out of the closet and was looking for the life he was owed.

Violet swallowed as she burst into her house, kicking aside pebbles.

She rushed for the kitchen cupboard and flung it open so hard the door snapped off. It clattered to the counter, tipping the saucers off the tea-cups, and everything smashed over the floor as Violet grabbed her bottle of iron supplements and twisted off the lid. She knew she needed to run, to possibly never come back here. It was the only logical thought racing through her spinning mind as she threw a pill into her mouth and guzzled water from the kitchen faucet.

"Well, you can't go back to your human home now that it's been fairy tricked. Anything you touch will alert the Shadow Fairy that you're there, even nudging a single pebble."

She looked around at the mess as she wiped a drip from her lip. "Well, that's problematic," she muttered to the Master of Doom's voice in her head. She raced for the hall closet and yanked out her pre-packed overnight bag. Then she turned and took one last look at her garden home she shared with Zorah. As soon as she could, she would call her aunt and tell her to stay away from the house.

Minutes later, Violet was blinking rapidly at the busy downtown street, begging her supplements to kick in. The stress made everything worse—Violet was sure she would pass out on the roadside and end up in an ambulance. And she didn't doubt the Shadow Fairy's ability to stalk her all the way to the hospital.

She had to get back to the café. She took a few wrong turns, thinking they were right turns, certain she had the worst sense of direction of an-yone in Toronto when her mind felt like chalk and clouds. She knew she wasn't going to figure anything out until she could think straight, so she half-crawled into an alley to wait it out, shoving her overnight bag ahead of her. She sat back against the cold brick wall, hugging her knees to herself and clutching her purse.

Someone walked up to Violet with a weird glare and a questioning face. The young woman looked to be in her late twenties or early thirties with a long braid of red hair roped around her neck and resting over a green knit vest. A name was carefully stitched across the left bust pocket of the vest: GRETCHEN.

"Where'd you get that sweater, Human?" she snapped in a high voice. "My sisters and I agreed not to make you one. That faeborn assassin didn't ask politely." She moved in to block the morning light from Violet's eyes, and Violet squinted up at her. She recognized her from the knitting store Mor had brought her to yesterday.

"I smelled our yarn on my way by," the young woman added. "That sweater doesn't belong to you. Give it back."

"I... I can't..." Violet choked out.

A cool breeze brushed through the alley, running along Violet's neck and sending a shiver down her spine. She watched the wind flutter Gretchen's red hair, and Gretchen stiffed. The woman's nose wrinkled like she smelled something bad, and she turned her head toward the end of the road.

Violet's gaze followed. She was too dizzy to scream, but her fingers tightened around her purse when she saw the redhead guy there.

He stood, eyeing Gretchen. A bead of dark blood ran down his chin, and a swelling bruise covered half his jaw, but he looked strong.

Violet jumped to her feet, gluing herself back against the wall. She stuffed a hand into her purse, searching for anything she might use as a weapon. Her fingers curled around a fountain pen, so she tore it out and ripped off the lid, holding it high above her head. She wouldn't go down without a fight—a fountain-pen-stabbing *fight*.

Gretchen looked the Shadow Fairy over the same way he studied her. There was a strange tension in the air that was so thick, Violet almost choked on it.

"Step aside," the redhead said. "I want a conversation with that human."

Gretchen's nose wrinkled again. "Can't you see what she's wearing, you foolish male?" Do you want the whole Sisterhood coming for your throat?"

The redhead glanced at Violet's pink sweater. "Yes, I did notice that delicious little fact," he said. "Perhaps we can make a bargain for her?"

Gretchen's hands slid beneath her knit shirt at the back, and Violet's eyes widened as the motion revealed two long, silver knitting needles flush with her spine. "No bargain," Gretchen said. "She's wearing our yarn, which means she's under our guard. Even if we didn't agree to it." The last part sounded bitter.

The redhead guy's broad, diabolical smile returned. "Too bad you're here alone, then," he said to Gretchen, his eyes glittering.

Gretchen's jaw tightened. She clasped the needles behind her back and drew them out, making it clear she wasn't planning on running. "Let's go, then," she stated.

The redhead guy vanished, and Violet gasped, her eyes darting around the alley until Gretchen stabbed backward into the air. He reappeared behind her and nearly took her needles into his neck. He dropped to a knee to avoid them and thrusted his boot into Gretchen's side. It happened so fast Violet almost missed it.

Gretchen slid over the asphalt, ripping the fabric of her pants at the knee. Her head whipped back to stare the redhead down with a look of menace. She jumped and kicked off the wall, soaring high into the air, and she *shrank*. Violet watched with wide eyes as the young woman transformed into a winged creature the size of her thumb that darted back and forth like a bullet. The two went at it—vanishing fairy and tiny fairy—until Gretchen reappeared in full size with a swinging kick that caught the redhead in the leg.

He stabbed backward as he took the hit...

The blade went into Gretchen's stomach.

Violet shrieked and dropped the fountain pen as Gretchen released a high, raspy gasp. The redhead yanked his blade back out and Gretchen tumbled to the ground in a heap. She didn't move after that. The redhead turned on Violet before Gretchen's blood even started leaking onto the asphalt.

Something flashed in his brown and silver eyes as he drew a step toward her. "Take off that sweater," he insisted in a sweet, articulate voice.

Violet pressed back against the wall as hard as she could, shaking her head and clutching her collar. Her skin was useless—this sweater was the only thing she had left to protect her.

He leaned in, trapping her there as his cold and musty earth scent filled her senses. "Take it off, *Violet*. Or I'll take it off you myself."

CHAPTER

18

Mor Trisencor and the Path that Led to Nowhere

By the time Mor reached the alley filled with his secretary's scent, Violet was already gone. A feral ache he didn't know he could feel blistered over his hardened heart, and he braced a palm against the brick wall to support himself. She was only his secretary. Truly, he hardly knew the human, and death was not a new thing to him.

But.

Seeing the pink sweater lying abandoned at the foot of the wall in the alley empty of life, hope, and promises... Queensbane, it was over.

He'd gotten a human killed.

A human who had trusted that he wasn't the monster tearing through the city. A human who had spent her last months writing articles about that same monster, knowing her work could put her in danger.

Mor's fist pounded once over his furious heart as he tried to dull the unwelcomed feeling, bringing himself back to his senses even though death had caught up with him—*again.*

Perhaps Violet was right to call him 'Doom.'

Since the moment she'd shown up at Mor's cathedral door looking for a job and was mistakenly marked as his lover, death had been following Violet the same way it had always followed him. Only, he'd been able to dodge it—*had* been dodging it for quite some time. But it had caught Violet in its snares.

Mor bit his lower lip until he punctured the flesh and tasted his own sweet fairy blood. He imagined Violet becoming one of the many victims lost to the forest, a body Luc left for Mor to find, leaving behind thoughts meant to torture him every morning to come.

Why hadn't Violet stayed at the café like she was told? Why didn't his secretary listen when he instructed her not to go to her human home? Why did she take off her faeborn-cursed sweater?!

He lifted the sweater from the ground, running his thumb over the soft material. It was torn clean down the middle, hanging open and mangled. A smell lifted from it; the sharp, fruity smell of fairy blood. Mor furrowed his brows as he turned the garment over, but he couldn't spot the blood. It took him a moment to realize that what he was smelling wasn't on the sweater at all.

A drying puddle lay at his feet. He sprang back a step, searching for traces of Shadow Fairy in it. But it wasn't Luc's blood—it smelled nothing of the Shadows. In fact, it smelled of...

Yarn.

"Queensbane," he cursed. The blood smeared into a trail that led out of the alley. He followed it, drawing one of his fairsabers, skin tingling with the sensation of pins and needles even before he reached the front door of the Yarn & Stitch minutes later.

He barged in, and angry female eyes fired all sorts of silent insults and horrific curses in his direction.

"Where is my secretary?" he demanded. "Is she here?"

Freida rose from her seat on the couch. The coffee table had been swept of yarn projects, and upon it lay Gretchen, bleeding all the way to the carpet, eyes closed, a gaping hole in her stomach.

Freida grabbed a needle from the pile on the end table. The female's heels clapped over the floor, her gemstone earrings glistening in the storefront lights. It appeared she'd rushed here straight from her day job. "You dragged us into your war, Assassin!" Her shout was magnified by magic, booming over the yarn-filled shelves and far out into the street. "You nearly got one of my sisters killed!"

Mor took a step back as the old woman reached him, her fist tightly wound around her needle. He glanced at Gretchen on the table again as the story in Freida's tone came together. He shifted his approach, allowing his shoulders to lose their ice-hard rigidness.

"I did not know that would happen," he promised.

"What did you think would happen, you fool?! Gretchen had to intervene on your human's behalf! Now she may die here on my table!" Freida barked. "Stay out of our way now—we will go deal with the Shadow Fairy ourselves!"

Mor's shoulders hardened again and he wobbled a little, feeling his own faeborn blood leaking down his leg from the deep wound in his side. "He will take you all down," he warned in a low growl. "You are out of practice, Sisterhood, and you are no match for someone of that Shadow Fairy's bloodline. He's no ordinary fairy!"

"Then why don't you tell your Prince to stop him? If Alabastian's reputation has any morsel of truth to it—which I know it does—he should be able to put an end to all this." Freida's words were cold, cutting, and clear, and Mor's face fell. He staggered a step, only to realize he'd lost feeling down the right side of his body, all the way to his toes.

"I cannot ask him to do that," he said in a quieter voice. "That Shadow came here for me. I will deal with him. Do not get involved, and don't you *dare* make a suggestion to Cress."

Freida pointed in his face. "No, you foolish male. That Shadow is mine to deal with now. You stay out of my way!"

Mor inhaled an aggravated breath. "I apologize for Gretchen, and I will make it right if it's the last thing I ever do, but..." The room teetered and Mor tried to blink away the hallucination of moving shelves and couches. "But you can't…"

He noticed Freida's gaze sweep down him to the widening puddle of fairy blood at his feet. He tried to take a step, but everything around him tilted fast. Before he knew it, he was being caught by several sets of treacherous female hands before his face hit the floor.

"Pearl," he heard Frieda snap as darkness painted itself over his mind, blotting out his thoughts. "Get him out of here."

For the first time in a long while, Mor dreamt in colour and taste. He dreamt of cool green water, tasted thin grains of salt, and listened to a herd of navy water dragons tell him a story beneath the sea where no one could find him.

It had been years since he'd visited the dragons. He was surprised they still remembered him, still spoke his real name with fondness. They invited him into their circle amidst silver reefs and pale stone statues, where the undersea light glimmered off their deep blue scales.

The story they told was of a young fae male who carried a blessing of the sea inside of him for the sacrifices he had made, and the evil he had stood against. A blessing kept secret for numerous faeborn seasons, that not even the stars or the sky deities would whisper about for its preciousness.

One that had kept him alive when the shadows of the air had come knocking. It was the first time Mor knew for certain that the water dragons had been looking out for him all these years by imparting the gift of never being able to forget.

If it could still be called a gift at all.

In the middle of his slumber, he asked them, "Why can I not just forget the bad memories and keep the good ones? Wouldn't that make things easier?"

An old dragon laughed, a booming echo through the water. "I think you will soon find that you need the bad memories, too. They can tell you things. They can give you answers, and sometimes they can solve problems. You must allow yourself to think of them every now and then, Son of Pane."

Mor's salty tears mixed with the sea water

"But it's hard to think of those memories. It hurts," he admitted.

The dragon's long tail swished behind him as it leaned forward, coming eye-to-eye with Mor like Mor was still just a childling of the village, and hadn't left and grown up. "The hurt is why we need those memories. The hurt is what makes us understand others who are hurting, dear Son. If we grow numb to the hurt, we become shells with no hearts. And your heart is what has saved you," the dragon said. "Don't despise your hurt, and most importantly, don't despise your heart."

19

Cressica Alabastian and the Whole Three Days,
Starting at the Beginning

The trio of days had started all wrong.

First:

In the middle of the cursed night, Shayne had lunged off the couch in Kate's apartment—still sleeping—and tripped over the area rug in the small living space. It had turned into a full-fledged fairy-splat after that. Shayne became one with the rug, moaning loud enough to rattle the building.

Cress released a huff as he tore off his sheets and strutted out of the bedroom. "You'd better be dead," he warned Shayne as he entered the living space. "Or I'll kill you for waking me up again."

Shayne rubbed his face and shot Cress a look. "I fell," he said.

Cress blinked slowly. "How enlightening. I hadn't noticed."

From the chair by the door, Dranian's snoring hitched. It wasn't fair that the fairy was able to sleep through anything these days, and Cress was left to deal with Shayne's horrendous sleep noises.

Shayne picked himself up off the floor, rubbing his backside. "I had a bad dream," he explained.

"I'm having a bad dream *now*," Cress growled. "Is not even a prince of the North Corner permitted to get any sleep here?"

"Aren't you going to ask me what my dream was about?" Shayne asked, flopping back onto the couch. The white-haired assassin adjusted the pillow behind his head, already seeming ready to go back to sleep.

Cress hesitated. He opened his mouth, then shut it again. He folded his arms. He shifted his weight.

"What was it about?" he finally asked.

"I'm not telling," Shayne said.

Cress grumbled a curse and turned to head back into the bedroom. Kate was lucky to be sleeping at Lily's apartment these last months. At least she was able to dream without waking to Shayne's midnight madness.

"Cress," Shayne said before Cress was out of sight.

The Prince poked his head back into the living space. "What?"

Shayne tapped a finger against his stomach and stared up at the ceiling. "I dreamt about home."

Cress watched the assassin for a few moments. He didn't need to ask why that would have resulted in a nightmare. Why it would have made Shayne fling himself off the couch in a fitful sleep. He knew full well.

He also knew that comforting his Brotherhood of Assassins had never been his strong suit. Cress was made to demand their attention, equip them with skills, and when necessary, strike fear into their hearts so they would obey. It was Mor who had become the fairy to march into their sleeping caves and give them a good talking to when needed, or an inspiring quote, or an ear to listen. Cress never had to think twice about his assassins' worries or feelings. He fought for them, he saved their lives, and he taught them to defend themselves when he wasn't around. He hadn't had time for much else while enemy war fairies knocked at the

North's door and enchanted sea monsters lurked below the North Corner waters. Cress had been sent across the Corner to slay fae and monsters. Negotiating wasn't in his skill set.

But Mor would have known the right thing to say to Shayne in this moment. Cress could only think to swat at Shayne's head until all of his obnoxious dreams fell out.

Cress's gaze dropped to the floor. It was getting increasingly difficult to do as Mor had asked. There were only so many wedding preparations that could distract a powerful assassin prince.

He remembered the day he first crossed Mor on a golden field. The curly-haired fool had been different then; wild. A bit lost. A smidgen out of his mind. It was only after a heart-pounding battle Cress had dragged that Shadow rebel back to the Silver Castle with him, and Mor had turned into the thing the Brotherhood of Assassins didn't know they needed.

Cress found himself smiling briefly at the precious memory. He dropped the look from his face though and folded his arms to compose himself.

"I love the café, but I'm bored," Shayne said. It seemed his mind had gone to the same place Cress's had. "I was an heir to the House of Lyro, remember? You know I wasn't made to sit things out."

Cress's sigh filled the apartment. "There has to be a reason Mor told us not to become entangled. I've gone over it a thousand times, and I can't figure it out. But there must be a faeborn-cursed reason." He rubbed his eyes, realizing he was still so treacherously tired. "Now, if you wake me one more faeborn-cursed time, Shayne, I'll toss you off the balcony," Cress threatened.

Shayne's eyes were already closed. It was painfully obvious that the white-haired assassin was only pretending to sleep. He released a teeny tiny snore that was orchestrated to the highest degree, and Cress grunted. The Prince rolled his eyes and marched back to bed.

He didn't sleep a wink after that.

Second:

Mor had surprised everyone by showing up at the café on day two. A colourful human was on his arm with bright lips and shimmering eye powders. A new friend, it seemed. Cress glared at her with all the coldness of the North. How dare she be accepted into Mor's confidence when Mor already had perfectly good friends he was avoiding?

Cress quickly turned toward where Kate was crouched down by the low cupboards and began rattling through his latest wedding plans in a loud voice so Mor might hear all he was missing out on. From the corner of his eye, he saw Mor head through the café toward him.

Kate looked up at Cress like he was crazy. With her eyes alone, she cast him the sort of adorable, *"What in the human realm are you doing?"* look that could have melted his faeborn heart on another day. But her face changed when Mor appeared at the counter.

"Cress," Mor's voice seemed to fill the whole room.

Cress ignored him.

Kate cast Cress a crossbeast-fang-sharp look. She stayed where she was, crouched before the cupboard. Not getting involved, apart from nodding her head toward Mor, saying something to Cress with her eyes that had an entirely different vibe than their lovely wedding plans.

Cress huffed and turned to face the deserter. "May I help you, Mor?" he asked, flashing a wicked smile as he waited for an apology, which would be undoubtedly followed by Mor's grovelling and begging Cress to take him back.

"I'm not staying," Mor said, and Cress's smile fizzled out. "I just came here because I need Kate's sweater."

Cress blinked. Once. Twice. Thrice.

"Give it to him." Kate's treacherous decision ruined Cress's cold behaviour performance.

"I don't particularly want to," Cress said back to her.

"Give it to him, Cress. If he came here asking for it, it's because he needs it," Kate said. Then she muttered, "Seriously, you're so moody when you miss sleep."

Cress had half a mind to explain to his betrothed that his reasons for missing sleep had only half to do with Shayne's noises. The other half had to do with the stress of planning a wedding to *her*. She ought to be grateful for his sacrifice.

For a brief moment, the corner of Mor's mouth tugged up. But the almost-smile vanished before it set in.

Cress flung open the cupboard doors below the sink where those at Fae Café stashed everything of the important and magical sort, and he yanked out the sweater made of the Sisterhood's fairy yarn. "For your new friend?" Cress asked as he tossed the sweater over.

"She's my secretary," Mor stated without explaining further.

"She's pretty," Kate commented, rising from her crouched position just enough to spy on the human over the counter.

"She's vile and hideous. I hate her," Cress stated.

Mor rolled his faeborn eyes as he turned away with the sweater.

The hardness on Cress's face melted off as he worried that was it. He hadn't seen Mor in months and suddenly Mor arrived at the café after all this time and there was no, "How are you, Cress?" or, "Are you well?" or, "Are we still the best of fae-friends?" or even, "That human woman I brought in means nothing to me and I wouldn't dream of replacing you with her." Truly, Cress fought the impulse to chase after the fairy and do all the grovelling and begging himself. He opened his mouth several times to call things as Mor slipped away, moving further and further through the tables, becoming more out of reach by the second.

"Mor," Cress said. Just his name. Nothing else felt good enough.

Even though Mor's back was turned, he slowed his escape just a little. Cress knew Mor's fairy ears would pick up on his next words past the distance between them. "You have one more week to settle this. Then I'm coming for you."

By the grace of the sky deities, Mor did not react.

Mor did, however, leave his human behind in the café for Cress to glare at for the next twenty-four hours. The Prince of the North could hardly keep his distance. It took every faeborn ounce of his self control not to pin her in the corner and release a mountain of questions about what Mor was doing, where he was going, and what was so good and magical about her that Mor had let her near him in the first place?

Third:

The human had escaped. Cress didn't hear about it until he came down from the apartment in the morning and learned that Dranian had taken Violet Miller out on a cursed stroll. Shayne was nowhere to be found, and Kate... Well. She'd orchestrated the whole evil plot to let the human go.

"Are you out of your faeborn mind, Human?!" Cress said to Kate in a fit of panic. "You helped her escape?"

"She's not our prisoner, Cress," Kate rebutted as she dusted the café bookshelf with a large, plush fluffy thing.

"That is *precisely* what she is, Katherine!" He only used her real name anymore when she'd done something he adored or disproved of. It seemed she knew it, too. She paused her dusting and turned to face him with her hands on her hips.

"She needed her medicine. It was important," Kate stated. "You can't deprive someone of their health. It's a basic human right in this country."

Cress huffed and spun toward the door, dragging his hand through his silken hair. He spun back to her again.

"Where did they go? I cannot let that human escape *or* come into harm's way," he said.

"I thought you found her vile and hideous," Kate challenged, going back to her dusting.

"I do. But Mor asked us for this *one* thing, and if we fail, he won't ask us for help again." Cress looked around for his fairsaber handle. "I'm sure she's fine," he coached himself. "She's probably fine." He did another full spin, making himself dizzy. He could not remember where he'd left his faeborn weapon.

The café door burst open; both Cress and Kate jumped.

Dranian marched in, spear in his hand, fairy sweat on his brow, his chest pumping.

"Queensbane, what happened?!" It was more of an accusation than a question. "You lost her, didn't you? Oh, sky deities have mercy, we're doomed!" Cress moaned. Yes, now was the right time to panic.

"I'm afraid I failed to protect Mor's human," Dranian stated, and Kate dropped the fluffy dust thing.

"What?" Her weak human-y voice lifted from beside Cress. "Seriously?"

"I will take whatever punishment is necessary." Dranian dropped to a knee. "I forfeit my right to guard humans ever again in this lifetime."

Kate shook her head. "Dranian, this isn't your fault! You don't have to—"

"I should make you eat rocks!" Cress bellowed.

"What? No way!" Kate swooped in and dropped beside Dranian, and soon Cress had two subjects kneeling before him. Kate clasped her hands together in a begging sort of way. "Cress," she reasoned, "this is my fault, not his."

"Then *you* eat rocks," he said to Kate. But his mouth twitched as she gazed up at him with her large, hazel, human eyes. He could never truly make her do that. Queensbane, he hated the thought of it. "Oh, forget it!" he said, marching back to the counter to hunt for his fairsaber. "I'll fix this myself."

"Mor was there," Dranian said, and Cress stopped.

"You saw Mor—Where?"

"In the street. And the Shadow Fairy showed up. I saw him with my own eyes; the one Mor has been hunting."

Cress came right back, slower this time. "You saw the Shadow."

Dranian's green gaze flickered up to the Prince. "I did. I smelled him too, even past his dandelion cloak. This war fairy..." Dranian looked off, his green eyes glazing over like he was in another place. "I've never crossed a scent like his." His gaze shot back to Cress. "He's not quite like us. We've faced many fairy kinds before, but this one makes me afraid."

There was a shift in the café's air. Cress felt the old North magic murmur over his flesh. "What exactly are we dealing with, Dranian?" he asked his assassin.

Dranian's ever-scowl twisted as he seemed to think how best to describe it. He finally settled with, "Something as powerful as you, Cress. Possibly even more powerful."

Kate began looking back and forth between Dranian and Cress. She was going to make herself dizzy if she didn't cut it out.

Dranian stood, and Kate scrambled to stand beside him.

Cress realized his jaw was dropped, leaving his mouth hanging open. He closed it when a human realm fly buzzed by and threatened to sail right in.

So, there was a Shadow Fairy in the human realm terrible enough to have driven Mor mad and make Dranian believe such things. Cress's hand idly went to Kate, and he tugged her to him by her sleeve. He stared out the café window as he hugged his human to himself. She blinked up at him in question.

"Where is Mor now?" he asked Dranian over his prized human's head.

Dranian's gaze fell to the floor again. "He vanished as soon as the Shadow Fairy did. I was left in the street with no rival, no ally, and no human to guard."

So, that pretty much summed up Cress's last few days.

CHAPTER

20

Violet Miller and the Doctor of Lies

There was no obvious reason why Violet should have returned to the cathedral. No one would have blamed her for quitting her job after she'd nearly been sliced to death with a mythical-style weapon. It wasn't like the benefits were good here, or her coworker was easy to get along with, or the office environment was safe.

Yet here she was. Waiting at the Master of Doom's bedside as he slept.

He hadn't been bandaged up when the knitting store women dumped him on the cathedral's front steps. For a split second after Violet had found Mor like that, basking in the shadow of three yarn-adorned ladies all sneaking away faster than a speeding bullet, she worried he was dead. She was lucky the cathedral doors were unlocked for once, but the second she dragged Mor inside, they'd slammed shut—seemingly on their own—and when she tried the handle, they were locked again.

It had been no easy feat to carry the muscular fairy-creature up the flight of stairs and haul him into his room, dragging him the whole way by the sleeves of his coat. She was shaking with fatigue when she finally got him onto his bed where she wrestled off his coat and rolled him onto his stomach. Her heavy breathing filled his dark, creepy room now, and she was relieved he wasn't awake to notice how out of shape she was. She told herself that the first chance she got, she was going to take up jogging.

Violet assessed Mor's blood-soaked shirt. She wasn't exactly known for her first aid skills. She thought about calling Zorah to come do her doctor thing, but Violet trespassing in this cathedral in the first place was what had made her "smell" like Mor, and that one little fact had been the cause of her almost dying more than once since. She didn't feel the need to bestow that honour upon Zorah as well. And besides, she'd just sent a very convincing text to her aunt, saying she was on a work trip. Which, in all technicalities, wasn't actually a lie.

Violet got down to business trying to get Doom's shirt off by herself. Her fingers swiped over his bare back beneath the fabric, and she halted. A pink burn mark appeared on his skin almost instantly. She blinked at it, then she tore her hands back and lifted her fingers, staring at them.

"Why do I hurt you again?" she asked Mor, as if he might suddenly pop awake and answer.

She glanced at her overnight bag. She'd spent the night at the café. She'd run away from the fight in the street. She'd gone home and taken her iron supplements. She'd met the redhead villain in the alley. She'd come here.

It didn't matter. It seemed her superpower had returned, and she couldn't touch Mor now.

She jogged down to the kitchen and rummaged through the drawers until she found a pair of oven mitts. With her ridiculous lobster claws on, she tried to pull off Mor's shirt, struggling to pin the fabric between her thumb and single giant finger. When that failed, she tossed the mitts aside and carefully pulled his shirt away from his skin, no longer caring about saving his clothes. She chopped the whole shirt off with a pair of kitchen scissors like a maniac, and she tossed the fabric over the side of the bed.

A surge of nausea crossed her stomach when she looked at his wound; dried red blood delicately splattered out his side like a blooming red flower. She flung herself toward the bedside, sure she'd barf. But after a few inhales and loud exhales, she drew back, her hand pressed tightly over her mouth.

A collection of tattoos adorned Mor's skin. Five dragon-like creatures filled the canvas of his upper back with detailed, scaled bodies and long, serpentine tails. She leaned over the artwork to see better. The dragons almost looked blue, shimmering in the dull light creeping around the drapes of the bedroom window. She'd never seen tattoos before that could shimmer. Her gaze travelled to his arms covered in the boxy text of a language Violet didn't know. It wasn't written in straight lines; the columns were in random places—on the inside of his wrist, on his forearm, over his bicep.

Violet sat straight again. For the first time since she'd met the Master of Doom, she was curious about his story. Well, maybe it wasn't the first time she'd been curious about him. But it was the first time she'd looked at someone's skin and had desperately wanted to know more about dragons and foreign languages.

After hours of Mor not moving a muscle, Violet left his bedroom, collecting all the "medical supplies" and bringing them out with her. She hadn't been able to do much about the wound with the ancient first aid kit she'd found in the basement that looked to have expired decades ago.

Violet was exhausted by nightfall. She searched the halls for a spare bedroom, finding a bathroom instead. There was no light switch, so she flicked on a lamp by the door. The light revealed a spectacular ironclad tub resting in the corner. She gasped into the quietness, dropping her overnight bag to the floor and rushing to the beautiful bath. The air lingered with the scents of soap and soon-to-be-fulfilled, muscle-relaxing dreams. When she spotted a bottle of bubble bath on the vanity, she could have cried.

It took her all of ten minutes to fill the tub with steaming water and bubbles, shed her clothes, and sink into the glorious hot liquid. She tried to massage her tight shoulders as she sat there. She'd never worked so hard to move anything in her life, though it was probably a good thing she didn't have experience moving bodies.

After scrubbing her hair and face clean in the bath, Violet dried with a towel and poked around in her overnight bag. She didn't have much— just some undergarments, a pair of comfy weekend shorts, and a loose t-shirt. A toothbrush, toothpaste, and some emergency makeup. She didn't bother with the makeup since she imagined she was going to bed soon.

Bed. Where was she going to bed?

She cracked the bathroom door open and peeked into the hall. Nothing stirred, and there were no lights on apart from the bathroom lamp. Cool air rushed against her skin from the hallway, and she stifled a shiver. She ducked back into the bathroom, grabbed her overnight bag, and crept on her toes back to Mor's room.

There was no light switch in the bedroom, either. Violet bit down on her sigh and felt her way in until her hand came against a small lamp on the dresser. She flicked it on.

Mor hadn't budged.

So, she headed for his antique dresser and quietly pulled the drawer open. Inside, his clothes were neatly piled and organized by colour—if you could call black, white, and gray colours. She took the first sweater she saw—a relaxed gray one—and pulled it on with a sigh of relief, hugging her arms to herself to try and restore some warmth to her skin. She looked back toward the dark hallway, thinking of navigating this unlit cathedral at night.

She realized candles were stationed around the room—one in a holder—and a book of matches rested on the nightstand by the bed. She huffed a laugh and headed for it. "Sleep tight, you creepy vampire," she said to the Master of Doom as she reached for the candle and matches.

A hand appeared and took a fistful of her sweater. Violet shrieked as

148

she was yanked into the bed, her head hitting the pillow, her body pinned beneath a forearm. She dragged her wide eyes over to see Mor, holding himself up by his elbow, his eyes going in and out of focus. He held her to the mattress by his grip on her sweater—well, *his* sweater—and he gazed at her with half-open, still mostly sleeping eyes.

He gazed at her for a long time.

Violet swallowed, unsure if he was awake. Maybe he was one of those people who did things at night without knowing it. It seemed he wasn't seeing anything, even though he was looking right at her.

But then he said, "You look pretty this way, Human."

A bead of warmth dropped through her stomach where his arm rested. His stare was so brazen, so fearless. So totally asleep. Violet held her hands up slowly so she wouldn't touch him.

"Doom," she said. "I can't touch your arm—"

Mor fell onto the bed, face into the pillow, and didn't move again.

Violet released the breath she'd been holding and shook her head. She tried to use her sweater-covered-forearms to pick up his arm and move it off her. "Is he joking?" she muttered when she realized his fist was still tightly wrapped around the fabric of her sweater.

So much for being delicate.

Violet grabbed his bare arm and flung it off. She slid out of the bed and scooped up the matches, glancing back at her crazy boss one last time, only to see four pink fingerprint burns forming on his forearm in the exact place she'd grasped him. He hadn't even reacted.

Once her candle was lit, Violet slipped back into the hallway and headed to the big open space where the stairs led down to the lobby. She felt very small in the enormous, dark room, lightly stepping over the creaky wooden stairs with her candle's tiny light.

She reached the living room where Mor had left everything spotless. A blanket was tossed over the back of the nearest couch. She took it and laid down, then she blew out the candle.

The morning came with a rainstorm.

Violet tiptoed up the stairs to check on her boss. The Master of Doom was still fast asleep in the same position she'd left him in. She exhaled loudly. Then, instead of tiptoeing back down the stairs, she stomped and smacked the walls on her way, banging off everything in her path.

Still, the fairy didn't wake up.

She made herself tea as the rain pounded on the foggy windows, and she carried the steaming mug to the living space. She'd found one of her old journals in her overnight bag, one she'd used when she first started at The Sprinkled Scoop. It took her a few tries to get the fireplace going. But when she did, she snuggled under the blanket in the fireside chair and sipped her tea as she flipped open her journal. She scribbled the first things that came to mind:

My name is Violet Miller.

I live with Zorah Miller, my aunt. I work for a crazy legendary creature boss who talks in his sleep and may erase my memories at any moment. If he does, this is a reminder of my name and whose family I'm a part of.

Mor probably can't be trusted.

His weird fairy friends probably can't be trusted either.

Violet tapped her pen as she thought about what else to write. She puzzled over everything she'd been through in the past week, from losing a job, to getting a job, to learning fairies existed, to having met the serial-attacker in person. She jotted a few notes down—everything she'd learned so far about fairies and the memory-thief.

After several minutes of writing, she set the journal aside and blew lightly on her tea. The rain raged against the cathedral, echoing in the ceiling heights, the sound mixing with the low crackling fire. Yet, as the fire's warmth breathed over her, Violet realized she was relaxed. She should have been scared out of her mind with all that had happened.

Her gaze drifted out of the living space toward the stairs in the lobby. All was still, apart from the rain on the windows and the moving flames before her.

She headed back to the kitchen to make more tea and went up to the office.

Articles covered the room like wallpaper, uncategorized. A puddle of ink still stained the floor, along with half a dozen scattered pens from when she'd thrown them at Mor. She sighed and began tidying up. She carefully pulled articles off the walls and organized them into piles based on topics. There weren't any file folders, so she set each pile evenly spaced apart atop the desk and started reading through them one by one.

The redhead guy's face filled her whole mind, all at once. He seemed like a lunatic. Violet was sure she shouldn't even be alive after she'd crossed him in person. A chill rushed up her spine as she thought about it. As she went over his words from their conversation in the alley; words she'd dwelled upon for nearly twenty-four hours.

Just like that, she was sucked back into it. Lost in the story. In the evidence that didn't add up. In the absurdity. The young women who had been carefully left in different parts of local park woods. Never in the same spot. Never on the same day. Everything seemed spaced out, evenly. She lowered her handful of articles to her lap and stared at the wall.

It wasn't like the redhead was physically harming the young women, apart from leaving them asleep for too long. It wasn't like they woke up with broken jaws, or broken legs, or other more horrific violations.

It was like…

Violet looked at the piles of articles on the desk, neatly spread apart. Organized.

"He's organizing them," Violet said to herself.

He was a fairy, like Mor. What if being a folklore creature gave all of this a different meaning? What if he had some fairy purpose to fulfil? She slapped her hand on the desk as the thought slid into place. "He's collecting something." Her chair screeched back as she stood, and she raced out of the office, down the hall, and into Mor's bedroom.

"Doom!" she shouted as she came in. "I don't think the attacks are random! There's a purpose..." Her voice trailed off when Mor didn't move. Violet scratched behind her ear, looking at the bedside clock. It was nearly noon. She sighed. "Do fairies just sleep forever?" she muttered as she walked back out.

Two. Whole. *Nights.*

Violet was ready to yell at the Master of Doom by the morning of the second day. She'd done her hair into a lazy bun and had put on makeup, just because she'd been bored. She'd already consumed three cups of tea and had typed out a whole article all before ten a.m. based on her theory of the redhead having "an end goal" in mind. After, she found herself in a rickety chair by Doom's bedside, waiting, because she had nothing else to do.

Mor stirred.

Violet grabbed the side of the bed, thinking she was imagining it.

His eyes peeled open. Mor stared at the canopy above his spoked bedframe for a moment. His gaze dragged over to Violet. She dropped her grip on the bed and sat back in the chair, suddenly aware of her hair being messier than normal, and the fact that she wore comfortable shorts and his oversized sweater. She oddly brushed a hand over the hair that had fallen out of her bun.

"You're alive," he said, realization crossing his groggy face. "Thank the sky deities. I was afraid my soul was ruined."

Violet slow-blinked. Did he really not remember seeing her the other night? Grabbing her and yanking her to him by her sweater? Going on about how pretty she was and all that—not that she needed to be told to know it.

The dummy actually tried to prop himself up on his elbows like he wasn't recovering from being stabbed. His curly hair stood on end in places, but it didn't make him look bad. It probably wasn't possible for Mor to look bad.

"Thank the sky—what? Are you joking?" Violet almost glared. If he wasn't so helpless and hurt and sleepy, she might have. "You nearly got me *killed.*"

"No, you nearly got *yourself* killed, Human," he said right back. He rubbed his eyes and shook his head a little like he was warding off the tiredness from sleeping for three million years. "I told you to stay at the café. You do reckless things, and it gets you into trouble. That's not my fault."

"This is *all* your fault," she corrected, folding her arms. "You have a past with the attacker I've been investigating, and he came after me because I smelled like you. How does that translate into me almost getting *myself* killed?"

Mor released a grunt. "Humans," he muttered to himself as he pulled back the sheets and began inspecting his bandaged side. He didn't even ask who'd bandaged him up. Violet's jaw slid to the side so she wouldn't blurt out the obvious—that she'd done it. Like a hero.

She released a huff and sat back in her chair. She would literally bite her tongue to keep her thoughts to herself if she had to. She would bandage up this ungrateful fairy a dozen times over if she must. Because she couldn't go back to being jobless again. She told herself that was the reason.

Mor tried to sit up all the way—he winced, and Violet jumped forward, grabbing his shoulders. "You were stabbed, you idiot," she said. "You should rest."

Mor went still. He blinked at where her fingers wrapped tightly around his bare shoulders. "My bones have melded, and my flesh is healing fast. I'll be fine," he said like he hadn't noticed that she could touch him again. He nudged her hands off and sat up. "Why are *you* frail? You're speaking in a tone that makes me think you'll collapse at any faeborn moment," he asked, looking her over.

Violet cleared her throat as she sank back into her seat. "I didn't take my supplements," she admitted.

"Why?"

"Because I think I figured out what's hurting you every time our skin touches." She dragged the bottle of iron supplements out of her purse at her feet and held it up.

Mor took the bottle and read the label. Then he opened the lid and sniffed inside. He carefully tipped the bottle over, and a pill rolled out onto his hand. He snarled as a sizzling sound filled the room, and he hurled the pill toward the wall, shaking out his hand now blemished with a dark red circle where the pill had landed.

"Oh my gosh," Violet whispered. "I wasn't even sure if I was right until this minute."

"So that's why your flesh feels so faeborn-cursed hot," he said, more to himself. He shoved the bottle back toward Violet. She took it and was about to put it back in her purse when he said, "Keep taking them. They might be the only thing stopping that Shadow Fairy from snatching you; not that a pair of gloves wouldn't solve the problem." He muttered the last part more to himself.

Violet raised a brow and shook the pills. "You *want* me to take these?"

"Won't you have fainting spells if you don't?"

"Maybe. I'm anemic," she explained. "Like, really, *really* anemic. I never get enough iron—"

"That's not what those pills are for," Mor stated. "And for the faeborn record, that's not how iron works. Edible iron comes from generous plants. Cold iron isn't meant to be eaten."

Violet grunted a laugh. "Well, I'm different than other anemic people. I had a special doctor prescribe these for me, and you might lack understanding of basic human medicine, but trust me, these pills work," she said, and Mor rolled his eyes.

"That doctor is a liar. These are killing you." He nodded to her bottle as he threw his legs over the bedside and stood. "And you've also become wildly addicted to them. But they're your best protection against my enemies. So, take them, for now," he said, opening his dresser drawer and pulling out a white shirt. He paused, still staring in the drawer. He glanced back at Violet. At her sweater.

Violet shifted in her seat and looked off, hugging her arms to herself.

Mor released a sigh and pulled his shirt over his head as he walked across the room, appearing at full strength out of nowhere. "When all my problems are sorted out," he went on, "I'll pay a visit to that doctor myself." His voice was low, and Violet got the strangest feeling she should high tail it to the doctors' office and warn her doctor to run for his life or something.

Mor stopped by the bedroom door. He turned back with a strange expression. "You didn't take one of those pills last night?" he asked again.

Violet shook her head and stood, too. She chose not to mention that *'not taking one of those pills last night'* had left her dizzy this morning, and she was doing everything she could not to show it.

It looked like Mor had a question on the tip of his tongue.

"What?" she asked, nudging her purse away with her foot. It was only then that she remembered she was wearing Mor's slippers. He seemed to notice the fluffy pink things with the cute cat ears cradling her warm feet. Violet quickly moved on, "Spit it out if you have something to say. I already told you I don't like it when people beat around the bush."

Mor seemed to let the slipper thievery go as he drew back into the room. "How did you escape the Shadow Fairy in the alley?" he asked. "How are you alive, Violet?"

Violet huffed an odd laugh that was a total misrepresentation of how she felt about what had transpired. "I hardly remember," she said. "It all happened so fast." She cast him an odd look when he came to stand in front of her. It reminded her how tall he was.

"May I see?" he asked.

"See what?" Violet almost backed up a step when he lifted his hands toward her face.

"Hold still, Human. It won't hurt." His voice was gentle as his fingers came over her temples. She held perfectly still when he touched her as light as a feather. But she gasped, warning bells going off in her head.

A rush of warmth flooded her mind as he slid into her memories faster than she could form a response—she could feel him there, inside her mind. It was *terrifying*. She reached to smack him away as it awakened a feeling she knew she'd felt before.

"It's all right," he said before she could hit him off. "I'm not stealing anything. Every memory will still be here when..." His face changed, his calm mouth sinking to a frown.

Violet's mind filled with the memory of the alley, the redhead's echoing voice getting sharper and sharper as the memory became clear. She suddenly worried that if Mor saw the memory, he might also somehow be able to tell her feelings about it, and all the things she'd thought about it since.

CHAPTER

21

Violet Miller and the Thing that Happened in the Alley Two Days Ago

It took one quick swipe of the redhead's fairy sword to slice the front of Violet's sweater in half. Strands of pink yarn flew to the ground, one landing in a small pool of Gretchen's blood behind him. Violet raised both hands in surrender before he might start hacking at her sleeves, too. "I'll do the rest!" she volunteered, quickly yanking the sweater's remains off her arms. She carefully set the heap of ripped yarn on the ground at her feet, then stood tall again—still with her hands raised.

Her throat constricted when the fairy leaned in, tilting his mouth toward her neck. He inhaled deeply.

A second too many passed of him standing that close. When he pulled away, his evil leer was gone. His mouth twisted to the side like something was bothering him. Like maybe he totally forgot Violet was even there and had gotten lost to his manic, murderous thoughts. But then he said, "You're not what I expected, Violet."

Violet blinked. She didn't dare lower her hands. "You're not exactly what I expected either," she rasped.

The crazy thing was that close up, the redhead didn't look like a psychopath. He definitely gave off "dark villain" vibes, but when he spoke, it made Violet feel like he'd known her forever. Like they were old friends, trusted allies who had things in common. She wasn't sure how she connected the dots, but it occurred to her that maybe his easy familiarity was because he was reading her articles on him... And also, that he was totally flattered.

What gave it away was when he said, "You must like me a lot to obsess over every one of my victims the way you do."

"You must like me a lot to have read all my articles on those victims," Violet said back, her voice coming out with less force than she would have liked. She cleared her throat. She was already pressed back against the cold brick wall. There was no more moving back for her.

She stole a glance toward the end of the alley, hoping to find a healthy Master of Doom figure standing there, or even Dranian with his spear. But all she saw was a gentle breeze rustling some debris and filling the alley with a shallow whistling sound.

"So, we like each other, then," the redhead said. His smile returned, broad and provocative. "I'd invite you to seal our discovery with a kiss, but I have a feeling that would go just as poorly as last time." He drew a sparkling red gem out of his pocket and placed it in his teeth, biting down to hold it in place and smiling around it. "I don't want you to forget this anyway," he added.

Violet's arms grew numb; she slowly lowered them as it dawned on her that this redhead fairy still thought her skin was untouchable. He mustn't have seen when Violet had touched Dranian's fingers in the street. She swallowed, trying to think of how to use that to her advantage.

"You're right about that," she said. "I'm special. I hurt fairies who get too close. You might want to take a step back," she said to him.

He raised a scarlet eyebrow and didn't budge.

"You don't believe me? Fine. I'll prove it." Violet lifted a hand toward him, and sure enough, the Shadow Fairy took a step back, bringing the ruby into his mouth and closing his lips. Her hand hung in midair, her chest filling with relief. She lacked a lot of basic life skills due to her situation, but she was good at bluffing.

The redhead eyed her, his mouth tipping down at the corners. He spat the ruby back out into his hand and shoved it in his pocket. "What," he began, braving another step back toward Violet, "in the name of the sky deities—" he stopped before her again, nearly pinning her against the brick wall, proving he was less afraid than she thought "—is that scent doing on you?"

"Mor's scent? I thought you already knew about that when you mistook me for his girlfriend or whatever—"

"Not Trisencor's scent, Violet. The other one."

He looked back and forth between her eyes.

Violet debated how to even reply to such a question.

"Listen, you might not believe me, but I actually have no idea what you're talking about. Why does everyone keep telling me I smell?" Violet asked.

He tilted his head, his broad smile finding its way back like he knew something she didn't.

"And if you're going to kill me, just get on with it. Seriously, the wait is murdering me all on its own. This is worse than actually dying!" she said to him, and he burst out laughing.

His laugh was buttery and smooth—Violet couldn't help but notice. He didn't sound like a psychopath either. That was a double threat.

"Oh dear, Violet. Trust me, the dying part would be infinitely worse than this," he assured. "But I won't kill you unless I decide I want to bring Trisencor anguish. You understand," he drawled, flicking a bug off the shoulder of his black coat.

"Well, you got it all wrong. I'm not Mor's girlfriend or lover or anything. I'm just his secretary, and he doesn't think about me like that. I don't even think he's capable of those sorts of feelings," Violet said with slight sarcasm.

The redhead chuckled again. "Oh Violet, you foolish, little, naïve human. Let me tell you something about Mor Trisencor." He took yet another stride in, and this time the buttons of his coat brushed her shirt. He slapped a hand against the brick wall beside her head, blocking any escape path, forcing her to stay put and listen.

"Mor feels things, *deeply*," he said.

Violet wasn't sure she was still breathing. She tried to avoid looking right into his dark eyes.

"Because of those *feelings*, Trisencor will forever be marked as a traitor to the Dark Corner, forever hunted, forever despised. He's a slave of the North, bound for death by even his own Queene. Death will forever follow him." The redhead's expression turned cruel. "He will always feel strongly, yet his heart will never be able to truly love anyone, lest what he loves be stolen away and ruined as his past continues to catch up with him the way I did." The fairy's metallic-scarlet hair glistened in the sunlight as he whispered, his breath scented of sweet roses and sugar. "What you need to understand, Violet, is that Mor is not *allowed* to love. Everything touched by his heart will be destroyed. Fairy forces have sworn to make it so."

The silence filled with thick, dismal notes and a warm wind swept into Violet's hair. Even if she could have formed a response, she didn't want to. What kind of person would say such a terrible thing about someone else?

Shuffling sounds filled the alley, and Violet looked to the entrance with hope. But it wasn't Mor or Dranian.

Fairies Violet recognized from the knitting store filed in, two of them appearing via teleportation with a popping sound around the redhead. One of them dropped to assess Gretchen who still laid motionless on the pavement.

The old woman who'd heckled Mor in the yarn store, the one Violet now knew was named *Freida*, called from the end of the alley where she stood with the other women, "If you take her, Shadow Fairy, we'll follow you through the wind. But if you leave her behind, we'll stay put. It's your choice, but you had best decide quickly," she said.

The redhead's hand slowly slid off the brick wall beside Violet's face. "I don't want any trouble, females. I'm not here for you." He didn't look or sound afraid; frankly, he looked ready to fight them all. He even drew out his sword handle. But he seemed to take inventory of all the women, and he slid his handle away again. He turned back to Violet and looked deeply into her eyes in a way that made her sure he never intended to really let her go. He smiled.

"You can call me Luc, dear Violet. We might as well be on a first name basis since we'll be seeing a lot of each other."

Without another word, he stepped back and vanished into the air.

CHAPTER

22

Violet Miller and the Present

For two days Violet had let those dreadful words play over in her mind. For two days she'd tried to keep herself from thinking about the fact that Mor wasn't allowed to love. Violet's heart broke further with each passing second she spent thinking of what her boss must have endured to be labelled in such a way in his lifetime.

Violet watched Mor's bothered expression as he dropped his fingers from her temples, and the memory of the alley fizzled away from the forefront of her mind. For a moment, they both stood there in silence, looking at each other. She wished she knew what he was thinking, now that he knew what she'd been told about him.

Finally, Mor said, "He's not lying. Death does follow me."

Violet looked between his dual-coloured eyes. "That would make a catchy article title." It was all she could come up with. She hadn't even said it with enthusiasm.

Mor exhaled a deep breath and turned back toward the door. If he was upset about what the redhead had said about him, he hid it well.

"Mor... I don't care about what he told me. I don't believe him," she tried.

"I don't care what you believe. Believe whatever you want, Violet," Mor said back, and something sank through her stomach. She wasn't sure why it bothered her. She didn't care what he believed about her, either.

She cleared her throat and followed him out of the bedroom. He moved slowly enough for her to catch up.

"Let's discuss The Fairy Post," he moved on.

"You seriously want to talk about the newspaper right now?" she rasped, smoothing down a wrinkle in her sweater that wasn't really there.

"Let's have the secretary job interview we never got around to before," he finished as he headed down the hall toward the stairs. "But I need to bathe first. It feels like I've been hibernating for a faeborn year."

"An interview? But I'm already your secretary," she objected. "I've been taking your calls, writing articles, I organized your office, and I even almost scheduled an interview with The Sprinkled Scoop. I told my old workplace that I'm the Secretary of Doom, too."

Mor bristled as he descended the emerald-carpeted staircase. "If you're going to call me *Doom*, then I'm going to call you *Paint-Face*," he stated.

"Paint-Face?" Violet released an odd chuckle. "Why?"

"Because of the colourful paint you put on your face. The peach cream, the rosy lip stain, the black ink on your lashes," he rattled off as he reached the bottom of the stairs and headed toward the kitchen.

Violet stopped walking on the stairs. "You. Are. *Seriously*. Terrible," she stated to his back. "Do you know how rude it is to say that to a girl? And for the record, I wear makeup because it looks good on me," she snapped.

"Hurry up!" he called, and she started moving again, a scowl etched into her *painted* face.

Thirty minutes later, after Mor was bathed and squeaky clean, they sat across from each other at the kitchen island. Mor held a latte, and Violet sipped a tall tea with sugar and plenty of ice. The kitchen was a quaint space with a dull window and a few bunches of herbs drying in the muted light. They were spread out on towels, categorized by plant. Baking supplies filled the rest of the countertops: measuring cups, muffin tins, and a spatula, all set in a neat little tower.

"You bake?" Violet asked.

"I worked in a café for numerous months. Baking is in my faeborn blood now. Tell me about your past, Violet Miller," Mor said, changing the subject. He sipped his latte, waiting.

"My past?" she asked. "Oh, you mean like my work experience?" She scratched her head as she thought. "Well, I was in high school up until two years ago, and you already know I took an internship at The—"

"No." The simple word cut Violet's work experience story off at the knees. Mor slid the latte to the side and folded his hands on the countertop. Suddenly it started to feel like a real interview, and Violet's grip tightened on her iced tea. She wasn't great at actual interviews.

"The part about you waking up," he said.

"Oh..."

That was totally *not* an interview question, but Violet swallowed and cleared her throat. "Um... I was around thirteen years old when I woke up. I don't remember anything of my life before that, but I remember what it smelled like when I opened my eyes."

Mor tapped his fingers against his knuckles. "What did it smell like?"

"Well, there was a strong aroma. It was like flowers, and sweet cotton candy, and an earthy tea-like fragrance. Like a circus had passed through while I was sleeping. The grass was damp, and the sun was so bright that it turned the leaves above me fluorescent green. That's what I remember waking up to—sweet smells and bright leaves."

"Leaves. So, you were in a forest like the others." Mor's hands tightened together.

"I was one of the victims. Maybe the first one, I'm not sure," Violet admitted outright. There was no point in avoiding it now—Mor had already looked her up on the internet. "It's why I followed the story when it started happening again to other women this year."

Mor chewed on his lip. "But the other victims only lost their memories of the twenty-four hours prior to waking up. The human internet told me that you lost all your memories. Every single one up until that day."

Violet nodded. "I don't know if it was your friend's doing or not."

"I imagine not," he stated.

"Then we feel the same. I think we're dealing with two different criminals. Your friend—"

"Enemy," Mor corrected.

"—being the second one, and my memory-thief being the first."

Mor let out a long breath and tapped a finger against his folded hands. "There's something else that's different. You said you were thirteen years of age. All the human females being targeted now are several years older than that," he pondered.

"Yes, but we all lost memories. That's the worst part—the not knowing. Regardless of how long a period of time it was for each of us. You can't imagine how valuable your memories are until you've lost them." Violet gently banged her toe against the island cupboards when a quiet pause fell between them.

"You talk like you *want* to remember your past. But sometimes it's better to forget," Mor finally said.

"Of course I want to remember."

"Why?"

Violet tsked, wondering how he could be serious. "Because what if I lost something huge from that life? What if I was… I don't know… a foreign princess or something? Or my parents were government agents, and that's why they couldn't come forward and claim me?" she asked.

Mor raised a brow, a teeny smirk pulling at his mouth. "You think you were a human realm princess?"

"I don't know! But wouldn't it be better if I at least knew for sure?" she asked.

Mor stared, his dual-toned eyes seeming slightly unfocused. "What if it wasn't like that?" he asked in a low voice. "What if it's better to forget, Human? What if your life was dreadful, and no matter how much you tried to forget, you couldn't?"

Violet felt a heavy weight linger in his words.

"Do you have something you wish you could forget, Doom?" she asked, and his attention snapped back to the present.

"That's none of your business." He took a swig of his latte.

Violet mirrored him, sipping her tea. She thought about how he'd so easily looked into her memory of the alley with a simple touch of his fingers. Mor wasn't the first fairy she'd ever met, and that realization alone sat like a weight on her chest. After all this time, she had an answer about what had happened to her that day in the forest. After ten years of searching, she now knew she'd been right to suspect the folklore and not the science. She'd been laughed at, she'd had her writing ridiculed, and she hadn't been taken seriously because of it. Yet... Here was a creature of legend who could steal memories, sitting right across from her.

Violet studied the beautiful, tanned fairy on the other side of the island. "If you can take memories away from people, can you also return the ones they lost?" she asked. Suddenly she couldn't believe she hadn't thought of that until now. If Mor could let her see what had happened that day, and her whole life before that day, the mystery of who she was would be solved. She sat up straighter in her chair when he didn't immediately say no.

"What happened when you woke up on the first day you remember? Tell me that bit," Mor asked, ignoring her question.

Violet slumped back in her seat. She worked her jaw and smoothed down her shorts over her legs. She fidgeted with the handle of her mug, deciding she would try asking again later.

"I wandered from the park forest onto a busy street and into the nearest building, which just happened to be a local news station. It was a zoo after that. I became the mystery girl—a puzzle the whole city tried to solve. *'Who is the girl in the purple dress?'* That was the first headline.

The next was, *'Why doesn't a single person recognize her?'* It became like a game. Rewards were offered to anyone able to solve the puzzle, and I was hounded by private investigators."

Mor folded his arms and leaned back in his seat. "The Shadow Fairy you met is named Luc," he said. "He's a nine tailed fox—something of an anomaly among fairies. It means even if I kill him, he'll keep coming back. And I believe he didn't arrive in the human realm until six months ago. That's proof that whoever stole your memories was someone else." He paused, chewing on the inside of his cheek. "And what is a *zoo?*"

Violet wasn't sure whether he was being serious. "You know, a zoo. Like where they keep animals in cages and people can walk around and point at them," she said.

"Ah. Of course." Mor nodded. "We have those in the Ever Corners, too. We call them *stables*. The royals go there when they wish to select a crossbeast to ride. They point like this." He stuck his nose up and pointed at Violet. "And then the lesser fairies must get the crossbeast fitted with reins." He took another sip of his latte. "Unfortunately," he went on without missing a beat, "some of the lesser fairies don't survive that part. Crossbeasts are quite temperamental." He set his mug down and flicked a dollop of whipped cream off the brim.

Violet's mouth hung open. The crazy part was that she still couldn't tell if he was joking. When he didn't crack a smile afterward, she grew more afraid he wasn't.

"Okay. Anyway…" She pushed a loose hair behind her ear. "As for the actual newspaper stuff, I know I'm not the ideal journalist, but—"

"You're perfect," Mor stated. "You're perfect the way you are. Don't change a thing, Violet Miller."

Her chest tightened. He hadn't even batted an eye when he'd said it.

"…reading your articles is like reading a bad fiction novel." Cedric's words collided with Mor's in a strange battle of voices in her head.

Violet dragged her mug up to her mouth and took a long gulp. She spied on him over the cup as he pressed his fingers against his bandaged side like he was testing the pain—he winced.

Violet set her tea back on the counter. "What do you need me to do for this job?" she asked.

Mor shrugged. "Keep The Fairy Post alive when I'm busy. Simple," was all he said.

A disbelieving chuckle tumbled from her. "Simple? You think being around you is going to be simple?" She laughed for real now, filling the kitchen with cackles. Mor set down his drink.

"No, actually I think it's going to be rather terrifying. This job doesn't just come with a quiet office and fancy ink pens, Human. You'll also be required to take annoying phone calls, clear my schedule at a moment's notice, and eventually, help me bury a body."

Violet blanched. "You see the thing is, I'm having a hard time telling if you're joking today."

"Once I catch the fox and kill him eight more times," he clarified. And then, "Don't worry your pretty little painted face over it. No one will miss him. He has no friends." He sipped his drink again, tilting the mug to get the last drops. Violet's jaw dropped.

"That's a terrible thing to say," she scolded.

Mor looked up at her in surprise. "Is it? It's true."

Violet's mouth moved a few times. "You know, I didn't think it was possible to feel bad for that redhead, but you're starting to make me sympathize with him a little."

"What?" Mor blinked.

"You know, like when you're watching a horror movie and you accidentally start rooting for the crazy axe-murderer because he has a sense of humour. I think Luc could be viewed as cool, in a psychopathic, dark villain sort of way."

Mor slammed his mug down on the counter, making her jump. "Don't do that, Human," he warned.

"Do what?"

"Start to like him. He will enchant you if he finds out, whether he has to burn his face off to do it or not."

Violet released a sound and rolled her eyes. "As if." Honestly, she had no idea what weird fairy nonsense he was talking about. But she stole another look at Mor as he stood and carried his empty mug to the sink. He didn't seem like the naïve sort, but the fact that he thought she could actually fall for the sinister redhead was astounding.

Violet tore her eyes away from his perfect skin and interesting tattoos to look out the window. She didn't see him approach until he was already on her side of the island. He reached for her iced tea glass, leaning over her where she sat, and her heart fluttered into a wild, startling dance when his face brushed within an inch of hers.

Mor froze with his hand on the cup. Violet nearly jumped when his gaze cut over and he looked right into her eyes. He was too close to be looking at her like this, yet he stared. Then he said, "Don't do that either, Human."

Violet's cheeks flushed. She didn't know for sure what he was talking about—she'd never said a word of her thoughts out loud. But if her tumbling heart had any guesses…

"Let's go steal some books from the library," Mor said, changing the subject to Violet's relief, and drawing back to stand. "There's something I need to look up."

CHAPTER

23

Mor Trisencor and the Limitations of Touch

The library roof was painted gold from the sun when Mor and Violet arrived with their pockets full of pens and notebooks. Of all the libraries in the city, this one had become Mor's favourite due to its size—he could get lost inside with few humans noticing he was there—and its vast collection of myth and fable literature that ranged from ancient times to various human cultures. He'd avoided the academy library ever since he left the café to track Luc, fearing he might run into Kate there. Or Cress. He'd been using the literature at this library instead when he needed to do research for his articles.

Even though he was doing all he could to avoid those working at Fae Café, there were times when Mor wished he would run into Cress here by accident. Once or twice, he'd seen a pair of blue eyes through the shelves, and he'd scurried over to the next aisle only to discover a plain old human that didn't resemble Cress in the slightest. He felt foolish for thinking Cress would ever come to a library he knew nothing about.

A slow ache grew inside Mor when he remembered the moment he'd seen Dranian battling Luc in the street. It had been a nauseating yet... *invigorating* sight for his sore, tired eyes to behold one of his brothers fighting his nemesis. It had both filled him with pride and terrified him in the same moment.

For a faeborn-cursed heartbeat, Mor missed the taste of enchanted coffee and sweet cookies so terribly that he stopped walking.

"What?" Violet staggered to a halt. She had an impatient look, which was astoundingly hypocritical.

Mor grunted and started walking again, taking the steps two at a time while Violet tapped her way up, making a clamour in the heels she insisted on changing into after she'd already insisted on changing everything else. Mor already missed seeing his sweater on her. Since the moment he'd opened his eyes and beheld Violet Miller in the middle of the night, fashioning dripping wet hair and cloaked in his garment at his bedside, he'd been battling between annoyance at having his sweater taken without permission and a sheer desire to put an enchantment on the material so she could never take it off. He'd been too poisoned by his injury to think clearly when he'd grabbed her and pulled her to him—sweater and all, overcome with some foolish need to see her up close without her face paint on.

Mor rubbed his eyes at the recollection, glad his secretary had believed his act about not remembering what he'd done. How shameful of him, after he'd been so adamant about keeping their relationship professional and making her work life miserable just for fun while he was at it.

Now his secretary wore that same pink dress she'd been wearing for ages, as though she refused to be seen in anything less extravagant while out in public. Her hair was braided to the side—something that had taken her a whole faeborn hour. Mor had gotten so tired of waiting, he'd nearly barged into the bathroom and shaken his hands into her hair to turn it wild again.

The great stone library's front doors were pegged open at the top of the stairs, inviting them in. A sweep of cool air from cold air machines brought relief to Mor's warm flesh as he strutted past the desk where kind human servants checked out books, and he made the long trek through the shelves toward the back.

Violet's breathing grew heavy, and Mor snorted a laugh.

"If you wanted to be able to keep up, Human, you should have worn reasonable shoes like me," he said back to her.

"I don't have any other shoes," she said.

Mor's smile fell. "Queensbane," he muttered, slowing his pace a little.

The section of back shelves was dimmer than the rest of the library, but a narrow, gated window allowed a sliver of light to spill over the space, giving magic to the air where dust particles floated in the stream. Mor breathed in the warmth of the well-used area. Libraries often told stories, and it hardly had anything to do with the books themselves. He took in the whispers of time, the fragrances of enjoyable tales tucked into the pages of the books. He wished he had the ability to look into the past of a space the way Cress did.

"I could seriously go for a bubble tea." Violet stretched dramatically with her arms high in the air like she'd just climbed out of a cave after a season of hibernation. "Someday I'll get you to try it. It's delicious. Also, what exactly are we looking for here?" Violet asked, practically yelling.

Mor shushed her. "This is a library, Human. There are rules." He was astounded that she didn't even know the binding laws of her own species.

Violet sighed and flicked her braid off her shoulder as she reached for the books, pulling one out at a time to read the covers. "There's no point in looking for fairytale books since *you're* a fairy. You should already know all the fairy stuff," she said as she reached for a tome on a high shelf. "And you don't have to keep reminding me that I'm a human. You can just call me *Violet* since that's my name—*eek!*"

A book spilled off the ledge above her, and Mor watched it smack the top of her head, spin off, then slap the floor. Quiet conversations throughout the library went silent as every human within hearing range undoubtedly stopped to wonder what fool had broken the binding silence law of the sacred building.

Violet rubbed the top of her head. "Ow!" she said, even though it was seconds too late.

Mor huffed and folded his arms. "I think I regret bringing you with me. I should have locked you in the office while your hair was still wild and unruly. Bringing you out in public is an enormous hassle."

Violet shot him a look. "You didn't even try to catch that book before it hit me!" she accused.

"I'm standing over here," Mor pointed out with a shrug.

"You're tall. You could have smacked it off course before it smoked my head. My…" She teetered, her lashes fluttering, and Mor's arms dropped. Her feet wobbled in her heels, and when one of her legs gave out, he sprang to her side, catching her waist and steadying her on her feet.

"Queensbane, Human!" he whispered loudly at her.

"I told you to call me *Violet*," she had the mind to say even while she teetered.

"Why are you so weak? And…" Mor glanced off in thought. "How did I not notice that you were in this state when we left?"

Violet tipped forward, her cheek coming against his chest. Mor looked around to see if anyone had noticed. 'Lovey dovey shenanigans' were against the law of the library as well, as was scribed upon the list of rules by the door where they came in. Violet's closeness to him might be considered such a thing as a shenanigan of the 'lovey dovey' sort.

Mor cleared his throat when Violet didn't move from him. "Human," he said. She remained still and rebellious. "*Violet*," he tried again, hoping her name would make her snap out of it. A thought crossed his mind, and he released a huff as he realized. He took hold of her arms—his bare hands against her.

Nothing happened.

"Violet!" he snapped again—only this time it was him who broke a sacred library law with his shout.

She flung her head up, her eyes wide. She seemed to try and blink away her dizzy spell. "What?" she mumbled.

"You didn't take your cold iron, did you?" he scolded.

Her mouth moved as she sorted through responses, and she looked around like she was trying to come up with a blatant lie.

"Vi-o-let." He growled through his teeth. "You can't imagine how tempting it is for me to enchant you right now. I'm typically too considerate for such a thing, but I don't like bickering. It would be easier if you would just do what I told you."

A laugh lifted from her as though she'd come back to her senses. "You want to enchant me?" she asked doubtfully. "How would you do that? With a magic wand?"

"With a kiss," Mor corrected. He leaned in and looked into her eyes, feeling the warmth of that little flare that arose in the greens of her irises. Her rhythm galloped when his gaze dropped to her mouth, tracing over it.

"Don't even think about it!" She stepped back, pulling from his grip. She folded her arms.

Mor gave her a look that promised he'd more than thought about it. "I'll wait until you're not expecting it," he promised.

Violet's face twisted into a scowl. "I'll take double my iron pills every day then. We'll see how it goes for you when you try!"

Mor nodded, satisfied. "Fine then. Do that."

He marched around her with a sigh. Some humans were far too easy to manipulate.

He came to the shelf with dozens of books that told tales from all over the human world. One in particular caught his attention above all the others. One he'd been eying for months but had never wanted to touch.

He pulled the book out. A picture filled the cover of a white fox with nine long, luminous tails all with deep red tips. The fox held a ruby in its teeth.

A stifled moan brought him back around to observe his human secretary. She held onto the shelf with one hand for balance as she adjusted her shoe with the other. Mor hadn't noticed how sharp and deadly those shoes were until she held one up in her hand. He caught a glimpse of torn flesh at her heel before she put the shoe back on. She stood tall again, still wobbling a smidgen when she let go of the shelf. She leaned her back against the bookcase and... her eyes closed.

Queensbane, was she going to take a cursed nap right here in the library?

Mor dragged a hand through his curly hair. "Wake up, Human," he said, tucking the book under his arm. He walked over to her and dropped to a knee to reach her feet. Violet started when he took hold of the first shoe and tugged it off.

"What are you doing?" she asked as he pulled off the second shoe, too. He stood and handed her the pair of deadly foot weapons—which seemed to really only be a weapon against *her*.

"Hold these," he said. She took them by the stabby points and held them to her chest as Mor reached around her legs and lifted her into his arms. He would have carried her out that way if he wasn't worried about the wrath of the librarians who might consider his noble act a 'lovey dovey shenanigan' and cast him out of this building for eternity. He vanished from the shelves instead.

He put Violet to bed when they returned to the cathedral. She tried to object, but all it took was a little nudge and she'd toppled onto his duvet. Her eyelids didn't protest—they closed immediately as she mumbled something absurd about bubble tea again, and Mor sighed, fighting the impulse to point out that she was of no use to him in this state. He dug through her purse for her cold iron pills, and he set them on the pillow beside her face so she could find them when she awoke. As he pulled the blanket around to tuck her in, he eyed the scrapes with leaky blood on the backs of her bare heels. No wonder she'd had such trouble keeping up to him on the walk.

Mor left Violet there to sleep off her dizzy spell and he flipped open his library book. He read as he puttered around the cathedral and cleaned with his free hand. The book told stories of nine tailed foxes among humans. Fun, thrilling stories. Completely unrealistic stories. All of the foxes in the tales were cunning females. None of the stories told how to defeat or outsmart a fox, though one told of a human stable boy who swallowed a female fox's bead during a kiss and stole her powers. Another one told of a great fox feast where the foxes tricked humans into eating poisoned food, then made them bargain to get their lives back. Yet another told of a lonely female fox who stole one thousand secrets and transformed herself into a human. The last two tales he didn't bother to read. It was all nonsense anyway.

Mor slapped the book shut after several hours. He used both his hands to clean after that.

The cathedral was in much better shape by the end of the day. Mor's back had grown stiff from all the sweeping and scrubbing and window washing. Even the wooden rail of the stairs was polished.

It didn't look perfect, but at least the lobby and the living space were shiny. He hadn't gotten around to sweeping the dusty hallways or stabbing the spiderwebs in the corners with a broom. That was a job for another day.

He stopped at the office to straighten the papers but found that everything had already been tidied up. The articles were organized on the shelf, the desk was clean, and the floor looked to have been scrubbed of its ink stain. Mor ventured in, his fingers trailing over the empty desktop. He paused at a freshly printed paper still sitting in the mouth of the ink-giving machine. It seemed Violet had forgotten to come back for it. He slid the page out and began to read the article, already having every intention of publishing it, but no intention of letting her know that right away. She'd come riding into his cathedral on such a high horse, he was determined to make her work hard for her accolades at The Fairy Post.

Violet's words soared off the page. A slow smile crept over Mor's mouth when he reached the end of her work. "Secretary" didn't feel like a fitting title for the human female scribe. Not that this was the first time he'd read her articles. Perhaps he had been a little obsessed with Violet

Miller's writing even before he saw what she looked like on TV and had been nearly assaulted by her in his bell tower. Though her prettiness had nothing to do with anything.

Mor cleared his throat and stuffed the page back into the printer's mouth where it lay flat on the tray. It wasn't like her articles were the only ones he had been saving all this time. It wasn't like the thought of her writing columns alongside him made him feel warm and cozy and happy on the inside. It wasn't like that.

Dusk came over the human city before he knew it, and Mor headed to the upstairs closet to fetch a blanket so he could sleep on the couch.

A sound emerged from his bedroom—muffled voices. He chose a thin blanket from the stack in the closet and headed to peek into his room. He'd assumed Violet would wander to the office after she woke, but when he cracked the door open, he saw her sitting on his bed staring at her phone, her covers off, her hair tousled, and her cheeks... stained with tears. His fist tightened around the door handle as he debated whether to announce himself and go in.

He spied a human news reporter on Violet's phone screen. Mor tilted his ear to listen.

"...and the whole hospital is sympathizing with thirteen-year-old Sophie Ellis as we all hope and pray for her to wake up. The girl lived at the Moon City Youth Home along with fourteen other kids. The accident occurred early this morning when a passing truck lost control and struck her. Sophie Ellis's injuries are critical, but the doctors say she may pull through." The voice changed, and Mor guessed he was listening to the doctor now. "Miss Ellis may never be the same if she wakes up. In some head injury cases like these, the victims must deal with repercussions their entire lives."

"Violet." Mor stepped in to interrupt her show.

Violet glanced up from her phone, revealing a look of torment on her face a split second before she dragged the back of her hand over her eyes and wiped it away. Her black eyelash paint stained her knuckles. She cleared her throat and tried to smooth down her disorderly hair.

Her watery green gaze darted back to his. With her face paint smudged, Mor could see her freckles—the same freckles he'd spotted the other night and had needed to see up close.

"If you break every time you see someone who appears as helpless as you felt in your childling years, you'll never be able to survive," he said. He came to the bedside, having the strangest overwhelming impulse to push her hair behind her ear. As it was, half her face was covered in stringy, tear-drenched hair strands. But his hand pulled into a stubborn fist at his side so he wouldn't be a fool.

Violet looked down and nudged her bottle of cold iron. At least she was taking her supplements.

"She's just thirteen years old. And she lives in a youth home, so even if she wakes up, she has no one. Those are always the worst stories," Violet rasped.

Mor swallowed, his throat a smidgen tighter than normal. In the beginning, Violet had appeared quite strong and goal driven. But in this moment, she looked like a lost childling who couldn't figure out where she belonged. Perhaps he should have never prodded into her story while he interviewed her in the kitchen. Perhaps this unearthing of her feelings was his fault. Perhaps he hated the way it felt to see tears on her face, even if their relationship was professional.

He didn't feel like being professional at the moment.

She wiped the damp hair away from her face on her own, and he was relieved he didn't have to do it. Though, one measly rebellious strand still stuck to her freckled cheek. Mor's fingers twitched. He couldn't stop looking at it, feeling its call to be dealt with. She was not his to hold, or to comfort, or to fix up. Queensbane, he would plunge himself into an ice-cold shower after this until he started thinking reasonable thoughts about his secretary again.

Her lashes fluttered when her eyelid paint got in her eyes. She tried to wipe it away, but she missed a gleaming black spot entirely, and Mor fought an exasperated sound, clasping his hands together. "I know I'm the one who told you to take your cold iron, Human, but I'm pretty faeborn frustrated that I can't touch you right now," he blurted at her. He didn't mean for it to come out hoarse, or with begging, or laced with a tone of desperation that surprised himself.

He was relieved humans did not hear stories in the tones of speech. He may have had a faeborn heart attack if she'd caught what his had just said.

Violet's expression was unreadable. It was somewhere in the vein of startled, but there was something else hiding in the cracks of it all, too. Her slender throat moved as she swallowed, and she shoved the blankets aside. Heat rushed through Mor as he realized he couldn't tell what she was thinking, and he worried perhaps she had picked up on the story in his words after all.

"I want to go back to work," was all she said. She slid off the bed, dragging over Mor's-Kate's slippers and sliding her feet into them.

Mor breathed a silent sigh of relief. He glanced at the window where the stars were beginning to show. "This late?"

"Writing about facts is how I relax. I just want to read some mindless information for a while." She brushed past him, the scent of her garden house going with her. Mor's gaze was left on the bottle of cold iron pills. Pills that made her a weapon against fairies.

Pills that had been the only thing stopping him from making an utter fool of himself this evening. He might have held his secretary against his chest like a real faeborn lover until the ache left her voice. He might have clung to her all night if she hadn't mended fast enough, or any number of other disastrous things. Thank the sky deities for those pills.

Though, it was strange how putting one little object in her mouth could give her so much power.

"Violet," Mor said before she reached the hall. She turned back. Mor stared hard at the pills on the bedside table as his head blossomed with another thought. A great, wild, heavy idea. He tore his gaze away and landed it on her, though his attention was long gone. "I'm going out in the morning. I may leave before you're awake. Don't open the door for *anyone* while I'm gone."

179

CHAPTER

24

Mor Trisencor and the Ruby

The first time Mor ever saw Luc's sparkling red ruby was on a cold day when the Shadow Army division was training in the forest. The overcast had made it almost pitch black, but fairies, especially Shadow Fairies, often saw best in the dark. Fairies were sectioned off into pairs to battle, and in some cases, to release all the anger and fury they had bottled up since the beginning of the day. Night training had transformed into the thing the most vicious fairies looked forward to.

Mor, on the other hand, despised the evening battles. Fairies from across the Shadow Army came through the forest to challenge him. Ever since Mor had joined High Prince Reval's division, he had become a target; the strong village boy who the Prince had selected to join his ranks. Sometimes he won against the Army's great war fairies. Sometimes he was left hardly breathing, unable to move from where he'd fallen until sunrise after his bones had melded.

But on this night, Mor had overheard whispers of Westra—a newer, terrible war fairy that had recently transferred to Prince Reval's division—who was salivating at the chance to battle the village boy the rest of the fairies were lining up to fight. Mor waited for the fool to emerge from the woods and challenge him. But it wasn't Westra who spoke over the division and made a challenge.

Luc sat high upon a large rock, his knee propped up, his arm draped over it. The moment Westra appeared, Luc stole him. "I've been waiting for you," he said to Westra. Luc's lush hair glittered in the muted moonlight. "Forget the village boy. Fight a real war fairy this eve." Luc slid off the rock and approached Westra with all the sly movements of a fox. "Unless you're afraid of the Dark Prince's son?"

Westra's thick arms flexed. "I fear no fairy," he said in a horridly deep voice.

Seconds later, the pair stood across from each other in the clearing. Luc turned away, seeming to take a look at the foggy stars. Mor caught sight of him sliding a red gem into his mouth. When Luc returned to face Westra, something strange came over the ruby-haired fairy. It was like Luc could see Westra's strikes before they happened. The nine tailed fox blocked before Westra struck.

Luc left Westra a broken-boned mess in the grass in exactly eleven seconds.

Afterward, the notorious fox sauntered through the division as they marvelled at his brutal, fast success. No one had seen Prince Reval's son enter a night challenge before. War fairies became respectful in his presence in the days that followed. Only the bravest dared to challenge Luc beneath the stars. And he always won, leaving his opponents with snapped bones and teeth, and sometimes killing them outright.

Night after night, crowds of Shadow Fairies gathered to watch the battles where Luc hungrily stole the attention of his father's division. Mor saw more fairy blood in a single faeborn week than he had in his whole lifetime. He knew the challenge was coming; Luc would challenge Mor before the Army, and possibly kill him. That's what this was all leading up to. Yet, Mor didn't run away.

But every eve that came, Luc fought someone else, and Mor watched from a distance. At first it was a relief. Then it became mildly frustrating.

Finally, on an evening where the stars struggled to peek through the toiling haze above, and the forest beasts hushed in unison, Mor challenged Luc himself. Luc had been drinking silver water from a crystal vase at the woodside. The Shadow Fairy slowed his chugging, staring off into the darkness of the forest. He lowered the vase and wiped a bead of silver from his lips.

When he turned to Mor, his gaze was sharp. "You wish to challenge me, Trisencor? Haven't you seen what I can do?"

"Let's get it over with," Mor said. He stretched his arms as he headed toward the clearing. He rolled his black fairsabers in his grip.

When Luc appeared across from him, the fairy's feet seemed sluggish. He eyed Mor, tapping a long finger against the fur tails hanging from the chain around his throat. His chain was down to only eight tails now. The fox stared until Mor crouched into a ready position. And finally, Luc drew his fairsabers. He lowered himself into position, too.

Mor looked at Luc's pocket. Then back to the fairy's face.

"Where's your ruby?" he asked.

Luc's broad smile appeared, growing slowly. "I don't need it for you, Trisencor."

Mor grunted. "Very well. I'll challenge you again tomorrow since I'll still be alive. Perhaps you'll change your mind by then." He lunged, and Luc blocked, beginning what would be a three-hour battle late into the gloomy night. It ended with Mor on his back in the grass with Luc's fairsaber at his throat. "Do you have a death wish, Fairy?" Luc asked when it was over, his chest pumping, fae sweat glistening on his scarlet brow.

Even though his faeborn bones felt weak and his body threatened to faint, Mor cast him a gloating smile from the ground.

Three faeborn-cursed hours. No one had lasted that long against the fox.

Mor challenged him again the following evening. And the one after that.

Night after night went by. Luc never used his ruby to face Mor, never pulled it out again for a fight. And it seemed he was right about not needing it.

Mor never won. Not once.

Mor didn't see Luc's ruby again until they were on a hunting mission. Mor and Luc travelled across three villages to find a certain rogue fairy, all the while bickering over who was going to kill who first. Every morning, Luc informed Mor of how he planned to kill him that day. And every morning, Mor listened, and by evening he usually came up with a witty response of how he would return the favour. They never walked anywhere in silence—Luc had far too much to say for that.

"You talk too much," Mor grumbled as they arrived at the cliffside village where the rogue resided. Crisp jade water stretched as far as the eye could see, and Mor had a brief touch of homesickness—hot like an elfshot, something he had not felt for many years.

He slid off his crossbeast and patted the creature's head around its horns, avoiding getting too close to its dagger-sized teeth.

"And you don't talk enough, Trisencor. But don't worry, I'll chat enough for the both of us," Luc said. "I have a feeling I'll like this rogue anyway. Rumour claims he's a troll fairy, and most trolls can sense treasure. Did you know that?" Luc slid off his beast and marched to the twig house of the rogue. He rapped on the door, then in the same heartbeat, he kicked the door in.

Mor sighed and waited outside while Luc stormed into the house. Mor examined his nails as he listened to the shouts. He flicked off bits of lint and dirt from his shell armour. He looked up at the dark sky, wondering if a storm might blow in later.

The rogue came flying out the front door. Mor snatched him by his collar and dragged him toward the cliff. Luc emerged from the house, brushing the dust and triumph off his hands. He kicked the dirt from his boots and followed as Mor reached the cliff and held the rogue fairy half over it.

The rogue squirmed, trying desperately to cling to the cliff's edge with his toes. "I have gold!" he promised Mor and Luc. "I can make you the richest fae in the Dark Corner!"

"Can you?" Mor kept his face dull and straight with his sarcasm, making the rogue believe for a second that he was serious.

The rogue nodded but seemed to realize Mor was playing him for a fool when Mor tilted his head and smiled after all.

"Give up the weapons you stole from the Shadow Army troves," Luc demanded in a bored voice. "And perhaps we'll forget what you did for a little while."

When the rogue refused to speak, Luc nudged Mor's side as though he wished to take over. Mor yanked the rogue back to land and handed him off to the fox. From there, Mor folded his arms and waited.

"I wish to make a bargain. One that will surely benefit you the most!" the rogue fairy blurted, trying Luc instead.

"Sky deities," Luc cursed in amusement. "You're just full of deals, aren't you? Shall I take out my coin purse and pay you for your kindness?"

"I *am* kind! You should have mercy on me for how kind I am!" the rogue exclaimed.

Mor snorted a laugh.

"You stole weapons from the Shadow Army. *Our* army," Luc corrected.

"And you use them to rule over your village," Mor added—the part he found the most important of all.

"Not all of them," the rogue protested. "Some of the weapons I sold!" He leaned toward Luc as if meaning to whisper. "Let's make a bargain. I can fill your pockets with real gold, no rocks—enough to rule any village in the Corners of Ever as a noble. And I'll give you a fairy trick, too! One that will destroy your greatest enemy in his sleep!"

184

Mor laughed louder this time. "You should take the bargain, Luc. Perhaps you'll finally go through with it and kill me."

"Don't tempt me," Luc muttered back with a smirk.

The rogue kept talking. "In exchange, you must forget about the weapons. You must forget about me, and I can run off and live happily with my childling son. All it would require is for me to be able to steal your memories of this conversation so I cannot be tracked."

Luc's smile faded. "Oh dear." He angled his head, his eyes turning sharp. "And what shall I tell my commanders when you rob us again and they realize I didn't do my job?" he asked.

The rogue fairy looked off as he thought about that. His eyes widened as though he'd come up with another cursed idea. "I can draw you a map to my personal storehouses of gold!" he offered. Then he smiled, wide and wicked. "I would trade everything I have for that tiny little ruby you have hiding in your pocket."

Luc stared; not blinking, not moving a muscle. He said nothing for a moment as he slowly reached into his pocket, drawing out his ruby, and held it before the rogue fairy's nose. It sparkled even in the dim light. "This ruby?" he articulated slowly.

The rogue fairy's eyes turned wild as he gazed at it. "Yes," he breathed.

Luc hurled the fairy off the cliff—one swift movement that left the rogue no chance of catching himself.

Mor folded his arms and waited to hear the splash at the bottom. It was a faint sound when it finally came; the cliff was quite high.

"He will live, you know. That fall won't kill the fool," Mor pointed out.

Luc shrugged and began heading back to the village. "I hope he does. I hope he crawls out of the sea and warns every fairy he meets about me."

Mor released a grunt. "You could have taken his bargain and ruled over this village as a *noble*."

"Yes, I find it rather amusing he tried to tempt a rich noble with the idea of becoming a rich noble." Luc's sarcasm was straight-faced, too.

"How did you manage to refuse?" Mor followed, snatching a handful of rose grass off the path to feed his crossbeast before the ride back.

Luc didn't answer right away, and Mor looked up to see him solemn; the jokes vanished with the wind. "I never take a bargain where I could lose something," Luc said, stopping before the rogue's house. The door was wide open. The son the rogue had mentioned was nowhere in sight, and Mor wondered if the childling even existed or if the rogue fool had been sputtering nonsense to try and buy himself sympathy.

Mor sighed and shook his head. He spotted a nest of sea snails on the front stair. He reached to pick one up, eyeing the slug peeking out from its shell. "Why is that, Luc?" Because you can't stand to lose?" he guessed. He turned and hurled the snail toward the cliff, aiming for the Jade Ocean to set it free.

Luc turned away from the house. "My mother once made a bargain like that," he said. He snatched half the rose grass from Mor's hand and headed toward the crossbeasts. He fed his beast the grass.

Mor followed and did the same, careful to keep his fingers from getting too close to his creature's teeth. "What did your mother lose that was so faeborn important?" he asked.

Luc brushed the grass remains from his hands and rounded his crossbeast. He pulled himself onto its back in one motion and reached for the reins. Then he said, "Me."

CHAPTER

25

Mor Trisencor and Brunch with the Nobles

Two days sleeping and one day cleaning was two days and one day too many.

Mor scaled the early morning shadows, becoming a vapour in the wind. He moved across the sidewalks, in and out of normal speed, and finally he shed his dandelion-dusted jacket when he reached the walk-ways by the harbour. He folded it and hung it on the rail. And he waited.

The water sparkled with early light, rippling too far into the distance to see even with fairy sight. Human-speckled boats drifted by, and loud white birds squawked overhead.

A breeze ruffled Mor's curls, and he glanced over to see Luc standing a few feet down the rail in a loose, light blue tunic, appearing nothing of the shadow-dominating war fae he was. He licked a cone of pink ice cream, dropping a dollop onto his shirt. In one swipe, he scooped the drip up and sucked it off his finger, rattling the pendant of eight tails hanging faithfully at his throat. His ruby was nowhere to be seen.

"Have you tried this, Trisencor?" Luc asked, holding up his ice cream cone. "It's like a cold, sweet, cloud of icy honey."

"Where's your coat?" Mor asked as he glanced back out at the water. Luc answered his question with another question. "Did you hope I would come running the moment I realized your scent was no longer masked?" He stuffed a large bite of ice cream into his mouth. Then he got to work crunching the cone.

"You did though, didn't you?"

"And *you* came alone." Luc looked at Mor for the first time, his silvery eyes sparkling in the sunlight and outshining the human realm waters. Mor stared back at him.

"Don't you wish to know why I decided to shed *my* dandelions?" Luc asked, raising a scarlet brow. He flicked the rest of the cone over the rail and Mor watched it fall all the way down into the harbour.

"No, not really." Mor traced a finger over his folded jacket. "But I imagine it was for the same reason I did."

"Yes. And now we're both here, like we both wanted." Luc's cold, beastly smile was the darkest thing about the morning.

"You know I've been tracking your movements," Mor said. "You probably knew it would drive me mad, too, trying to figure out what you were doing. I've tried stopping you with force and that didn't work, so now, I'll just ask. Tell me—" Mor turned to face him, "—what are you collecting, Luc?"

Luc's smile almost fell. He kept it pasted there, just a straight line.

"What makes you think I'm collecting something?" he asked after too long a pause.

Mor searched the fairy's face, his stance, his tone. Violet's article wasn't wrong; as soon as Mor had read it, he knew she'd pegged the fox correctly. "Why steal those human females' memories of a single day of their life? What will those memories give you that you don't already have?" he asked.

Luc's gaze grew sharp for a second, then he tore it away and looked out at the sunlit water. "I know Violet isn't your lover, Trisencor," he said, but his smile broadened again. "She's so much more special than that."

Mor angled himself toward the fairy. "What in the name of the sky deities are you talking…" It dawned on him a little too late. He'd seen the traces of Luc's attempted kiss on Violet from the day they met at the bus stop. He knew Luc had tried to get close to Violet, but Mor hadn't considered…

"Did you steal something from her?" Mor asked, his hands twitching toward his fairsabers as he thought about how desperately she clung to her recollections. "At the bus stop… or in the alley?"

All Luc replied with was, "Too bad she doesn't remember."

Mor's flesh tightened, his vision melting to a shade of red. Violet was *his* secretary. His responsibility now. And she'd been in Luc's clutches, possibly more times than she realized. Luc had been playing games with her—the same way he'd played games with rebellious Shadow Fairies in their Army division.

Luc licked the sweet bits of ice cream from his lips as his smile faded. "I imagine only one faeborn Shadow Fairy will leave this street alive today. Let's get it over with so I can be on my way."

Mor reached behind him for his fairsaber handles as he drew closer to the fox. "Don't hold anything back." Mor eyed Luc's pocket, waiting for him to draw out his ruby. "Give me your best fight—"

"But, Trisencor," Luc scratched his head, feigning bafflement, "aren't you wondering why no one you care about is dead yet?"

"I'm not interested." Mor let his blades slide out from their handles to prove it.

"You might be," Luc challenged. "Did you think I wouldn't find out where your High Court was hiding? Did you think I wouldn't be able to identify your allies simply because you had kept your distance from that café?"

A rock sank through Mor's stomach. "My… what?"

"Your watchdog raised his spear at me in the street. You might have been careful to mask your scent all this time, but you never told that fool to mask his. I walked right up to Fae Café's front door. I almost went in too, but the strangest thing happened." Luc glanced off in supposed bewilderment. "A human girl came out. What did she say her name was again?" He snapped his fingers. "Ah, that's right! *Lily Baker*."

Mor dropped one of his fairsabers and grabbed a fistful of Luc's collar.

Luc only grinned. "I bet that's her real name, too. I wonder if she'd walk into the harbour for me and drown herself if I told her to," he said.

Mor's blade found Luc's throat. Terrible thoughts of murder surged through his mind until a familiar voice brushed over him.

"Actually, I wouldn't, even if you said please," she said.

Mor's gaze ripped over to a blonde-haired human in a police uniform with her gun drawn. She had it aimed for Luc's head and, sky deities, she looked ready to shoot. "I knew what you were the moment the wind blew your hair off your ears," Lily said to the Shadow Fairy in Mor's grip.

To Lily's credit, Luc seemed surprised to see her there. But his surprise wouldn't save her. Mor was about to shout for Lily to run, but Luc spoke first. "Lily Bak—"

Mor punched his mouth with the hilt of his weapon.

Luc grunted and drew a fairsaber, the blade forming and swinging all in one motion. It nearly sliced Mor's head clean off. Mor ducked and blocked, picking up his other handle and forging the blade while attempting a stab at Luc's midsection. But the fox kicked him backward, and Mor was caught by a pair of strong hands.

"Queensbane, Mor. Is this the sort of humiliating nonsense you've been up to?" Cress's icy voice took up every ounce of space in Mor's ears.

"No..." he whispered. "No, no, no!" Mor spun to see the Prince of the North Corner for himself.

There Cress stood, his dark turquoise gaze sailing past him and locking onto Luc. Cress's gold and silver fairsaber handle was in his hand.

Luc surveyed Cress with a strange look. It was possibly the first time

Mor had seen the ruthless Shadow Fairy hesitate. Luc had never crossed Prince Cressica Alabastian in person, but it would not stop him from recognizing who Cress was.

"Lily, leave." Cress's words were cold.

Lily glanced at him, and her gun wavered. She looked like she might protest—but she obeyed. She jogged down the street toward the police car parked on the curb where her partner waited.

"Cress." The name cracked in Mor's throat as he looked at the one fairy he did *not* want to see, now doomed alongside him. "You should not have come here!" he rasped through his teeth.

Power rippled ever so slightly off Cress's skin. The tension in the air was suffocating, and Mor tightened his grip on his swords, preparing to flood Luc with a thousand cold iron stabs. There was no letting the fox get away alive now after what he had seen.

But Cress spoke before Mor could move.

"How about brunch?" he said. It was the most unexpected suggestion said in the darkest, most cruel voice.

"*No,*" Mor growled.

"You're out of time, Mor." Cress finally tore his gaze off Luc long enough to settle it on him. "You knew I was coming to handle this," he said.

Luc still stared; his smile gone. He seemed to weigh his odds as he sized Cress up. Calculating how he might run Cress through. But instead of stabbing, he said, "What an excellent idea, Prince Cressica."

Three tense fairies were led to a table in the corner of the breakfast diner with a view of the harbour. Mor and Cress took seats on one side, and Luc took a seat on the other against the wall. Mor looked around at all the humans. Humans that would run in terror if this brunch did not go well, and chances were, it wouldn't.

Mor glared at Cress. "You promised to stay away," he said.

Cress was no fool. He must have realized the Shadow Army would come for him now that he was revealed. That they would storm the human realm, crushing anything in their path to execute Queene Levress's ward—the exact terror Mor had spent the last months trying to avoid.

"Nonsense, Mor. All I must do is kill him. A dead fairy speaks no secrets." Cress settled his stare on Luc. He didn't take his glower off the Shadow Fairy even when a human arrived to pass out goblets of water. A slow, wickedly broad smile spread across Luc's face in response.

"I'll be right back to take your orders!" the human promised. She was ignored.

"Mor must have forgotten to mention that killing me doesn't keep me away." Luc angled toward Mor. "Right, Trisencor? You saw me die once."

"You're a nine tailed fox," Cress said, and Mor's head snapped toward Cress in surprise. "I did my research. I know how many times I must kill you for you to stay down."

Luc released a chuckle. "You may try then if you'd like, but my war isn't with you, Prince. It's with the one who abandoned his people," he said, nodding in Mor's direction.

"I am his people," Cress stated, sharp and deadly. "So, if you touch him again, I will gut you on a table like this one."

Luc's dark smile spread. "Has Mor not told you about me? Or about himself, then?" he asked. "About how he turned coward and abandoned his army? Has he not told you the story of how he—"

Cress shoved the table forward and pinned the fox against the wall. Luc's breath caught as his lungs were crushed. His wild silver-brown eyes fired up to Cress.

"We're in public," Mor reminded Cress with a mutter.

Luc's skin was tight beneath the pressure, but he didn't move, or push back, or disappear like every fairy at the table knew he could. "Are you trying to make enemies, Prince?" he asked Cress coolly.

"It's in my nature," Cress returned. "Along with assassinating my enemies."

Luc nodded, then whispered in a tantalizing tone, "Mine, too." His warped smile returned, and prickles skittered across Mor's back. "And if you think that Trisencor and I are the only Shadow Fairies in this realm, you're in for a surprise. We're an army, after all. We live in the shadows. We watch from a distance. We creep into your lives and homes and minds. And if you betray us, we destroy the things you love." He angled his head like a crossbeast, his gaze snapping over to Mor. "And we enjoy it."

Mor's heart tried to beat its way out of his chest.

"It sounds like we're a good match, then." Cress shoved the table a little harder, turning Luc's next sound into a growl. "But you're lying. I would see the Shadow Army coming long before they entered this city. You're alone here, Fairy."

Luc released a raspy chuckle. "Maybe. But you're doomed, Prince of the North. In the same way you plan to kill me, I cannot let you live now that I've seen you," Luc promised. "My tongue is burning from the false-hood of saying my war isn't with you. *That part* was a lie. I planned to kill you the moment I saw you. And the lovely truth is that you will have to kill me several times to keep me down, but I only have to kill you once."

Mor broke. He grabbed Cress's arm and they slipped into the air.

They were already shouting at each other when Fae Café appeared around them. Humans at tables shrieked and spilled coffee or halted their conversations mid-sentence as two fairies appeared out of thin air, yell-ing at the same time:

"Are you out of your faeborn mind?!—"

"I told you to stay away!!—"

"That Shadow Fairy has plans to torture you to death, Mor!—"

"I had a *good faeborn-cursed reason* to do this by myself!—"

Mor couldn't remember the last time they yelled at each other this way, or the last time he truly lost his temper and yelled at all.

"That is *preposterous!*" Cress shouted, swatting a mug off a nearby table. It shattered against the wall.

"Why can't you ever listen?! Being a prince doesn't give you the right to deal with *my* past when *I told you to stay away*—"

Cress put his finger in Mor's face. "It has been you and me together for all these faeborn years! I gave you the space you asked for, but this has gone on long enough! If that Shadow Fairy is not dead in the next twenty-four faeborn-cursed hours, I swear I will begin snapping necks, starting with *yours!*"

Dranian moseyed out from the kitchen. He folded his arms and watched, muttering something about how Shayne had left and asking if Cress or Mor knew where he was. But neither Mor nor Cress heard him.

"You're out of your faeborn mind," Cress growled at Mor again. "Ask me for help," he demanded.

Mor's jaw tightened. He had half a mind to draw his fairsabers right here in the human-filled café.

Cress's gaze flared when Mor said nothing. "Ask. Me. For. Help. *Mor.*"

"We have customers," Kate's small voice said from where she stood by the wall. Mor hadn't seen her sneak up.

"Some things are more important than customers, Kate." Mor articulated it cruelly, like she was daft. It was mean—and he wanted it to be. He wanted every fairy and human in earshot to hate his words. To hate him.

Cress's eyes narrowed. "Nothing is more important than our customers. That's the first rule of business," he bit out.

Mor took a threatening step toward his dearest friend. He rarely used his power of the Dark Shadows, but he did it now, letting the coolness slip over the floor and meet the frost crawling from Cress's own feet. And Mor said the thing that would seal the deal.

"Stay away from me, Cressica Alabastian. Or I'll destroy this place with fire magic and shadows." He flicked a nod at the café. "This is your last warning."

He took to the air, the colours bleeding around him, the wind scarcely cooling his fire-hot heart.

CHAPTER

26

Violet Miller and the Presumptuous Assassin

Loud knocking startled Violet awake. Early afternoon light sifted through the office curtain cracks, patching over the desk where she'd stacked piles of Mor's research. His written notes covered everything, and Violet had read enough of them that she was sure she could identify his handwriting anywhere. They mixed in with her own notes from the research she'd stayed up late doing online on memory-loss-related fairy folklore.

She peeled her cheek off the desktop. She couldn't recall exactly when she'd fallen asleep at Mor's desk—it must have been after midnight. Apart from the knocking, all was quiet. Mor must not have been back from whatever business he'd said he needed to take care of.

The knocking sounded again, and Violet stumbled from her chair as the noise echoed through the cathedral. She rubbed her face, mumbling,

"It's too early for visitors."

"Don't open the door for anyone while I'm gone." Mor's final words from last night shook her awake as she realized no one should be knocking on the door at all, regardless of the time. Violet blinked the sleep away as she scooted out into the hall, tapped her way down the stairs, and crept toward the large entryway doors as quietly as possible.

"Mor!" someone shouted from the other side. He sounded bored and on the verge of getting annoyed. "Moooorrrrrrrr!" And then, "Mor, I missed all the drama this morning! Don't you feel even a smidgen bad for me?"

Violet slinked to the nearest window to peer out.

Shayne—the white-haired fairy—stood on the front stairs. He wasn't in an apron anymore. In fact, he was decked out in glistening black and navy leathers, and a *crossbow* was strapped to his back. He was probably sweating buckets in the summer heat, although he didn't have boots on, at least. He stood on the stairs in bare feet.

Violet sighed. Mor had told her not to open the door for anyone, so Shayne would have to melt out there. She turned to head back upstairs when a wall-rattling knock boomed through the lobby this time.

"I'm not leaving!" Shayne shouted. He began drumming his knuckles against the door to the rhythm of a song Violet didn't know. A second later, he started singing—loud and painfully off key.

Violet huffed and went back. "I can't open this door. It's locked from both sides!" she called to him.

"Ah, hello, pretty Human. Then how did *you* get in?" he asked right back, seeming unfazed by the fact that they were yelling through a door.

Violet thought about it. Would Mor really be angry if his friend came in? Shayne was the one Mor had trusted Violet's life with, so it wasn't like Shayne was one of the bad guys. "There's a ladder out back that takes you up to the second-floor balcony. I scaled the eavestrough to the roof after that. Once you're on the roof you have to be careful because it's a steep slope, but if you can get to the bell, there's a staircase below it that leads inside."

"You did all that?" Shayne's response was immediate.

"Yes. And in heels, I might add," Violet bragged. She smothered her smile.

There was a long silence on the other side of the door. Violet thought maybe he'd left to go try out the obstacle course, but he piped up again, "Queensbane. You're the craziest human I've ever met. I think I'm in love with you. Might we share a kiss when I get inside?"

"No!" she stated, though her cheeks warmed a little. Three different fairies had thought about kissing her in the past two weeks. She flung her hair over her shoulder and smirked. Mor could call her *Paint Face* all he wanted, but she clearly wasn't repelling anyone with her looks.

Since Shayne didn't specifically say if he was going to brave the climb and come in, Violet wasn't sure if she should wait. She didn't hear anything clanging around on the cathedral's roof, so she ventured back to the office. She sat down in the desk chair and dragged her newest version of the upcoming Fairy Post to herself to look it over, worried it would be garbage since she wrote it while she was so tired last night. She had a gift for spewing embellished nonsense when she did midnight writing sprints.

"Human women like me." Shayne's voice broke the silence and Violet glanced up from her articles. "But not you. I wonder why." He was lounged against the doorframe. He'd come in as silent as a mouse.

Violet cast him a look and went back to her paper. Shayne sauntered in and sat on the chair across from her desk, dragging his crossbow off his back and resting it along his lap. Violet tried not to stare at the shining weapon that looked unsettlingly stabby.

"What are you doing?" she asked him.

"I'm watching you, Human. I'll just sit here and watch you all day." Shayne batted his eyelashes.

Violet made a face. "I won't be able to type another word if you do that."

Shayne slid his crossbow off and set it against the chair, then leaned forward with his elbows resting on his knees. "Why ever not? Most would love having a strong assassin gaze at them longingly while they do their work."

Violet shifted her weight in her seat. "Let's just say I'm not interested in…" she waved a hand toward his leather Catwoman outfit, "…crazy."

Shayne sat back in his seat, face pensive. "You like someone else," he realized.

Violet's eyes widened. "No, I don't!"

But Shayne was already grinning—too widely. "You can't fool a fairy, Human. Not on matters such as these. You just lied and said you don't long for someone crazy like me, but you're the spitting image of crazy yourself, and in my experience, crazy calls to crazy. So, the only explanation is that you already have strong affections for someone else." He tapped a finger on his knee, and suddenly his face changed. "Queensbane, is it Mor?!" It came out with a horrifying level of excitement.

Violet stood. She was sure her cheeks were hot enough to fry an egg on.

Shayne sprang from his seat and gasped. "It is!" He pointed at her. "It's Mor!"

Everything inside of Violet told her to shout protests. To deny it to her death. But when her heart took on an extra beat, she was suddenly very afraid to ask herself why. Why was her heart beating off its rhythm? Why did the accusation make her blush so hard?

Violet abandoned her work and beelined for the door. For the first time in days, she had a reality check. She asked herself what she was even doing spending time in this place after she'd almost died because of it. She needed to go home to Zorah, pack their bags, and convince her aunt to move somewhere remote with her—like she should have done right from the beginning.

Shayne was faster than lightning. His body cut her off and he slapped a hand against the opposite doorframe before she could leave. He bit his lower lip over a grin. "Don't go anywhere, pretty Human," he said. "I didn't think it was possible for someone to fall for Mor. I must know everything."

Violet set her jaw and grabbed his bare hand with hers.

Shayne released a low-toned shriek and tore his arm away. He cast her an accusing look. "That was mean," he stated.

"*You're* mean!" she countered, suddenly feeling like a child in a fight. But Shayne grinned.

"I know. It's part of the reason you females like me, I presume," he said.

A crash sounded down the hall, halting their petty fight.

Mor marched around the corner in his vampire coat, and Violet held her breath, suddenly afraid he'd heard their conversation. She wanted to melt into the floor—right into that unmarked grave she'd been so worried about the first time she came here.

Shayne's smile widened. "Mor!" he greeted. Mor grabbed Shayne by the arm and yanked him away. "Ow!" Shayne protested as Mor dragged him to the end of the hall and down the stairs. Violet rushed after them but stayed at the top of the staircase as Shayne was tossed toward the front doors.

"How many times do I need to tell you fools not to come after me?!" Mor sounded furious—Violet staggered back a step.

Shayne rolled his eyes and patted off his leather suit as though Mor had spoiled it. "I wanted to see your lightless hermit hut for myself, Mor. You can't keep secrets from us anymore, you know. If you're really fighting a nine tailed fox, you need us."

Mor's jaw flexed. "I *must* do this on my own. Don't make me keep saying it."

Shayne's smile was gone. "Then why did you bring her to the café before and leave her in our care?" He nodded up the stairs toward Violet. Both fairies glanced at her at the same time, making Violet want to shrink into the floor all over again.

Mor opened his mouth twice before coming up with an answer. He dragged his gaze back to Shayne. "I didn't mean to get her involved. She broke in and now my scent is on her, you know that."

"Yes, I gathered she'd broken in when she told me all about how she brilliantly did it. And of course she smells like you, Mor. She probably likes it." He couldn't stop his smile from breaking out at that last comment.

Violet considered pulling off one of her heels and throwing it at his white-haired head.

"Go back to the café where you belong and tell the others to *stay away* until I finish this. I swear, if I have to have this conversation one more time—"

"Absolutely not," Shayne stated. "You might be able to spit on Cress's parade because of your adorably chummy history, but I'm here now, and I'm far more difficult to get rid of. I'm not leaving until you let me help you. Even if it's just to wash your faeborn stockings." Shayne held up both hands like he was ready to do the dirty work.

"You hate stockings!" Mor snapped.

"No, I hate *wearing* stockings." Shayne pointed up at Violet. "Do you really want to watch that human die? Just because you're stubborn, Mor? What if she's the price you pay for not letting us deal with your problem? Don't you remember what almost happened to Kate?"

The air seemed to stop moving in the cathedral. Mor said nothing and glanced up at Violet again instead. Violet lifted both her hands.

"Oh, I definitely don't want to get in the middle of this argument," she said. She had no idea what had *'almost happened to Kate',* but she became acutely aware it must have been something terrible. "Feel free to finish your pleasant chat. I'll be in the office." She turned to go, but Mor materialized in her way at the top of the stairs.

"You're already involved," he said bitterly. "My brother is right."

"Of course I am," Shayne said from below as he picked nonexistent lint off his shoulder.

"Not about everything," Mor shot back at him. He looked at Violet. "But he's right about you. You shouldn't be here with me."

Shayne loudly sighed. "I'll leave for now, Mor. Only so you can finish your lovers' quarrel. Bring her to me when you change your mind and find your faeborn brain. I will protect her." He kept talking as he walked up the stairs, passed them, and headed down the hall. He dipped into the office and came out with his crossbow and a handful of pens. "Also, I'm stealing these." He waved the pens in the air for Mor to see. "They're small and pocket sized, and I can't resist," He winked at Violet and headed down the hall toward the hidden stairs to the bell tower. "See you soon, Human," he added.

Violet turned to Mor. "I shouldn't have to point out how you leaving me with him ended last time." She jutted her thumb after Shayne.

"That wasn't my fault, that was Dranian's!" Shayne's voice boomed from down the hall, and Violet shut her mouth, baffled he'd heard what she said from that far away.

A crease formed between Mor's brows, and he frowned. "I need to think."

Violet grabbed his sleeve. Something heavy sank through her as she imagined him disappearing like when he left her at Fae Café. "What do you need to think about?" she asked. She sounded strangely like she was pleading. She didn't know why she wanted to beg him to stay. Wanted him to talk his next move through with her. "We're coworkers," she reminded him. "We should come up with a plan together."

Mor looked down. "You and I..." he started.

Violet inched in, waiting. She didn't risk blinking, afraid she'd miss something on his face.

When Mor looked back up again, his expression was harder. "I went to your house and gathered your clothes. They're on the bed in my room." He took a hold of her covered wrist and tugged until her hand lost its grip on his sleeve and slipped off. "But maybe I shouldn't have. I apologize, Violet, but things have changed."

Violet's mouth parted in disbelief. "Mor," she tried again.

"Don't wear those heels anymore. I bought you reasonable shoes. They're with your other belongings."

Mor took a step back. Violet couldn't read his expression as he vanished in a wisp of wind, leaving her standing there with questions she could only ask the empty cathedral. She had a sinking feeling she'd just lost her job. And possibly more than that.

Cedric's rash comments found her all over again as the realization settled in. As the familiar feeling of belonging nowhere waited just below the surface, threatening to sprout. The dread of going through that again was too much. She couldn't lose The Fairy Post. Her hand found the stair railing and she squeezed, clinging to it like she was holding onto the entire cathedral itself.

Getting let go from The Sprinkled Scoop had been terrible.

But she had a feeling being let go of by Mor would be so much worse.

CHAPTER

27

Cressica Alabastian and the Fate of the Cards

The day felt far too long, as though the sky deities had stopped the heavens from passing over, holding the Prince hostage in time. Cress paced by the café windows until Shayne returned in the afternoon. The white-haired assassin brought little news, saying only, "I think I might have gotten to him."

Cress rolled his eyes. Shayne meant far less to Mor than Cress, and Cress hadn't been able to convince him. Cress was nearly insulted when Shayne had stated his preposterous plan to visit Mor's tacky cathedral and try to convince him with his words alone.

But still, as the hours passed by, and hot coffees were brewed, and customers left happy, Cress paced by the door. Out there, Mor was fighting the battle of his life—in his mind and with his hands. It had been a while since Cress had killed something, leaving an itch on his palm where his weapon belonged, but more importantly, Mor had never, *ever* snapped at Cress the way he had after his fox enemy had learned of Cress's existence in the human realm. Mor was not himself and all was wrong in the games of fairies.

Cress tapped his forefinger against the fairsaber handle in his side pocket as he stretched his neck back and forth and paced some more. The early afternoon turned to a warm late afternoon, then to a golden evening. The sun was setting when Kate finally cut off his relentless pacing.

His human stood in front of him, her arms folded, her big hazel eyes trying to look strong and mighty and tough. It was adorable. And astoundingly pathetic. She'd just coloured her hair this month too, so it was a luminous black-blue now. He would force her to change it back to burgundy before the wedding. She just didn't know it yet.

"Cress," Kate said. The word was stern, spoken like a batty, old-aged woman chasing hogbeasts off her front porch so they wouldn't eat her nectar berries.

"Mmm?" was his only response.

Kate sighed and dragged a coffee over the nearest table which it seemed she'd strategically hidden with her body until now. "Drink this if you're going to be up late waiting. And stop pacing by the door; you're seriously making me restless."

She extended the coffee toward him in her delicate little fingers. Kate Kole was a good many things. She was sweet, soft, and acceptably pretty. Perfect for him, apart from only six major flaws he'd counted over their months of human dating.

He offered her the first smile he'd mustered in hours. His most handsome one.

It didn't faze her. "You should really get some sleep though," she said. "Promise me you'll go to bed if he doesn't show up by ten—"

"Twelve."

"No. *Ten.*" Her hazel eyes told stories of wrath to come if he didn't comply. As if she could hurt a moonbug.

Cress took his smile back. She didn't get to have it. "I haven't been sleeping anyway, Human. I'm too bogged down by wedding plans and business decisions, and what recipe to make next for my show." It was half true. He didn't mention the real reason he laid awake each evening.

Her expression softened, and she stepped toward him. "All right."

She batted her eyelashes as she came right up against him on her tiptoes. She puckered her human lips and...

Cress smooshed his hand over her face and pushed her backward. "Yuck," he stated.

Kate gasped. "Yuck?!"

"Yes. Yuck. Your antics repulse me. If you think you can lure me into an enchantment to get me to go to bed against my will, you're out of your human mind, Katherine Lewis." He quickly brought the hot coffee to his lips and began to chug.

Kate's jaw dropped as he gulped down the whole thing and passed the empty mug back to her, wiping a bead from his bottom lip. "There will be no sleep for me tonight," he announced. He fought the impulse to make an anguished noise in reaction to how the coffee had burned his throat on the way down.

Kate grunted and took the mug back. "Whatever. It was decaf anyway." She stalked off with all her non-caffeinated trickery.

"Don't you have anything to say?" he called after her. "Anything at all, Human?"

Kate made it to the kitchen door without a reply, so Cress helped her out.

"*Un-real*, Cress!" Cress mimicked her in a high, human-y female voice. Kate glanced back with an irritated look, and he flashed a gloating smile.

Dranian emerged from the hallway in graceful strides, followed by Shayne shuffling a deck of cards. The two planted themselves at the feasting table closest to the fireplace. "You in, Cress?" Shayne asked, and Cress saw him slide an ace card up his sleeve when Dranian wasn't looking.

"Yes. Deal me in. And Kate and Lily, too," Cress said. "And I spotted a fresh pie on the counter in the kitchen. Let's split that."

Shayne grunted a laugh. "You're going to get chubby if you keep eating pie," he warned.

"Impossible," Cress said back, heading over and yanking the hidden card from Shayne's sleeve. He added it back to the deck.

"Lily made the pie for her human police department's summer fund-raiser," Dranian muttered, taking the cards away from Shayne to shuffle and deal them himself.

"Ah. Then let's eat it *quickly*," Cress decided. But his smile faded, his ear twitching toward the street. The shadows outside began to call his name.

Cress moved through the tables and pushed out the café door, rattling the bell. He looked into the darkest corners of the street as the door swished closed behind him. There were no human chariots on the road. Most of the storefronts were shutting down for the night even though the street lanterns weren't lit yet. He searched the alleys of the breakfast tavern until he spotted a hooded shadow, and Mor stepped into the last blink of light the human sun would give for the evening.

Cress said nothing as Mor approached. As Mor stopped before him. As Mor pulled down his hood, revealing his curly hair and a face that looked to have been wrestling all day with whatever decision he had come to.

Cress stared at the brown-and-silver eyed assassin. Wind whistled through the street. After several beats of silence, Cress nodded. "Come inside. I'll tell Dranian to deal you in."

Cress led the way into the café, and Mor followed without a word.

Shayne's eyes widened. The white-haired assassin stood until Cress lifted a hand and gestured for him to sit back down and shut up. So, Shayne sank back into his seat, biting back a smile. He would definitely try to take credit for Mor's return, even though it was likely Cress's and Mor's unmistakeable bond that had done the trick.

Cress looked around for the pie he'd ordered. He didn't see it on the card table. He eyed the kitchen, but he didn't want to leave Mor alone, worried one of his assassins would bring up the topic of his Shadow Fairy nemesis. Cress would force them to avoid the topic for the first while, at least. Mor being here was enough.

"Mor!" Lily jogged from the kitchen. She came over and punched

207

him in the arm. "You should have let me shoot that Shadow Fairy by the harbour. I'm a good shot. I would have gotten him right between the eyes." She smiled and poked herself between her brows to show him. Little did she know that no fairy in the room believed she could take out a Shadow Fairy with a mere human weapon. Mor was too nice to point it out though.

Cress huffed. So much for avoiding the topic. Count on humans to make things weird.

Lily scooted into a chair, followed by Kate. Cress and Mor sat also. Finally, Cress couldn't take it anymore. "Where's the pie?" he asked.

Lily tensed. "Don't you dare touch my pie, Cress," she warned. She appeared quite serious.

It was fine. Cress would pretend to have to go to the bathroom soon. He would have no trouble sneaking into the kitchen to eat it.

Dranian passed the cards around and everyone picked theirs up.

"Aren't you going to apologize for avoiding us, Mor?" Shayne asked and Cress thought about punching him through the window.

"No," Mor stated. "I told you to stay away, and you didn't." He splayed his cards in his hands and began sorting them. "I should rip you apart, limb by limb, Shayne. And stop trying to flirt with my secretary."

"Limb by limb?" Kate asked in disgust. "Do you guys always have to be so gross when you make threats?"

"Oh, they're not threats," Cress promised. "I assure you, almost every act you've heard us speak of is one we had to perform at one time or another."

Kate and Lily looked up from their cards.

"Seriously?" they both asked at once.

"Even when you threatened to spoon feed Dranian flesh-eating ants that would 'devour him from the inside out?' You actually *did that* to someone before?" Kate no longer seemed interested in the card game.

Cress blinked. "Did you think we were *nice* assassins?" he asked with mild sarcasm. "Did you think we danced around to flute music and strummed songs of the Jade Ocean on golden harps for a living?"

A look was exchanged between the human females.

"You just said you wanted to kill a faeborn Shadow Fairy," Mor added toward Lily. He poked himself between the eyes, mimicking her. "Remember? How absurd for you to be queasy now."

"Well, I *would* have taken him out if you'd let me," Lily said, and to Cress's surprise, she didn't drop her gaze like she was uttering a falsehood. Still...

"Killing is easy," Cress said. "Killing Shadow Fairies is not. But I'm well practiced," he bragged. "I watched dozens take their last breath because of the poison I put in their drink, or the fairsaber I plunged through their faeborn heart, or the water I held them beneath until their faeborn lungs—"

"Stop it, Cress!" Kate smacked the tabletop. "You're going to give us nightmares. Un-*real*."

Cress shrugged. "Mor once chucked a fairy into a pit of childling crossbeasts so he'd die slowly," he said.

Everyone at the table looked at Mor. Mor seemed like he was about to protest the claim, then he looked like he was about to explain himself like there was a perfectly good reason for what he did, then he seemed to realize it was better to not say anything at all.

Dranian, who'd remained quiet during the whole conversation, piped up and said, "Shayne once dragged a faeborn fool through a village by his nose. Broke it right off in the end."

Shayne grinned. "I did. It was hilarious."

Kate became a strange shade of flushed. Lily put one hand over her eyes and the other over her human belly. Mor, Cress, and Shayne took turns pinching their mouths shut to hide smirks.

Suddenly Lily stood. "Excuse me while I go barf," she said, rushing for the stairs to Kate's apartment.

"Humans have such weak stomachs," Dranian murmured.

Shayne nodded. "You'd think the ugly one would have a higher tolerance for punishments. She is the human version of a guard here in this realm."

Kate put the backs of her hands against her cheeks. "Lily is *not* ugly. She was the prettiest girl in our high school. All the guys liked her."

Shayne chuckled and laid a card to start the game. "That's why I call her ugly. She thinks she's tougher than me, prettier than me, and better at café-ing than me. And besides, she told you to send us away in the beginning, remember? One of us has to put her in her place for that," he said.

Kate poorly stifled an eye roll.

"I think when she comes back, I'll tell her about the time I caught an elf spy and flicked out his eyeballs—"

Kate smacked her cards down on the table again, cutting Shayne off and revealing her cards to everyone else playing. Cress leaned forward a little to see before she could pull them back to hide them again.

"I can't hear any more!" she said. "If any of you say one more word about death, or killing, or torture, *I'll* be the one to send you away this time. Got it?"

All four fairy assassins scowled and snuggled deeper into their seats, eyes dropping to their cards. Dranian laid a card, taking Shayne out of the first round.

Cress waited a few seconds for the game to go on. Then he leaned over to Mor and whispered loudly in his ear, "Remember that time you fired a flaming arrow right into that fool's open mouth while he was shouting—"

"Out!" Kate stood and began collecting the cards. She yanked Dranian's right out of his hand. No one moved. "No more '*warm beast milk*' for any of you. Sleep on the street tonight for all I care! You're not allowed in this café tonight!"

"But—"

"Humans only!" Kate pointed at the door, and four disgruntled fairies slowly lifted from their seats.

CHAPTER

28

Mor Trisencor and the Big Fairy Sleepover

Dranian appeared the most horrified by the cathedral. He grunted toward the dust, he grunted toward the bugs, he grunted toward the unlit hallways.

Shayne, on the other hand, stretched and yawned as he headed up the stairs. "I'm the only King here so I'll take the comfy bed." He stole a subtle look at Cress as if to see whether Cress would challenge him on it.

"Whatever, *Your Majesty*," Mor said from the dim living space off the lobby where he tossed a blanket on each of the spare couches for Cress, Dranian, and himself. Mor was used to sleeping on the couch anyway since it was where he'd decided to sleep from now on until...

Shayne's bare feet slapped over the hardwood floors of the upstairs hall, and Mor's eyes widened. He sprang back into the lobby and called up the stairs in a loud whisper, "Stay away from that bed!"

From *right outside* Mor's bedroom door, Shayne glanced back down the hall. The white-haired assassin had to lift to his tiptoes to see Mor at the bottom of the stairs. He raised an eyebrow at first, until a look of realization filled his face. He pointed toward the bedroom door. "Is *she* in there?"

Mor bit down on his thinned lips. "I... I don't know. I think so," he admitted in a panicked whisper.

Shayne took a patronizing step toward the door and flittered his fingers over the handle. Mor airslipped so fast he sliced dust particles, cutting between Shayne and the door and tossing Shayne across the hall before he inhaled another full breath.

"I'll snap your fingers off!" Mor warned with a voice that sounded calmer than he felt.

Shayne sighed. "You'd better have a guest bedroom fit for a king," he said.

Mor nodded to another bedroom down the hall where he knew an old mattress rested in the corner. To his relief, the white-haired assassin released a dramatic sigh and headed that way.

Only when Shayne moseyed down the hall and into the other room did Mor return to the stairs. He waited a moment at the top, listening to see if Shayne was about to come back out and complain about the accommodations. When all seemed still, Mor returned to the living space where Dranian was already snoring on one of the couches.

Mor sat on his couch parallel to Cress's. "It's not like I care about that human," Mor felt the need to clarify, "it's just that I can't stand the thought of her being tormented more than she already has been. Though, I'll admit, I don't know why it bothers me so much," he added. "I never would have even looked twice at her before I realized she was writing the articles I was reading, and then I discovered there was fairy trouble in her past. The more I'm around her, the stronger I can feel it, and the more it bothers me."

Cress just sat there with his arms folded, listening. A second later, he swatted a spider off his shoulder.

"And I can't even touch her, so trying to slip into her human mind and see her memories is out of the question. Not that I would try without her consent anyway. I mean, unless she was in peril, of course, and I *had* to... *Queensbane*," Mor cursed and dragged a hand through his hair, pulling strands from the tie. "I can't decide if I want her to keep taking her cold iron or to stop altogether. It's driving me faeborn mad."

When he looked up, he found Cress smirking. "You're mad because you can't touch her, Mor?" he challenged.

Mor sighed. "It's not like that."

Cress's wicked smile widened. "I can't begin to express the joy and merriment it would bring me to learn that you *like* a human after all the harassment you bequeathed me for it."

Mor shot a doubtful look across the living space. "This is not like your situation. You were enchanted in the beginning and even if you hadn't been, you fell like a delicate forest flower." He leaned back on the couch and rested his arm across the backrest, splaying his impressive assassin muscles. "I'm nothing like that."

Cress's smile dropped. "Careful," he warned. "I've been stress eating and losing sleep for two months over these dreadful wedding plans and I'm one ripe comment away from ripping your tongue out from your head."

Mor stuck out his tongue and spat a little in invitation. Cress's fingers twitched like he was truly thinking about doing it. Mor's face broke into a smile around his tongue.

"One of these days..." Cress mumbled to himself, tearing his gaze away to look out the window. A second later, he said, "What spell does that nine tailed fox have on you, Mor? What about him are you trying so hard to hide from us?"

"I wasn't trying to hide anything from you. I was trying to hide *you* from *him*." The humour left Mor's face.

"Very well. Then what does he know about you that's got him pulling your faestrings and has you bumbling around like a fool?" Cress's turquoise gaze cut back to Mor.

"He knows everything about me, Cress. He knows my birthstory, my childling story, my Shadow Army story, and what I did to the army the day I left. He knows why I left. He knows how I fight and how I think."

Cress tapped a finger on his knee. "I also know all of those things. Let me handle him for you."

Mor shook his head. "It's not just that I must do this myself, Cress, it's that I *want* to do this myself. He is my greatest enemy, and I am his. This has always been between me and him, and I wish to defeat him fairly."

"That sounds like a statement that's about to get you killed," Cress remarked.

Mor ran his fingers through his hair again. "I want to deal with my past and burn it with my own two hands. I wish I could forget it all, but I can't. And I'll never feel settled about it unless I end things."

Cress nodded slowly. "I suppose I can allow that. But soon, I'll have to get involved against your wishes, Mor. And when that moment comes, I will do whatever is necessary to keep you. I will even trade that human for you." He nodded toward the stairs, and Mor's eyes flashed at the words. "He seems to want something from her," Cress added.

Mor shook his head. "Don't." A half growl, half plea. "Don't do that. That is not a noble trade."

Cress studied Mor. "Is that really why you don't want me to? Because I couldn't care less about being noble these days."

"I would consider it a betrayal." Mor clasped his hands together and squeezed them. "Because you know I want to keep her alive."

Cress stared too long and hard until Mor dropped his gaze again.

After a moment, the Prince's low voice filled the living space. "You know you have to send her away if you want her to live. Keeping her in such an easily penetrable place is like dangling hogmeat before a starving crossbeast. Send her to Shayne. He's secretly worried about her survival, you know."

"Why?" Mor sighed.

"Because Shayne knows you. He knows what it'll do to you if you get a human killed."

Cress had a look in his eye, one Mor had seen before. One that promised the moment Mor gave the go-ahead word to Cress, this war would look very different.

Mor dragged his blanket over and unrolled it. He kicked off his boots and laid back on the couch, draping the thin fabric over himself.

"You three better make sure you're out of here early in the morning. I'm not sure how I'll explain this absurd sleepover if Violet wakes up and catches us all," he said to change the subject.

Cress smirked and unfolded his own blanket. "Tell her to mind her own human business. Tell her it's brothers before lovers and all that."

Mor rolled his head to glance at Cress. "I don't think that's how the human expression goes."

"It is. Kate's-brother-Greyson said it," Cress said.

It took Mor a moment of thinking before he spoke again. "I think it's *bros before hoes*. I heard Greyson say it also."

Cress's face scrunched. "Hoes? What are hoes?"

Mor shrugged. "It must be how human males refer to their women."

Cress was quiet for a long while, nodding and thinking that over.

CHAPTER

29

Violet Miller and a Morning Sip of Fun and Doom

Violet had possibly gone too far, but she needed Mor to keep her. She wasn't sure how he'd react once he found out what she did. He'd been so adamant about keeping everyone away from his cathedral, and Violet had flushed that hope of his down the toilet. He'd find that out soon enough.

The morning was cooler than normal, leaving the bedroom window covered in dew. Violet sifted through the duffle bag Mor had packed of her clothes until she found a clean shirt, a loose pink sweater, and a pair of blush jeans. Thus far, she'd tried to stay somewhat decorated with her clothing—if wearing the same dress for days on end could be considered decorated—but she didn't have many options with the clothes he'd chosen. Everything looked... comfortable. Relaxed. Totally not workplace appropriate. Also, everything in her duffle bag had a strange grassy smell. Violet lifted the collar of her sweater and sniffed with a wince.

Her scathed bare heels were happy when she traded her usual stilettos for the shoes he'd bought her—boring white things with laces and zero added height. After she slid them on, she raked her fingers through her loose hair in the bathroom. There was no point in trying to doll herself up this morning when she still didn't have her curling iron, so she stuck on a cute, salmon-coloured sunhat instead.

She headed downstairs to the kitchen to make tea, but she paused in the doorway when she saw four used mugs on the countertop. They hadn't been there last night. When she peered inside the cups, traces of milk were left in the bottom. She looked back toward the hall, wondering if Mor had company while she'd been asleep.

Violet's suspicions were confirmed when she spotted several sets of muddy shoeprints, and one set of dirty bare feet footprints around the kitchen. She squatted down to examine the bare foot one, trying to measure it against how big she remembered Shayne's feet being.

"Did you drop something?"

Violet yelped and stood-spun all at once. One of her shoes caught on the other and she tripped forward, her hat flying off. For the first time, Mor didn't let her tumble to the floor in a heap at his feet—his arm came around her waist and he yanked her against him to balance.

Violet was sure she could hear her heart beating in her ears. She was also sure he'd just discovered she hadn't taken her iron supplements last night. That she'd secretly decided to try and ween herself off them forever, despite his instructions. In about an hour, she was going to start getting dizzy, and if it was an unlucky day, the stomach pains would begin, too.

She hoped maybe she could pull away before Mor noticed their skin was touching, but his vampire coat hood was down, and her cheek pressed against his warm neck. Also, his hand held gently against her lower back, his fingers grazing her midriff where her shirt had lifted during her epic tumble. He must have *noticed* he wasn't screaming, so likely the cat was out of the bag.

Mor's hands found her sides and he slowly pulled back. His gaze darted over her outfit, her relaxed, uncurled hair, her new flat shoes. Violet awaited her lecture about the cold iron, but he didn't give one. Instead, he looked at her with a bothered face and said, "Who are those humans knocking on the front door of my cathedral?"

Ah. It was time he learned about her late afternoon betrayal from yesterday.

Three and a half minutes later, two high school students stood in the open cathedral doorway, peering in at the peculiar, creaky lobby floors, the antique emerald-green carpet up the staircase, and the high shelves lined with half-melted candles. They both clutched notebooks and suitcase bags.

This was the first time Violet was seeing them in person. Their interviews over the phone yesterday had been short but promising when she'd asked them a variety of questions that ranged from, *"Are you squeamish about blood?"* to *"If you happened to meet a vampire in real life, would you be terrified or excited?"*

"Remi and Jase, right?" Violet asked, clutching her hat tightly in her hands before her. "Am I remembering your names correctly?"

The guy and girl were only a few years younger than her, but Violet suddenly felt like she was a hundred years old as she waved them further into the cathedral. She warily turned to Mor. "These are our new interns!" she told him with as much enthusiasm as she could muster while melting beneath his silver-brown gaze.

Mor stared at the interns and said nothing for several seconds that felt like years. Violet was sure she was going to have a panic attack if he didn't speak. Finally, he turned toward Violet and said, "Put on something discreet. Black, preferably." He pulled his hood on over his head.

Violet blinked a few times over. "I don't have anything black."

"You have no garments that are black?" Mor folded his arms.

She shook her head. "You're the one who packed my bag; you should know most of my clothes are pink, white, floral, or green. Not all of us want to dress like Masters of Doom, you know."

He stifled an eye roll and headed out the front doors, brushing past the interns. "Come with me."

The interns looked to Violet as if to ask, *"Is he talking to us?"*

Violet forced a smile. "The office is upstairs. I've added two new desks for you, so go make yourselves at home and get familiar with The Fairy Post style. I left all the past issues on your desks."

The interns exchanged a look, and the girl shoved her glasses further up her nose. That was goodbye as Violet trotted down the cathedral stairs after Mor.

The doors slammed shut behind her, trapping the interns in, and Violet winced, wondering if she should mention to Mor that locking them in might frighten them the same way it had frightened her on her first day inside the gloomy building.

"Doom?" she asked as she followed him down the sidewalk. "Where are we going?"

"We're going for bubble tea," was all he said. The cape of his jacket fluttered behind him.

Violet had to run to keep up. This was the first time she'd heard Mor mention liking bubble tea. But she wanted to know how he felt about the interns, if he was secretly happy she'd taken initiative. Happy enough to want to keep her around forever. "Okay. Why? And are you really going dressed like that?"

"My jacket protects me," he said. "Your clothes protect you, too, Human. I dragged them through a dandelion field before I brought them to the cathedral."

Violet looked down at her outfit, thinking of the grassy smell.

Her phone buzzed and she pulled it out, seeing another message from Zorah. She chewed on the inside of her cheek as she thought about what to say to her aunt. She'd been adding flourishing details about her work trip every time Zorah asked a question, trying to keep the conversation going every morning so that she knew Zorah was still alive and breathing. But it was only a matter of time before Zorah realized Violet was lying through her teeth.

"Just tell her the truth," Mor said without looking back at her.

Violet blinked at the back of his head, positive he had eyes there. "Have you been reading my texts?" she asked, and he pulled one shoulder into a shrug.

"You don't guard your phone well enough. It's too easy."

Violet halted, bringing Mor to a stop. He turned back and seemed to take in her folded arms, her scowl.

"First, that's totally an invasion of my privacy," she said. "Second, I can't tell Zorah the truth about this because she would lose her mind if she learned about you fairy people. And third, you haven't said a word about the two awesome interns I just hired to keep The Fairy Post running. You could at least say thank you, even if you're not sold on the idea yet."

"You've doomed them," Mor stated plainly.

Violet huffed and started walking again, shoving past him a little. "You're so dramatic."

"Think what you like, Violet. You might be pleased with yourself now, but you'll feel differently about it when those two humans are rotting corpses left for me to find on the cathedral stairs."

Violet gagged on her own spit. She whirled, but Mor strode past her, taking the lead again. "Arm them with dandelion coats and cold iron daggers, at least," he muttered. "All they have back there are ink pens and note-taking books."

Violet shuddered and released a sigh. "You can do a lot more damage with a pen than you'd think," she mumbled.

Mor snorted an almost-laugh. Then he reached back and took her hand—her bare hand—and the world around Violet turned to blurs of colour.

She landed on her feet beside a front porch. Mor marched up the stairs and knocked on a yellow-painted door. Violet's eyes widened. "This is my house!" she said.

"Yes." Mor waited.

The door swung open, and Zorah stood there with a spoon sticking out of her mouth and a half-eaten cup of yogurt in her hands.

"Apologies, Human. Violet is not on a work trip," Mor stated to Zorah.

Violet gasped. She shoved him, but he barely moved. "You're such a tattletale!"

"Yes. Most of the time," Mor agreed. "I despise being forced to keep secrets unnecessarily."

A metallic clang brought her attention to Zorah again where the spoon seemed to have fallen out of her mouth and now rested on the floor by her feet. Zorah's jaw hung open as she stared at Mor.

Violet jumped into the house, shoved Zorah's mouth shut, and pushed her aunt backward into the kitchen. "Don't make a big deal of this, *please*, and yes, I was lying about the business trip thing but there's a totally reasonable expl—"

"Is he your boyfriend?!" Zorah asked. She hadn't looked away from Mor yet. She batted her eyelashes, making the mood weird.

Violet glanced back at the fairy to find a small, egotistical smile on his face. "Don't be so flattered, you tattletale vampire," she muttered in a whisper, and Mor's smile fell, confirming he'd heard her from across the room.

"Is he the reason you've been sneaking around?" Zorah finally turned to Violet. "You have a boyfriend?"

"I—It's not like—We're not…" Violet dropped her head and looked at the crumbs on the floor. "Whatever. Yes, he's my boyfriend." She shrugged, casting Zorah a tight-lipped smile. It was as good a story as any, and one that Zorah would actually believe—

"No, I'm not," Mor said from the door.

Violet huffed in disbelief. "I'm hiring more interns," she threatened.

Mor smiled. "Go ahead," he invited. "See how it ends for them."

"Sorry, Zorah, but we really need to go." Violet patted her aunt on the shoulder and marched for the front door, practically shoving Mor back out of the house with her body. "I'll call you later!" she shouted back to her aunt.

"I'm not surprised you have a boyfriend, but he's not the guy I expected you to bring home!" Zorah called after her with a grin. "What about that other handsome, bright-eyed guy I keep seeing you with?"

Mor's hand flashed out and grabbed Violet's arm, stilling her in the doorway.

Violet twisted back toward Zorah with a raised eyebrow. "What guy, Zor? I'm not seeing a guy." She was intensely aware of Mor's existence beside her. "I'm not seeing anybody." She was also sure she was blushing.

Mor didn't seem to notice. He strode into the house, approaching Zorah in the kitchen, appearing tenser than a moment ago. "What did you just say?" he asked in a serious voice. "You're certain it was Violet you saw?"

Zorah snorted a laugh. "Um, yeah. I can recognize my niece from a mile away."

Violet rushed to Mor's side. "She's totally making this up." She forced a ridiculous laugh in a terrible, tacky attempt to convince him she wasn't seeing anyone else. But the look on Mor's face when he turned to her made her stomach drop.

"No. She's not," was all he said.

Zorah's smile fell, too. "Sorry I blabbed in front of your boyfriend, Vi, but I thought I taught you better than to see two guys at once. That's not okay."

"I'm not seeing any guys!" Violet said in exasperation.

Zorah's smirk returned. "Okay." She seemed to forget she was scolding her niece, and she winked at Violet the moment Mor turned around and headed for the door. Violet released a huff and followed him outside, taking in Zorah's eyebrow dance a second before she shut the door behind her.

The sounds of cars passing by filled Violet's ears as she stood on the front steps of her house, trying to remember to breathe for a moment. The backs of her hands found her hot cheeks, but it did little to cool them down.

"I don't know why my aunt said those things," she said. "I don't have a boyfriend—not that it's any of your business, technically. And as if she thought *you* were my boyfriend. Horrifying." She choked the last word out.

Mor studied her from where he stood at the bottom of the stairs. He seemed particularly interested in her flushed cheeks, in how she interlocked her fingers, and how she tapped her toes against the top stair. He sauntered up a step, his height bringing him eye-to-eye with her. "Does thinking about me being your lover frazzle you, Human?" he asked.

The simple words sent Violet's heart into a new tempo.

Mor cracked a smile, making it clear he was both flattered and was messing with her.

Violet released the breath she was holding. Her hands formed fists at her sides as she shooed away her nerves. "Doesn't the thought of being my boyfriend frazzle *you*, Mor? Even a little?"

Two could play this ridiculous game. Violet slid her hands into his hood and deep into his hair, making Mor flinch. She brought her face to his, their lips just a breath apart. She'd hardly been able to go near him when she was taking her iron, so the touch of her palms against his skin startled her more than she expected.

Mor's lips peeled apart. His throat bobbed. "Violet," he rasped in a whisper that sounded like a warning, or a plea, or some sort of pain, and her act faltered, her smile wavering.

She almost tore her hands back, almost said she was sorry for being stupid and unprofessional. But Mor grabbed her wrists before she could pull away. Violet held in a gasp as he came to the top step, pinning her wrists up beside her shoulders against the front door and forcing her to lean back. He brought his face in, and he kissed her.

He *kissed* her. Gradually. Deliberately.

Mor dropped her wrists and slid his fingers into her loose hair, shifting her hat off balance and sending it tumbling into the garden. He didn't take his mouth off hers; he didn't pull his body away. Violet's chest pounded as she realized he didn't *want* to.

She pulled her mouth off his and rasped out, "Mor."

His body flexed; his hands went still. It was like he'd gotten lost for a moment and had just come slamming back into himself. He pulled his face back, his silver and brown eyes a brilliant shade of wild as he stared at her. She didn't know the feeling of being looked at in a way that made her feel so... wanted. Loved, maybe. Needed. Like if she woke up in a forest tomorrow with no name and no memories, he would show up to claim her.

Violet was sure she'd lost her voice. His hands were warm where they were tangled into her hair. He looked back and forth between her eyes and inhaled.

"I..." he stuttered. His mouth formed the start of words he didn't finish. "Queensbane..."

It didn't seem real. Violet had to ask herself if this was a dream or a cruel joke. But nothing about the way he was looking at her felt pretend.

"Mor... do you want me as more than a secretary?" She somehow found the voice to ask. Her pulse doubled over as she feared the answer—either way. A second of silence passed by, and her knees threatened to tremble.

Mor dropped his hands and took a wide step back, landing halfway down the stairs. "It's... complicated."

Violet trotted down after him. "I'm not complicated. I'm as simple as it gets. If you want me as more than a secretary, you can take my heart, Mor."

His eyes widened. "Stop, Violet."

She didn't know what had come over her, or why she was willing to say such things. She'd guarded her heart fiercely for ten years only to offer to toss it away to him now.

"I've been on my own for a long time. I haven't belonged to anyone. I could belong to you." She surprised herself again, but it was like once she started, she couldn't stop. "I don't want you to keep disappearing from me. I want to know what's going on inside your head when you look at me like you are right now."

She reached the bottom stair and Mor grabbed her wrist. He tugged her forward and put a hand over her mouth. "Stop, Violet," he repeated. "I'm not the one you want this with." He was far too serious to leave any hope behind.

A well emptied in Violet's chest, draining out fast. She couldn't look away from him, couldn't even blink. Strain blanketed his face along with a flicker of fear that went away when he swallowed and composed himself.

"What you need to understand, Violet, is that Mor is not allowed to love. Everything touched by his heart will be destroyed." Luc's words in the alley danced through her mind. She wanted to yell at that redhead fairy right now.

Mor hesitated to remove his hand from her mouth, but when Violet said nothing for several seconds, he dropped his arm back to his side. "Let's get bubble tea," he said.

They were back in the wind in a heartbeat. Blurred colours turned sharp, and Violet found herself in front of the bubble tea shop. Cars passed where they stood in the parking lot. She looked around, worried people had seen two beings appear from thin air.

"You really shouldn't teleport like that in public," she mumbled at Mor. "You're going to start rumours."

Mor dug a hand into his pocket, keeping his gaze down. "I'll get you anything you like. What kind of tea do you want?" he asked, pulling out a wallet that looked made of wood.

"Mor," Violet whispered. At his name, Mor stopped fidgeting with his pocket change. He didn't look up. "You can't possibly believe that you're not allowed to love," Violet said. A coin tumbled from Mor's hand and rolled down the sidewalk.

"Violet," he said again, this time with warning.

"If you're so afraid of your enemies catching up with you, we can keep it a secret."

Mor shut his mouth. He blinked at the asphalt in the direction of his lost coin. When he lifted his gaze to her, his mouth was tight at the corners. "Don't tempt me. I've hardly got any control with you as it is." Violet's mouth parted. "Don't you understand? You're already doomed, simply for being in my company. Getting feelings involved will only make it worse."

They stared at each other, both refusing to break eye contact until a passing car honked.

Mor took in a deep breath. "I'll get one of everything," he said, turning for the bubble tea shop.

"Mor." She stopped him one last time. "Are you treating me to bubble tea because you're going to send me away today?"

Mor didn't reply, answering her question well enough. Violet's lungs grew tight. She'd just hung her heart out in front of him, and he'd been planning to kick her out the whole time. She nodded, her only response as Mor continued into the tea shop.

Violet released a strained breath, slapping both hands over her face and feeling the weight of her words pulling her toward the ground. That seed of fear—the gutting dread of being cast out again—sprouted within her from the shallow place she'd tried to bury it.

When she dropped her hands, someone was standing in front of her. Or so she thought, but she blinked, and he was gone. Her eyes fired up; the clouds in the sky had jumped—appearing in new places. The wind seemed to have started and stopped suddenly, too. Almost like someone had pushed a pause button on her and the rest of the world had kept moving for a moment.

Violet whirled, scanning the crowds moving down the street. She caught sight of a scarlet-haired figure among them, sliding a ruby into his pocket as he walked. She took a step after him, but Luc was marching away at a graceful, inhuman speed and was already too far off to yell after.

The dizziness returned like a punch. Violet grabbed her forehead and winced, cursing her anemia for having terrible timing. But her iron deficiency felt like the least of her worries as she scanned the groups of people, no longer seeing any traces of Luc. For a moment, she debated if he'd even really been there.

Mor came out of the bubble tea shop with a tray of four different tea flavours. He slowed his walk as he reached her, sniffing the air and tugging his brows together.

"Mor," Violet said. "I think I just saw Luc. I think…"

The flashes of him there and gone.

The clouds snapping into different places.

The feeling of the wind changing in a split second.

"I think I may have spoken with him," she rasped.

Mor dropped the bubble teas. They splattered over the parking lot as he took her shoulders and looked her over. "Queensbane, Violet, has this has happened before?" The way he asked made her wonder if he already knew the answer.

Violet swallowed, thinking of Zorah's comment about seeing her around with another guy. "I don't know."

Mor released a heavy breath, an anguished expression twisting his face as he turned her away from the bubble tea shop and ducked them between two parked trucks. "It has. At the bus stop, and in the alley, and likely other times when you didn't even know you met him. He's been doing this for a while."

Sickness filled Violet's stomach as she realized. All those times she'd met Luc, he'd made her forget part of it. She pressed a hand against her chest when it felt too tight to breathe.

It had happened again. She'd had memories stolen again—and this time she had no idea how many or from when.

"Mor…" she rasped as her hands began to shake, as her heartbeat elevated. As a fresh wave of terror coursed through her veins. "It doesn't make sense," she said. "He never tried to kill me… right?"

Mor's hand came out toward her, but he hesitated and dropped it back to his side. He squeezed it into a fist, his body rigid. "No. But he kept coming back," Mor said. "Encounters are different with foxes. Any number of things could have happened. But he didn't want you to remember—as if he was worried I would find out if I looked into your mind. So, he was after something."

"What could he possibly be after with me?" Violet hugged her arms to herself.

"Queensbane, I don't know. But if he's still coming back to you, I imagine he didn't get it yet." Mor finally took her hands. "What I do know is he's doing this because of me. You need to leave me alone. And I can't send you to Shayne anymore because I need him now. So, you'll have to go to the Sisterhood."

"*Mor*—"

"I'll take you back to the cathedral first. Fire the interns. Pack your things. I'm not sure how much time we have," he said, closing his eyes and dropping his head. "Take The Fairy Post firm with you. You can have it."

"No." The statement was simple. "I'm your secretary, Mor," she objected with half accusation, half insistence.

Her words brought his face up slowly, and in it, Violet saw a strange monster she hardly recognized. A hardness covered his gaze, his expression sending nausea rolling through her stomach. It was like he'd turned into something else in the blink of an eye.

"Are you?" he asked, taking a step back. "Are you my secretary, Violet Miller? Apart from writing a few mediocre articles that are utterly bland and read like poor fiction, and causing me more trouble, what have you done?"

His words rang in her ears, and she closed her mouth. It was a cold punch to her gut—the one thing she dreaded hearing—and he'd said it. If Mor wanted to cut her confidence off at the knees, he'd done it well. Those words would haunt her.

Violet slid her jaw to the side. "Don't send me away. I need this job," she said, quieter this time. Though, this hardly had anything to do with The Fairy Post anymore.

"No, you need coin. The Fairy Post will give you plenty of that," Mor stated. He opened and closed his mouth like he was deciding exactly how to put his next words. He swallowed, he hardened his jaw, then he looked her dead in the eyes. "I don't want you as more than a secretary, and after that outburst of your feelings earlier, I don't think I even want you as that anymore. Apart from that one disgraceful moment of curiosity on your porch stairs, I don't have any interest in having your heart. We needed each other in the beginning, but now I don't need you anymore. I'm relieved you're leaving so you can stop getting in my way."

Violet was quiet through his speech. She waited with her arms folded. Waited, as his words burned over her skin. Waited.

And then she smiled with tears in her eyes. Smiled, because she was sure that was the biggest, most pathetic lie he'd ever told. Tears, because a small fragment of her worried certain parts of it were true. He'd always pushed her away, he'd looked horrified when she'd suggested they love in secret. He'd been planning to send her away all morning, and she'd babbled on about how she felt, like an idiot. The thin layer holding back her seed of fear finally snapped, and the weight of abandonment settled in, filling her chest with coldness. She was sure she would never look at Mor warmly again.

"I hate you," she reminded him quietly. "I hate all fairies. I hate the games, and the memory stealing, and the manipulation. You have nothing to worry about. It's easy to stop caring about you." Violet swallowed. "You owe me a paycheck for the work I've done," she said from a thick throat.

Mor folded his arms. "I'll pay you another way, Human." Not Violet, *Human.* "What do you want from me?" He waited, and when Violet didn't answer fast enough, he went on, "Do you want me to try and find who you were in your past? Do you want to learn who you really are, Violet Miller? Do you want me to go into your mind and attempt to locate whatever's left of the memories from the years you lost and give them back to you so you can see them? Will that satisfy you enough to part ways?"

A streak of realization made something squeeze in her chest. "You can... find my memories?" He'd never told her that. In all their time side by side, he'd never once mentioned he had the ability to give her back the one thing she'd lost. The one thing she craved.

"Maybe not," he stated. "It depends on the skill of the fairy who stole them. It's a difficult feat, but I'm special. If the fairy left any threads of the memories behind, I may be able to start from the day you woke up and work backward—if there's anything left." He came back toward her, rolling up his sleeves. It was all business to him. He hardly looked her in the eyes as he lifted his hands. "This is my parting gift to you for the work you've done for me so far, Human. There's no reason for us to see each other again after this."

She didn't move away, so he placed his fingers along her temples.

Instantly, Violet's mind filled with a different day, with new surroundings from another time. Her eyes opened like she was really there, and she saw the same forest. A gasp escaped her as she recalled that moment, ten years ago, when she first woke up in the purple dress. A strange panic returned at the familiar smell of cotton candy and earthy tea. She heard the wind rustling the leaves above. Saw the bright light soaking the backs of the leaves and turning them fluorescent. She almost felt her stomach flexing with the motion of sitting up. She looked down at her violet dress and summer shell sandals.

Mor's fingers tightened ever so slightly on her temples in real time.

Violet watched her memory unfold of how she climbed to her feet and looked around the forest. How she started running toward the distant sound of cars. How she came out of the trees on the cusp of a city and stopped in front of a modest news building with a glass storefront.

How she stared at her reflection in the windows, not even recognizing herself.

Mor ripped his hands away. He staggered back, breathing heavily as he looked at Violet with wide eyes like he was seeing a ghost.

Violet's mind spun so fast from his exit, she teetered. Her hands couldn't catch anything to steady herself as dizziness rushed in, and she tumbled toward the ground. She was hardly aware of him catching her. One single memory slipped in as everything went black.

THE
BACKSTORIES
THE &
FRONTSTORIES

CHAPTER

30

Haley Whitefield and How it All Began Ten Years Ago
in the Violet Dress

It was raining the hour Haley Whitefield stood in a green forest with mud gushing up between her sandalled toes. In the distance, sounds of humans lifted from the city, humans who had no idea what sort of madness was hiding in their local park. Her stomach clenched with the need to heave up its contents, but she held them in—determined not to spew into the grass until the being before her departed.

Her dress was damp, and her hair was even wetter, sticking to her face in strings. She'd destroyed her beach sandals—the one's she'd stolen from a street cart moments before she was taken to…

The *other* place.

She could still hear the music. Could still taste the sweet flowers. Could still feel the nausea of it all.

She could still see his face.

The boy had seemed older than her, likely a teenager already, with sharp, metallic eyes, detailed tattoos, and sun-kissed skin. But his age hadn't mattered. He'd still been able to tear his way through the other beings like him. He'd still been able to get her out. Haley looked back toward the way she thought the *other* place was, but truly, she had no idea which direction they'd come from.

"This is where I leave you, Human," the being said. The man before her was tall and fair-skinned with pointed ears. Just like the ones who had captured Haley in the first place. "I was paid for two tasks though. First, to deliver you home, and second, to steal your memories of the Ever Corners so you won't try and find your way back."

"Find my way back?" Haley placed a hand over her restless stomach. "Why would I ever want to go back?"

The being shrugged. "Perhaps to find the fairy who saved you?" It seemed like a guess.

Haley pushed a strand of her wet hair behind her ear and stole another look in the direction she thought the *other* place was. No, she did not want to go back there. She did not want to experience the horrors ever again.

But she would think about that boy.

"I never want to go back to the other place. But I don't want to be here either," she admitted. "Isn't there somewhere else I could go?" She folded her arms and squeezed them to herself. The rain had finally stopped, but she still shivered as beads of moisture rolled down her bare arms.

"I was not paid to deliver you beyond this forest," the being said, scratching behind his pointed ear. "But if you dislike your life here, I can perhaps help with that. I can give you a new start." He fiddled with a large, flat pendant at his throat. "I am a pauper, after all. I assist when I can, and I will be taking your memories of your time in the Ever Corners anyhow. Perhaps if I take *all* your memories, you won't dislike the human realm so much when you wake."

Haley stole a look toward the city where sounds of car horns and emergency sirens trickled through the trees. The city she'd been hiding in for too long. The city that didn't want her. The city whose streets had become her home and had kicked her out again and again.

What would losing her memories accomplish?

Her fingers pressed against her slow-beating, sad heart as the blurry faces of her parents filled her mind. Two people she hardly remembered yet remembered all too well. Maybe a fresh start would be nice.

"Do it," she said. "I don't want to remember how hard everything is."

The being tilted his head. "You won't remember who you are," he warned. "You won't remember who you belong to."

Haley cracked a weak smile. "It's all right. I don't belong to anyone."

For a moment, the being chewed on his lip in thought. "If that's your wish, Human. Hold still."

When the being placed his fingers along Haley's temples, she felt the strangest rush of hot liquid into her mind. It drew back out just as quickly as it had flooded in, and with its exit went everything she knew. As her identity washed away with the rain, Haley heard someone say, "You might faint, Human. But when you wake, you'll be better."

CHAPTER

31

Mor Trisencor and the Thing that Made Him Destroy Everything
Ten Faeborn Years Ago

The evening was firelit with barrels and magic lanterns, casting rippling light along the underside of the cave. Mor sat several seats down from Luc. It didn't stop him from hearing Luc's argument with Sireling. But Mor's sharp ears had gone deaf to the bickering fairies down the table the moment the human girl had arrived.

He had not taken his eyes off her when she was brought in. A human. A real, breathing, living human.

The Shadow Army had done a thing so forbidden; it would certainly bring the wrath of the sky deities down upon the Dark Corner of Ever. The fools. Mor wished he didn't have to be here when this dreadful army was punished.

A youthful fairy took the last empty seat beside him. Mor believed his name was Zarus, but Mor had never cared to learn the names of Prince Reval's division. He called them all *"Fairy"* on the rare occasions he did open his mouth to address them at all.

"I found the human myself," Zarus bragged to Mor like they were allies as he brushed a lock of his cream-coloured hair aside. Mor was certain he'd never shared a conversation with this fairy before this moment. "I think the Prince will give me a reward for it."

At the front, the human girl was offered fairy food, and Mor stood from his seat, startling Zarus.

The girl reached for the food as Mor watched. She brought a sugar blossom to her lips, nibbling on the end to taste it.

Mor moved. He rushed around the table until he stood before her, far taller and stronger than her delicate, thin frame. "Don't eat it," he commanded in a low voice. The fairies at her sides glared at Mor, raising brows, setting their jaws, one even barring his teeth.

"What do you think you're doing, Fairy?" the barred-teeth one asked.

"It will make you ill and then it will make you want to dance," Mor warned the human again, ignoring the Shadow Fairy's question.

The girl looked up at him from large green eyes, surrounded by a scatter of freckles. Her brown, messy hair was damp. The purple dress she wore appeared soggy, and her toes were covered in dirt. She didn't look clean, or well fed, or decorated beyond her strange, purple garment.

"Eat it," the Shadow Fairy at her side demanded, flexing his fists. When the girl still didn't obey, he asked, "What's your name, Human?"

"Don't answer that," Mor said. Still, he had not taken his eyes off the human. And since he'd arrived before her, she had not taken her eyes off him, either.

Both Shadow Fairies shoved Mor back at once. His feet shuffled a step off balance, but he kept his gaze locked on her, his expression saying, *"Don't do it."*

At first, the human appeared too afraid to heed his advice. But there was a look in her eye—a resilience Mor had not seen in a single war fairy he'd spent the last faeborn years fighting alongside.

The human dropped the sugar blossom to the floor. She stomped on it with the wrath of the sky deities, crushing the petals beneath her shell-covered feet. Mor breathed a sigh of relief until her green gaze sliced up

237

and locked back onto his. She uttered two words. Two pleading words that sailed through the wickedness of the air and landed inside Mor's ears:

"Save me," she said.

She was grabbed by a multitude of fairy hands. A Shadow Fairy stuffed a handful of blossoms into her mouth while another held her still and pried open her lips for more. And something deep inside Mor, a doomed monster that had been hiding since the day he'd been recruited to fight for the Shadows, *snapped.*

He found his faeborn hand around a Shadow Fairy's throat. He found bones snapping beneath his strength. He found his fairsaber blades plunged through bodies. He found a barrel of fire kicked over at his feet. He found the banquet tables set ablaze before him. He found a trail of lifeless Shadow Fairy bodies tossed to the floor, flung over the tables, and smashed against the walls in his wake.

He hardly knew he'd done it all himself until the cool night breeze washed over him on his way out of the cave. The human girl's hand was in his.

The entire cave was on fire behind them.

The human girl asked a dozen questions that Mor didn't answer.

"Are you evil? You don't seem evil."

"Are you going to send me back home?"

"Are you a vampire or an elf?" She'd eyed his ears.

"Is this place sort of like Neverland in Peter Pan?"

Mor led her to a pauper fairy and paid every coin he had on him for the fairy to take the girl back to the human world and erase her memories of this dreadful place. He prayed to the sky deities that the pauper would keep his word.

It took Mor three weeks to catch enough whispers of the Dark Rebel

Movement to track them down. For months, he fought alongside the rebels against the Shadow Army, guarding the village borders, right up until the Shadow Army declared war on the peaceful, unguarded South Corner of Ever. The North had rushed to the South's aid, but not before many small-self fairies had been killed.

It was upon the grassy fields of the South Corner, while the North Army was attempting to drive the Dark back into its corner, that Mor crossed a young, legendary fae Prince named Cressica Alabastian on the battlefield; a fairy who was powerful enough to burn entire plains to ash, shoot himself into the sky like a bird, and turn his body to faestone when he wished, striking terror into the hearts of all who heard of him.

CHAPTER

32

Luc Zelsor and the Week His Father Took Him

"I want you to take in a ward," Luc said to his mother as he sat back in his father's throne with folded arms. He was only half his mother's size, his voice young and high. No one else was in the cold throne room while Luc's mother offered a tribute of wreathes to the sky deities. She hung one on the back of each throne.

"Why is that, Luc? Won't you be jealous if I give you a brother or sister?" his mother asked. Her mouth moved in silence as she counted the chairs.

Luc pulled his legs up on the large seat to cross them. "Not a sister— that would be useless. I want a brother." He scratched his chin as he thought it through. "I want a brother who isn't afraid of anything."

"That's strange." His mother pushed her pale hair behind her pointed ear and lifted the brightest wreath of all to hang upon the back of the Dark Queene's ceremony throne. "Why would you ever ask me for such a thing?" she asked. She pulled the next wreath out and studied its thorny black rose stems.

Luc looked down and twisted the laces of his boots. "All the other childling males are afraid of me."

His mother lowered the wreath, finally looking at him. She released a chuckle as she came over and patted him on the head, scuffing his ruby hair. "You're a fox, Luc. That's nothing to be afraid of. Besides, you have the power to make them like you, don't you? I thought foxes could lure others in. If you pull them in and show some kindness, they will like you as I do."

Luc released a large sigh and folded his arms again. "I don't know how to be kind. And father wants me to be cruel."

His mother's light laugh drifted through the throne room as she went back to her wreathes. "So be cruel to others when you're with him and be kind to others when you're with me. I will teach you kindness."

Luc glanced toward the tall murky windows. The cloud of torment raged in the sky above the palace, ever swirling, ever restless. He thought of what his father would do if he ever caught Luc being *kind.*

A day later, Luc's father returned to the palace with a deep frown and a look in his eyes that made the palace fairies stay far out of his way. High Prince Reval slammed his chamber door shut, trapping Luc's mother in the room with him. Luc waited in the hallway, sure they did not realize he was out there. He turned and pressed his thin ear against the door to listen. His stomach dropped when he learned his father meant to cast his mother out—out of the palace, out of the capitol, out of the Dark Corner of Ever. His father did not even give a reason why.

"I'll only leave if I can take Luc," his mother's voice sailed through the door, and Luc went still, his thoughts falling away until his mind was empty and listening and waiting and desperate. He pressed a hand against the door, imagining he was reaching for his mother through it.

But everything that followed was unexpected.

Luc did not expect his mother to make a bold bet to win him so he could leave with her.

He did not expect his father to agree.

But most of all... In the day that followed, he did not expect his mother to lose the bet.

He did not expect to have to watch his mother walk away from the palace with a straw basket of her belongings and a black rose wreath upon her head.

But what Luc did not expect the most was to be trapped with Prince Reval forever. To forever be cruel, instead of liked.

33

Violet Miller and the Present

Violet awoke in a comfortable bed surrounded by the smells of fresh coffee and sugary baking. Her chest ached and she brought up a slow hand, pressing it over her heart. Her first thought was of Mor—the look on his face before she'd passed out. The wideness of his eyes, the surprise, the fear. It was the last thing she'd seen. Something had happened to Mor when he'd tried to find her memories.

Her second thought was of the bizarre dream she'd just had. She was sure it was a dream because none of it made sense. She'd dreamt of a place with strange, vivid sights; potent, syrupy smells; and sweet, unfamiliar foods.

Violet pressed her hand harder into her chest, fighting to take in full breaths.

A young woman walked by the open bedroom door, and Violet sat up too quickly. Her head spun, and she moaned, making the woman stop and come back to the door.

"Finally," the woman said and folded a set of tattoo-covered arms.

Violet blinked up at her, trying to place where she'd seen her before. It hit her as soon as she pictured the blonde woman in a fitted police uniform. "You're that cop!" Lily Baker—that was her name.

"Save it," Lily Baker said. "There are weirder things to worry about right now. Trust me."

The officer disappeared from the doorway and came back a second later with a steaming mug of coffee. She extended it to Violet. Violet stared at the drink for a moment. Then she glanced around at her immediate surroundings to see if Mor had left a note to tell her what had happened.

She realized she was in a small apartment with pink bedsheets over her legs. A window was cracked open to let a breeze in. She spotted her phone resting on the nightstand, but there was no note anywhere. Not even a clue Mor had been here.

Violet wasn't prepared for hot, angry tears to fill her eyes, or for her hands to start shaking.

"Take your time. What you've been through so far is pretty unreal," Lily said, holding the coffee steady. "Getting preyed upon by that Shadow Fairy and everything."

Violet inhaled sharply. "Officer..." Her voice came out raw. She swallowed.

Lily gave up and set the coffee down on the nightstand. "Yeah?"

"You're friends with Mor, right?" Violet dragged her watery eyes up to the policewoman.

Mor.

No, Violet could not think about him right now. She had to push him far out of her mind. He'd cut ties with her, then dropped her off to wake up without him, and he hadn't left a note. But still, she wanted to ask. "Did he say anything when he left me here?"

Lily folded her arms and tapped a finger against her bicep. "He said a few things," she admitted, though it didn't seem like she was planning to spill those *things.*

"You need to leave me alone."

It seemed Mor had said everything he needed to say to Violet.

"He's really done with me," she realized. "I didn't think he'd actually go through with it." How cruel of him. He could have at least left a note after the way he'd looked at her the second before she'd fainted.

Lily sighed. "Mor said you might ask me some strange questions." She dragged a chair over from the corner of the bedroom and sat down, then she pulled out a notebook, flipped to a new page, and clicked the back of a pen. "Tell me everything that's happened so far with that Shadow Fairy. I promise I'll believe you."

Violet swallowed the lump in her throat and shook her head. "I can't."

Lily tapped her foot against the floor. After a moment, she nodded. "You don't know me yet. I get it." She tucked the notebook away, slid the coffee off the nightstand, and tried handing it to Violet again. "Drink this. It'll make you feel better. Though, I should warn you that it's totally enchanted, so you'll desperately want to come back here for more over the next few days."

Violet reluctantly took the coffee, and Lily stood to leave.

"My aunt," Violet blurted after her. "Her name is Zorah Miller. Please keep an eye on her."

Lily paused by a bathroom door, a sympathetic look crossing her face. "I know your story. It's seriously the worst that you've had to go through all this. If you need any help, you can always find me here or at the station," she said. "I'll sit outside your aunt's house in the squad car today if that'll make you feel better."

The moment the bathroom door was shut with Lily inside it, Violet set down her coffee, grabbed her phone off the nightstand, and dialed the interns. She bit her nails as she waited for the call to go through. Remi picked up on the second ring.

"Hang on," Violet said, dialing Jase next to form a three-way call.

"Hello?" Jase's voice filled her ear.

"I need you two to meet me back at the cathedral. I don't know what Mor said to you, but this is *not* over. We're going to write this story. The world needs to know about the fairies." And their heartless tactics. How they could give false hope and abandon people all in the same breath.

Lily came out of the bathroom in her uniform and Violet hung up the phone. She tucked it away and climbed out of bed, looking around at the small apartment with a tiny kitchenette as she came out of the bedroom. Bar stools lined a short island that was covered in tiny piles of trinkets—coins, marbles, pens, straws, and other random objects. Violet recognized some of the pens from Mor's cathedral office.

There were also personal belongings strewn everywhere like many people were living in this space.

"You can stay up here if you want to be alone, or you can come down if you want to be around other people. Just don't leave the building or you might get whacked with a macaron," Lily said, leading the way to a stairwell.

Violet followed, overcome with the sounds of cutlery and chatter in the stairwell. At the bottom, she found herself in the café—the one she'd been in last time. Coffee drinkers were scattered around the tables, some chatting in pairs, and others reading novels by the fireplace as they sipped iced lattes. A bookshelf was behind the counter and Violet wandered over to it. She hadn't noticed the books in Fae Café before. Some of them were scuffed like they'd been read a hundred times.

A loud *smack* sounded through the shop, and a few customers jumped. Violet turned toward the noise, spotting Shayne's white hair through the window. He stood on the sidewalk outside, his arm winding back with a muffin in his grip. It looked like he was about to hurl it at the Yarn & Stitch store across the street.

Violet rushed through the café and pushed out the door, knocking it off a small bell. "Wait!" she shouted at Shayne.

He paused, mid-throw. He looked surprised to see Violet there.

A pink pastry fell out of the sky and pelted Violet on the cheek. "Ugh!" She whirled at the impact. When she pulled her hand away from her face, her fingers were sticky with icing.

Shayne grinned. "That's what you get for getting involved," he said.

"Involved in what? And Shayne, why are you doing this? One of those women is dying because of me," Violet objected, wiping the icing from her cheek with her sleeve. She looked up at the clouds, wondering where the pastry had even come from.

Shayne snorted. "Of course she is, Human. That's why they're mad!" He carried on with his throw, hurtling the muffin at the Yarn & Stitch window. It splattered into three pieces against the glass. Across the road, a girl in yarn clothing with big curly hair and bug-eye glasses gasped and cast Shayne a horrifying death look. Four women from the Yarn & Stitch were outside in total—one of them held a basket of macarons. The others reached into the basket and threw the desserts back at Fae Café.

Shayne sprang over to Violet and yanked her out of the crossfire, nudging her back into the café ahead of him. He shook crumbs out of his hair as he came in. Then he declared to the room, "I'm tapping out."

Dranian nodded from the counter. He removed his apron and walked by without a word, grabbing a tray of pudding cups on his way out to the street. Violet watched as Dranian started throwing them at the knit-covered women, splattering the bug-eyed glasses girl right in the mouth.

"How long has this food fight been going on?" Violet asked, eyeing the tea stains and spongy macaron splatters smearing the windows.

"It'll end soon. It's going to rain any minute. They'll give up and go inside to save their ugly knitted vests." Shayne dragged a half-empty coffee to himself and sipped.

"Who's going to clean all that up?" Violet asked.

"Oh, we will—Dranian and I. We don't have a choice. Kate was our master a while back, and she told us we had to clean up the messes we make here. Though, technically she let us off the hook, but we like to pretend she didn't." Shayne headed to the counter, and Violet followed. "Anything to drink, Human?" he asked her, and Violet shook her head.

By the café door, Lily tugged on her police vest. She pushed the door open a crack and yelled, "Coming out!"

All the fairies on both sides of the road paused, lowering their arms and their dessert ammunition. Lily walked down the sidewalk, nodding 'good morning' to one of the gaping neighbours as she passed. The second she was out of range, the macarons and pudding began flying again. "I don't get it. Why all the hatred between you and the knitting store?" Violet asked.

"Oh, this is nothing. You should have seen the snowball fight we started with them back in February when they first moved in across the road." Shayne drank his coffee again. When Violet brought her attention back to him, she saw he was eyeing her over the mug. He licked his lips and sat on the nearest barstool, turning to face her and patting the stool beside so she'd sit too. He started talking before Violet was seated. "Are you all right, Human? And what exactly happened to Mor?"

Violet cringed at the mention of his name, trying to push thoughts of Mor away. "I don't know," she lied, turning to face the counter. "Are you actually concerned about me? Or are you really just making conversation to learn about Mor?"

Shayne shrugged and ripped a paper towel from the roll by the sink. He handed it to her and nodded to the drying icing on her cheeks. Violet accepted it and began scrubbing.

"Maybe a little of both," Shayne said.

Dranian took a macaron right in the nose outside. He growled a slew of unusual curses so loudly that everyone could hear it through the windows. Violet wondered why the customers weren't weirded out by the catastrophic food fight outside, but maybe the regulars were used to it.

"Where is Mor?" she finally asked flat out, hating herself for caring. "Why isn't he here?"

Shayne shook his head and looked down at his coffee. "Apologies, Human, but Mor made it clear he didn't want me to tell you anything— not that I know anything important. I'm surprised he even brought you back here again after what happened last time, even though I told him already that it wasn't my fault." He drank the last gulps of his coffee, then scowled. "It seems like no one around here even respects the opinions of a High King."

Violet chewed on her lip. She wrang her fingers together and kicked the underside of the counter island. "I remember something," she said. "About my past."

"Oh? And what's that?" Shayne turned away and reached for the coffee pot. He poured himself another full drink and began scooping in *heaps* of sugar. He finished it off with enough milk to turn the coffee beige.

The memory flooded in with wisps of colours, sounds, and smells, and Violet's mouth went dry. "I remember being harassed by people who look like you and Mor. With sharp ears," she whispered.

Shayne slowed his coffee stirring, the spoon dangling from his frozen fingers.

"I remember being in a strange place with gold fruit and a bright green lake," she added.

Shayne dropped the spoon against the rim of the mug. He twisted on the stool to face her.

"I was dragged into a black cave and told to eat flowers. They wanted me to dance to weird music—"

"Siren song," Shayne whispered, more to himself, like he was reliving a memory of his own from long ago.

Violet sat up straighter. "You know where I'm talking about?" It was a plea. She couldn't decide if she was relieved or terrified that the place from her dream existed.

Shayne slowly nudged his coffee away like his thirst had died. "No wonder Mor seemed so strange." He scratched his chin. Suddenly, he slapped a hand over his eyes and moaned. "This isn't good, Human," he said.

Violet sank into her seat. "What isn't?" She hadn't even told Shayne the worst part yet.

"This is the exact sort of situation that will destroy Mor. I'm worried he's just made avenging you his priority if he knows you were harmed by fairy folk like that."

"Avenge... *me*?" she rasped. "I doubt it."

"I'm relieved you're leaving so you can stop getting in my way."

Shayne lazily dropped a flat hand onto the counter. "Mor was right. I should have sent you to the Sisterhood as soon as you woke up like he asked. I can't stay here and protect you, Human," he said.

"What?" Dismay sank through Violet's stomach. "You're going to kick me out, too?"

Shayne flashed a dull smirk. "Never." He stood and tugged her sleeve to pull her up with him. "But Mor is vulnerable, and that fox is likely going to use your past to rattle and trap him. I have to go help Cress and Mor. My brothers need me." He guided her through the café and out the door.

Pudding splashed through the air outside in an arc. Shayne batted a macaron out of the way before it could hit him as he walked past Dranian. He pulled Violet across the road, right up to the Yarn & Stitch front door. He respectfully stepped aside to let a fairy woman pass with a fresh basket of desserts that were certainly meant to be used as ammo against Dranian.

"Here," Shayne said to the knitters. He nudged Violet toward them, and Violet looked back at him in question. "You need to take her. I have other things to do."

One of the women sat on the front step, blowing a bubble with her gum and watching the dessert battle while she knitted. She snorted. "What are we supposed to do with a human—"

Freida pushed out the front entrance, the door slapping the opposite wall from being opened aggressively. "Come in, Violet Miller," she said.

Violet looked from Freida to Shayne. Shayne extended a hand toward the Yarn & Stitch like her next step should be obvious. She didn't know how to tell him that she was meeting her interns at the cathedral and needed to leave immediately.

Violet slowly walked to Freida, who put an arm around her and brought her inside. She didn't have a chance to look back at Shayne again before the door swung shut behind them. "Don't get any ideas," the old woman said. "The moment you step out of here, you'll be taken by that nine tailed fox. He's watching you, you know."

Violet swallowed. She patted her pocket for her phone so she could call the interns who were likely already on their way to meet her at the cathedral. Maybe she could tell them to meet her at the Yarn & Stitch instead. But her hand stopped over her flat pockets. She held back a moan as she realized her phone was still in the apartment where she'd met Officer Baker.

She had to get out of here. She had to reach the interns. Now that she knew exactly who the serial-attacker was, she had to finish her story.

Gretchen lay across the coffee table in the same spot Violet had last seen her. The fairy woman's eyes were closed, her limbs hanging limp. No wonder the knitters were mad at the baristas. They were probably the maddest at Mor.

Maybe they were mad at Violet, too, since she was the one Gretchen had been defending when Luc had stabbed her.

Violet moved in and sat by the table, taking Gretchen's hand. "I'm so sorry," she whispered, even though she had no idea if Gretchen could hear. "I hate myself today," she added. "For so many reasons."

Freida went to an end table and poured a hot cup of tea. She added a few pinches of powder from bowls on the table and a large leaf. "Nonsense, Violet Miller. You only hate what others have told you about yourself. You are just fine the way you are." She brought the tea over and set it on the coffee table. Violet stared at the antique teacup but didn't touch it. "Drink this," Freida instructed. "It will help with your stomach-ache, and I imagine it may also clear away some of your mind fog."

"You don't understand," Violet said, ignoring the fact that Freida somehow mystically knew her medical condition. Her throat constricted as she turned toward the old woman to admit the one terrible thing she hadn't even been able to tell Shayne. "I blamed the universe for making me wake up with no memory of who I was," Violet rasped. She wished she'd never let Mor try and find her past. She wished she'd never wanted to know in the first place. "But it was me who wanted to forget. I made a deal with a fairy. I did this to myself."

Rain began to pelt the windows, and sure enough, the knitting store members trickled back inside, swatting the raindrops off their knit vests and sweaters.

Freida rested her teacup on the saucer and came to sit on one of the couches. "You're an odd one, Human. You did this to yourself, and yet, you believe your assassin is out there getting revenge on your behalf because he thinks you were taken advantage of? Are you quite sure that's what he believes?"

"I *was* taken advantage of!" Violet said, though again, she had no idea how Freida had known what she was thinking. It was like the old woman could read minds. "I was thirteen years old, and I was taken to a weird land of fairies and harassed! Trust me, if a guy tried to kidnap me now, I'd kick him in *an area* that would cause him pain. But I was young and didn't know any better back then."

Freida cackled. "*An area,* you say." She wiped an escaped tear from the corner of her eye as her laughter rang through the store. "I think I like you, Violet Miller. If I was still a recruiter for the Sisterhood of Assassins, I might have tried to bribe you to join us." She sat back and sipped her tea. "But watch your mouth in here," she added as the rest of the women found spots on the couches and pulled out their knitting. "We're not supposed to speak of anything of the magic or faeborn sort at the moment." She nodded toward a video camera in the corner of the store but didn't explain what it was or why it was there.

Violet looked back at Gretchen. It seemed like the red-haired fairy wasn't breathing, but her eyes moved behind her eyelids. "I wish I could stay with her until she wakes up, but I have somewhere to be," Violet said.

"No point in staying by her side, Violet Miller," Freida said. "She's in a fairy coma. She's likely dreaming of pretty green seas and whistle flowers. I don't think she'll want to come back. She may stay that way forever." Something sank in Violet's stomach. "However…" Freida set down her tea and folded her aged hands. "You shouldn't try to leave. As I said, you're being watched."

"I told my interns to meet me at the cathedral," Violet admitted. "They're probably almost there already. I need to go stop them so they don't get into danger, and we need to write our story." She glanced off toward the pudding-covered Yarn & Stitch windows. "Even if Mor has left me for good."

Freida stared at Violet for several moments. Finally, she leaned back against the couch, snuggling in and pulling a ball of ivory yarn from an end table.

"Mor Trisencor is someone you should forget, Violet Miller," she began. "That fae is a gifted, dangerous Shadow Fairy who was not only trained by the Shadows but also by the vicious North Brotherhood of Assassins." Freida looked Violet dead in the eyes, then added, "But he is absolutely in over his head. He will die soon. And likely, he will die terribly."

Violet stood, her knee bumping the side of the coffee table as she did. "What do you mean?" Her breathing staggered. "He... He knows what he's doing, and he's got his brothers..." It came out like a plea instead of a question.

Freida sighed. "Do not defend him, Human. He severed you from his faeborn life and wishes to never see you again. He is not worth your worry. Now, let me teach you how to knit." She pulled a lob of yarn off the table and lifted two fresh needles. "It's always beneficial to know the ways of the yarn."

Violet looked toward the door where rain began pelting against the glass, thinking of things beyond yarn and needles.

CHAPTER

34

Mor Trisencor and the Museum of Shadows

The sky growled, spitting water and fog over the downtown streets and ushering humans indoors. A handful of watchful people still carried on in the rain, scrambling for their umbrellas or pulling up their hoods. Pools of water dotted the roads, dark and cold in front of the Museum of Ancient Egypt. Several humans who looked toward the museum screamed and raced for cover.

Two Shadow Fairies waged war upon the front stairs.

Purplish fairy blood leaked into the crevices of Mor's hands beneath his fairsaber handles. He blocked Luc's right saber and kicked for the fairy's knees, but Luc swiped his free blade across Mor's kneecap, and Mor released a growl as a spray of his blood painted Luc's rainwater-drenched summer shirt.

Neither fairy wore a dandelion coat. They'd raced across the city toward each other, fairsabers out. This was the end, and it seemed they both knew it.

The large, wooden front doors of the museum burst open. Cress marched out, shouting, "Stop airslipping away from me, you fools!" He swung his sword, locking it against one of the fox's blades. Mor stabbed at Luc's lower sections, his sword brushing the fox's hip before Luc vanished back into the air and appeared behind Cress.

Mor punched his blade over Cress's shoulder, narrowly missing Luc who airslipped again, leaving Mor and Cress alone on the museum stairs.

Cress tilted his ear toward the wind. He did a full turn, then he shot up into the heavens like an arrow. Mor gaped, watching as Cress snatched at something in the sky. Luc reappeared—half strangled in Cress's grip. Cress threw the Shadow Fairy down toward Mor, and Mor raised his fairsaber, ready to deal a lethal hit.

Luc caught his senses during his fall and vanished. Mor raced into the wind after him, channeling over fog and rain, following Luc across three streets in a heartbeat.

Mor leapt out of the airslip, pinning Luc against a street lantern. The stem of the lantern bent from the impact, and the light flickered above. Luc kicked Mor back a step and slashed the air, barely missing Mor's throat. He marched after Mor, grabbing his collar.

Mor was tossed back against the lantern post this time. The light finally went out, blanketing the two Shadow Fairies in rainy dimness.

Why her? They were the two words burning through Mor's mind with each swing he dealt and hit he took. He gritted his teeth, timing his wild rhythms. He ducked just before Luc's fairsaber struck the lantern post and carved into the metal where Mor's head had just been.

Mor snatched Luc's ankle and tore him back into the air, rushing fast through the city as Luc fought to regain his balance. Luc punched his blade forward, catching Mor in the side with a shallow cut, and he ripped himself from Mor's grip as they landed in the lobby of the dark museum that one sign claimed was closed for renovations. Luc rolled over the tile floor, and Mor skidded to a stop on one knee.

Luc laughed, uncurling himself to lay flat on his back. "Have you had enough yet, Trisencor?" he asked.

Mor stood in the light spilling in from the open entrance doors. He tightened his grip on his fairsabers and marched to stand over the nine tailed fox. "Never," he stated.

"Good."

Luc vanished and appeared standing before him "Me neither," he said.

Their fairsabers collided, sending a sharp, metallic ring through the empty museum. Thunder howled outside, muting the next three swings and blocks. When the sky deities stopped roaring, the sound of someone sighing loudly came from a large, historic Egyptian throne at the far end of the room. A small sign said: NO CLIMBING ON DISPLAY. But it seemed Cress didn't care for human rules.

"You two took forever to come back," he remarked from where he was draped sideways over the oversized throne, his head laid back against the armrest, his legs crossed like he'd been napping for the three seconds Mor had been gone.

Cress pointed with his fairsaber at a picture across the room depicting a human female with an elongated skull from a distant kingdom called *Ancient Egypt*. "Look at that, Mor. There are humans with weird heads."

Luc smacked Mor's left fairsaber from his grip. Mor's blade tumbled over the floor, sliding until it hit the base of the display where the Prince of the North lounged. Mor tried desperately not to shout at Cress and point out that it was *Cress* who wanted to help—a thing the Prince seemed to have forgotten during his marvelling at human paintings.

Luc raised his blade toward Mor's throat and held it steady there before Mor could lift his right sword in defense. Mor swallowed, his neck grazing the sharp end of the Shadow sword. He couldn't even speak to ask the sky deities why in the faeborn cursed world he'd bothered to bring Cress along.

Cress dropped from the sky like a boulder.

Luc yelped as he was pummeled into the floor, his chest crushed beneath the weight of Cress's knee, his fairsabers clanging away. "You fool," Cress said to him. "You came to my café and threatened my High Court. I will enjoy killing you over and over."

Cress didn't hesitate. He stabbed Luc—straight and true—and though it should have been a sweet relief to Mor's eyes, something tightened in his stomach at the sight. An old memory rushed in of the last time he had watched this same fox die in front of him. Mor shook the thought away as he witnessed Luc take his last breath, as the fairy's ruby-haired head relaxed against the tile.

Cress stood and brushed a bead of sweat from his brow. "Queensbane, this fox is as faeborn tough as you said. But don't worry, he's still no match for me," he remarked. He walked across the lobby toward a human drinking fountain. After a few seconds of deliberation, Cress pressed a button on its side and a spout of water came out. The Prince ducked his face in and out of the stream a few times, grappling at the flying water with his lips before he finally figured out how to get some into his mouth.

Mor stood by Luc. Waiting.

The necklace of fox tails at Luc's throat shivered. One of them disintegrated, leaving seven behind.

A second passed before the colour returned to Luc's face. But the fool didn't open his eyes or strike or vanish, even when the wound in his chest closed and the fairy blood dried up. The faint movement of his lips was the only indication he was back.

"Bravo," Luc said, eyes closed. "Bravo, Trisencor. It seems you beat me for the first time."

Mor angled his blade so the tip was at Luc's throat. "All the things you've done to me... You'll pay for them now," he said.

Luc's slow smile spread over his face. "All the things I've done," he said quietly. His eyes slid open; he focused on the curved museum ceiling. "Your problem, Trisencor, is that you think everything is about you." He licked a spot of blood off his lips then turned his head and spat it out. "Do you know how long it took for me to convince the commanders to let me come here?" Luc asked. "How much talking, how much luring, how much baiting and convincing before I had the commanders wrapped around my finger at last?" The sound of the drinking fountain ceased, and Mor guessed Cress was coming back. But Mor couldn't take his stare off the nine tailed fox. "I never came here for you," Luc said. "I came here for something else. It was just by the meddling of the sky deities that I happened to see you and..." The fairy worked his jaw, his lips tightening, anger flashing over his silvery eyes. Quiet *popping* sounds filled the museum, like Cress was making noises with his lips on the other side of the room after his drink.

"And *her*," Luc finished.

Her.

Mor's mouth parted, the realization settling into place that Luc knew who Violet was.

"I recognized the old fairy scents upon her when she and I first met, but it took a few tries to establish exactly where those old scents came from. I'm ashamed I didn't figure out sooner that she was the same human from that day." Luc lifted a hand and delicately touched his freshly healed chest.

Mor blinked. "How did you find out?" he asked in a monotone voice—determined not to allow Luc the luxury of believing Mor was even the slightest bit interested. "When she has no memories of those things?"

Luc laughed from the floor; a coarse, bellowing sound that echoed over the wide space and bounced off the walls. "I wasn't after her memories," he promised. "But I was after *her*. And the beauty of it all is that our dear Violet thinks you'll keep her safe from me," he said, rolling up to sit and climbing to his feet. When he was eye-to-eye with Mor, he added, "You won't. I would very much like her to suffer for a long time, and then die."

Mor swung his fairsaber, but Luc grabbed Mor's wrist and held his arm in place. "Oh dear," he said, stealing a glance past Mor. "I don't think you want to bother me anymore, Trisencor. Or the next sound you hear will be your North Prince screaming through a deathblow."

Mor's face grew puzzled. He whirled to find Cress, his stomach dropping at the sight of Cress surrounded by two dozen Shadow Fairies,

258

armed and cloaked with dark iridescent shell plates of armour. It was a sight from Mor's childling days he thought he would never see again: His own division of the Shadow Army, wearing the colours he wore, holding the same swords he held in his own grip now.

Cress's fairsaber hadn't been torn from his hand, but he didn't dare move it. He stared across the museum at Mor with cold, turquoise eyes, saying only one thing in the tone of his expression: *"The fox wasn't lying about the Shadow Army being here."*

Luc stretched, working his arms, hands, and his fingers as though he was coming back to himself after being slain. He tilted his neck back and forth and smiled as he dragged his ruby from his pocket. The fox rolled the gem over his fingers and walked past Mor to where Cress was surrounded. He settled his dark gaze on the Prince of the North. "I warned you, Prince, didn't I? If we both kill each other once, I'll still be here, and you won't," he said.

Mor's hand tightened around the one fairsaber he had left. He tried to calculate his odds of successfully snatching Cress into an airslip and outrunning the Army through the wind.

Luc called back to Mor, "I wonder what secrets your Prince is hiding, Trisencor?" He held up his ruby in the muddied light from the doors. "Do you think he knows the hidden passages into Queene Levress' Silver Castle? Do you think he knows the weaknesses of the North Brotherhood of Assassins? I'd love the opportunity to destroy both." Luc paused before he spoke again. "Do you think he knows where our dear Violet is hiding?"

Luc shoved the ruby in his mouth and grabbed Cress's temples, sending Mor springing a step forward. He halted when the Shadows threatened to stab Cress through the neck. Cress's flesh tightened, but he didn't fight back.

"Luc…" Mor tried. *"Luc."* He said it again, darkly.

Luc frowned, and then nodded and dropped his hands from Cress's temples. "I suppose it was wishful thinking. I rarely get the secret I want on the first try." He lowered his voice to say quietly to Cress, "Shame on you for hiding all those cookies from your friends. But I imagine one of them will find your stash in the bottom of the freezer soon." Luc dug his ruby out of his mouth, and Cress glared.

It took a full second for Mor to realize what Luc had said.

"Secrets?" Mor growled when it dawned on him. "Secrets?! That's what you've been stealing?" He could hardly believe it. "You've been luring in human females and stealing their *secrets*? For what, Luc?! What do you need human secrets for?"

"Did you know I stole Violet's secrets exactly seven times before I got the one I wanted?" Luc disregarded the question and turned to Mor with one of his own. "Do you want to know what her greatest secrets are, Trisencor?"

Mor felt his last bit of life drain from him. He backed up a step, bringing his fairsaber up between them. "No."

"Yes, you do." Luc smiled, beautiful and broad. "The first secret— the one I stole from her at that bus shelter—was that once, she hated her life so much she wanted to forget it. How interesting is that? And why was it a secret?" He paced and tapped his chin in feign wonder.

"Vanish, Mor," Cress instructed from where he stood with blades at his neck. "He is trying to lure you in."

Luc chuckled. "Nonsense, Prince Cressica. Trisencor isn't affected by the lure of foxes. He's proven that enough times."

"What are you talking about?" Mor gritted out, and Luc looked at him doubtfully as if to ask, *"Do you really not know?"*

Mor blinked.

Luc released an annoyed sound like it pained him to have to explain. "I never had to force *you* to like me, Trisencor. You were never afraid of me to begin with," he said aloud, and there was a certain tone in the statement that left a ringing sound in the back of Mor's mind.

Luc worked his jaw with a look Mor couldn't read. After a moment, he turned away. "The second of Violet's secrets was that she was lying to her aunt about her job. The few after that were also a bunch of boring human nonsense I added to my collection. But after a while I discovered a secret I found interesting. You see, ten years ago, Violet made a deal with a pauper fairy to get rid of her memories. *All* of them. This was a secret she didn't even know or remember she had. Isn't that fascinating?" Luc went on. "And then I thought, 'Ten years ago... I wonder if by some miracle of the sky deities she could be that same human girl?' Because call me crazy, I thought she sort of looked like the human from that day. And once I noticed it, I could not unsee it."

Mor's voice shook. "Luc. Your war is with me, not with a human—"

"This was the secret that gave it away for me," Luc went on. "The one that told me she was in fact the human who you abandoned the Shadows for."

Mor looked over at Cress standing perfectly still. Cress seemed to have no reaction to the news, but he twisted his fairsaber in his grip like he was ready to turn and fight his way out.

Luc's face curved into a snarl. "But there was one more secret that I found the most interesting of all."

"Don't tell me," Mor said as his rhythms began to hammer.

"She's in love with you." Luc said it anyway, and Mor closed his eyes, trying to steady his breathing. "That was her greatest secret. That she was falling in love with her fated-to-suffer, very ruined boss."

The sound of Luc's footsteps stopped in front of Mor. When Mor opened his eyes, he saw revulsion in Luc's gaze. "And if I didn't know any better, I'd guess that flittering thudding in your chest is a sure sign of a fairy crush."

Why her? The words came back in full swing.

Why was Violet the same human girl that had sent him into such a frenzy on his way out of the Shadow Army? Mor's heart wasn't only breaking imagining Violet in that situation, it was aching, angry, set ablaze and feeling the weight of that horrid day all over again since the moment he'd first laid eyes on the human.

"Your war isn't with Violet," Mor stated again, clear and steady. "It wasn't her that made me turn on the Army."

261

Luc raised a brow in question, and Mor's gaze slid across the room to Cress, indicating it was time.

Then Mor said, "I was going to leave the Shadow Army anyway."

Cress turned and swung at the Shadows

Mor stabbed toward Luc—

His fairsaber sailed through empty air.

Luc was nowhere in sight. And Mor would have followed him, but he couldn't leave Cress alone to take on the Shadow Army division alone. The division of Mor's past who had finally returned for him.

35

Violet Miller and the Never-Ending Kiss Attacks

The Yarn & Stitch smelled like freshly brewed tea and the muggy moisture from outside seeping in through the cracks. There was no shortage of teapots—they were all around the store wherever they could fit; tucked into shelves around yarn supplies, stacked beneath the front window, spread evenly over the checkout counter...

Violet wasn't sure what anyone could possibly do with so many teapots.

The rain finally died down. Violet hadn't been able to stop thinking about her interns for a second over the last hour. She imagined they were at the cathedral, either waiting outside in the downpour, or if the magic of the temperamental cathedral front doors was feeling nice today, maybe the interns had managed to get inside. They were probably trying to call her on the phone she didn't have. Probably wondering why both days they'd shown up for work so far had been weird.

But more than that, she worried about Mor. Shame on her for it—she couldn't shake off what Freida had said. *"...he is absolutely in over his head. He will die soon. And likely, he will die terribly."*

She could barely breathe past the ache in her chest. She'd never felt more helpless, more angry. More desperate to run into a dangerous situation she didn't belong in, where no one wanted her.

Violet sat at the coffee table picking at a macaron, dissecting its fluff and icing. Her plate was on the corner of the table—the only space left that wasn't being occupied by Gretchen's sprawled body. Violet wondered why the knitters didn't put Gretchen on a bed somewhere. It seemed mean to leave her out in the open like this. The woman's mouth was hanging open and everything.

Every few seconds, Violet looked back at the front door. There never seemed to be a decent time to try and sneak out, and even if she did, she had a feeling these women took their job of guardians seriously. She'd probably be followed and dragged back.

She wouldn't go running to Mor, even if she was worried. She just wanted to meet her interns.

Violet sighed, rubbing her tense forehead. There were only so many conversations she could listen to about "Glenda" from the moped place who wouldn't give the knitting club a deal on mopeds, and the newest in-trend knitting pattern, and how long it would take the "barista-assassins" across the road to get fat from all the pudding they eat, and how much longer until Kate Kole's wedding.

Violet dug her fingers into her hair. She couldn't take it anymore. She stood and turned all in one motion. "Freida, I'm sorry, but I can't—"

Violet's words cut off; her vision filled with a mop of metallic-red hair. Luc stood over her, gazing down into her eyes, a strange wildness and anger on his face as he took her in.

One of the knitters screamed, and soon every fairy woman in the store scrambled for their needles. "Don't touch our human, Shadow Fairy!" one of the women snapped.

Luc cracked a small smile, indicating he intended to do just that.

Violet turned and grabbed the nearest teapot, holding it above her head to whack him with it. But she blanched when she spun back and found cold wind blowing an eerie shadow over the store. Luc kicked the couch to his left, and it struck the two closest women, tipping over and pinning them to the floor.

"I must take her." He said it almost apologetically. "So, feel free to try and stop me, Sisters."

Luc grabbed Violet by the waist and vanished.

Violet couldn't scream in the wind. She couldn't breathe, let alone make a sound as they swerved around smeared buildings and *through* things at warp speed.

The world finally formed around her as they came to a stop in an abandoned-looking street. Damp roads glistened beneath the sun breaking from behind the clouds, and tall buildings sheltered them on either side.

An arrow speared past Violet's shoulder, and she heard a thump.

Luc gasped.

His grip slid off her, and Violet slapped a hand over her mouth. She whirled as he fell flat upon the road, an arrow protruding from his chest. His inhales were ragged, his dark lashes fluttering until his eyes slid closed. It seemed he was no longer breathing. One of the silk fur pendants on his necklace shuddered and turned to dust before Violet's eyes, the twinkling hairs floating off in the breeze.

Shayne appeared at the end of the road, walking toward them with his crossbow raised, another arrow already loaded, and a satisfied smile across his face. He splashed through the puddles in his bare feet.

"Three down, six to go," he said.

But Luc's eyes flashed open.

Violet screamed and sprang back as Luc reached up and tore the arrow from his heart. He stood and yanked Violet to him, pinning her back against his bloody chest and forcing Shayne to stop walking. Dranian inched out of the nearest alley, spear raised, and came to Shayne's side.

Voilet was sure she could feel Luc's heart pounding against her back.

His breathing was heavier than before.

"Dear Violet." His voice was sweet and warmer than she expected, though there was a strange urgency he didn't have before. There was something in it that made her want to put her guard down, that same feeling she got the first time she met him like they were old, trusted friends. He reached around to nudge her face toward his. "Think of me beautifully for a moment." He pressed his mouth against hers, and Violet's heart doubled over. She tried to pull away from his kiss at first, but then...

Then...

Luc drew back slowly, the sun glowing behind his scarlet hair, making it burn like a bouquet of flaming gemstones. The silver in his eyes turned to vibrant crystals, gleaming and beckoning her to stare at them forever. She'd never loved a set of eyes so much—why hadn't she noticed them before?

"Violet." When Luc said her name, Violet felt warm all over. "Be my shield, would you, dearest? Take an arrow for me?" When he gifted her a smile, his face was perfection; soft, smooth skin, a heart-shaped mouth, and deep lashes unlike anything Violet had ever seen.

"Queensbane," Dranian muttered. "She's totally fallen for him like a weak-minded fool."

Luc turned Violet back toward Shayne and Dranian, holding her tight in front of him. "She has," he answered. "Luring in prey is what a fox does, didn't you know?"

"We've fairy trapped the street, Foxy," Shayne said to Luc. "There's only one place we discovered you frequent—and it's right here. It's you against the High Court of the Coffee Bean now."

Without warning, Dranian threw his spear. Violet screamed as it brushed past her cheek. Luc's hands disappeared from her waist—he reappeared behind Shayne. Dranian was already spinning, grabbing one of Shayne's fairsabers from his belt and stabbing toward Luc before Luc could swing at Shayne's back. Shayne bolted forward and grabbed Violet's hand, dragging her out of harm's way as Dranian and Luc swung swords.

Shayne placed Violet against the brick wall of the nearest building. He batted his eyelashes at her a little—it seemed forced. "Queensbane, Mor is going to kill me," he muttered. Seemingly out of nowhere, he leaned in and gave her a strong, swoon-worthy kiss. Violet gasped as he pulled himself off, leaving behind traces of warmth on her mouth. She blinked away all she'd felt for Luc a moment ago, and she stared at Shayne—at the pure diamond-white of his hair. At his crisp, blue eyes.

"Your hair is... luminous," she realized.

Shayne grinned. "I know." He stood a litter taller. "I knew you couldn't resist liking me a little, Human." He turned and shouted back at Luc, "You might be powerful, but I don't need fox magic to attract women!"

Luc threw Dranian down the road, sending the auburn-haired fairy rolling twice over. Shayne's smile dropped, and he spun back to Violet. "Violet," he said, and Violet stared, hanging onto his every word. "Run."

He pushed her toward the alley.

Violet found herself scampering away, but uneasiness grew inside of her with each step she took. She slowed to a stop, looking back at where Shayne raised his crossbow to block a fairsaber blow from Luc. And she realized she didn't want to leave. How could she leave Shayne when he was in trouble?

But he'd asked her to; it was what he wanted.

Violet almost turned away again when Shayne's deep cry boomed down the alley. Her flesh tightened—she gawked as Shayne was tossed to the pavement. In the same second, Dranian sprang over him to tackle Luc, and Luc disappeared into thin air. Dranian landed on the road with a thud.

Violet was grabbed. She shrieked as her body was turned. She faced Luc again—was kissed by him, *again*.

Suddenly she couldn't remember why she'd been so concerned about Shayne. She stared at Luc as his gaze flickered past her and took in the others. "Dearest Violet," he said. "Don't let him kiss you again." He seemed frustrated.

"I won't," she promised with all her might.

But a spear spiralled through the alley and split them apart—Luc pushed her away and the spear sailed between them. Luc reached into his pocket and drew out a small, sparkling red gemstone. Violet eyed it curiously. Trying to remember where she'd seen it before. He placed the gemstone into his mouth and turned to face the fairies moving down the alley toward him.

Shayne darted right while Dranian darted left.

Shayne went for Violet.

Dranian went for Luc.

Shayne reached her. He tried to kiss her, and she slapped him. "Violet," he said through his teeth like she was being unreasonable. He swatted her hands out of the way as she tried to keep him at bay. But in the end, he won. Shayne puckered up and smacked his fairy lips against hers. Violet stopped struggling, relaxing into his hold. When he released her, she forgot about Luc again.

Shayne grinned.

Dranian growled, an intense shout that boomed down the alley and made the hairs on Violet's arms stand on end. When she saw why, she screamed.

Luc's fairsaber protruded from Dranian's right arm, sprouting right out the bicep.

Luc dragged his wild gaze up to Shayne. "Not a step closer," he warned, and Shayne's bare feet went frozen to the ground. Luc's chest heaved—rage flashing behind his silvery eyes. "For the faeborn record, I didn't want to do this." He twisted the blade a little.

Dranian screeched, panting to catch his breath, and Shayne looked like he might scream, too.

"This is enchanted cold iron, fairy-mutt. That means this won't heal," Luc said to Dranian from a curled lip. "Now you're just a three-legged guard dog."

He tore the blade back out and Dranian roared.

Shayne charged, his fairsaber stabbing into the brick wall after Luc vanished, sending chunks of brick tumbling to the ground. Luc appeared at the end of the alley. He lifted the ruby off his tongue and placed it back in his pocket. Then he blew Violet a kiss and turned to walk away. No one chased after him.

Shayne dropped his weapons and crouched beside Dranian, his blue eyes watery with panic.

"I must kill him now. For my honour," Dranian rasped in anguish, clutching his useless arm to himself.

"You've lost your arm, you fool!" Shayne snarled. "Leave him to me." He grabbed his crossbow and whirled toward where Luc had gone. But when he jogged to the end of the alley and looked both ways, it seemed there was no sign of the nine tailed fox.

At least, that was how it appeared, until a cold hand grabbed Violet's arm and she was torn into speeding teleportation. A cruel voice breathed against her neck:

"I'm not finished with you yet, Violet."

CHAPTER

36

Mor Trisencor and the Day He Watched Luc Die for the First Time
Eleven Faeborn Years Ago

It was the week after Luc and Mor had gotten back from interrogating the rogue fairy. News had spread through High Prince Reval's division that the troll fairy had lived, and not only had the fool lived, he'd stolen from the Shadow Army once again. A whole basket of charmed arrows this time and a satchel of rare gold-peeled grapes.

Luc and Mor stood in the forest. Five more steps and Luc would be in the clearing where the commanders had set up their twig throne circle. The commanders would arrive any minute, and Luc would face their judgement for failing his mission.

But it seemed the fox's feet were stuck.

"I guess you should have taken the rogue's bargain. Perhaps ruling over the village as a noble would have been better than facing this," Mor said. He lifted his boot to Luc's back and shoved him into the clearing with his foot.

Luc stumbled into the throne circle, the muted daylight coming over him where he couldn't hide. He looked back with a glare, and Mor cast him a gloating smirk. But Luc's face changed when Mor walked into the clearing and took his place at Luc's side. The thrones were empty—for now. They'd be filled with very angry and very powerful fairies soon.

"I was there, too," Mor said simply in response to the look of question on Luc's face. "It's only right we face the punishment together."

Luc worked his jaw, then tore his glare off Mor and rested it on Prince Reval's twig throne. "My father will go harder on you than he will on me," he warned.

"Yes, well, I'm far more resilient than you. I can take it."

Luc rolled his eyes, and before Mor could see it coming, the nine tailed fox kicked him deep into a prickle bush on the cusp of the forest. Mor rolled over thrice before he caught himself on his palms, and he stifled a growl as he looked down at his hands now burning and red with little pins sinking in everywhere. He scampered out of the bush and onto a forest path, surveying the hundreds of thistles that would take him *hours* to pick out. He nearly stormed back into the clearing and dealt Luc a fresh punch, but when he looked up, he saw through the branches that the commanders had entered the circle. Prince Reval stood over Luc. Mor leaned forward with a spying eye and tilted his ear to eavesdrop.

He went rigid when the Prince of the Dark Corner drew a dagger and plunged it into Luc's heart.

Time seemed to stand still for a moment. Though it was Luc who killed, Mor felt he'd faced that fate himself. His hand had sprung to his faeborn heart—he was sure it had stopped.

Luc's body was pale and flat on the grass. The fox tails at his throat shivered in a shadowy breeze, the wind stealing one of them clean off its chain as its fur dissolved into nothing. Luc was a lifeless fairy corpse— Mor could not tear his eyes away. A second passed. Then Luc *moved*, flinging his arm up and ripping the dagger out of his own chest, sending Mor staggering back a step.

271

Luc sat, dragged his limbs beneath himself, and stood face-to-face with his father.

"You have only eight more chances. Don't disappoint me again." Prince Reval's cold words sailed into the forest, and Mor watched as Luc lifted his silver-brown glower to the Prince.

"I won't fail you, Father," he said. The words were clean and crystal clear, yet...

Luc had never looked at High Prince Reval the same way again after that.

CHAPTER

37

Violet Miller and the Master of Doom

Violet felt her body trying to faint, her mind sinking into darkness, her lashes fluttering, her limbs turning slack. The dizziness was all consuming as she was sped around and around the city, never stopping, her feet never catching on solid ground. The only thing solid around her was Luc's grip.

It went on for hours—it must have. She thought she would die like this, as a mere vapour in the wind.

Until she struck a wall of stone.

That was what it felt like when an extra set of hands showed up and Luc's grip was torn off. There was a struggle; Violet felt it past her bobbing head. And then her cheek came against a warm chest, and she was charged out of the speeding wind.

No… she was falling.

Violet snapped out of her dizziness as she sped downward. She shrieked and clung to her captor's fluttering shirt. He turned their bodies and wrapped his arm around her just as they slammed through a roof, his back shattering the wood and shingles.

They fell through the building and crashed into a floor, making the whole structure shudder. Cracks burst in every direction, and the floor nearly caved in. The only thing that wasn't broken was Violet.

Violet's heart pounded as she looked at the person beneath her whose shirt she gripped for dear life. Her pulse skipped a beat or two. Or seven.

Dust and wood chips were tangled into Mor's hair. He stared back at her for a moment. Then he slid his arm around her waist and rolled her over. She found herself beneath him, eyes widening when she noticed chunks of beam and brick detaching from the roof above—they plummeted down. She yelped as the debris smashed over Mor's back, his body tense while wreckage tumbled off both sides.

Their eyes met.

Violet felt like there were things she needed to say. But mostly…

"I miss Shayne," she croaked. She felt horrid for saying it, but elated, too. She hadn't even thought of Shayne since Mor had caught her, but now that she'd said the white-haired fairy's name aloud, she couldn't get him off her mind.

Mor blinked, his eyes squinting as he looked at her in question. He glanced at her mouth.

"Mor, I miss him so much my head hurts. Where is Shay—"

Mor brought his lips to hers, silencing her and filling her with a slow warmth. It trickled all through her chest, into her abdomen and down her limbs. It sent sparks into her brain, making her feel alive, and wild, and nervous all at once. She was sure this wasn't real. Her hands found his cheeks, drifting around to clasp behind the back of his neck. She pulled him in closer and he relaxed against her, crushing her beneath him enough to feel like a shield without cutting off her air. A tear rolled down her face, one lonesome, treacherous one.

What was so remarkable about Shayne anyway, apart from his delightful smile, handsome face, and witty personality? Sure, maybe he was a catch in some people's eyes for all those somewhat compelling reasons, but Violet had never been more sure that he was wrong for her. In this moment, she was absolutely consumed by the fairy above her.

Someone nearby cleared their throat.

Violet stopped her kissing.

Mor didn't.

He ignored the bystander and slid his dust covered hand into Violet's splayed hair, brushing away her tear with his thumb as he did.

The person cleared their throat again. Then someone else did it, too. Two bystanders, then.

"Excuse me, boss?" one of them squeaked from a dry throat.

Mor did stop then. It seemed to take him a moment to figure out who was talking to him as he held tight to Violet, his mouth barely off hers. He finally lifted his head and glanced over, so Violet did, too. And she realized, for the first time, that they were in the cathedral.

The broken-roofed, woodchip-covered, dirty-all-over-again cathedral.

Remi and Jase stood on the stairs, both pale and round-eyed. Remi held tightly to a frying pan like she'd been preparing to use it as either a shield or a weapon.

"Ah, right. Them," Mor murmured, more to himself. He eyed Remi's frying pan. "Don't even think about trying to hit someone with that, Human. Trust me; it hurts."

When he spoke, Violet pulled her gaze back to him, noticing how he glowed like the morning sun, and sounded like a smooth-running river when he talked, and—

"Don't mind Violet for the next few minutes. She's going to act strange," Mor added as a warning to the interns.

He climbed to his feet, pulling Violet up with him. Then he winced and released a moan as he stretched his back and neck. He reached over to his opposite shoulder and seemed to snap a bone back in place—Violet shrieked.

Jase fainted.

It was only then that Violet noticed Mor's hands were covered in dried blood, his t-shirt was sliced in five places, and there were gaping wounds over his abdomen, knees, and arms. The sight must have made her eyes wide and wild because from the stairs, Jase asked as he came to, "W... What's wrong with her?" The intern's throat bobbed as he swallowed.

Violet was baffled he didn't ask why she and Mor had just come plummeting in through the ceiling. There was no elephant in this room—just an elephant-sized mound of roof debris and weirdness.

Mor scratched the back of his head. "It's going to seem like she likes me, a lot. It may get a little unbearable for you to watch to be faeborn honest," he told Jase. "Normally when this happens to a fairy, we lock him in a closet for a while, but it seems cruel to do that to a human, so..."

"Mor," Violet stopped him. Mor glanced back at her. There was a strange look on his face, like he was trying to figure out what was compelling her to speak. There was also something else though—worry. Hesitation. Something that looked like fear. "I'm totally clear-headed," she stated. "I was kissed enough times to have caught on that my mind was being yanked around whenever it happened. I know I'm the victim of some sort of creepy kiss potion you all must have drunk today!"

Mor chewed on the inside of his cheek. It seemed like he was waiting for something.

"Should we leave?" Remi asked, clutching the frying pan to herself. "This seems like the sort of situation where we should leave—"

"I don't like you anymore, Mor," Violet stated, and her heart thundered. Every inch of her wanted to run to him, to clasp him, to beg him to never leave her side again, but those feelings weren't real. The muscles in her face twitched. She tore her gaze away so she wouldn't look at him, because something about the expression on his face screamed at her with the most compelling argument she'd ever battled. She clenched her hands into fists hard enough to make them shake. But she refused to reach for him or to acknowledge him ever again.

She didn't love him. She had to coach herself every second so she wouldn't blurt in his face that she could hardly breathe while standing this far away from him.

"You look astoundingly uncomfortable," Mor remarked, and Violet spun on him.

"Fine!" she shouted. "I've never wanted anything more than I want you, Mor! You big, stupid fairy! I can't even think straight right now!"

From the stairs, Jase paled again, but Remi snorted an unexpected laugh. "Yikes," she muttered.

Mor bit his lips together as Violet approached him. Even through the tangle of heart-pounding, fluffy emotions, she was still angry. "You left me!" she shouted, pointing at him.

He said nothing but his brown eyes flickered with guilt.

"I really wish…" Her voice turned dry. She dropped her hand back to her side. "I really wish I could hate you right now." Her eyes wetted with tears. "But all I want to do is ask you if you're okay, and brush the dirt out of your hair, and thank you for saving me, and bake you muffins *for the rest of eternity!*" She shouted the last part, turning on her heel and storming through the wood planks on the floor toward the kitchen.

Her chest pounded as she marched in and began throwing cupboards open to search for the measuring cups.

CHAPTER

38

Cressica Alabastian and the Thing that Happened
One Faeborn Hour Ago

The museum floor was wet with purple blood. Some of it was Cress's. Even more of it was Mor's.

They fought back-to-back, never closing their eyes, never looking down as Shadow Fairies airslipped in and out of their vision, knowing a single glance in the wrong direction could cost them their lives.

Cress's phone rang. He pulled it out, fighting with one hand as he pinched the phone between his head and his shoulder. "Yes?" he growled.

Mor released a baffled sound behind him—seeming to wonder why Cress had answered the phone at a time like this.

Shayne's voice came through. "I killed the fox once, but he got away with Violet! And Cress—Dranian is hurt."

"Queensbane," Cress gritted out. "How hurt?"

"He's down an arm. Where are you?" Shayne panted through the phone like he was running. "Are you still at the museum?"

"Unfortunately—" The phone was smacked off Cress's shoulder. At first, he thought it was a Shadow Fairy's doing, but he realized it was Mor who'd rudely ended the call. Mor didn't even look sorry for sending Cress's phone smashing to the floor.

"Focus!" Mor shouted at him.

"I am focused!" Cress shot back. He stabbed a Shadow Fairy and kicked him into the museum wall then turned his forearm to faestone and used it to block a swinging saber. He slashed the fool's knees, and the Shadow Fairy fell at his feet.

Cress's royal heart clenched, his mind telling him he and Mor weren't going to make it out of this as they once had fighting side by side against Shadows in the past. Though they fought hard now, Cress knew their skill had grown relaxed in the months they'd been among the humans sipping beast milk and eating pies.

He took down another foe with a faestone punch.

Something eclipsed the light from the museum doors. Even though it could cost him, Cress glanced that way.

A pack of females in hideous sweaters of all the ugliest colours of fairy yarn filled the museum's doorway. It was the most beautiful sight Cress had ever beheld in his entire faeborn life, and a beat of relief soared through him.

Cress drove his fairsaber into the nearest Shadow and shoved Mor toward the museum doors. He backed toward the Sisterhood himself, aiming his sword at his enemies, daring them to try and stab him while he closed the gap between his royal self and approximately a thousand pounds of bad smelling yarn.

Shayne and Dranian raced in right as the fight between sword and needle broke out. The two didn't even stop running—they sprang into the mass of Shadow Fairies, saber and spear swinging. Dranian fought with a terrible disadvantage, hugging one arm to himself. Knitting needles pierced throats and heads and thighs. Cress was about to join in, but… he hung back, wondering if he needed to.

Mor remained at his side. Cress caught him stealing a glance out the museum doors, looking toward the city.

The Prince sighed. "Just go. I need to stay and make sure Dranian doesn't lose his other arm," he said.

Mor disappeared without objection, and Cress stood his ground to ensure no fairies slipped into the air after him.

A Shadow Fairy bellowed over the museum, and all the Shadows stopped fighting, the knitters slowed their movements, and Shayne and Dranian caught their breath. The silver-and-brown-eyed fairy with the loud voice marched until he reached Cress. A black and red medallion of authority in the Dark Corner hung around his neck.

"Are you in charge of this army, or is it that female over there?" The Shadow nodded toward Freida.

Cress opened his mouth to announce that apart from the army of females, he was in fact in charge of mostly everything, but Shayne's white hair appeared before his face.

"Actually, that would be me," Shayne stated. "High King Shayne, right here." He pointed to himself. "King of the High Court of the Coffee Bean."

Cress stifled a grunt.

The Shadow Fairy looked Shayne over, and by some miracle of the sky deities he seemed to think Shayne looked the part, which was absolutely preposterous.

"We wish to make a bargain," the Shadow said.

"Oh?" Shayne folded his arms, his fairsaber tapping against his side. "A bargain that will force you to leave, I hope?"

"We've shed enough fairy blood today. We arrived only this morning, and already I have division fairies who may not survive the night." He stole a glance back at one or two of the Shadows sprawled over the tile floor. "We came here to check in with our liaison. We were instructed to get in without making it known to the humans we were here—"

"Too late," Cress mumbled.

"—and then leave. I will be punished for this."

"So, you *want* to leave?" Shayne asked. "Done. I agree. Go, then." He nodded toward the doors behind him.

"It is not that simple, North Fairy." The Shadow Fairy's eyes darkened, and a cool breeze rippled over Cress's skin. Cress tried not to laugh at how *not*-afraid he was of the fairy's threat. He thought about crisping the floor to ash and sealing the walls with frost—just to remind everyone he was there.

"Now that Queene Levress of the North has agreed to share her gate with us—" Cress flinched, "—the Dark Queene gave an immediate instruction to send a spy into this realm. She commanded a group from our division to come check on our spy every season to gather his reports."

"What do you wish for?" Cress cut in with a deep growl. "Now that you've told us your whole, boring, faeborn-cursed life story."

The Shadow Fairy's gaze cut over to Cress. "I want safe passage every season for me and my division. The wars are bad enough in the Dark Corner. There's no reason for us to come here and die at your hands."

"And in exchange, you'll leave?" Shayne asked, getting back to it. "That's not good enough. I want you to take your foxy friend with you."

A snarl crossed the Shadow Fairy's face. "Luc Zelsor will face a short trial when we find him. If he fails to persuade us of his innocence in this conspicuous catastrophe, he will be dragged back to the Dark Corner of Ever for punishment and stripped of his post. When he was appointed as a liaison spy, he was told to stay out of sight. But it's clear he hasn't followed the rules. Likely, he will suffer the strokes of iron."

"So, what's the bargain then? I let you pass through the human realm—preferably without you killing anything—once a season? And in exchange for that, you stay far away from the High Court of the Coffee Bean and our humans?" Shayne asked.

"And us," Freida cut in. She took her place beside Shayne, and Cress was beginning to think they really had forgotten the High Prince of the North was present.

The Shadow Fairy's gaze darted back to Cress, *finally*. There was enough recognition in his eyes for Cress to gather he'd seen Mor standing at Cress's side during the fight. That he knew exactly who and what

Mor was. "You are lucky I did not include Trisencor's death as part of my bargain," he said coldly.

Though the air was tense, a cruel, slow smile crept across Cress's face. It was an invitation to try and see what Cress would do about it. But then...

"You still can," Freida offered. "It's not too late."

Cress wouldn't dare to ever slap a female, but there were times when Freida made him wonder about it.

The Shadow Fairy grunted and went back to Shayne. "Do we have a bargain, High King?"

Shayne nodded. "I can agree to that."

There was no handshake or fae-grip or salute. The Shadow Fairy marched around Shayne, Freida, and Cress. His whole army followed in complete silence, the only sounds the thudding of their boots down the museum stairs. Some of the fairies carried their injured army members over their shoulders.

The Brotherhood and the Sisterhood watched them leave.

Dranian appeared beside Cress with a bothered brow. "So, they will take that fox back with them?" he asked in a low, grumbly voice.

"I doubt it," Cress replied. "If the fox planned to cooperate with the Dark Corner, he would have stayed here with his fellow Shadow Fairies. I imagine he'll run off for good, likely never to come near us again now that we took two of his sacred lives."

Dranian lifted his head high. "He stole my arm. I will make it my life's mission to hunt him down and make him pay," he proclaimed to all listening.

Shayne, Cress, and even horrid Freida rolled their eyes a little.

"I don't care if we made a bargain with those fools," Cress said, eyeing the army of Shadows marching openly down the street, turning human heads. News vans had already rolled up, and a few reporters with terror-stricken faces were bravely trying to approach the Shadow Fairies. "We are going to guard our café and our humans with our lives until the moment they're gone," Cress finished.

CHAPTER

39

Mor Trisencor and the Merry Batch of Muffins

There'd only been a split second to make a decision when Mor had finally spotted Luc, raging like a whirlwind in the heights of the city's buildings with Violet in his grip. Mor knew he could not take them both.

As Mor spied on Violet puttering around in his kitchen and tossing flour and sugar into a bowl, he knew he'd made the right choice. He left her to her baking and went to the office, inhaling the thick scent of ink, stock paper, and article ideas. The folktale book he'd borrowed from the library—the one with the white nine tailed fox on the cover—rested peacefully on his desk. He stared at the fox painting for a long while before he picked it up.

"You've been luring in human females and stealing their secrets? For what, Luc?! What do you need human secrets for?"

Mor's own enraged questions burned through his mind as he flipped the book open, looking for a particular story. The sound of ruffling pages filled the office until he came to a tale about a lonely female fox who stole one thousand secrets and transformed herself into a human so she could hide among the humans forever. Mor read the first few lines, then flipped the pages to skip ahead. A detailed painting of a fox offering her ruby to the sky filled a partially torn page. Her pure white hair was partway through turning nut-brown like a human's; her reward for her one thousand secrets collected.

Mor slapped the book shut.

He rubbed his temples and leaned back against the desk.

Was Luc trying to become a human? But why? Mor tapped a finger along the book's cover, taking in the silence of the room and the few articles Violet had left pegged to the walls.

"Do you know how long it took for me to convince the commanders to let me come here? How much talking, how much luring, how much baiting and convincing before I had the commanders wrapped around my finger at last?"

Luc had claimed he didn't come to the human realm for Mor. And for the first time, Mor started to believe him.

"Queensbane," he muttered, dropping the book back onto the desk. "Queens—*bane.*"

Luc was attempting to escape from the Shadow Army.

Mor had always wondered why in the name of the sky deities Luc had never killed him back in the Army when he'd had so many chances. And why the fox didn't even stop Mor the day Mor trashed the cave and escaped when all that time Mor had been losing in his nightly fights against Luc. Luc had the skill to stop and kill Mor during his escape, yet he never lifted a finger.

But it wasn't just that incident. Mor had to rethink every memory he had with the nine tailed fox. The one of Luc appearing at the nightly fights and challenging all the highest-ranking war fairies so no one remembered to challenge Mor anymore. The ones of Luc refusing to use the enhancement of his fox bead every time Mor challenged him to a fight. The one of Luc kicking him aside to take the punishment from Prince Reval alone for failing the troll mission...

Mor could hardly believe he hadn't seen it. Could hardly imagine it to be true—that Luc Zelsor had possibly been protecting Mor since the beginning.

And Mor had tried to kill Luc when they'd crossed paths here. No wonder Luc wanted Violet and everyone Mor loved to suffer.

And perhaps...

Perhaps Mor deserved to suffer. But Violet didn't—Violet didn't deserve another day of torture in her whole human life.

Cress seemed to think Luc had run far away and was too afraid to lose more of his lives to approach the High Court of the Coffee Bean again. But if there was one thing Mor knew about nine tailed foxes, it was that they found it extremely difficult to let things go.

Violet stayed up all faeborn night baking those wretched muffins. It drove Mor crazy at first. The interns had fallen asleep with their faces pressed to the countertop by midnight; the male human's arm was flung over the length of the counter. Mor came back every few minutes to check and see if Violet was *finally* finished with her baking masterpiece, but she never was.

Also, it bothered him a little that she was enchanted by him—compelled to want to be near him, to adore everything about him, to praise him like he was one of the sky deities themselves—and she hadn't even come desperately running through the cathedral to find him *once*. It was nearly insulting. The enchanted kiss had been strong; he'd felt it. Violet must have had the willpower of a stubborn wild steed.

He'd finally given up and gone to take a shower.

Once clean, Mor sauntered into the kitchen, eyeing the four bowls of abandoned ingredients on the counter from where Violet had started mixing flour before giving up and starting over.

"You must be having a difficult time trying to stay away from me," he guessed, putting as much sympathy into his voice as he could while he took in how much she'd trashed his kitchen. He'd likely be the one to have to clean it.

"Yes, *Doom*. I'm trying desperately to hate you," she admitted.

It was painfully obvious that she was avoiding saying his name.

Mor nodded, drifting in a little closer. He stopped directly behind her where her floral scent engulfed him—then he thought better of it and scooted back. He pulled out a stool and sat at the island beside the sleeping male intern before Violet could notice how close he'd come.

A few words rolled to the end of his tongue to be said, but he sucked them all back in again, one by one. He scratched his head. He ran a hand through his hair. He flicked an abandoned spoon on the island.

"I made a mistake," he blurted. He clasped his hands in front of him and squeezed them to near death.

Violet stopped her mixing. When she turned around, Mor nearly burst out laughing at the dollop of batter on the end of her pretty little human nose. "You think?" she said as she strangled the tea towel in her grip.

Mor took in a deep breath and let it out slowly. "I understand you're angry, but you're enchanted, and you *should* be racing for me with all the rage and passion of a thousand gazelles—"

"Doom." Violet said it coolly and straight-faced. "I liked being enchanted by Luc more."

Mor slammed his mouth shut and stood. "What?"

"It hurt less than this." She tossed the tea towel to the counter with an echoing slap and turned back to her mixing bowl. "You kissed me in front of my house, and then you left me forever. After I told you that I wanted to belong to you like a total idiot. You led me on then pushed me away. Who does that?"

"A pompous fae," he answered. "One who's doomed—"

"And *then* you dove into my memories and tore away suddenly like I had thirty contagious diseases, and you looked at me like... like..." Violet shook her head, unable to come up with anything. "And after that I got kidnapped! While we were apart!"

Mor wanted to go stand at the counter with her, but he sank back onto his stool again. "I'm not going to try and justify what I did. I know I hurt you when I left you to wake up alone. I did it because I thought Luc was after *me* and your proximity to me would get you killed, but I was wrong."

Violet glanced back at him again with her batter-speckled face.

"He was after *you*," Mor said, feeling the rush of nerves all over again. "He wanted *you*, Violet. Not because he thought you were my lover, but because he realized who you are."

The batter spoon tumbled from Violet's hand. She tried to catch it but it clattered to the floor, and the interns snorted and shuffled. Neither of them awoke. "Do you know who I am?" she asked, all the anger draining from her face, replaced by a flickering hope that twisted something in his chest. "Mor... did you find out who I was before?"

Mor stood again, shoving the stool away once and for all. He came to meet her by the counter. "I'm sorry," he said, and he swallowed. "I'm sorry, Violet, but you and I met before the day you came to my cathedral looking for a job. If you were ordinary, I might have sent you away and never thought about you again, but you had an aroma of fairy-meddling on you, and I think I accidentally kept you around because I wanted to know why."

Violet blinked up at him doubtfully. "We've met before." It was a question.

"The day before you woke up, you were taken from this realm and into the fairy one. You were brought to a feast for the Shadow Army in the Dark Corner of Ever. And you were saved by someone—a youthful male fairy who..." Mor forgot how to speak as her face changed.

"That boy..." she breathed. "I remembered him when I woke up from a strange dream yesterday. It wasn't a dream though, was it?"

There'd been a moment in the parking lot after Mor had seen Violet's memories, after he'd recognized her reflection in the window from her own recollection of the day she woke up in the forest, when Mor was sure he'd accidentally grappled a few strands of her lost memories and sent them back into her mind. He'd lost control—he'd wanted to scream. He hadn't been able to stop himself, and he had no idea what pieces of her old self he'd given back from that terrible day in the Ever Corners he'd once paid a pauper to make her forget.

Mor swallowed and carefully took her flour-covered hands. "I was sixteen years of age. I was wearing black shells on my shoulders. My shoulders weren't as broad, and my skin may have been lighter from living under a cloud, and my hair would have been short."

A tear broke from Violet's eye and skittered down her face. Mor swiped it away, a blend of things racing through him—mostly relief. He was sure Violet wouldn't have believed this story if she didn't have her own recollection of it.

Mor pulled her against him, wrapping his solid arms around her shoulders. There was nothing he wanted more in any realm than to keep her safe now. To tether her to him even. To never let anything happen to her like what had happened that day when she was among his Shadow Army division, and what had happened today when she'd been kidnapped by a Shadow Fairy all over again.

"I should have never left your side. Now that I know you're who Luc is after, I won't let go of you, Violet," he said.

Violet's arms slowly closed around him. Her fingers hesitantly dug into his shirt, taking handfuls in her fists like she was afraid to let go. "You want to stay together?" she asked in a small voice.

"Yes. You belong to me now," Mor promised. "You're mine, Violet Miller."

The morning crawled in with the smell of warm baking. Mor had just fallen asleep on the couch in the living space when the wild trumpet blasts of the oven rang through the cathedral. He started, flinging himself up to a sitting position and clutching his tiny little blanket. He slapped a hand over his faeborn chest and tossed the blanket aside, rising to stride to the kitchen. He was prepared to put an end to Violet's manic baking and mixing and wasting of supplies and colossal destruction of his kitchen. But when he entered—seeing that the interns had finally been shaken awake after their long night's sleep at the island—he saw Violet standing by the oven, holding a steaming tray of muffins in her mitten-covered hands.

She was beaming.

Perhaps he didn't care about the kitchen or the wasted ingredients or whatever. He slid onto a stool beside the female intern this time. The intern was looking around like she was trying to remember where she was. She gasped and looked at the time telling device at her wrist.

"My parents are going to kill me," she said.

The male intern's eyes rounded. "Mine, too."

"Here! Everyone try a muffin before you go!" Violet said, setting the tin on the counter and plucking out a few. After a moment of her teetering, during which time Mor became aware that Violet had failed to take her cold iron pills again, Violet popped the muffins onto a plate and carried it to the island. She slid into the seat beside the male intern and placed the glorious platter before Mor first. The smell was absolutely intoxicating, and Mor's stomach grumbled at the sight of a fresh breakfast.

He took one and carefully peeled off the papery thing. Violet watched his every movement, linking her fingers together and resting her chin atop them with a smile. Mor had a feeling that if he played his cards right and made sure she knew he loved her muffins, she would bake breakfast every day of the week, and he would live in the luxury of waking to this delicious smell for the rest of his faeborn life.

Mor shoved the whole thing into his mouth.

He smiled around the pastry when Violet's face lit up. He chewed a little. He stopped.

His face warped, and he tried not to cough.

Was that… *salt* he tasted?

A cough slipped out, and he covered it up with his fist. Was that some sort of crushed grass flavour?

He forced a wide smile over the glob of rot in his mouth.

It was the human realm's worst mud mixed with the taste of horror and misery.

"Mmmm," he said.

Violet sat up straighter. "Do you really like it?" She grinned.

Mor stared her dead in the eyes for a second. "Mhm." He grunted the sound out, but he gagged a little, and Violet's face changed.

She glanced at the plate of muffins. "Is there something wrong with them?" she asked, and Mor's hand flashed out to the plate. He dragged the whole platter toward himself before she could take one, and he forced himself to swallow the fungus—he felt it slide all the way down his throat like a rock in sticky mud.

"They're so good, I want them all," he declared, hugging the plate to himself. "And I'm faeborn starving."

"Mor, let me try one," Violet demanded. She glanced to the female intern beside Mor. "Can you grab one for me?"

But Mor shook his head and yanked the platter away when the young female tried to reach for one. The intern got a determined look on her face and tried again, and it was then that Mor jumped to his feet and exited the kitchen with a dozen garbage-worthy muffins pressed against his chest.

"I'll be in the office if you need me!" he shouted back.

FOUR
FAEBORN
WEEKS
LATER

CHAPTER

40

Violet Miller and the Interview by Idiots

The Sprinkled Scoop turds were rolling out fall decorations already—Violet eyed a garland of brown leaves wrapping the office window as she and Mor entered the news building with their heads held high. Former colleagues of Violet's turned their heads, and once they saw The Fairy Post owners, they couldn't seem to look away.

Since Violet left, The Scoop hadn't bothered to write a single article about all those women who'd turned up in the woods with no memory of how they got there. Not that there was much of a story anymore—there hadn't been another victim in several weeks. Mor claimed it was evidence the Shadow Army had found Luc and had dragged him back to the land of his fairy people. It took a while for Violet to be able to breathe easy again, but there hadn't been a single trace or sighting of the redhead, so she began to believe Mor was right.

Fil nearly spat his coffee when he saw them—first because of Violet, second because of Mor.

The tattooed assassin-fairy ignored the bumbling, gaping journalist sitting at his desk. He marched by at Violet's side, emitting an invisible shudder through the room that seemed to make Fil sink lower into his seat. Mor hadn't bothered to dress up for the occasion, despite Violet's prompting. He fashioned a fitted black shirt that he may or may not have realized showed off the muscles he'd once used to snap his enemies' bones with. Also, no tie, no blazer, no dress shoes. Not that he needed it—he seemed to draw attention just fine the way he was.

Violet, on the other hand, wore a sweeping black dress to match her boss, velvet red lipstick, smoky eyeshadow, and her sleekest pair of stilettos.

Cedric came promenading out of his office with a big, ridiculous, fake smile.

"Ah, you must be Mor Trisencor. And..." His face changed when his gaze darted to Violet.

"My lead journalist," Mor said in introduction.

"I'm his secretary," Violet corrected. "Also known as," she glanced back at Fil who was still gaping at his desk, "the Secretary of Doom."

Mor folded his arms and stood tall, dwarfing Cedric in his shadow. He took a slow, deliberate look around The Sprinkled Scoop office. "I thought this place would be bigger. It's quite small," he said. Then he turned to Violet. "Our office is at least seven times as big as this, don't you think?"

Violet nodded. "Didn't I tell you this place sort of felt like working in a closet?" she whispered to Mor loud enough for Cedric—and Fil at his desk—to hear.

Cedric let out an airy grunt.

"Anyway," Violet slid a folder out of her purse, "this is a list of the dates we're available to interview you for The Fairy Post. Feel free to get in touch. We'll get back to you if we feel like it and can spare the time." She handed the folder to Cedric who slowly took it.

With that, she turned and headed for the door, waving at Alice on her way by. Alice performed an awkward wave back like she wasn't sure if she was allowed to greet her former coworker.

Mor shook his head in visible disappointment. "I really thought this place would be nicer." He practically shouted it as he followed her out. "This office is painfully dull. No wonder we're catching up to these fools in subscribers."

The air outside was cool and fresh. Violet breathed it in as she descended the stairs of The Sprinkled Scoop office. "Let's go get an iced ca-fae mocha at Fae Café!" she suggested, spinning to watch Mor trot down the stairs after her.

When he reached the bottom, he wrapped his arms around her waist and tugged her against him.

"Hmmm." He looked around the street for a second, then eyed Violet suspiciously. "You know the only reason you keep wanting to go drink those mochas is because they're—"

"I know, I know. The coffee is enchanted or whatever." Violet waved a hand through the air. She slid her arms around him too, clasping her hands behind his back. "I don't even care. The coffee is so good. Sometimes I wake up thinking about the soft whipped cream and the dark nutty taste."

Mor sighed and patted her on the head. "I've now learned that there are two different kinds of humans in this realm. Some are very difficult to enchant, like Kate. Others are very easily enchanted," he said, then he lightly flicked her nose. "You, Violet, are the latter. Sometimes it makes me nervous." He mumbled the last part as he turned her toward Fae Café and put an arm around her shoulders.

"I told the interns to come up with a new crossword puzzle this morning," Violet said, changing the subject. "Remi seemed into the idea. Maybe we should make that her thing for the next few days." She moaned. "What are we going to do when they go back to school in a week? Should I ask them if they still want to work with us some evenings? On weekends, maybe? I don't know if I could start working on weekends though. Now that I'm living back home with Zorah, I feel like

I see her even less than I did when I was staying in the cathedral. We've just gotten so busy."

When Violet looked at Mor, she realized he was smiling. "What?" she asked.

Mor shook his head at first like he didn't want to say.

"What?" She pinched his side a little, and he yelped, making a passing group shoot them a look.

Mor swept in front of her, stopping her from walking. He put his hands on her shoulders, the traces of a smile lingering. "Violet," he said, his brown and silver eyes glowing.

Violet fought a weird chuckle. "What's gotten into you?" she asked.

Mor bit his bottom lip then released a sigh.

"I'm just happy. That's all," he finally said. Violet felt herself melt, and he laughed like he somehow knew her temperature had changed. "I've enjoyed working alongside you more than I ever thought I would. And um..." He looked off all of a sudden, scratching the back of his head. He closed his eyes like he wouldn't be able to tell her his next thought if he was looking at her.

Violet raised an eyebrow, wondering what in this world could rattle him so much. A second ago, in The Sprinkled Scoop, he'd been a vision of intimidating strength and power.

Mor pursed his lips, and his eyes flashed open. "I've accidentally made you my mate," he blurted. "Unalterably."

"Oh." She blinked a few times. She didn't get it. "A... mate?" she articulated. It felt like he was describing something from a wild animal documentary.

His gaze dropped to the sidewalk. "It just means I really can't lose you now. It will absolutely destroy me if you leave. I just needed you to know."

Without another word, he took her hand and led her toward Fae Café. For the entire walk, Violet couldn't come up with a thing to say, but she bit down on her lips to keep herself from smiling. She wanted to ask questions, but the more she thought about it, the more she put the pieces

together on her own. Maybe fairies didn't know how to say, "I love you."
It took nearly the whole journey for her heart to settle.

When they reached the café, Violet turned to Mor before they went in. "You're not going to lose me, Mor. I'll never run away," she said.

She couldn't believe they were really exchanging these words. They hadn't exactly been dating in the typical sense for the last few weeks, but the heart-fluttering tension between them every day had been so potent, Violet could hardly stand it. It was a miracle she hadn't burst yet from sheer joy. Mor had spent three days at her bedside while she'd suffered through the nausea and light-headedness of weening herself off her cold iron supplements. And once she was better, he'd hardly been able to stop touching her hand, tugging her closer, whispering against her ear even when it wasn't necessary to do so.

Mor's face broke into a smile as he reached past Violet for the door. "Well in that case, you can have my gray sweater," he said.

Violet chuckled as she stepped into the café and was instantly met with the warm, alluring fragrance of coffee. She spotted Lily behind the counter.

"I made muffins!" Violet announced to the crew of Fae Café as she drew a container from her oversized purse. Across the storefront, Shayne perked up in his seat by the fireplace. He slapped a book shut, eyeing the container, and followed Violet to the counter where she slid the muffins toward Lily.

A few morning customers were around, talking quietly or reading. Violet salivated at the sight of their lattes and mochas.

At a bistro table, Cress and Kate were talking about Kate's wedding dress. Well, *Cress* was talking. "No taffeta! Only silk or satin, maybe with an organza or chiffon overlay. Swarovski crystals are a must, or real diamonds; nothing cheap. Perhaps a sweetheart neckline and a puddle train as well, with plenty of rouching in the bodice," he stated while looking at a scribbled list in his hand. Violet would have thought the turquoise-eyed fairy was joking if he didn't look so serious.

Across the table, Kate stifled an eye roll and took a sip of her coffee.

"I'm just going to wear whatever's on sale off the rack," she said when she was finished.

Cress dropped the paper to the table. "You will *not* do that. You are marrying a Prince of the North Corner of Ever."

Shayne peeled the lid off the muffin container and sniffed the potent aroma of still-warm blueberries. "You can marry me instead if you'd like, Kate. I won't fuss about your dress," he called back and shot her a wink.

"You're such a flirt," Lily muttered at Shayne.

Mor suppressed a smile as he rounded the counter. He took a large mug from the cupboard and began making a hot drink Violet desperately hoped was for her.

Shayne settled his dreamy blue gaze on Lily. "And you're such a stiff statue, Human. I bet if you stood perfectly still on the street corner, other humans would walk past you and think you were part of the streetside decorations." He lifted a muffin from the container and peeled off the cup.

Lily cast Shayne a look. "Do we need to take this outside, Assassin?" She seemed to be only half joking.

Shayne grinned. "I'd love to. I do know your real name, after all. You don't know mine." He reached across the counter and stole a small plate from a pile then placed his perfectly peeled muffin in the centre, setting up his snack with care.

"Just because you read a few books on how to trap and kill fairies doesn't make you stronger than us, Human," Cress declared to Lily from his seat as he flipped through his book of wedding notes. Kate inconspicuously slid a novel out of her sweater pocket, opened it below the table where Cress couldn't see, and began to read.

Lily scowled. "You just wait," she mumbled as she hung up a washcloth. Dranian came out of the kitchen behind her and swept through the café, so graceful and silent that Violet wasn't sure anyone even noticed him.

Shayne's grin widened. "I'll wait forever, ugly Human. You know I will," he said to Lily.

Mor slid a piping hot ca-fae mocha across the counter to Violet and flashed her a smile. Violet took the drink, beaming in return. She turned toward the open table beside Cress and Kate just as Shayne bit into his muffin.

Violet walked away to the sound of Shayne choking. She heard a pronounced spitting sound. She smiled and took a sip of her mocha as she reached her seat, not looking back.

"What sort of crossbeast feces is this?!" she heard Shayne whisper to Mor.

Mor's low, quiet voice of warning sailed to Violet's ears. "You are going to eat that, and you are going to pretend you love it, or I'll slay you where you sit," he articulated to the white-haired fairy.

Violet shoved her mocha mug against her mouth to drink again so she wouldn't laugh. If Mor would just be honest and tell her that her muffins were disgusting, she would stop making them, and he could stop forcing everyone to eat them. But as it was, Mor hadn't admitted the truth yet, and therefore, everyone they crossed each day would continue to suffer.

"Kate and I will be living upstairs after the wedding. I'm invoking the human right of dibs," Cress announced to the whole café—even the customers.

"You can't call dibs on *my* apartment," Kate murmured too quietly for it to be a real objection.

Cress ignored her and pointed around at the other fairies with his pen. "So, all of you need to find another place to live."

Dranian broke his silence by bumping a table by the fireplace. "How are fairy assassins supposed to find a place to live among humans?" he asked Cress. His eyes seemed notably horrified for someone who hardly ever showed facial expressions.

Cress shrugged like it wasn't his problem. "Mor did. Go live with him," he said.

Dranian pointed at Mor and growled, "I will not sleep in that dark, infested cathedral ever again!" he promised.

"Of course you won't," Mor said. "You're not invited. I wouldn't let you live with me if you paid me." Mor took a long, slow drink of his latte without breaking eye contact with Dranian.

Shayne laughed, picked up his muffin, and sauntered over. "Here." He passed the muffin to Dranian like he was consoling him with it. Dranian took it with strange emotional gratitude and shoved it all in his mouth.

Violet waited for him to react. She struggled so hard to suppress her smile that her face hurt. But she didn't know what to do with herself when Dranian chewed the thing and swallowed it without batting an eye.

"Mmm. That was good," the fairy said in his monotone voice, and Violet's smile fell.

"Should we be roommates then, Dranian? Split our coins to pay for a box of space where the rest of the humans in the apartment building will be lucky to have us?" Shayne asked him.

Dranian growled under his breath and plunked into the nearest bistro seat.

Shayne sat across from him. "I'll make you pancakes," he lured, leaning toward Dranian with a grin. "And I'll soak them in human sweet syrup—"

"It's called *maple syrup*. Wow, this is Canada for goodness' sake—get it right," Lily interjected as she carried over a coffee and sat across from Violet. She flashed Violet a smile to say hello. Mor followed and slid into the seat beside Cress. He leaned a little to take a snoopy glance at Cress's wedding notes.

"—and they will be delicious, and you'll never want me to leave," Shayne continued without missing a beat.

Lily set down her coffee and turned to Shayne. "It seems like every time you talk, you're trying really hard to convince someone to want you."

Shayne released a loud laugh and dramatically swung around in his seat to face Lily. "Have you noticed I don't bother trying with you? I don't want everyone to want me, Human. Only people I *like*."

Mor snorted a quiet laugh, and Violet saw Kate kick his foot under the table.

"*I* like you, Shayne," Violet said. "I think I'll bake you your own batch of muffins." She took a long drink of her mocha as she let that settle in. She stole a look at Mor, whose eyes had rounded a little. Still, to his own demise, he refused to object and admit that her muffins were crap.

Kate finally closed her book beneath the table and slid it back into her sweater pocket. "Is anyone tired of talking about wedding plans?" she asked.

"I am," Lily admitted. "I think you guys should just toss your plans to the wind and let everything fall where it may."

"That would be fun," Kate smiled.

Cress released a loud sigh. "You shameless hoes," he said, shaking his head—Violet nearly spat her mocha. Cress pointed between himself and Mor with his pen. "You humans could learn a thing or two from us fairy folk. Planning is the key to success, whether it be for an event, or an assassination, or anything really." He clicked his pen and scribbled another note. Mor nodded at his side, leaning again to see what Cress was writing.

"What did you just call us?" Kate glared across the table.

"Hoes," Cress answered. He looked up and almost dropped his pen at the look on her face.

Mor didn't see it though. "Hoes. As in *bros before hoes*," he added, articulating so that she might understand. Cress's hand flashed out to Mor's arm, stopping Mor from continuing to educate all the stupid humans in the room.

Violet was astounded she wasn't the first to squeak out a laugh. Shayne took the gold medal for not-keeping-it-together when he burst out laughing, tumbled from his seat, and turned into a basket case on the floor.

"Unreal," Lily said, shaking her head and taking a swig of her coffee.

301

Cress looked at Shayne, seeming to wonder why Shayne had insight into this situation when he didn't.

The café bell jingled, and a teenager with scruffy hair walked in. Cress stood immediately. He rushed to the teenager and said—not quietly enough, "Kate's-brother-Greyson, what does it mean to call a human female a *hoe*?"

The teenager chuckled and looked at Cress like he was crazy. "Trust me, you don't want know," was all he said. The 'Kate's-brother-Greyson' guy fixed his eyes on the coffee pot behind the counter and headed that way.

Violet smirked and scratched her knuckles. Fall was coming with its colder temperatures, and her hands always suffered from the dryness the most. She pulled her purse up onto her lap and dug inside for lotion, but her fingers bumped something small and cold instead. When she opened her bag to peer in, she had to blink several times to convince herself what she was seeing, and when it dawned on her, she blanched.

Dozens of small, cold pebbles filled the bottom of her purse.

She couldn't move, couldn't pull her eyes away from them. Seconds passed where she hardly heard the chatter around the tables until Mor piped up from his seat, "What's wrong?"

Violet's head snapped up—she squished her purse closed. She met his gaze and flashed him a smile. "Nothing," she said, dropping her purse beside her chair. The sound of all the pebbles hitting the floor seemed to be the loudest thing in the room.

Shayne and Lily went at it again, bickering over some nonsense, but Violet's hands wrapped tightly around her mug, her palms sweaty as she stared out the windows of Fae Café. A strange phantom wind seemed to seep in from the street and brush over her bare shoulders like a hand swiping along her flesh, and through the late summer heat, she shivered.

It was a fool's hope. Violet begged the universe for it to just be a coincidence that pebbles filled her purse.

She shouldn't consider it a sign. It wasn't like it meant anything for sure—that *he* was back. That he was coming for her. That he'd gotten close enough to leave rocks in her purse like he wanted to let her know he'd been there. She hadn't seen red hair close by. She hadn't heard a sweet fox voice or smelled his fragrance in the air. The clouds hadn't shifted; the wind hadn't changed.

Yet, everything about the mysterious pebbles told her he was back.

She went home and got no sleep, imagining someone appearing at her bedroom window. After hours of restless tossing and turning, she got smart and closed the blinds.

Zorah made her toast with jam for breakfast, and they had a normal morning chat before work. Violet had finally told Zorah about The Sprinkled Scoop situation three weeks ago, and that she was now working for a new paper called The Fairy Post. So there were no more secrets between them.

Apart from the big one, of course.

For a moment, hope rose within Violet that maybe the pebbles were just that—pebbles. Maybe there hadn't been as many rocks as she thought. Maybe a few had fallen in here and there over the months and she'd just freaked out when she saw them because of all that had happened. Maybe seeing a pile of rocks would always be a trigger like that.

She made it to the cathedral to find that Mor was gone. The interns hadn't arrived yet, either. The doors had decided to shut her out today, so she sighed and walked around back. She climbed the ladder, scaled the roof, and made her way in through the bell tower, thankful to at least be in flat shoes this time.

She hung up her jacket and got the kettle going in the kitchen for tea. But when she turned around, she spotted a tiny gray stone resting on the kitchen island. Violet looked around. She couldn't hear another soul in the cathedral. "Hello?" she called, clasping her hands tightly together.

When nothing answered, she moved for the island and lifted the stone, turning it over in her fingers.

"It's just chance," she muttered, annoyed she was freaking herself out so easily. She tossed it in the garbage, fixed her tea, and headed out of the kitchen. But she stopped short when she saw another pebble on the floor. Past it was another pebble. And another one after that.

Violet's stomach dropped.

Two dozen pebbles made a neat path down the hallway, into the lobby, and around the corner toward the sanctuary. She swore they hadn't been there a moment ago.

She didn't realize her hands were shaking until she dropped her tea.

CHAPTER

41

Mor Trisencor and the Moment He Lost the Fairy Game

The cathedral repairs last month had taken only a few days, mostly because Dranian and Mor knew how to work hard. Cress helped a little but always seemed to find excuses to disappear. Shayne on the other hand didn't even hide that he wasn't helping. He showed up, though, and lounged against the rooftop, basking in the sun and talking everyone's faeborn ears off while Dranian handed Mor supplies by the strength of his one usable arm. In only two afternoons, Mor had patched the large hole he'd made when he'd fallen through with Violet.

The days went by without trouble after that. The air was clean of mischief.

The interns had fallen into their summer roles with ease. The sounds of clicking buttons from typing machines became the music to which those in the cathedral dwelled. The space often smelled of coffee, fresh literary dreams, and Violet's repulsive baking. The Fairy Post had released two papers in the past four weeks, the articles written mostly by

Violet, but a few by Jase and Remi as well. It freed up a lot of Mor's time.

Time which he usually spent cleaning up after Violet.

For four weeks straight, Mor had been cleaning up after his human. She wasn't a messy person, per se. She just had a habit of taking everything out from where it belonged and leaving it in random places for him to find, step on, kick, or accidentally crush.

Even though she'd moved back in with her non-blood-related aunt, she seemed to feel the need to keep most of her belongings in Mor's cathedral. He pretended to mind—sometimes he huffed, sometimes he made comments, sometimes he fluttered his dark lashes in an eyeroll. But in truth, he liked finding her face paints in his bathroom, and her colourful ink pen collection on his desk, and her hair pins absolutely everywhere. It made him feel as though she was always close by, even when she went out or headed home for the evening.

Some nights she stayed late. He caught her scribbling in a journal by the fireplace in the living area, wearing his slippers and snuggled beneath his blanket. He joined her occasionally, bringing a newspaper or a novel and sitting in the chair opposite to read. And a few times, the interns joined them too, hauling their "homework" into the living space. They usually got nosy and started asking questions they shouldn't about who Mor was, where he came from, why he was weird, and the like. Mor normally refused to answer, informing them that, "A little mystery is good for the human soul." It was an odd collection of beings together, doing different things, thoroughly distracting each other, and chatting into the evening until everyone started yawning.

Mor loved it.

There was nothing that would make him think it all might get taken away.

It was Dranian's designated birthday. Months ago, Shayne had discovered that humans celebrated the day of their birth every year over and over again, whereas in the Ever Corners, no one fussed about the date someone was born apart from using it to count their years of age. Mor thought it seemed like an unnecessary hassle, but he wore the party hat Shayne had provided and showed up at the breakfast tavern nevertheless to eat hog meat and cooked bird eggs with his brothers. He was sure someone was going to put an end to the long list of traditions King Shayne was forcing their High Court to adopt, especially since Shayne had designated himself eight birthdays a year, and the rest of the High Court only got one.

Mor's phone rang, interrupting their breakfast. He slid the device out of his pocket and pushed a button or two. He held the thing to his ear. "Yes?"

"Boss, someone from The Sprinkled Scoop just showed up asking for a word with you," Jase said from the other end of the line.

Mor smirked a little. "Does he seem... perturbed?"

"Yeah, a bit."

"Excellent. Tell him I'll be there in five minutes," Mor said.

There was a pause. Then Jase asked, "Will you really be only five minutes?"

Mor smiled. It seemed his interns were catching on to things. "It'll be closer to an hour. Feel free to tell him to wait by the front door—but don't give him a chair to sit in. Make the fool stand."

"Got it."

Jase didn't immediately say goodbye or hang up, so Mor waited as he watched Dranian shovel ketchup-covered eggs into his mouth. The auburn-haired fairy seemed entirely unbalanced since he'd injured his arm; even his eating was clumsy. A heap of eggs fell off his fork and landed on the floor. He seemed to debate whether or not he should pick them up and still eat them.

"What's the problem?" Mor finally asked Jase.

"It's just..." Mor could practically hear the human boy squirming.

"Can't you come back sooner, maybe? This journalist sort of gives me the creeps." Jase dropped his voice to a whisper.

Mor sighed. "Why is that, Human?"

"Well..." Jase's tone was odd. "He's got those same two-coloured eyes you have. Kind of like sparkly marbles or whatever, you know?"

The smile fizzled off Mor's face. "What colours are his eyes, Jase?" he asked, his grip tightening on his phone. "Specifically, which two colours?"

"Uh... I can't see from this far away," Jase admitted. "Do you want me to go check—"

"No. Be there soon." Mor hung up the phone and turned to Cress, Shayne, and Dranian. "This birthday party is over. Come to the cathedral. Bring your weapons."

Mor vanished before his brothers could ask questions.

The cathedral was quiet.

Mor crept over the creaking floors, peering into the various rooms. His interns were nowhere to be found. He had no idea where Violet was, either—if she was about to walk in. If she already had. Pebbles speckled the floor like they'd been kicked in different directions.

"Luc," he called into the echoey space. His heart twisted in his chest. Traces of fairy mischief laced the air, the coldness of the Dark Corner staining the walls and saturating the emerald carpet.

He finally found the fox in the sanctuary.

All the candles were lit. A pew had been dragged up onto the dais and sat there like a wide throne. Luc rested in it with his arm over the backrest, and Mor's chest tightened at the sight of the nine tailed fox, alive and well, and very much in the human realm.

"What did you do to my interns?" Mor asked in a low voice.

Luc cast him a dull, disgusted smile. "You'll never find them."

"Luc," Mor warned, "my brothers will be here soon, and you'd better tell me before then. Remember—you only have six lives left. I shouldn't have to remind you."

Luc's spiteful chuckle echoed through the large room. "Oh dear, it's like you're not even worried about Violet at all," he said, pulling out his ruby and rolling it between his fingers.

Mor's stomach tightened. He hadn't noticed Violet's scent when he'd walked in. Luc must have somehow erased it.

"And I shouldn't have to remind you—that's *six lives more than you*," Luc added.

"What did you do to my human?" Mor asked. When Luc didn't answer, he resorted to begging. "Luc, don't put her through anything more. I know you want to leave the Ever Corners and hide among the humans." He saw Luc's gaze flicker up to the wall. "I will help you."

Luc pulled himself off the pew to stand. "It's too late for apologies, Trisencor. I want you to hurt. I want her to hurt, too. It's in a fox's nature to want these things, I suppose. We're born to be cruel." He held his ruby up to the muted light coming in through the stained-glass windows.

"I despised your father, too," Mor said. "We were the same that way. Luc, if there is any kindness in you, give Violet back to me."

Luc placed the ruby in his mouth. He drew out his fairsabers.

Mor staggered back, reaching for his fairsaber handles, shaking his head. "Don't do this," he pleaded.

"Our dear Violet may be out of it for a while after what I've done. If you survive the next three minutes, you'd better find her before she starves to death like those other poor human fools." Luc dragged his silvery gaze up to Mor. There was no remorse in his eyes. There was no feeling at all.

Mor didn't have a chance to draw his blades before Luc struck. A cold-iron saber ripped across Mor's side, and he released a guttural sound as his purple blood sprinkled the floor.

Luc grabbed his hand from behind and twisted—Mor's wrist snapped. He growled as Luc landed strike after strike, dull punch after dull punch; torturing Mor slowly instead of killing him with one blow.

Mor didn't get in a single hit, even after he managed to forge his fairsaber blades.

He could hardly move when Luc was finished. He crumpled to a heap on the floor, wheezing from crushed lungs and broken ribs. Luc moseyed around and stood above him.

"That was too easy, Trisencor," he said in obvious disappointment. "I wasn't going to hurt you at first, you know. I wasn't going to hurt your guard dogs either, but you pushed me into a corner." Luc put his fairsabers away and crouched, bringing his face over Mor's. "Foxes become dangerous animals when they're cornered," he added. And then, "If I ever see you again, I'll run you through."

Mor's breathing staggered as Luc stood and walked away, pulling the bead out of his mouth and placing it back in his pocket. The fox headed for the hallway on foot instead of airslipping.

"I'm sorry," Mor said, bringing Luc to a foot-dragging, reluctant stop.

The ruby-haired fairy remained still for a moment. Then he said, "I told you it was too late for apologies."

Mor's eyes glazed over as he felt himself passing out. His hoarse breathing filled the sanctuary, mixing in with the dull hum of history making the air thick between them. "I know you let me live all those years. I know you're letting me live now," Mor rasped.

Luc turned around, and this time his smile was broad and terribly amused. "Oh dear. I'm not letting you live, Trisencor. Not this time. You'll see."

Mor watched the nine tailed fox walk away, step after step, until he was gone from the sanctuary.

CHAPTER

42

Violet Miller and the Absence of Everything

One Hour Ago

All sounds and sights had vanished. The girl was in a deep pool of water with coolness on her skin, blue behind her eyelids, and the distant peaceful sloshing of waves. There was nothing inside her, just an endless dark. No emotions, no familiarity, no memories. Until there was a voice.

"Haley," a woman called. The girl couldn't place the voice, but the sound of it sent a rush of warmth through her. It was like she'd entered a dream she'd forgotten about, a dream that was reaching out to her, calling for her to come back to something.

"Haley," the voice called again. *"Haley, hurry up. We're going to be late for our trip! Do you want to read Peter Pan on the drive?"*

She heard the distant slamming of car doors, the click of a seatbelt, and crackling music coming through a radio. She heard the voice of a young girl reading a book out loud about a magic boy named Peter speaking to a girl named Wendy at her window.

"Violet." A new voice called her name. This one was different—a guy's voice. Strange and cold, dark and alluring.

Violet? Who was Violet?

"That's you, dear Human," the voice told her. "I'm talking to you, Violet Miller."

The other sounds vanished. The girl opened her eyes, and new surroundings rushed in, sharp and clear. The visual hit her hard enough that she tipped over, but a strong arm caught her and helped her balance. Beneath her feet was solid ground, around her was... a warm, bright green forest.

"Oh dear," the guy said. "He really messed you up, didn't he?"

Violet—it seemed that was her name—blinked at someone standing before her. A young man looked back, casting her a sympathetic smile. He was tall and broad with fair skin, strange silvery eyes, heart shaped lips, and rich red hair.

"Who are you?" Violet asked as she looked around, trying to place where she was. They were deep into the trees, and nothing else was in view apart from a dirt path a stone's throw away. The forest appeared wild and unkept—roots plunged from the earth, tree branches were snapped off as though a great storm had rushed through, and shredded leaves were everywhere.

Signs of a struggle. Violet wasn't sure how she knew that.

The guy drew in a step and gave her a beautiful smile. "Don't you recognize me? I'm your lover, Violet," he said. When their eyes locked, Violet felt herself being pulled in, like he and her were two magnets and the universe was pushing them together. She found she couldn't look away, and though it made the hairs on the back of her neck stand on end, it also brought her a sense of comfortable familiarity.

"My... *lover?*" The word choice seemed odd.

He reached out, and she meant to take a step back, but he got to her first, wrapping his arms around her shoulders and holding her tight against his chest where a necklace of furry pendants tickled her skin. He had an unusual fragrance, like sweet sugar and tea leaves. And... vanilla ice cream?

"There, there. You're safe now, dear Violet. I rescued you from that monster," he said.

"What monster?" She had to admit, he was warm. She found herself relaxing in his arms.

"You don't remember what happened?" He pulled back just enough to look her in the eyes. He looked confused and slightly hurt, his heart-shaped mouth tipping down at the corners.

She wanted to ask what he was talking about. What had happened? When she tried to think back, she recalled nothing at all, no memories apart from a few seconds where she'd heard a woman's voice in her head.

Who was that woman? Where did she go? Violet looked both ways, but she didn't see a woman anywhere.

"I'm sorry," Violet said to the guy. "I don't remember." She looked off, trying hard to recall something. Anything. There was a deep sense of hollowness in her chest, like something had been dug out. The amount of confusion made her feel faint. She wanted desperately for someone to tell her what was going on and to answer all the questions looming at the tip of her brain.

The guy placed a hand on her cheek, bringing her gaze back up to his strange deep brown and bright silver irises. "I saved you, Violet." He brushed her hair out of her face. "A monster stole your memories and tried to kill you. But don't worry, I'll never let him hurt you again." He tugged Violet back against his chest, and Violet leaned against his frame as she realized her body felt so tired she could barely stand. Her mind worked hard though, going over what he said.

"A monster tried to kill me..." It was a question from a dry throat. Her pulse picked up speed at the realization.

"Yes, Violet. His unhidden name is Mor Trisencor—my enemy. It looks like he stole every one of your memories to torment me, and now you don't remember the things we've been through together. He was jealous that you belonged to me."

Heat touched Violet's eyes, tears forming at the sounds of those things—those beautiful words about being together. Belonging to someone.

"Thank you for saving me," she whispered, feeling the need to be polite. Because even after the feelings of familiarity, she felt a strange coldness toward this guy that seemed reserved for acquaintances.

She pulled back to look at his face again, trying to place it. Trying to memorize it so she wouldn't forget it again. His gaze dropped to her mouth and heat spread through her when he leaned in like he was going to kiss her.

She tore back a step.

He blinked, a flit of frustration crossing his handsome face, his mouth twisting to the side.

"I don't know you," Violet said, not sure if she was apologizing or explaining herself. "I mean I don't remember you yet. I don't want to do..." she motioned between his lips and hers, "...that."

The guy slid his hands into his pockets. He pulled a red gemstone out of one of them and rolled it over his fingers, but he didn't take his eyes off her. "There's something I need you to do for me, and I only wanted to kiss you before I asked." He reached for her hand, and she felt something cold slide into her fingers, but when she tried to look down, he pushed her chin back up and levelled her gaze with his. "But I understand your hesitation. You must be very confused. Why don't you come with me, and I'll brew you a tea and we can talk about it. You might change your mind then."

Violet shook her head. "No." Nausea crept into her stomach out of nowhere. She turned toward the path to walk away, placing a hand against her forehead as dizziness spilled in. None of this felt right. What sort of weirdo tried to kiss someone who didn't remember them?

She only took five steps before his voice snapped through the forest.

"Haley Whitefield," he said.

Violet's body went rigid. Her muscles felt ready, like they were waiting for something, eager to move. She looked down at herself, at her body that wouldn't cooperate. The guy sauntered around and came to stand in front of her again. He didn't look at her with sweetness anymore. Instead, a dark twinkle replaced the kindness in his eyes.

"When Mor comes for you," he started, "I want you to kill him."

Fire pooled into Violet's veins. Her hand tightened around something, and she looked down to find a dagger she didn't realize she was holding. She gasped at the most sudden, powerful, uncontrollable desire to kill the next person who walked into her view.

The guy leaned in, his face an inch away. "Don't move from this spot until he finds you," he added.

Violet watched in horror as the red-haired guy took a few steps back. A slow, sinister smile crossed his face. He disintegrated into thin air before her eyes.

CHAPTER

43

Mor Trisencor and the Hunt

The whole human police station went still and quiet when Mor barged in. Mor scanned the faces for one he knew, clutching his side where his fairy blood leaked out. Police officers dotted the space, some at desks, others escorting non-uniformed humans around.

"Lily!" Mor shouted, the sound taking flight and booming across the station, shuddering the curtains at the window and making every being in earshot jump.

Lily came rushing out from the break room, followed by her partner Connor. "What in the world..." She rushed over with horror-stricken eyes, taking in the cuts on his arms and abdomen, the bruising on his mouth. "Are you crazy, Mor?!" she exclaimed, looking back over her shoulder as she nudged him toward the door.

"I need the assistance of all the guardians at this station," Mor stated, addressing the officers around the room this time. "A human female has gone missing. Her name is Violet Miller. She could be anywhere in the city, and she's in great danger. Additionally, two of my interns are missing. I'll provide Officer Lily Baker with all the information I have."

"Seriously?" Lily whispered at him. "What happened?"

"I can't airslip," Mor told her in a low voice, looking down at his weak body. Anguish filled his chest, and he pushed his hand against his thudding heart.

Lily took his arm and headed for the door again, grabbing a folder off her desk on the way by. "You can ride with me."

"*Baker*! Wait for me!" Connor scrambled to catch up.

Lily led the way out of the station and to her chariot, flicking on the flashing blue and crimson torches as soon as she got inside. Connor went to the passenger side.

"Sit in the back, Connor," Lily told him.

Connor looked at Lily as if to ask if she was serious. He glanced over at Mor, scowled, then got into the back. "You two better not lock me in here," he muttered.

Mor climbed into the front beside Lily, wincing as pain shot through his middle.

"Mor, you look like you're about to die on the spot," Lily said. She tossed him the folder and crossed her arms. "You should read that. It took me a few days to dig this up. I think I figured out who Violet is."

Mor's fingers ran over the file on his lap. "Just take flight," he said. "We need to find her." He swallowed as Lily turned the vessel's gadgets and they began riding across the parking lot.

"Where are we going?" Connor asked glumly from the back seat.

Lily hit a button and a divider wall began to roll up in the middle of the car, blocking her partner off from the front seat.

Connor snorted. "Wow, really—?" But his question was cut short as the wall sealed.

"Okay, but seriously, where are we going?" Lily asked Mor when it was just the two of them.

"I'm not sure. She could be left on a rooftop, or in a closet, or beneath a bridge, or on a boat. She could anywhere. Are the rest of your allies participating in the hunt as well?" he asked. "We'll cover more ground with your whole brotherhood of human police officers."

Lily nodded. "I'll call it in officially, and we'll get all the city stations involved. We'll find your people, Mor," she promised.

Mor lifted the lid of the folder. He rubbed his side, shoving the ribs back into place so they'd heal faster. He released a grunt, making Lily glance over. But all his pain melted to numbness as he read the page before him.

He read for exactly four seconds before he slammed the folder shut again.

Lily pursed her lips. "I think her real name is Haley Whitefield," she said quietly. "Her parents died on a vacation when she was six, and she went missing afterward. Mor, it seems like she ducked the system. I think she might have grown up on the streets—"

"I don't want to know." It was cold and clipped. Mor felt his faeborn soul begin to tear apart. He could not imagine Violet in that situation— not right now. Maybe not ever. He handed the folder back to the human beside him.

Lily chewed on her lip. "Yeah. Okay."

Mor pulled out his phone and smashed several buttons. He listened to it ring until he heard Greyson's voice. "Hello?"

"Greyson, I need you to drive Cress, Shayne, and Dranian around the city to look for my human. It's an emergency. They'll be at my cathedral by now, wondering where I am," Mor said.

"You want *me* to drive them? Why?" Greyson asked.

"Because Shayne drives too recklessly, Dranian can't drive with one arm, and Cress drives too slow," Mor stated.

"Ah, you're doing the *safety-first* thing. Cool," Greyson said. "Consider it done, bro."

Mor hung up. After a moment, he turned back to Lily. "What does 'safety-first' mean?" he asked.

Lily sighed. "Don't worry about it," she said as she steered the vessel toward the park.

Mor was quiet for several seconds. Then he said, "When have my brothers or I ever done anything *safety-first*?"

The city streets were filled with blue and crimson flashing torches late into the evening. Lily's allies scouted the streets for the search. Mor imagined the most horrible scenarios, tormenting himself every moment of the night and into the morning. He didn't eat—unable to swallow food while he imagined Violet starving somewhere. He paced through the empty cathedral, tearing his hair out as he watched the photos of Violet, Jase, and Remi fill the TV on the late-night news. Violet was famous—again. He hated himself for it.

He called Shayne the following afternoon. "Forget the hunt for Violet. Find Luc if he's still here," he told his brothers. "Find him, Shayne. He's the only faeborn soul who knows where Violet is."

"We've already started looking for him. We've looked everywhere and there are no traces of the fox. I think he's long gone." Shayne didn't sound like himself.

Mor sat in silence in front of the fireplace after that. Violet's journal rested on the footstool before one of the chairs. He dragged it to himself and slowly flipped it open to read. He read thoughts and stories she'd written about him. The way she wrote in her journal was the same way she wrote articles; with flowery words and embellished sentences.

Mor was beside himself when he finally got the call in the middle of the night that Violet had been found.

His body was a broken mess when he climbed from Lily's vessel to a scene where yellow banners hung throughout the trees, blocking snoopy humans from entering the forest. He, Lily, and Connor marched through the wooded area. Mor's insides groaned, his mind screamed, his faeborn blood ran hot.

A forest. Luc had left her to wake up in a forest—again. Of all places. He should have known.

He broke into a run when he saw Violet. She stood in place, not moving a muscle even as human officers tried to coax her to follow them. Her body trembled from the cold and exhaustion. Her hair was damp from evening dew and sweat. Mor slowed as he realized...

"Violet," he said, keeping himself at a distance.

Her watery gaze slowly slid over to meet his. There was no recognition there, just a blank stare. She shivered. Then, from a dry throat, she asked, "Are you Mor?"

Mor saw the trick upon her limbs as she reached for something hidden in her pocket. The trees were filled with police officers. A dozen witnesses, or more.

Yet still... he said, "Yes."

She took her first step, struggling on tired legs. Mor sprang forward as she drew the thing out, and he wrapped his arms around her, hiding her weapon. He slipped her into the air as she plunged the death-enchanted dagger into him.

44

Violet Miller and How She Became a Murderer

A wide, dark building formed around her—wood floors, a deep green carpet, many unlit candles. Violet's hands were wet.

She looked down. Sickness pooled into her stomach.

Blood. So much blood.

She tore backward, staring with wide eyes at the dagger she'd thrusted into the body of the person before her. The guy was on his knees, battling to breathe. He pulled the blade out of his stomach and dropped it on the floor. Dark branch-like veins spread over his body from the wound. He tried to hold himself up on his palms.

But he looked up. He looked at her.

"It's all right, Violet," he said quietly. "I know he made you do it."

They were the only words he said before he dropped to the floor. And then he didn't move.

Violet's chest pounded. She looked down at her shaking, blood-soaked hands where the liquid was cooling and becoming sticky.

The hollow building was silent. No lights were lit, nothing but faint moonlight showed the silhouette of the body on the floor.

Violet took a cautious step toward him. She knelt and brought her wrist above his mouth to see if he was breathing. She felt nothing. So, she turned her ear toward his chest to listen.

Still, nothing.

She came back up slowly as it sank in what she'd just done.

This guy was gone.

CHAPTER

45

Luc Zelsor and the Fox Tail

Luc leaned back against the large wooden door. He waited there with his arms folded until the human came out.

Dear little Violet pushed the door open, peeking out at the night like a timid bird. Fairy blood soaked her fingers, glistening in the moonlight as she crept from the cathedral. Her feet were still bare like they'd been the day before. She closed the door softly behind her without looking back at it.

"Did he make it?" Luc asked, making her jump. Her rhythms fell all over the place as she whirled. She looked like she might run, but instead, she blinked at him.

She shook her head a little.

Luc's jaw tightened. He tried not to growl as he ripped the cathedral door back open and muttered, "Fool."

He marched in to where Mor lay on the dirty wooden floor. Mor's muscled body was very much dead, and Luc sighed.

What sort of elite Shadow Fairy couldn't avoid being stabbed by a human?

Luc unearthed his necklace from his shirt. He scowled as he tore one of the fox tails from his throat, shaking his head as he dropped to a knee and held it firmly against Mor's lifeless chest.

The cathedral doors squeaked. Luc could hear the human trailing in behind him.

A dark breeze flitted through the lobby. Wax candles shook upon their shelves, and loose papers took off in flight. The fox tail dissolved, the fur splitting away.

Luc rose again. He took one last look at Mor Trisencor.

Five left.

He turned back to Violet.

"Haley Whitefield," he said, and she stiffened. "You are never going to tell him that I came in here and did this," he commanded.

She didn't respond, but her attention said enough.

Luc released a heavy breath. He pulled up his sleeves and took hold of Violet's head with his bare palm, leaning around to whisper against her opposite ear. She gasped as he told her a secret.

The nine tailed fox dropped the human and headed for the door. The cool night rushed over him as he stepped outside, and he pulled up the hood of his scent-concealing jacket.

"You're cruel." Violet's small voice followed him.

Luc looked out at the moonlight and breathed in a deep lungful of human realm air.

"I know," he said.

He walked into the shadows of the night. This time, he did not come back.

CHAPTER

46

Mor Trisencor and the Dragons

Time was frozen beneath the Jade Ocean. Mor wasn't sure how long he'd spent underwater with the dragons, swimming and listening to them sing. They gave him wise council, and he told them stories of the Shadow Army and of the North and of the human realm. He told them what had become of him since he'd left the village. But after a while, the oldest dragon shook his head as though Mor was being absurd.

"Why are you here, Mor?" the old dragon asked.

Mor glanced at him strangely. "I'm here to tell you what happened to me."

The creature's deep blue scales shimmered in the muted sunlight as he leaned in to look Mor in the eyes. The dragon's eyes were as large as Mor's hands. The old dragon was a vicious creature, but his gaze had always been soft.

"You're not supposed to be here," the dragon said. "We gave you the dragons' gift so you could face this life on your own. But why do you keep coming back?"

Mor looked around at the dragons—his first family—and something sank to the pit of his stomach. "I think he beat me," he admitted. The realization came flooding in all at once; brief recollections of a recent fight, and memories of a lifelong rivalry. "The nine tailed fox defeated me, once and for all. I suppose this is where I wanted to come when I passed on."

The dragon nodded, but he didn't look convinced. "But you're not dead, Mor. You're simply dreaming."

"What?" Mor blinked at the great creature. The rest of the dragons nodded as if to say that the old dragon told no lies.

"Wake up, Mor," the dragon said. "You're not finished."

A slow beeping sound filled Mor's ears. His eyes peeled open, and he saw a face before him he didn't expect; a human with large glasses and a sloppy bun of hair atop her head. At first, he couldn't remember the human female's name. But it came back to him when he imagined visiting Violet's house.

"Zorah." His throat strained to make the noise.

She said nothing. She stared with round eyes that looked even bigger in her glasses. Then she ran out of the room, her white medical coat flapping all the way.

Mor blinked and looked around, finding white walls, white machines, white bed linens. It was a lot of white. Then he heard Cress.

There seemed to be a verbal dispute going on outside. Mor tilted his ear to hear the Prince of the North arguing with a human doctor. For a moment, Mor just listened, a funny smile finding him. But a thought trickled in—a face.

He sat up in his bed. Tubes ripped from his flesh; machines beeped. He tore off his covers and marched from the room. Half a dozen doctors were stationed in a line just outside his door, seemingly to try and keep Cress at bay. Mor looked past them down the hall but saw only Dranian sprawled over a row of chairs, snoring in his sleep. No one else was around.

"Where is my human?" Mor asked Cress over the doctors' heads.

Cress threw up his hands. "Well, you could at least say *hello* first, Mor. Or possibly, *thank you for coming* even though these fools don't want to let me pass. Can you tell these humans that I'm your legal-guardian-person? Or at least explain to them that I'm your Prince. Perhaps that would do it." Cress put his hands on his hips and waited.

"He's my legal-guardian-person," Mor said to the doctors, then to Cress in the same breath he said, "Where is Violet? Is she all right?"

Cress's turquoise eyes softened a little, and Mor shook his head.

No. No, he did not want to see Cress's face go soft, or worrisome, or concerned. The Prince hadn't shared a concerned look for another soul in nearly his whole faeborn life—why was he doing it to Mor now?

Mor pushed through the human doctors. A small bead of blood rolled down his arm from where he'd yanked out a needly thing when he'd left his bed.

Cress took Mor's shoulder, stopping him with a strong grip before he could pass.

"Your human is with Shayne," the Prince said. "Mor, she doesn't remember anything. She doesn't remember you."

Mor's throat swelled. He swallowed. "I know."

Cress didn't release him right away. But finally, his fingers loosened and he dropped his hand. "Shayne is with her at Lily's apartment," Cress said. "She may be compelled to try and kill you again when she sees you."

Mor nodded. "I know that, too," he said again.

"Shayne would have enslaved her with her real name, but he seems to think he's already going to be dead at your hands for enchanting her with a kiss before. He wanted you to be her master. If one of us has to do it to stop her from killing you, Mor, it should be you."

Mor glanced at the floor. The white tile was dirty. "I don't want to enslave her."

Cress flicked a hand through the air and cast an easy smile. "Oh, it's not that big of a deal, Mor. I enslaved Kate. And I only abuse that power when it's absolutely necessary—"

"It's never necessary." Mor shot him a look. "Don't force Kate to do things, Cress. Don't you remember how long you had to try and make up for the book release incident?"

Cress's smile fell.

Mor shook his head and mumbled as he headed down the hall, "Why does that human want to marry you?"

"I'm strong, and powerful, and sometimes, I'm even adorable!" Cress called after him.

"You're spoiled, you think you're the best at everything, and you're completely blind to your own weaknesses. I'd have told you that years ago if I didn't think you'd cut out my tongue for it," Mor called back, startling Dranian awake on the chairs as he passed.

When Cress didn't reply, Mor glanced over his shoulder, fighting a smile. He realized half a dozen human doctors stood by the door of the room he'd abandoned, gaping and looking between him and Cress. Mor made a face, thinking about the loud 'enslaving' conversation he'd just had in front of them.

Mor shook his head and left anyway. "Humans," he muttered as he rounded the corner, sniffing his way to the exit.

Shayne answered the door at Lily's apartment. Mor took in the white-haired fairy's wide smile.

"Welcome to our home—"

"Don't even try that joke," Mor said, shoving past him and searching the room. His heart did a double leap when he saw her.

Violet stood at the window. Her chestnut hair was down and loose without an ounce of styling. If she was wearing face paints, he couldn't tell. Her freckles were prominent in the direct sunlight, and she wore flat shoes that looked comfortable and didn't suit her. Her green eyes slid over to him standing there.

She had nearly no reaction; her face stayed the same. Her hands though...

Her grip tightened on the windowsill. Her throat shifted as she swallowed, and her gaze didn't leave him. In her masked expression, he saw the hints of desperation not hidden well enough. The desperation eating away at her like a poison, making her muscles want to jerk toward him.

She wanted to kill him.

"Where's Lily?" Mor asked Shayne as he watched Violet.

"She's interviewing your interns." Shayne moseyed over and stood at his side. His pockets looked stuffed with things that he no doubt stole from Lily's apartment. "They're fine, by the way. The female one looked a little shaken up, but there isn't a single bruise on them."

Mor nodded, biting back his relief. But his mind was occupied by the hundreds of memories, big and small, that he had with Violet, right from the day they'd met in his bell tower, and every day he'd spent with her after she'd thrown herself off his roof. "Where were they?" Mor managed to ask.

"You're never going to believe it." Shayne grinned and shook his head. "Your interns were tied together—his arms around her and her little arms around him—and locked in an ice cream shop downtown for two days. They were forced to hug each other in the beautiful, cool sanctuary of sweet ice cream and crunchy cones. It's actually a little romantic when you think about it."

"They were kidnapped," Mor corrected. "They were probably terrified."

"Yes, well, they ate ice cream and hugged for two days. I can think of worse ways to be trapped than in a delicious shop with my arms around a pretty female," Shayne said. He grabbed a thin blanket off the back of the couch. "Speaking of which..." Shayne snatched Violet as she took her first leap and rushed for Mor.

Mor was too distracted to notice Violet rip a panel of wood from the windowsill as she charged. The point of the stake came within an inch of his throat before Shayne wrestled Violet into the blanket, tying it around her so her arms were strapped down. Violet stared at Mor as the panel of wood dropped from her fingers and clattered to the floor.

Tears sprang into her eyes. "Please leave," she rasped. The first words she said to Mor.

Mor studied her shaking hands, the pleading in her voice. Her tone told him that his presence was making her lose control, and he didn't need the senses of a fae to know why that was difficult for her. But he had to hear her say it herself...

"Do you really remember nothing?" Mor asked her.

Violet didn't blink, even when a tear broke loose and rolled down her freckled cheek. "No," she said.

"Enslave her, Mor. It's the only way," Shayne said, holding tight to her shoulders to keep her in place. "Undo what that fox did, or she'll keep coming at you like this."

Mor took in a deep breath. "Do you want me to?" he asked Violet. "Do you wish to be enslaved by me so I can command you to stop trying to kill me?"

Violet's mouth moved. It looked like she was struggling to say something important. But try as she may, no sound came out. Finally, she closed her mouth and gave up.

Shayne sighed. "All right, I'm giving you exactly five seconds, Mor. Enslave her, or I will."

"Do it, and I'll throw you through the window," Mor threatened.

"One," Shayne said anyway, and Mor's face changed.

"You'd better be joking, you fool."

"Two," Shayne went on, wrapping his arm around Violet and giving her a little squeeze as if to assure her he had her best interests in mind— which he didn't. "Three..."

"*Shayne*," Mor warned.

"Four!" The white-haired assassin was practically singing the digits now.

There was a pause after that. Shayne didn't say the last number. He looked at Mor, waiting. Testing him. Mor stared back, positive Shayne wouldn't dare.

Shayne's smile widened a little.

"Queensbane," Mor cursed. "Shayne!"

"Five!" Shayne shouted, spinning Violet toward himself, and Mor charged. "Haley Whitefield, I command you to stop trying to kill Mor!" Shayne blurted it just as Mor ripped him back. Every muscle in Mor's healing faeborn body flexed as he lifted Shayne, turned, and hurled the white-haired assassin through the window of Lily's apartment.

Glass shattered to the floor; fresh wind rushed into the living room.

There was a light thump below, and a car trumpet began to sound.

Shayne's cackling laughter flitted all the way back up.

Mor's chest heaved, even as he stepped to the window to steal a glance down, hating that he was too concerned to move on without making sure the fool was all right.

Shayne lay back against the roof of a human vessel, bringing one arm behind his head like he planned to take a peaceful nap there. He'd dented the roof—all the blue metal was warped, and the vessel sang its trumpet alarm without ceasing. The fairy waved up at Mor with a wink that seemed to say, *"You're welcome."*

Mor huffed, gripping the sill of the broken window. First, he had to deal with his human forgetting him. Now he would have to deal with Shayne's fairy shenanigans as Shayne would no doubt play tricks on Violet at every turn with his new power. Mor only had one choice; to enslave her himself. Perhaps that was precisely what the white-haired assassin was hoping for. But Mor considered how much easier it would be to just take out Shayne's tongue so the fool couldn't command Violet to do anything more. He doubted the enslaving rule would still work with hand-gesture instructions.

It was settled then. Shayne was going to lose his tongue.

Mor turned back to Violet, not sure whether to apologize or to explain why he'd just thrown someone out a window or if he should start by trying to tell her everything she'd forgotten about him. But he started when he saw streams of tears wetting her face.

"Violet—" His heart did a double flip when she stepped to him and slid her arms around his middle, hugging herself to him tightly.

It didn't seem real. She didn't know who he was; why would she—

His phone rang. Mor would have ignored it, but he had a special musical flute that played whenever Shayne was calling him, so he'd know not to answer. But he'd just tossed Shayne through a window and—what if the fairy's faeborn legs were broken and he needed help snapping them back into place? Mor bit back a growl, yanked out his phone, and hit the green button, but before he could ask Shayne what this nonsense was about, Shayne yelled through the phone, "Haley Whitefield, I want you to tell Mor the truth about what you can remember!" The sound almost burst Mor's faeborn eardrum—he yanked the phone away from his ear and stared at it as Shayne's words settled in.

"I lied," Violet cried from a coarse throat. Mor's gaze fell on her. He wasn't sure he'd heard her correctly. At the look on her face, he dropped his phone to his side. "I lied, Mor!" she said again, the words nearly indistinguishable past her sobs.

Mor couldn't stop the wild thudding of his faeborn heart at how close she came against him, how she gripped him, how she said his name. He wrapped an arm around her slowly, sure he was imagining it all. He placed his other hand on her head, brushing her hair away from her face so it wouldn't stick to her tears.

"Violet," he whispered. "What did you lie about?"

Violet unhooked her arm from him just long enough to wipe the sleeve of her shirt over her eyes. "I love you, Mor," she blurted. "All I wanted to do was race to the hospital to see if you were all right!"

Emotions danced in Mor's chest. "You remember," he breathed.

There wasn't time to ask her how. There wasn't enough space in the whole human realm to have her explain or reveal how in the world

Shayne had figured it out first. Time had vanished as she lifted onto her toes and pressed her soft lips against his. It was so much more than a simple kiss.

The kiss told stories.

CHAPTER

47

Violet Miller and the Fox's Secret

Two Nights Ago

Midnight was dark, and only the moon showed what was happening in the cathedral.

After the redhead had revived the curly-haired guy on the cathedral floor with a strange fur charm, he turned, pulled up his sleeves, and put his palm against Violet's temple. He brought his mouth around to whisper in her opposite ear.

This is what he said: "You aren't going to tell a soul I gave your memories back either."

Violet gasped as something rushed into her mind like hot water—places, people, faces, memories. *Everything.*

No, she would not tell Mor that she remembered him. She would not tell a soul.

Warm tears filled her eyes. Her gaze flashed to the guy on the floor. Mor...

Luc headed for the door, but Violet didn't turn to watch him leave. It all sank in slowly, everything at once. And she said aloud the realization that should have come much sooner, "You're cruel."

The pause afterward was brief. Luc's voice sounded far away when he replied.

"I know."

Violet rushed to Mor's side. She searched his pockets for his phone, but when she tried to dial all the numbers of the people who might come help him, her fingers didn't seem to work. And she realized it was because she couldn't let them find out that she remembered. She had a secret to keep now.

She dialed Zorah instead.

CHAPTER

48

Mor Trisencor and Doom First Thing in the Morning

Mor stared evenly at the male faeborn doctor across the room. Dr. Wendal.

It surprised Mor to cross another fairy in the human realm, but perhaps he should have expected it. The doctor wore casual human-y clothes and fashioned long gray hair pulled back into a bun just like Mor's to hide his pointed ears, though the doctor was considerably older than Mor by the looks of it. Perhaps around Freida's age.

Neither fairy spoke as the human receptionist tidied up a few things in the room and left so that Mor could 'have his appointment' first thing in the morning with the doctor.

The moment the door to the doctor's room closed, the old fairy lifted a hand with his palm up as if to stop Mor—as though he expected some sort of reaction. Which he should have, since Mor was ready to grab the fool, airslip into the clouds, and drop him from the sky.

But Mor folded his arms, quite aware of his fairsaber handles in his pockets. "I was wondering what sort of doctor in their right human mind would prescribe cold iron as a supplement," Mor said to him. "But I suppose I should have guessed that no human doctor would."

The doctor's face squinted in confusion before he seemed to put the pieces together. He dropped his hand and folded his arms, mirroring Mor. Mor was slightly surprised to see muscles appear on the fellow. The doctor's casual clothes hid them well.

"I only prescribe cold iron to humans who are in danger of fairy meddling," the doctor explained. "And I only did it once. You must be here about Violet Miller."

Mor itched to bash in every cupboard of supplements in this doctor's office. "What in the name of the sky deities would make you tell a human to consume cold iron? The pills aren't only hurting her insides, they're going to shorten her human life, possibly by years!" Mor growled.

The doctor sighed and slid his hands into his pockets. "Judge me if you'd like, Shadow Fairy, but until you just said that, I didn't even know if you were a friend of Violet Miller's or a foe," he admitted. "I prescribed Violet cold iron to save her life. Yes, she may live a shorter human life if she continues to take those pills forever, but I deemed the risk worth it. It's better for her to live a slightly shortened human life with the occasional stomach-ache than to be hunted down and probably killed by fairies at thirteen years of age. Wouldn't you agree?"

For a moment, Mor didn't have an argument. But even so, he had to put an end to this.

"I will not allow her to live a shortened life because of cold iron," Mor stated. "You can prescribe her regular iron from now on if she has a low-iron condition."

The doctor nodded and chewed on the inside of his cheek. "The first time Violet Miller came in here a decade ago, I nearly slapped my hand over my nose. The scent of fairies was so strong on her, I worried every fairy hidden in the city for miles would be drawn to it. Even after all these years, when she comes in here, I can still smell it." He released a huff and eyed Mor. "Fairies will come for her—always. She's too interesting to let pass by. I am not young anymore, as you can see. And I already have a job, so I could not take on the role of following her around to ensure she was left alone. Cold iron enhancements were the only way I could be certain she would not be touched, even if the fairies did find her. So, I stand by my decision. For her own safety, I believe she should keep taking them."

Mor shook his head. "She doesn't need them anymore. Fairies won't touch her, whether her skin will burn them or not," he stated.

"How can you be so sure?" the doctor asked. "I may not be human, but she is still my patient. And I take my job seriously." His narrowing eyes emitted a warning.

"Because she has me now." Mor sauntered in a step, standing slightly over the doctor so the intent in his tone would be clear. "Her forever mate."

The doctor's face changed. He drew back a little then looked Mor up and down. At first, he appeared doubtful, but then... a gradual smile spread across his face. "Ah, I see." He nodded once. Twice. "Very good then."

The doctor turned and fetched a notepad from his table. He scribbled something on it. Mor leaned to try and read what the doctor-fairy was writing, but the scrawl was horrendously messy. He straightened when the doctor tore the sheet from the notepad and handed it to him.

"This is a new prescription for Miss Miller. As her guardian, please ensure she takes one every evening before she sleeps. I'm counting on you, Shadow Fairy," the doctor said.

Mor took the slip of paper. He couldn't have read the prescription if his faeborn life depended on it. But he folded it and tucked it into his pocket with his fairsaber handle, trusting it was for plant-based iron that had nothing to do with fairies.

The café was empty apart from a lazy fae Prince by the fireplace reading a book he claimed to have written. The fire was lit, breathing warmth through the space. The mornings were just beginning to get cool as fall approached, and the crackling fire brought a soothing music into the room.

Mor closed the door behind him. Kate's novel, *The High Court of the Coffee Bean,* hovered in Cress's hands, and Mor considered that the Prince would do well to let the story go and write a new one, instead of constantly going back to his and Kate's origin story to relive it.

Cress released a chuckle from the plush chair as he read, making Mor realize Cress had no idea Mor was even there.

"You've been in the human realm too long," Mor said to him, and Cress glanced up in surprise. "Your senses have turned to lakeweed mush. I could have crept up behind you and run you through." Mor kicked off his shoes and slid on the fresh pair of cream-coloured slippers someone had left by the door.

"Those are Kate's," Cress informed him as he eyed the slippers.

Mor wandered over to the fireplace chairs regardless, sat, and put his feet up on the stool between them. "Kate has big feet," he remarked.

"No, she doesn't. You're stretching her slippers." Cress closed the book and rested it on his lap, leaning back against the chair's headrest.

"Why are there no customers today?" Mor asked, eyeing the empty tables.

Cress sighed and shook his head. "Well, I did a rather exceptional cooking show yesterday, and I invited all my human subjects—"

"Subscribers," Mor corrected.

"—to our café to try my latest cupcake recipe. Unfortunately, Dranian mucked up the enchantment, and all who ate my delicious cupcakes were hit with unstoppable, raging diarrhea," Cress said. "It was an absolute mess, Mor. You can't even imagine."

"That's horrifying." Mor hid a smile.

"So, we shut down for the rest of the day. Shayne's been having nightmares anyway and wanted to catch up on sleep," Cress finished, and Mor raised a brow.

"Nightmares?" Mor wanted to ask how he hadn't heard about this until now.

Cress sighed again. "All those poor humans." He shook his head. "They must be devastated they don't get to eat more of my cupcakes."

"Yes. I'm sure that's what they're devastated about the most," Mor said with little enough sarcasm in his tone that Cress wouldn't know if he was being serious or not. "But on the note of that thieving pickpocket, I've been meaning to ask how in the faeborn world Shayne figured out Violet had gotten her memories back?"

"It sounds like Violet gave Shayne hints while she was under his care," Cress said.

"Hints." It was a question. Mor folded his hands on his lap, trying to imagine Shayne being the wise detective of the group. It didn't make a lick of sense.

"Shayne secretly followed her to the cathedral once where she stood outside and stared at the bell tower for hours. Then he caught her reading a Fairy Post, of all things. And last, he saw her running her fingers along the heels of her flat shoes. She even put on your favourite sweater, Mor—Don't ask me how she got it," Cress said. "It was all very confusing because every time Shayne asked her if she remembered you, she said *no*."

Mor tapped his fingers together as he thought about that. "She was doing it on purpose," he said.

Cress nodded. "It would seem so. It appears your human wanted Shayne to know she remembered everything. But for some faeborn reason she couldn't tell him. I sniff a fox trick on that one." Cress leaned back in his chair and folded his arms. He kicked his legs up onto the footstool, shoving Mor's feet out of the way and making one of Mor's legs drop. Kate's left slipper flew off and Mor scowled at his cold fairy foot.

"Were you as startled as I was to learn that nine tailed fox returned her memories?" Cress asked flat out.

Mor looked over at the fire. He hadn't stopped asking every moment of the day why Luc would do such a thing when he hated Violet so much.

Cress was quiet for a while, staring at Mor with his naturally cold eyes. Finally, he said, "Are you sure the reason you wanted me to stay out of your fox hunt was because you were worried about what would happen to me if he discovered I was here?"

Mor blinked in astonishment. "Of course! Why else would I have tried to keep you all away?"

Cress made a face, but it didn't reveal whether he believed him. "The thing is, Mor," Cress pulled his feet off the footstool and leaned forward with his elbows on his knees, "I could have killed that fox another seven times. In the museum, I could have waited for him to come alive, and slain him over and over before he even had a chance to gain his bearings," he said.

"What's your point, Cress? Why didn't you finish him off, then?" Mor asked, hugging his arms to himself.

Cress hadn't blinked once in the last minute. Mor felt like any little move he made now would be scrutinized by the North Prince. He kept his gaze on their shared footstool.

"I wanted to. He was messing with you. His presence took you away from us," Cress admitted. "But the thing is…" He tilted his head and squinted his turquoise eyes a little. "I think part of the reason you didn't want me to get involved in the first place was because you didn't actually want that fool to die."

Mor's wide gaze snapped back up. "What would make you say that?"

Cress relaxed back into his chair again, seeming satisfied. "I've known you a long time, Mor. You're bad at keeping secrets to begin with, but you especially can't keep secrets from me."

Mor didn't find the voice to object. He glanced over at the fire then out the windows, taking in a deep breath and letting it out slowly. "I suppose it doesn't matter anymore now that Luc is long gone. He wanted me dead in the end, and I imagine he's already vanished into human life somewhere. He probably thinks he succeeded in killing me. It's probably best to let him believe that."

Cress said nothing. He reached for a nearby mug on the windowsill and took a long drink of beast milk.

"Though I'm worried about Dranian," Mor went on. "The fool has declared an oath to not sleep until he's hunted the nine tailed fox down and finished him off. He wants revenge for his arm that was stolen."

Cress snorted a laugh through a gulp of his milk. "Good luck to him. I would pay every coin to my name to watch him try to fight a nine tailed fox with one arm," he said, wiping a milk stain off his upper lip.

Mor smiled at the thought.

"Fool," Mor and Cress muttered in unison.

CHAPTER

49

Violet Miller, Secretary of Doom

Cool air trickled in off the harbour sending a shiver up Violet's back. All week the weather had grown colder, often starting with a chilly morning and sinking into a hot afternoon. Soon it would stay cool all day long, and the leaves would start to turn. Violet wondered if Jase and Remi were having a good first day of school. If they were thinking about her as much as she thought of them, or if their summer of terror and mysteries had left them never wanting to think about Violet, Mor, or the cathedral ever again.

"You can take your time," Lily said from beside her on the bench. The officer took a swig of her latte in a burgundy Fae Café paper cup. "I know it's a lot to take in," she added after.

Violet scanned the papers on her lap. Papers that told a story about a girl who once had parents, once had a life. A girl who once belonged to someone.

"Haley Whitefield." Violet uttered her birth name. She'd said it a hundred times over since she'd heard Luc use it. "So, I guess my parents weren't government agents," she thought aloud.

Lily cracked a smile. "Not exactly. But listen, if there's one thing I understand, it's wanting to duck foster homes and stay off the radar. I was eight when my parents died, and I had no other family. My parents didn't even have any friends close enough to want to take me in. I was on my own for a long time until I met the Lewis's and joined Kate's family," she said, kicking a loose rock with the toe of her uniform shoe. "I can't judge you for choosing to stay invisible back then. Sometimes hopping from home to home is no better."

Violet pursed her lips and closed the folder. She handed it back to Lily. "The truth is, I don't remember any of this. I think it's worse for you because you remember."

Lily took the folder slowly. "Are you sure you don't want to keep it?"

Memories. What was the exact worth and weight of a memory? Violet thought about Mor who'd spent years wanting to forget his past, while Violet had spent years trying to get hers back. But in the end, it turned out they'd both wanted to forget, and she'd been the only one lucky enough to be able to do it.

Violet shook her head. "If things were so bad back then that I wanted to have my memory erased, then there's no need to dig up the past. I like my life now." Violet didn't tell Lily the part where she remembered her mother's voice—that distant woman calling her name, urging her to get into a car and read Peter Pan. She smiled when she thought about it. It was a good memory. Maybe one of the only good ones of her past life, and therefore, it was the only one she wanted.

Lily flashed her a smile. "So, what's next for you and Mor, then?" she asked, changing the subject.

Violet chuckled. "What about you, Officer Baker? Anything going on between you and Shayne?" she asked, and Lily made a repulsed face.

"Don't make me gag this early in the morning," she pleaded and stood. She brushed the dust off her police vest. "Shayne is already fake dating me for the sake of my coworkers, and he's become terrible. I get in more trouble from his messing around than anything else on the job.

It's unreal."

Violet raised a brow. Shayne didn't seem like the sort to be a terrible boyfriend. Maybe the fairy had sharpened up his troublemaking especially for Lily.

"Anyway, here comes Mor. I'll see you guys at the café after my shift." Lily pulled on her police hat as Mor appeared casually walking down the sidewalk with his hands in his pockets. "Don't let Cress near my lemon pie, Mor!" Lily called to him before heading in the opposite direction. "I expect it to still be there when I get back! Westbow is going to kill me if I show up for a community bake sale empty-handed again."

Mor cast Lily a smile that made no promises, and Lily grunted as she broke into a jog toward her squad car at the curb.

Violet took in the sight of the curly-haired guy she'd once been convinced was a vampire. The Master of Doom. The person she belonged to.

Mor came to the bench and stopped in front of Violet, blocking out the sun with his body. "Secretary, would you mind assisting me on my walk along the harbour?" Mor asked. His hand came out of his pocket and extended toward her.

When Violet took it, Mor lifted her to her feet but didn't let go of her hand. They walked for a few seconds, his side warming her from the chilly air. Birds squawked along the distant shores, and boat horns sounded from the lake.

"Where are we going?" Violet asked to break the comfortable silence.

Instead of answering, Mor pulled an apple from his pocket. "Would you like a shiny human grape?" he asked, holding it out to her. It glistened in the early sun.

"Is this breakfast?" Violet asked through a smirk as she took it.

"It's our first real date, Human," Mor said. "In fact, as per human date customs, I've provided dinner *and* a show." He slowed his walking, and Violet realized they were across the street from the building where she used to work. The large *The Sprinkled Scoop* sign hung out front for all to see.

Yelling erupted from inside.

Violet's smile faded. She dropped her hand without taking a bite of the apple.

"Mor…" she said in a warning voice. "What did you do?"

Mor appeared to be flexing every muscle in his body to keep from laughing. He made a strained sound and pushed his fist against his mouth. "You'll see," he squeaked.

Violet's gaze fired back to The Sprinkled Scoop in time to see Shayne and Dranian come bursting out the front door in their burgundy Fae Café aprons clutching empty delivery boxes.

In the second before the door shut, Violet heard cries and shouts such as, "Why can't I stop?!" and, "What's happening to us?!" and "Don't you *dare* sit on my chair!"

Violet's mouth parted, her jaw hanging open as she watched Shayne and Dranian race off in a speed walk. Dranian was straight faced as usual, but Shayne was grinning from ear to ear.

"I suppose I should have warned you," Mor said when he finally got it together. He handed Violet a small card. "The delivery note I attached to the boxes of Cress's legendary new *Unfortunate Mudslide Cupcakes* is a replica of this one."

Violet read the note that said:

I COMPLETELY UNDERSTAND YOUR DECISION TO DECLINE
TO BE INTERVIEWED BY US AT THE FAIRY POST DUE TO
YOUR BUSY SCHEDULES, AND I EMPATHIZE WITH HOW
YOU MUST BE SO *BACKED UP* THESE DAYS.

IN THESE SORTS OF SITUATIONS, I FIND CUPCAKES HELP.

SINCERELY,
SECRETARY OF DOOM.

Violet's loud gasp filled the street. "Mor!" she shouted at him. "Were those cupcakes the same ones that destroyed the café?!" Her hand flashed to her stomach as she imagined.

Mor shrugged and grinned. "I still think they're safer to eat than your repulsive muffins."

Violet tried to flick his nose, but he maneuvered out of the way and planted a quick kiss on her mouth. Then he took the apple from her hand and bit into it.

"The first bite is the hardest. I find once you break the grape's skin, the rest of the bites are easier," he told her, ignoring the look of disbelief she gave him. "Don't worry, Human," he added, nodding toward The Sprinkled Scoop where people inside were beginning to throw open all the windows. "It'll wear off in a few hours."

She huffed, thinking of the damage that could be caused in just *a few hours*. Then, she reluctantly laughed. "Whatever. I hope Cedric and Fil both ate the cupcakes first," she mumbled as they headed in the direction Shayne and Dranian had taken off.

Violet snagged her apple back from Mor and took a bite, savouring the crisp, juicy taste. "Mmmm," she said, nodding. "This is delicious." She chewed for a moment, thinking. Then she said, "I'm relieved you finally admitted my muffins were disgusting. I was getting tired of making them every day."

Mor nodded. "I know." He put his arm around her as they headed back down the harbour sidewalk. "You know what would be really humorous?" he asked, and Violet raised a brow. "If we used the same enchantment on Lily's lemon pie that she's taking to the human police station—"

"You're not doing that," Violet said, though she was already grinning. "It would be hilarious, but you're not doing it."

Mor walked in silence for about seven seconds.

"We'll see," he said, waving to Shayne and Dranian as they crept out of hiding from behind a sidewalk planter.

Shayne jogged over and threw an arm around Violet's shoulders, smooshing Mor's arm beneath his. Mor shoved Shayne's arm right back off.

Shayne sighed. "Don't be so territorial, Mor. I'm Violet's master, so technically she's *my* human—"

Mor pushed Shayne over the rail and into the harbour.

The Faeborn End, For the Second Time

(But read on for an extra chapter)

THE EXTRA ONE

Shayne Lyro and the Nightmare that Wouldn't Cease

Here he was again. Cold rain drenched his shoulders, turning his white hair glassy and warping his vision to melted colours as he blinked back downpour, blood, and sweat. Shayne's grip on his fairsaber was slick. He lifted his weapon and looked at his reflection in the blade, hardly recognizing himself with his bothered face and no smile.

Yet, it was him. Here, at the House of Lyro, outside its eight-tiered pagoda of the sky deities, fighting the one person who had taken everything from his childling hands, then cast him out, and now dragged him back.

"Raise your sword at me, Brother." That painfully familiar accent sailed through the thunderstorm. "Let me ascend in peace."

Shayne lowered his blade, setting his reflection aside. For the first time in months since Kahn-Der had dreamslipped into his mind and filled him with nightmares, Shayne looked up and met his brother's gaze. He'd been avoiding this bloodbath. He'd been frightened of it, even—not because he was scared to fight, but because he was afraid to lose all the simple things he had gained, all to this heartless fool who had never cared for another fairy a single day in his faeborn life.

Shayne raised his fairsaber.

He took in his long, last free breath.

He did it all knowing that for his brother to ascend to the highest chair in the House of Lyro, Shayne would have to die. And Shayne could not smile about that.

For, all good things come to an end. That included the legacy of once-smiling fairies.

Thank you for reading *Sincerely, Secretary of Doom*!
If you liked this book, please leave a review!

Not finished with the assassins?

Join Jennifer Kropf's newsletter at JenniferKropf.com to be alerted to all new books, including book 3 of the *High Court of the Coffee Bean* series, *Wanted: A Roommate Who Isn't Evil*.

Do you want to be a part of a **Fae Café contest**?
Post a book photo/video/quote/favorite moment of your Sincerely, Secretary of Doom book to Tiktok or Instagram and use the hashtag #faecafecontest in your post.

Every season, a winner will be chosen, and a special fairy present will be mailed to someone's door!
(open internationally)

Christmas fantasy books by Jennifer Kropf:

A SOUL AS COLD AS FROST

A HEART AS RED AS PAINT

A CROWN AS SHARP AS PINES

A BEAST AS DARK AS NIGHT

CAROLS AND SPIES

See more info:

ACKNOWLEDGEMENTS

Acknowledgements are so weird, am I right? One minute you're reading a funny story. The next, you're expected to read a bunch of mushy, sappy, heartfelt things that would probably be considered as 'lovey-dovey shenanigans' in libraries.

Here it goes anyway.

Thank you to God from whom all blessings flow. I still wake up every day and am overwhelmed by the opportunities you've given me.

Thank you to my editor, Melissa Cole, for your time investment and your epic eyeballs that see things I don't. We make cool books. Go us.

A big thank you to my agent, Brent Taylor, for believing in this book series enough to bring Welcome to Fae Cafe to other countries so it can be translated into languages I never imagined my stories would be told in.

Thank you to my Patrons: Sarah Breed, Laman Samo, Lydia Woodward, my girl Lyndsey Hall, Redlac (my bro), Amanda Shafer, Vickie, Stephanie, Jess, Amy, Ira, Bella, Austengirl, Thiccteacup, Nebula,

Judy, Amber, Erin, Fiona, Cheryl, Yajaiara, Jodi, Anastassia, Courtney, Elle, Mimi, Lydia, Mae, Kendra, and Kanyon for brainstorming, cheering me on, and giving me the fuel to write books! I don't even remember how many times I posted things about this book in our Patreon chat—ideas, chapters, covers—and asked for your opinions. You guys are the dream team.

Thank you to my beta readers Sarah, Lydia, and Kelly for your valuable thoughts and feelings about this book! You always baffle me with your awesomeness and willingness to read the scrappy first drafts of my work.

Thank you to Astrid Johnsson for all your hard work reading through this book and giving me the most in-depth revision advice I could have asked for. You are remarkable and this book is so much better now that you've been through it.

Thank you to my street team, to every single one of my ARC readers, and to the team at Book of Matches Media for all you've done for me. Every one of you is a gift.

Obviously a big thank you needs to go to the amazing and hilarious readers on BookTok who jumped onto this book series idea in the first place and offered ideas and so much joy. You are the reason I wrote Welcome to Fae Café in the first place.

And I need to thank my husband Phil for making it possible for me to write books to begin with. I never would have taken the first steps to publish something if you hadn't told me to go for it. And I probably would have gone back to work and ended up at some super lame job if you hadn't nudged me to try doing the author thing full time. AND LOOK AT WHERE WE ARE NOW. I still can't believe I get to do this as my job.

Thank you to Chase, Ellie, and Austin. To my mom, my dad, Grandpa John, my weird siblings, and their even weirder spouses. Kelly Clarkson says it best: My life would suck without you.

And last, thank you to you, the reader, for being a part of Mor's story.

Made in the USA
Monee, IL
07 January 2025

76235101R10215